Rahul
A Different Love Story

Ashis Gupta

RAHUL: A DIFFERENT LOVE STORY

Cover Image: "Horse" by M.F. Husain. Photography: Alexandra Palko. From the private collection of Gautam and Manu Chakravartty, Hawaii, with permission.
Book design by Fiona Staples.

Published by: Bayeux Arts, Inc., 119 Stratton Crescent SW, Calgary, Canada T3H 1T7, www.bayeux.com

Library and Archives Canada Cataloguing in Publication

Gupta, Ashis, 1940-
Rahul : a different love story / Ashis Gupta.

ISBN 978-1-897411-00-1

I. Title.

PS8613.U68R83 2008 C813'.6 C2008-905981-6

First Printing: November 2008
Printed in Canada

The publishing activities of Bayeux/Gondolier are supported by the Canada Council for the Arts, the Alberta Foundation for the Arts, and by the Government of Canada through its Book Publishing Industry Development Program.

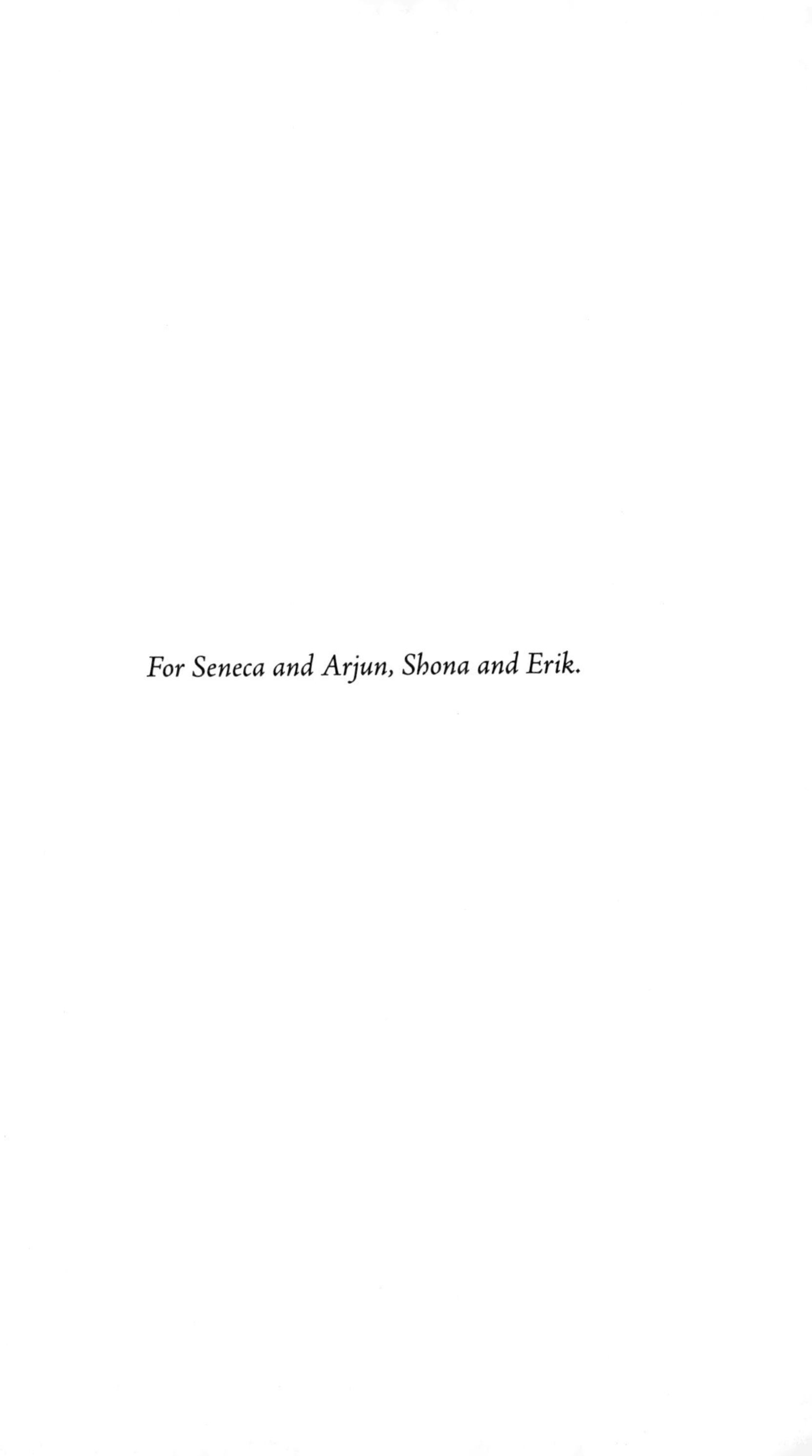

For Seneca and Arjun, Shona and Erik.

One

It started off as just another morning, simple and nondescript. But it ended with a miracle. Sambhu Narain stepped out of the mist and shadows until he could clearly see his home. He stood there a long time. Yes, the house was alive once more. Rahul was back, this time to live in it. He might someday find a woman to share his life, but that seemed unimportant. His heart was filled with pity for his son, so mangled he would never have a family of his own. Still, he also found a curious happiness in the thought, for there was a blessing in it too. To Sambhu Narain, this now seemed the only sure path to salvation open to man.

Something had gone wrong with the lives of men. Darkness had seized their souls, and injustice had become a way of life. That life, he was convinced, must end. At least, it must not be knowingly perpetuated any longer. The realization had dawned upon him suddenly, repeatedly, as he saw the senseless end to the lives of a son and a daughter, and stood watching as healing hands brought back to life the broken body of another son. Sambhu Narain saw no hope except in turning back.

Ah! but who was that little figure standing against the railings of the verandah?

The house remained dark and silent, and Sambhu Narain drew near for a closer look. He quickened his steps as he realized it was Malini. Briskly, silently, he climbed up the steps to her. He called out her name, and Malini recognized him instantly. She clasped him tightly in her arms, crushing her face against his body, sobbing out the words, "Grandpa, Grandpa, Grandpa."

"Don't cry, don't cry," he whispered, kneeling, touching her eyes with the tips of his fingers, gently kissing the tears away from both eyes. "You'll see before the morning is done," he said, embracing her once more.

"I know" she said, smiling, whimpering. "I think I can."

Sambhu Narain gently moved away the dark curls of hair away from her eyes, her forehead, her cheeks. He held her face in his hands for what seemed, measured by the intensity of his look, an eternity. He kissed the trembling girl once more. Then he straightened himself and started to walk down the steps of his home. Malini stood by the railings, smiling, speechless, as Sambhu Narain disappeared into the mist still surrounding the village.

The dew was wet and heavy on the dirt tracks and the neighboring patches of grass. Sambhu Narain lingered for a moment near the open-air stage, the handsome platform he had ordered made with such care and precision many years ago. It now leaned blackened and rotting on its side. Other structures lay strewn around. A wrecked podium and sprawling enclosures put together for the Farmers' Convention remained just as he had seen them four months ago. The fairground looked dirty and neglected, the weeds sprouting with impunity. A solitary child wandered naked through the grounds and stopped in front of a peeling and discoloured wooden ferris wheel. There was no one who could give him a ride. Sambhu Narain walked over to him thinking he would treat the child to one. The little boy began to cry, and ran away in the direction of the village. With his matted hair, his beard, his loincloth, and the trident in his hand, Sambhu Narain was the terrible bogeyman his mother, grandmother, and aunts had warned him against.

The morning had yet to shake off the spell of sleep. The village was silent. Sambhu Narain stopped and looked back at his house. Somewhere inside it, he knew his wife would be praying before her gods. He could almost hear her murmuring her hymns beside the flame of a single oil lamp, praying for her sons, her daughter, her daughter's daughter, and her husband.

Sambhu Narain slowly turned his eyes, clouded with a gentle and faraway look, to the rising sun. Suddenly, he heard a familiar voice singing in his ears. It was the voice of Kali, and it cried, "O Summer! rein in your terror. Listen to me. I am Annapoorna, Kanchenjunga, and the emerald lake at Manas. Come play with me behind my curtain of clouds, under my mantle of snow. Spare the fields, my womb, the shining blade of your wrath. The plain is a cradle and a tomb. Why stir the bones of dead men? Why sully yourself in their ashes? Come to the clouds, to the pinnacle sublime, to my cool lips."

He smiled as he heard the words ringing in his ears, for it sounded like the echo of his own voice, his own words.

Summer was never too far away on the plains. To the silent Sambhu Narain, the next summer would be the summer of the next plague, the summer of the next pestilence. It would be the summer of the shepherd playing his flute in ruined temples. It would be the summer of doors unchained and windows forever open. But summers really didn't matter to him any more. Neither did spring or winter. He could feel the seasons converging into one incandescent point of light which dissolved all time and brought every memory back to life. He knew the time was near when he would enter that point of light, and he longed to be one with that light.

Sambhu Narain looked back at his home for the last time. Then he started to walk towards the dark outline where the unseen hills tore open a jagged scar between earth and sky. There was healing in that scar, as well as pain and burning. Sambhu Narain walked determinedly towards the wind that crept up the bald hills and swept down to the plains, the wind that blew the dark clouds to briefly crown the hills and come hurtling down in a flood. He would renew himself in the wind and the rain. They sang the same songs his heart sang and whispered the same incantations that poured from his lips.

A few years later, Sambhu Narain would come back to Bishnupur one more time, to die. But, for the moment, he thought he could be one with the wind and the rain, for did they not destroy even as they healed? He craved destruction as much as he needed healing. Always had.

When the time finally came to part with him forever, almost everyone felt troubled in the midst of sadness, secretly ashamed that the pain they felt might suddenly dissolve into surprise, even delight. In the end, the end is nothing, simply a fraud, a divine sleight of hand, something of a cosmic deception, he was fond of saying. Those who knew him often wondered if it might not after all be true. Janaki Devi, his wife, seemed to believe it to be so. She saw the men carry away the bier without a drop of tear in her eyes. She showed no more emotion when she bent down to wash with holy water from the Ganga the stone steps along which they bore her husband's body. As they turned past the narrow path winding through the fragrant rose bushes into the dust swirling over the clayey fields, they looked back and caught her eyes briefly before she receded into the shadows of the old bungalow. Soon she receded even deeper into the tomb-like serenity of her prayer room where burning incense curled up and wreathed a majestic portrait of Sambhu Narain seated on a horse, as if nothing had changed, as if it was just another glorious, terrifying day in her life and the life of her husband. It was as if the shadows made sickly sweet by the rose petals and the sandal-wood incense were about to melt away at the touch of the light and heat radiating from the egg-yolk orange body of the sun exploding into a new day.

It was in the prayer room that the men found her when they returned later that night. She was standing at the door, gazing as if in a trance at the smiling, unblemished face of her husband. Everyone knew for certain that it was his ashes they had gathered together with the fading embers and scattered into the wind driving to a frenzy the waters of the river sliding past the cremation grounds. But they could not shake off a lingering doubt that his face in the picture looked real, too real, and that he might nimbly dismount from his horse any moment and take a seat in their midst once more, carefully folding the *zarda* laden, lime stained *pan* leaves and placing them in his mouth. And he would drink spiced tea by the pot and frighten his friends with tales of the supernatural until their blood ran cold and the hair stood up on their skin during the icy pauses when no one uttered a sound, when he himself would break the silence saying, "This is the way it happened," and lapse into an even deeper silence, more chilling than the silence of death, whose very fragility drove them back from trying to shatter it with idle talk or inconceivable skepticism. So the silence lingered on, thickened, and poisoned every sense with such an euphoria that there was little for the men to do except surrender themselves eventually to heavy, langourous sleep on the very mattresses on which they reclined as they listened, propped up by spotless pillows.

Some of the men stood at the door of the prayer room, overcome by the sandalwood smoke rising from the incense, driven to madness by the smell of roses seeping in through the shutters, lulled to a consuming sleep by the prayers Janaki Devi murmured softly, full of devotion. As they stood there, the seemingly impossible seemed to be happening. The men heard his voice echo, "This is the way it happened, only like this, like this." At the time, no one imagined that it was perhaps an echo from the past, his voice reverberating through the shell whose ridges and arches framed the eternity into which he had slipped, and out of which he could slip back into their midst with equal ease, perhaps to extol the virtues of Mister Forster, best damned English writer there ever was, by George! isn't that how you say it. Of course, second only to Shakespeare, and maybe a little behind Dickens too, but the man's vision of mosque, cave, and temple - so unifying and noble, and yet so unutterably tragic. And since there is no space in the universe that can hold such an unlikely unity, it is best that Muslims and Hindus stay apart, and Christians too, and Sikhs and Buddhists, for the shadow of intolerance lies directly behind the certitude of one's deepest convictions, and all that a writer can do is hold up that certitude so that the slimy ooze clinging to it can strike readers with horror and send them to seek out and nurture such things as love and family and nature, for they all pass, slip through our mortal fingers, except where they are enchanted and frozen by the magic of the poet.

They all knew he too was something of a poet as he skillfully unravelled life's surprises, sorrows, and contradictions and continued to move towards some visionary horizon when weaker mortals slipped away from their moorings, drifted aimlessly on heaving oceans of fear and oblivion, and sank. The messenger from Calcutta was one such drifter, full of pity instead of courage, well-meaning but incapable of action. He had been sent to break the news of Sambhu Narain's elder son's death. But the wind was still, the village hushed, and he was afraid to open his mouth lest his words brought down a sudden plague upon this pastoral remnant from days gone by, the kind of plague and pestilence which is always a threat posed by those who run with messages.

The poor man greeted Sambhu Narain with the rising sun and was welcomed politely by him, without undue enthusiasm, as a friend of his son, Rahul, who was too far away for him to reckon with in the events of the day that lay ahead, too far away for him to be concerned with thoughts of his life or death. Nearly two hundred miles away to the north of Calcutta, Sambhu Narain Chaudhury seemed ill prepared to contemplate anything other than the lazy peace of his ancestral home as he sat in his dark office, as was his custom every morning, ready to fulfill his obligations as the largest landowner of Bishnupur.

The office was part of the shorter arm of a large L-shaped house. Sambhu Narain was quick to point out that if the gentleman had come during the month of August he would have found the room brightened by the sun at that hour and could expect it to remain that way for several hours. Unfortunately, at other times the choice lay between shades of darkness and the pale yellow light from a kerosene lamp. So the stranger sat silently and uncomfortably in the half darkness and looked out through a single doorway with two sets of doors—one glass paned, the other with slanted wooden slats — which opened onto a large verandah. Below the verandah was a dirt road at the end of which, about a quarter mile away, there were some thatched huts. Most of what the stranger could see were silent fields, weighed down under the ripening late winter harvest, that separated Sambhu Narain's brick house from the modest huts.

It was a listless world, and the listlessness of the world outside drifted easily into the room. While it was beginning to touch the guest, it seemed almost to have overcome Sambhu Narain in his chair where he looked up from yesterday's newspaper and yawned with boredom.

He had once been a political writer of sorts – something of a hobby - but had now grown totally indifferent to political news. What was political and what was not, he asked, when even day to day two bit murders were being reported as political assassinations? So what was there left to interest him in the newspapers when the cartoons he no longer understood, and the entertainment ads irrelevant because the movie theatres were in Calcutta and his visits to the city more and more infrequent, and so he yawned a second time. Did anyone dare shatter this mood? Did anyone dare contaminate this illusion of continuity, of eternity, with word on the death of sons and daughters, violent deaths to which panderers of the news flew in the line of duty like vultures, and waited to burrow into motives and evidence, emotions and autopsies, like rats?

The mood did not last. Sambhu Narain suddenly called out to his servant, Panchu, by his name. Like a small but sustained roar, the voice rolled out of the room in every direction, out through the single window overlooking the stables where, under the shade of a *lichi* tree, a young stable boy rubbed down an aging horse with a handful of straw. As if in response to Sambhu Narain's voice, the animal shook his scraggy mane and neighed imperiously. Sambhu Narain turned his head to the window, nodded and smiled, and the stable hand paused in his work, flicked the sweat off his brow, looked around, and returned to his slow, rhythmic grunts as he kneaded the horse's flesh with straw.

Panchu shuffled into the room, walking with a childhood limp. He coughed politely, and waited. A short, slightly built man, remarkably youthful for his fifty years, Panchu had been part of the household for almost four decades. He was therefore the undisputed leader of the servants and enjoyed many privileges which the others didn't, one of them being unfettered access to his master at all times. After a brief conversation during which Sambhu Narain asked if Panchu was busy and Panchu replied, no! he was only cleaning up the master's shaving gear, the master said, good! and asked him to massage his feet for a while and then go and finish whatever he was doing. Panchu sat down on the floor, lotus position, gathered his master's feet into his lap, and without another word, started poking, pinching, and slapping his master's body with his hands. Peace and silence returned to the room once more.

From time to time one could hear Janaki Devi's voice deep inside the house. But her voice was too soft, too muffled, to disturb the peace. Sambhu Narain remarked with what the visitor imagined to be a touch of sadness how much his wife seemed to be on top of her emotions, how much in control. Yes, one could hear her voice. She had every reason to be excited since her daughter, Krishna, was coming home in two days for the festival of Saraswati, and there was much to be done. Saraswati would come like the tide, like the seasons, like day follows night. This the visitor knew as well he knew that Krishna wouldn't, as well he knew that he would never bring himself to break the news of Sanjit's death to Sambhu Narain. He couldn't understand how he had accepted his friend Rahul's errand in the first place. This was no task for a stranger.

I will tell you something, said Sambhu Narain, which my godless sons could never have mentioned to you, how Saraswati occupies a special place in our hearts, especially since the family was forbidden a hundred years ago from worshipping the formidable Durga. At the mention of Durga's name he raised his hands to his forehead in silent homage to the goddess. The last time the family had worshipped Durga was the time the eight-year old daughter of the house vanished mysteriously. She was a princess to the family. Since then, every daughter in the Chaudhury household was to be worshipped like a queen. It was the final night of the festival of Durga, and the word Durga was a passionate prayer on every lip when, at the end of hours of fruitless search, men and women lay weeping at the feet of the clay goddess. Then someone noticed a corner of the missing girls' *sari* inside Durga's mouth. When the time came for the inevitable immersion of the goddess, women beat their breasts and men wept shamelessly for it seemed that it was not only the goddess of clay that was being cast into the murky waters of the river, but the young princess as well. Living flesh and blood had become one with clay.

Sambhu Narain puffed deeply on his *hookah* during the pause, looked at his visitor with amusement, and asked if he, with all his obvious education and wisdom, knew what really had taken place. The visitor replied that all his wisdom could not compare with a single spark from the magical heart of *Ishwara*. The answer pleased Sambhu Narain. He closed his eyes and smiled to himself. While Panchu worked silently on his toes, Sambhu Narain described how his ancestors had locked up the house the same night and gone away on a long pilgrimage to Hardwar. When they returned, there were things to be rearranged, things to put away, things like brass plates, copper glasses and silver vases that had sparkled in the light of the festivities and had now to be stored away in enormous wooden chests, forever. The chests were so large, the servants needed ladders to climb in and out of them. It was in one of these chests that they found the body of the young girl, dead in a secret hiding place she had chosen while playing hide-and-seek with her friends on the last night of Durga. I do not know whether the family did right in ending their domestic worship of Durga, said Sambhu Narain, do not know whether it befits mortals to be vengeful towards the gods. His voice trailed away into silence as the delicious pleasure flowing through Panchu's virtuoso fingers settled heavily on Sambhu Narain's eyelids.

The visitor became aware once more of Janaki Devi's presence in the background as she moved from one end of the house to the other, casting a watchful eye on the scrubbing, the dusting, the peeling and chopping of the vegetables, all in preparation of her daughter's visit. Once or twice he reminded himself of her inner strength and felt that he should tell her the truth about her son, the truth he had been asked to bring to Bishnupur. But he was too much of a coward, knew he was far from ready, and so retreated into his tortured thoughts about the family.

There was a time when Sambhu Narain's holdings were five times as large as the meagre six square miles he now possessed. That was when he first came to Bishnupur, many years ago, upon his father's death. A time when nothing lay beyond the reach of his authority, when every birth, every death, every marriage, every transgression, every punishment touched him in some way. Although his little empire had no legal authority over his tenants, there were hundreds of ways in which he could still exercise influence as serious and potent as anything the law courts could devise. So it was not difficult to understand why his friends believed that it was the promise of power which swayed him more than anything else into giving up a colourless, if casual, journalistic career and moving from Calcutta.

Many events had changed people's lives around Bishnupur since the days of India's independence in nineteen forty seven. But Sambhu Narain's family was still the richest in the district, and in matters affecting the economic and social life of the village his voice was still respected as no one else's. The Nehru government had passed legislation forcing the princely *zamindars* to give up large parts of their estates. These legal irritants seemed irrelevant to Sambhu Narain who took pride in saying he thought nothing of land. When the younger of his two sons, Rahul, pointed out the contradictions in his life as a *zamindar*, Sambhu Narain was quick to retort that there was nothing inconsistent about being a landlord and being indifferent to the possession of land. The one is my destined role, he said, the other simply an illusion. As if to prove his point, well before Nehru's edicts could overtake him, Sambhu Narain voluntarily signed away hundreds of acres of his property, many to destitute farmers.

Each year, from February to October, since the day he had come to live in Bishnupur, Sambhu Narain sat behind the same teakwood desk, in front of the same petrified, leather-bound volumes of Johnson, Boswell, Scott and Dickens, telling whoever would listen how much he liked Dickens and how he would gladly give the others away to friends and relatives except for the lingering memory of his father whose books they were. Secretly, he wished his sons would lay their hands on the books, but that was not to be. Of his sons, Sanjit only had jet planes on his mind. Sambhu Narain admired his courage but doubted that he would ever do much reading. The younger son, Rahul, was a puzzle he had given up trying to understand a long time ago. In spite of the finest English-medium education one could buy under the shadow of the Himalaya, Rahul, whose current tastes ran to Mao, Marx and Marcuse, never betrayed the slightest interest in the noble authors languishing behind his father's desk. So the novels remained where they were and gathered dust.

From eleven to twelve each morning, Sambhu Narain sat in front of the books, ready to sign papers, any kind of document conceivable, for the sheer joy of it. While a succession of horrified estate managers watched helplessly, Sambhu Narain signed and signed and signed. Within the first five years of his stewardship, he had signed his name to every piece of paper placed before him. Now, when there was little left to sign away, fewer hopefuls dropped by at the appointed hour. Still, Sambhu Narain remained as unconcerned as ever, never bothering to read anything that he signed, deaf to whether someone entreated, "Respected Sir, please be kind enough to put your good name on this paper and oblige your humble servant", or whether someone mixed craft and cunning and said, "It's a blessing you are in our midst; please sign this paper for the matter needs immediate attention". It hardly mattered what one said, so that there was never any danger of having to explain whether a piece of paper was a share certificate, an affidavit, or a rent waiver. Sambhu Narain had wiped off all such distinctions in his mind. The request and his response to it were all that mattered. Head cocked to one side, he would slowly begin his signature, labouring over every flourish which had to be executed to perfection, until the signature was finally complete. At that point, he would throw his head back and gaze at his name for a moment or two, a piercing gaze which was always the same, always intent on delving below the name as if searching for some secret once revealed to him in a dream, until the moment passed and, freed from his spell, Sambhu Narain would slowly push the paper away from him.

Had it not been for his wife, he would probably have signed himself out of his very home, a possibility which Janaki Devi guarded against by controlling every item of correspondence now entering or leaving the house. She had herself placed before her husband many documents for his signature and had succeeded in transfering large tracts of land and other assets to her own name. Those who found their lust for land or money blunted by her cunning called Janaki Devi a heartless witch and swore behind her back that she was slowly poisoning her husband. They said it was evident to all that his mind had already gone, and that it was a matter of time before his heart, his eyes, and his feet gave way altogether, and then people would see his wife for what she was, a covetous woman who would share nothing with her children, a wily woman who claimed she was perpetuating the old tradition of living primarily for her husband when she was doing everything possible to hasten his end. If her chief concern lay in outwitting her relatives and protecting her childlike husband from total ruin, what had she accomplished, they snickered, when the truth was that the entire village had seen through the fool and no longer had any time for Sambhu Narain's eccentricities. Except one, perhaps, one event in which they willingly cooperated with him — the plays Sambhu Narain helped stage each year at his own expense, sometimes even scripting the plays himself.

Little by little, he had overcome the skepticism of the villagers, until skepticism gave way to curiosity and even amusement, until a few years later the event turned into something of a festival attracting audiences from miles around. More and more peasants began taking advantage of the large crowds to sell their wares, their weavings, their produce, until in nineteen sixty three there came the cows, the buffaloes, and the goats. After that, there was nothing to stop the jugglers, fire eaters, stunt cyclists and dancing girls with long, braided, perfumed hair to transform the humble village playhouse to a brief but spectacular carnival. This didn't bother Sambhu Narain at all, for there always remained a hard core of the faithful who drew their excitement not from the ferris wheels or the whirling skirts but from the fire and passion of his plays, their lofty themes drawn from the *Ramayan* and the *Mahabharat*. Sambhu Narain always reserved a major role for himself, not those of the classic hero but roles evoking the maverick, the outsider. He was Karna, pursued by the divinely guided Arjun on the battlefield of Kurukshetra. He was Ravan, the abductor of the chaste Sita.

His many tumultuous deaths always moved the audience to tears, especially his young children who were among his most ardent admirers. But there came the day when the oldest, Sanjit, began to scoff at the epics for their coarse simplicity. Rahul, upon turning twenty, said he could no longer stand the social hypocrisy of his father performing for the peasants, pretending to entertain while preserving an outdated code of morality and control. But Krishna remained steadfast in her loyalty from the day she could sit by herself on the rug spread in front of the stage to the day she stood up and clung mesmerized to the edge of the platform which served as the stage, until the day she went away to her in-laws and talked them into letting her return to the village for a few days in October each year so that she could laugh and clap as her father roared across the stage and then cry over his shoulder afterwards when the play was over and everyone had gone home.

Then it was time for father and daughter to remember, for her to tell him of her in-laws, some of their dark secrets and human frailties she had discovered through living with them; for him to tell her, and repeat year after year with fresh embellishments, his memories of her magnificent wedding. The *shehnai* wailed its plaintive notes from dawn to well past midnight for three days, and a fire, fattened by offerings of butter, burned night and day in everlasting witness to Krishna's union with Vikram. While one frail, silver-haired priest who could barely lift his head chanted the wedding prayers in inaudible murmurs punctuated by gasps to suck air, the other, Durga Chakravartty's father from the village of Bishnupur, droned out his incantations from the innermost folds of his overhanging belly with a flair which warmed every traditionalist's heart and filled their ears with the noble resonance of Sanskrit But the purists were few and far between, and hardly anyone understood the prayers any more. The one person who could be expected to wax eloquent over them was Vikram's uncle. A scholar of the highest order, he had retired from the University of Calcutta, a much admired professor of Sanskrit. This venerable scholar was too overwhelmed during most of the wedding to lend his presence to what, in an unguarded moment, he described to a shocked audience as no more than a crock of priestly mumbo jumbo. Having thus created some emotional distance between himself and the ceremonies, Professor Das was discovered, at that moment when the smoke was the thickest, the fire brightest, and the priests racing through their invocations like men possessed, tremulously clutching with one hand the rim of a toilet bowl deep inside the house while his other hand was moving blindly all over his face trying to locate his elusive mouth. The ultimate objective of this solemn ritual was to stick his fingers deep inside his throat and thereby throw up the countless *burra* pegs of Old Smuggler and other peripheral appetizers consumed earlier in the evening. An ancient colonial rite, the practice was guaranteed to make room for more of the same.

It was a lot of fun, said Sambhu Narain, remembering, how Krishna's father-in-law, the colourful Sir Ajoy Mukherjee, kept insisting, as he paced up and down his marble floors and planned the wedding, that there was to be nothing but the very best for his only son and his bride. Money was no consideration. So, while the guests drank to their fill and slapped each other on the back and the elders of the community hinted darkly that the country was going to the dogs, while the ladies paused in their social crucifixions to comment on the bride, while Sambhu Narain pretended to look somber and religious and Professor Das spewed all over the bathroom tiles, in a strange and mysterious way Krishna passed out of one life and entered another. And Krishna's mother lapsed into prayers from time to time, for she was in the habit of breaking away from the company of others to lose herself in prayers.

Jerking himself free from Panchu's seductive fingers, Sambhu Narain startled the visitor by suddenly asking, "What good are prayers when we are no more than puppets on a string, and the string, my friend, is not our prayers." He laughed and continued, "For I do not pray, and she comes to me still, do not sing to her but can hear her still."

He described how he had seen her as a dark woman holding her breasts in her outstretched hands, streaks of blood smearing her naked body and the earth she stood on, dark clouds hanging over her head, and bloodstained men prostrate at her feet. And what she said to him was this: 'My words are the only words there are; mine is the wilderness of words forever crying to be heard, not knowing who will hear, not caring if no one hears, for salvation lies in the crying, not in being heard.'

And he was full of fear and astonishment as she cried: 'Pity the power that's deaf, not the voice that cries; for our voices erupt from the heart of Brahma, set to words by Brahma, consigned to time past forever by Brahma, words without music — harsh and troubled, words without shadows — unwritten and uncommitted, words that are no more than the substance of dreams, dreams of Krishna on the battlefield of Kurukshetra, muddied by the blood of brothers, poisoned by the wisdom of the gods, dreams of the Siddharta wasting away under the lush banyan tree, dreams of the apostle to the east washing his ivory feet upon our shores. Listen, she said, to the voice of the Emperor Shahjahan awakened to a sigh by the muezzin's call, his sorrow unanswered by his beloved Mumtaz. But listen, the Taj remains, silent echo of the emperor's longing, the sharp, irrefutable edge of mortality, like this vast land which is my echo. That is all that matters. So tread upon the land if you must, fearlessly, but only if you'll make it a home like one of us, shred the skies with your claws like us, and sing my song of revenge silently with us.'

Sambhu Narain paused, laughed once more, looked hard at the visitor, and turned his head towards the open door which now framed the sudden apparition of the village postmaster, Gaur. He stepped out of his shoes at the threshold, carefully placed his umbrella against the wall, and walked inside to Sambhu Narain's warm greetings. Meanwhile, Panchu was up on his feet, waiting for the nod from his master that would send him scurrying inside for the inevitable sweets and tea for the postmaster. When Panchu had left the room, Sambhu Narain shook his head thoughtfully as was his habit and asked the postmaster, "And how's your wife today?"

Gaur replied that she was about the same as before, considering the heavy fog that choked up the morning air, and that his wife was unlikely to improve if she wasn't able to go to the hills. But where was the money?

Sambhu Narain kept shaking his head and remarked that the wife's condition couldn't be doing much good for the daughter, and asked when her new baby was to arrive.

"Today or tomorrow, there's no telling when," replied Gaur, then added with a lowered voice that her husband should've been up from Calcutta by now, and wondered if there was any point in suggesting the new surgical procedure to his son-in-law, this to be his fifth child, what with the price of rice soaring, and sugar practically disappearing from the market, and fish and vegetables almost luxuries...

"You weren't thinking of a vasectomy, were you?" asked Sambhu Narain, gently interrupting his friend.

Gaur came back saying yes, yes, that was it, and then, looking cautiously at the stranger in the room, he pulled up his chair a little closer to Sambhu Narain's and asked, "What do you think, can it stand up after the operation?"

Sambhu Narain's face grew a little serious. "Yes, my friend, they say it can'" he replied. "But I honestly don't believe them. Can you see as well after your cataract operation as you did before?" He paused and added with a smile that of course one could, but not without thick glasses. So that if Gaur really wanted his firm opinion, he would have to say that self-discipline and yoga would be infinitely more desirable than vasectomy.

Gaur couldn't help a note of exasperation from creeping into his voice as he cried, "You and your self-discipline. If we had self-discipline why do you suppose we wouldn't stop eating every other day and save a little on our grocery bills?"

Sambhu Narain began to laugh even before Gaur had finished, and told him it was not his money that he was proposing to save, but his life itself, that what he was suggesting would prolong one's life almost indefinitely, would take man further away from the animals and closer to the gods.

The laughter died down. During the silence that followed, the two men sat contemplating the delicate issue until they were awakened by the figure of Durga Chakravartty, the priest, arching his neck from the road outside and trying to decide whether anyone had preceded him into Sambhu Narain's office. Sambhu Narain looked at Gaur and said that the priest was the man who ought to be able to answer his question with a lot more authority and knowledge. Then, raising his voice, he called out to Durga Chakravartty not to strain his neck, but to come in instead.

The old man needed no further prompting as he quickly scrambled up the steps, walked into the room breathlessly, and announced that he couldn't stay very long as he had to arrange for the last rites of Chandra Babu's mother who had finally died of tuberculosis the night before. As the priest hitched up his *dhotie* to his knees and sat down heavily on the cot, Sambhu Narain asked how old the lady had been. The priest replied that she looked a hundred though she must've been a lot younger. Life really hadn't been too kind to her. The postmaster added softly God bless her soul.

The talk of death brought the visitor momentarily back to his senses, reminding him why he had come to Bishnupur in the first place. But the priest had other things on his mind. Having gotten the introductions out of the way, he began, "What I wanted to see you about this morning, Sambhu Narain, was the stage. It's been nine years since you had it built for us, but have you seen what last month's storm has done to it?" Sambhu Narain looked genuinely concerned and asked what had happened. The priest explained that all the struts from the eastern side had collapsed, which was not wholly unexpected since he had informed Sambhu Narain the previous summer that sections of the main platform had rotted away.

Sambhu Narain sighed. A great pity, he said, then added somewhat sheepishly that only one person could decide the cost of repairs, his wife, but that could wait since the more important problem they had before them was the question of vasectomy and one's ability to perform successfully after it. He informed the priest that Gaur had a serious question and asked if he would be able to give him a clear answer.

"Let me know the question first," demanded the priest. Sambhu Narain began by stating that the problem was as follows: Gaur's daughter was about to give birth to her fifth child, and would the priest therefore recommend vasectomy for the husband.

The priest was outraged. He cried out that he would never recommend it to a Hindu as long as he lived. But yes, if anyone needed it, it would have to be the Muslims, for with their four wives and God knows how many concubines did they not produce four times as many children as Hindus? Surely, if anyone had to be penalized, it had to be the Muslims.

Surprised by the priest's passion, Sambhu Narain seemed ill at ease with the general drift of the conversation. It was common knowledge that the priest was a vicious hater of Muslims who had, in nineteen sixty four, led a murderous raid on a nearby Muslim village called Hazariganj. Before Sambhu Narain had a chance to change the subject, Gaur, the village postmaster, seized the theme and commented that Chakravartty Mahashai, the priest, was absolutely right. The latter continued that he was beginning to find the Muslims getting rather cocky again, but what could you expect when the Congress party decides to make one of those untouchables the president of the nation. Gaur commented that they could of course do something to put them in their proper place, adding that the priest should speak to some of the young men in their village about teaching Hazariganj another lesson since the cow killers had obviously forgotten what happened to them four years ago.

Durga Chakravartty shook his head and admitted that he was getting too old for that.

Sambhu Narain nimbly stepped into the ensuing lull to announce that he had something to show them all, two of the most exquisite English blankets he had bought in Burrabazaar the last time he was in Calcutta. He was almost sure they were the last of their kind in all of India. While Sambhu Narain went inside the house to collect the keys from his wife, open the steel almirah, and get the blankets out, Gaur, who had looked somewhat uncomfortable discussing vasectomy, now turned to the visitor for a discussion on the decline of British trade in India. It didn't matter that the others were unwilling to come up with details that would fuel the conversation along. Still, the priest was quick to point out that the British certainly knew how to make things strong and durable. Them, and the Germans, for his German Solingen razor shaved as beautifully today as the day his father put it to his face forty years ago.

Gaur's voice was full of mockery as he swore that those great days, those fine things, would never come back. For why talk of blankets and razors, did folks know that the last time he went up to Siliguri and asked a pharmacist for a packet of English letters, the pharmacist said something to the effect that they had either stopped making them in England or stopped shipping them outside their own country. This left him no choice but to buy a packet made in India which he doubted would last very long, not that he was critical of things made in India for they were certainly much less expensive than the English ones, but he believed that there were certain things in which it was foolish to economize. Certain traditions were important.

Durga Chakravartty solemnly pointed out that times do change and we have to change with them, noting he had heard that ever since England had been driven out of her colonies she herself had been colonized by natives and niggers like us. So much for tradition.

Nothing is impossible, said Sambhu Narain, returning with the blankets. He presented the two pieces proudly, one checkered green the other brown, draped across each arm, and asked anxiously if they didn't think the two would make really nice suits.

Gaur got up from his chair. The village priest adjusted his bifocals. The two men brought their faces almost against the blankets, feeling them with their fingers, sniffing them for the fragrance of wool, finally pronouncing their verdict in unison: Oh most marvellous.

Sambhu Narain looked genuinely pleased with this response. When he turned to the visitor for his comments, the stranger remembered how much of a passion clothes were to him, remembering with fondness the laughter Rahul and he had shared over the old man's eccentricities. Sambhu Narain's finest suits dated back to the days when he was a journalist, and he was secretly proud of the fact that they had been tailored in London. Because he wore them less and less after India won her independence in nineteen forty seven, they seemed indestructible and lasted him into the sixties when he finally abandoned them, with some regret, as his daughter's wedding brought home to him how shabby his older clothes had grown.

Several years earlier, he had walked away from his career in journalism where sartorial standards were far from the highest. It was clearly something of a shock to Sambhu Narain to realize that there existed a world of fastidious dressers like the one inhabited by the friends and family of Sir Ajoy, Krishna's father-in-law. It was then that Sambhu Narain suddenly turned to dressing like a traditional Indian aristocrat, explaining his departure from western clothes as being the only proper way to express his nationalism.

In Calcutta, Sambhu Narain presented a picture of elegance in flowing silk shirt, fine handloomed dhotie, embroidered Kashmiri shawl. But there were two days each year when he would relent and wear a suit. This was during the theater season, and it never failed to awe the villagers.

Under the pretext of buying blankets, Sambhu Narain would bring back woollen material from Calcutta and permit them to be crafted in fear and trepidation by the village tailor who, in sixty five years, had never fashioned any western clothes other than some shirts and the odd pair of trousers for the more *avant garde* among the village thugs. Sambhu Narain felt somewhat diffident about having his suits tailored by the faithful Farookh Rahman from Calcutta's fashionable Camac Street who had urged him for twenty years to get some new suits made. He had finally grown weary of repeated alterations to old suits until, driven to blindness by age, he had given up tailoring altogether.

On theater nights, Sambhu Narain would finish his act and, while the others sang or danced or recited poems, he put on his suit and joined his family in the audience. At the close of the second night, it was always his custom to rise for a brief speech. After that, farewell suit for another year.

Smiling and appreciative of the visitor's compliments, Sambhu Narain folded the blankets and neatly placed them on one side of his desk. As he did so, he murmured that they should all see the suits his son Sanjit wore. He was getting to be quite a famous fellow, no doubt about that.

At which point, the visitor could only turn his head towards the window in a futile attempt to gather some courage and break the news to the father, except that the priest suddenly asked Sambhu Narain for news of Rahul and was rewarded with a distasteful glance from Sambhu Narain. He did not wish to discuss his second son, saying that he'd rather talk about Sanjit. He told them about the new Russian planes he was flying. He was also learning ballroom dancing for it was a big thing in the armed services, necessary for promotion and all that. Truly, he was proud of his son, what nerves of steel.

Of course, of course, noted Durga Chakravartty warmly. Why else would they take him into the air force, for that was no place for women and ninnies.

Wistfully, Sambhu Narain said yes and then began to smile. Everyone was certain there was something stirring his imagination. They were startled when he suddenly asked what they thought of the idea of putting on a ballroom dancing performance for the villagers that year. His eyes moved from the priest to the postmaster. Durga Chakravartty evidently did not understand the full implications of the question, pointing out to Sambhu Narain that the stage had to be repaired first with Janaki Devi's permission. Sambhu Narain ignored the suggestion. Turning his eyes to the open fields in the distance, he wondered whether Janaki Devi could be persuaded to dance. Even before the postmaster and the priest had finished exchanging looks of horror, Sambhu Narain let out a cry of delight as he looked triumphantly at Gaur and said, "Hey! they tell me you were quite a dancer when you were young. How about that."

Gaur grinned in embarrassment and pleaded with Sambhu Narain not to believe anything he had heard on the subject. "I only knew some native folk dances," he said. "What do I understand of the English ways you pick up every time you go to Calcutta." As an afterthought, he asked, "Have you done this dance yourself?"

Sambhu Narain replied emphatically that of course he hadn't. But a year or so ago, Sanjit and his sister had given him a demonstration and had playfully insisted on teaching him some of the rudiments. He would therefore be very pleased to show them what little he remembered of those lessons.

Unable to decide how to react to this, everyone chose to remain puzzled and silent. Sambhu Narain pointed out that there had to be some music as an accompaniment. Since the household His Master's Voice gramophone had snapped its mainspring several months ago, it was unanimously decided that the services of the village harmonium expert were essential. Gaur suggested that Chakravartty Mahashai could perhaps ask Biren to drop by with his harmonium in the afternoon. At this point, the priest gathered his *dhotie* around him and started to get up. He said he had indeed been thinking of Biren that very morning, that he would be pleased to ask him to come, but that he must now take his leave to attend to the peace of the old woman's soul.

God bless her, murmured Sambhu Narain, reminding the priest who was already at the edge of the verandah to be sure to drop by himself, tempting him with the promise of tea and biscuits.

"Yes, yes, we shall see," said the priest, clattering down the steps in his wooden *kharams*. As his footsteps died away, a strange silence returned to the room. The visitor began to contemplate the wooden rafters laced over with cobwebs, while Gaur began to show the first signs of dozing off.

Sambhu Narain's voice was soft and gentle. "Perhaps we should forget staging a play this year," he said.

"Why, why?" asked Gaur, suddenly awake and stopping himself from lurching forward into the desk just in time. He reminded Sambhu Narain that the village would probably have the largest crowd ever that year. He had been informed by Chanchal, the village Youth Congress leader, that the Congress party was planning to hold its annual district convention in Bishnupur during the October fair and that peasants would come to the village by the truckloads.

Sambhu Narain smiled ruefully and asked if that wasn't another reason not to stage a play. He would like to stay as far away from politicians as he could. He paused and added that was not the real reason. Which was that lately he had found himself increasingly indifferent to public exposure, increasingly under emotional pressure to look inside his soul and read the lines fate had been plotting and charting for him, to walk away from the peace that lay all around him. Somehow, it had to be a mistake, a deception.

Gaur stifled a yawn and assured Sambhu Narain that he still had many years left to begin contemplating such a sense of mortality. A distant look crept into Sambhu Narain's eyes as he confessed that, unlike other years, he had been unable to work up a script so far for the October play. He wondered whether Gaur and the visitor would be interested to hear what he had been writing of late. Not a play, nothing with a mythological flavour, just something that seemed the only way left for him to draw closer to his god. Did they want to hear that?

The visitor remained silent. Gaur replied that since he was sitting there and since he had nowhere else to go that afternoon, perhaps it was just as well that Sambhu Narain had something to read.

Sambhu Narain opened a small wooden cupboard behind him and carefully pulled out a sheaf of loose papers. He lifted up a single sheet, looked at his guests with some uncertainty, cleared his throat and, reminding them that what he was about to read had been born of a deep sense of frustration, he started:

"There must be something one can ask for
Something plentiful
Something no one needs or misses
Save the one who asks. . . .
Like the first note of a bell
Inviting other notes to gather, follow, echo
The asking.
But our questions lie exhumed
And consecrated
As longings unfulfilled,
Affronts to the perfect conscience
Unaccustomed to leaving stones unturned
Or resources unexploited
In service of human wants
To fatten the flesh on sorrow,
Grow monstrous, fearful,
Envious of homage to any force
But its own,
Oblivious of mean passions that give shape
Or careless fancies that breathe life."

Sambhu Narain read with a beautiful voice. As he finished the poem, his eyes met Gaur's and found there a look of utter bewilderment. Sambhu Narain probably found it disappointing, for he did not care to look at anyone else. Panchu had silently entered the room in the middle of the poem, but there was no need for him to announce his mission. Sambhu Narain knew what he was about. It was time for lunch, and Sambhu Narain slowly put the papers back in their place. He invited the visitor to stay for the meal and as long as he wanted to afterwards.

"That was a very difficult poem," said Gaur, "and I am not a very educated person you know." Sambhu Narain laughed and led the postmaster inside the house, his arm encircling Gaur's shoulders.

During the entire meal, they never saw Janaki Devi once. But one would occasionally hear her voice, and everyone was somehow aware of her invisible presence throughout. Later, they dozed through the warm afternoon, the rice and fish heavy inside their stomachs. The visitor went over a hundred ways in which to break the news of his son's death to Sambhu Narain. Even though the next train to Calcutta was not till the following morning, it was not until people began to arrive for the evening's gathering that he realized how helpless, weak, and cowardly he was.

Dusk came quickly to the village and he finally roused himself to join the others in Sambhu Narain's office where he introduced the visitor collectively to everyone, including some newcomers. They grew quiet in his presence. When they heard the sounds of an approaching bicycle shortly afterwards, the conversation came back to life. People knew it was Biren who never travelled along the village paths, especially after sundown, without sounding his bell continuously.

Biren stepped down from the bicycle in front of the verandah. Everyone had come out of the room to greet him. He explained his behavior about the bell, perhaps for the thousandth time, by telling the gathering, "I do not wish to have the blood of a snake on my hands, nor do I wish to give my blood to one. So I will stay clear of their paths, and let them stay clear of mine."

Biren rested the bike against a wooden post and carefully loosened the ropes which held the harmonium on the rack at the rear. He called out to Panchu in a loud voice at the same time, waited for an answer, then feigned an air of outrage as he caught sight of Sambhu Narain. Biren shouted to him that he had almost carried the instrument across the seven seas and was no longer prepared to haul it over the steps into Sambhu Narain's house. Never, never, Sambhu Narain assured him, trying to sound equally serious, for have we not an obligation to look after our artists, he asked his guests. Then, noticing one of the servants smoking in the dark near the stables, he yelled at him, "You scoundrel, can't you see there's this harmonium waiting to be carried up?"

The boy leapt up from under the *lichi* tree and darted towards the verandah, his half finished *biri* moving in a brief arc through the air until it fell dangerously close to a stack of hay, prompting five voices to bark at him simultaneously, "You imbecile, do you want to roast us alive? Go put out that flaming *biri* first." Even Sambhu Narain went after him lightheartedly, reminding him of the many times he had asked him not to smoke. Did he wish to remain a midget for the rest of his life? The mortified stable boy knew better than to answer back. He quickly went about the business of carrying the instrument into Sambhu Narain's office, wondering where to put it down.

Suddenly the evening came alive as everyone started to speak at the same time, someone ordering the servant to put down the harmonium on the cot, someone on the floor, someone on the table. Another voice began to insist on tea and sweets. The postmaster chided Biren for taking so long to come, unmindful of the anxiety he was causing the wives, his own wife probably wondering if the postmaster had slipped into the pond and drowned. Biren laughed at this and commented that it wouldn't be such a great loss after all. Sambhu Narain asked Biren to make himself comfortable and, seeing that Panchu had not yet shown up, wondered aloud where the bastard had disappeared to. Finally, he cleared his throat and called out to the servant in his most resounding voice. This seemed to provoke an immediate response as an unseen woman's voice asked from behind the curtains, "What's the problem? One would think the house was being raided by a band of robbers."

Everyone fell silent. Nobody answered. Just then, Panchu slipped past Janaki Devi to present himself inside the room. This immediately prompted Biren to demand which corner of hell he had been grazing in while Biren had been screaming his lungs out for him. Taking liberties which a younger servant would not have dreamed of, Panchu explained, "Sir, you must be a little patient at sunset. I was just finishing my last *chillum* of *ganja* and surely you would not expect me to break off in the middle of my euphoria."

"Enough," interrupted Sambhu Narain imperiously, ordering Panchu to bring another round of sweets and tea for everyone. He added that if Janaki Devi had moved away from the next room she should be told that they were soon to have some music which she might like to listen to. Biren called out after the departing Panchu to make sure the tea was piping hot or he would break his legs.

Apart from the priest, the postmaster, and Biren, three other prominent villagers had dropped by that evening. Devdulal Banik, an enormous man, owned the local grocery store and, on the side, loaned small sums of money at exorbitant rates. Chanchal, something of a budding politician, was actually a government appointed social worker and a self-trained irrigation expert who never lost an opportunity to declare how much he loved staying in the village rather than the nearby town of Siliguri where he supposedly had a large ancestral home. And finally Batuk, a person of no fixed occupation, pathologically inclined to help others in every way conceivable. All these men cast enormous shadows on the wall, against the light from the majestic brass lamp in the centre of Sambhu Narain's desk augmented by two common hurricane lanterns. His fat neck quivering with excitement, Devdulal's voice was like a duck's as he expressed his delight at the unexpected pleasure of dropping by for tea and finding himself served with music as well.

"And dancing too, I understand," added Batuk.

No, no, protested Sambhu Narain immediately, gesturing defensively with his hands, saying it was all a joke. Could they really imagine him dancing without forcing Janaki Devi to have him locked up behind bars by nightfall?

"But you can't disappoint us now," cried Chanchal, "not after all the snakes and crocodiles Biren foiled in trying to get here."

Sambhu Narain did not answer. Biren had meanwhile finished his tea and, placing the plate of sweets squarely on the harmonium, he quickly struck up a series of chords. It was not long before he started to sing, singing of spring, of rain, of lovers, and the land. Everyone withdrew into the secret recesses of their minds. Sambhu Narain gazed pensively into the darkness where the lights from distant huts were mere specks in the night and the crickets were busy with their own songs.

At some point in the evening, Panchu had taken care to pull the curtain right across the door leading into the house. A slight movement behind this now signalled Janaki Devi's presence there. Whenever the men sang in her house, she had Panchu pull her a chair behind the curtain where she could hear without being seen. At other times she would gladly meet the men, talk and even joke with them. But she felt these occasions had special meaning for the men and imagined that her presence there would be uncomfortable and unwelcome. Other servants, stray peasants, their wives and children had also materialized like phantoms. These now sat huddled together in the dark verandah, listening and watching.

From time to time, the ubiquitous Panchu moved quietly through the guests, carrying a silver tray, collecting empty tea cups and replacing them with cups freshly brewed. Biren sang at a stretch for an hour or more. When he finally stopped and picked up the plate of sweets off the harmonium cover, everyone knew he would sing no more. So they turned to Sambhu Narain. He looked very uneasy and began to protest, "No, no, it's impossible." They kept on urging him until he finally relented. "All right, all right," he said, "I'll show you a few steps of ballroom dancing."

From behind the curtain, Janaki Devi promptly exclaimed, "Good God, the man has taken leave of all his senses." She made no secret of her irritation as she stood up noisily from the chair and withdrew into the house. Devdulal had a silly grin on his face as he suggested that Sambhu Narain get on with the demonstration for surely Janaki Devi would come round in a few minutes. Sambhu Narain shrugged helplessly and asked Biren to give him a nice catchy tune. After a few hesitant attempts, Biren settled down with a popular film song. Sambhu Narain rose from his chair and started shuffling through the empty spaces in the room with something that looked like a one-two-three one-two-three waltz step.

It didn't matter that the music fought the steps all the way. Biren had no idea there existed any music other than the one he knew. When he saw Sambhu Narain gliding and shuffling with his arms extended forward, the grocer asked in a puzzled voice what had happened to Sambhu Narain's hands, why he was holding them stretched in front of him. He asked whether he was supposed to be doing some symbolic dance *mudras* with them.

"No, you fool," answered Sambhu Narain, dancing towards him. "I'm supposed to be holding a woman in my arms." At which several voices asked him what precisely he meant. Sambhu Narain stopped and called out, "Would you please come here, Gaur?"

As soon as Gaur stepped in front of him, Sambhu Narain asked Biren to resume his music. Then, without allowing Gaur the slightest hint of what was to happen next, he embraced his uncomprehending friend and began pushing him across the floor with his body. The spectacle gave rise to a shocked silence at first and hysterical laughter later as toes were bruised, slippers torn, and knees became hopelessly entangled in *dhoties*. In a minute or two, Sambhu Narain crashed into the cot, pinning Gaur between himself and the jelly-like mass of Devdulal Banik. When the bodies disentangled themselves, the grocer remained dazed and panting, the priest angry and disapproving, and the others doubled over with laughter.

"Heaven preserve us from such obscenities," exploded Durga Chakravartty, unable to believe that white folk danced like that in public.

"But it's their custom, Chakravartty Mahashai," explained Sambhu Narain apologetically. He added that it might surprise the priest to know that many of their own people danced like that these days. Sanjit, for instance, as Sambhu Narain had taken care to point out earlier in the day.

For a moment it seemed the priest would almost choke with disbelief as he asked, "You mean in public? With their wives?" Yes and no, replied Sambhu Narain, explaining that sometimes people even danced with women who were not their wives. The priest spoke up with derision, "No doubt with whores then."

Sambhu Narain began to lose patience with the man as he told him sharply that the priest was behind the times, that there was a world outside Bishnupur many knew nothing of, another world of men and women all of whom were not animals. "Ask Chanchal," said Sambhu Narain in conclusion. "He probably knows the big city better than any of you."

Realizing that he had to make some sort of a statement, Chanchal looked from one face to the other and began, "I had a teacher in school who was fond of saying that an Englishman's home was his castle. But the only castle I know of is one that is locked within me. As for my home, it really belongs to others and so I can be in touch with concerns that are not my own. As a public servant, I must of necessity make these concerns my own. You see, when President Johnson sneezes in America, Ho Chi Minh trembles in Hanoi. And that is because there are no castle walls, no castle gates any more. This is what Mrs. Gandhi has been trying to tell the nation, and as a Congress worker I believe her. I believe that she can bring about a new order, closing the gap between rich and poor, the educated and the illiterate, the farmer and the city dweller."

"And Hindus and Muslims and Christians, I suppose"' asked the priest with a sneer. Chanchal groped briefly for an answer, ending up explaining to Durga Chakravartty that the new order didn't mean he would have to eat in a Muslim home or pray in a Christian temple. He was about to add that there was a compelling need to live together with millions of people when he was rudely interrupted by the priest. "Enough, enough of that," he said.

Everyone lapsed into a brooding silence. It was clear that Chanchal's observations satisfied nobody. The visitor wondered whether Chanchal had intended to rebuff Sambhu Narain or had merely seized an opportunity to spill out some undigested garbage. There now began an exodus with the priest taking the lead. From inside the house Janaki Devi sent word that the image of the goddess Saraswati was to be installed the following morning. When the craftsmen brought the image to the house she would like the priest to welcome her across the threshold, even though the actual worship would begin on the day after.

Durga Chakravartty promised Panchu that he would definitely be present the next day and the following day, for even though there would be otherimages to be installed in the village, the one in Janaki Devi's house would be the most important, the most sacred. Then he turned to Biren and asked, "Are you taking your bicycle or walking with us?"

"I'm taking the bicycle and also walking with you," replied Biren, trying to blow away the tension in the air. He asked Sambhu Narain if he might leave the harmonium in the house for the night, just in case it became necessary for him to carry the priest who had had so many of his precious illusions shattered that evening.

Sambhu Narain turned to Chanchal who alone had no wife waiting for him at home. He suggested that he stay back for dinner and chat with the visitor.

"So much the worse for him," said Gaur, asking whether any of their daughters would ever manage to capture the castle of Chanchal's heart. "Who knows where his heart is?" asked Biren, shaking his head thoughtfully.

Batuk joined in the banter by suggesting that there was no need for it to be anywhere but in Gaur's house. He asked Gaur if there was any point in sending his daughter to college. Would that make her a better wife or a patient mother? Finally, he offered to play the matchmaker between Gaur's daughter and the young man who seemed to be wasting away.

Chanchal said nothing. When asked why he was silent, he replied that there was little he could say to a venerable man like Batuk. He who could barely afford to live decently could never afford a matchmaker of Batuk's eminence.

Then it was the grocer Devdulal's turn. He asked Chanchal to forget about the money since a simple promise by Gaur to provide Batuk a dinner of fish or mutton for the next six months would be enough to get him working as a matchmaker right away.

Their laughter mingled with the shadows and spread new life into the darkness surrounding them. It seemed to conjure up another spark of existence in the night as a pale dot of light and the sound of a bicycle bell approached the house and came to a halt in front of the verandah. "Telegram," cried the shadowy mailman as he briskly climbed up the steps shining his flashlight. He waited as Sambhu Narain signed a customary receipt with all his flair and deliberation. He picked up the yellow envelope and opened it impatiently. While everyone stared silently, he read the message at a glance and turned ghostly white as he read it again.

After what seemed an age, Sambhu Narain pushed the telegram away from him, covered his face with both hands, and began to sob uncontrollably. When the news of Sanjit's death reached Janaki Devi a few moments later, a single piercing cry escaped her lips as she fell to the floor and lost all consciousness.

Two

MOLLY MUKHERJEE heard not a word about her mysterious grandfather's death, although she could remember a time when the total senselessness of her uncle's death was all the family could talk about for months, and the impenetrable silence that followed her mother's death as if she had never even been one among the living. From a lonely hospital bed in New Jersey she remembered her Grandpa and his gentleness and wished miracles were fashionable in the new country her father had chosen.

She was cold, she shivered all day. From one moment to the other, she didn't know whether her body would explode or simply give up without protest. She was a prisoner to a tide that rushed in and out of her veins each day, and a day without it seemed like the end of the world.

To this day, some say her beauty was her undoing. Her beauty and a certain aloofness that made her hard to befriend. She was pretty, sweet-natured, and liable to melt if touched, or so her friends thought. So they called her M'n M.

Two years ago, Molly wore an off-shoulder slinky satin dress for her high school graduation party and picture. The dress drew wistful glances from the boys in her class. Boys and girls alike talked about her dress for days, how the peach colour of the dress blended magically with the olive, Mediterranean glow of her young and succulent skin to give her an almost ethereal status. She was the dark, silent woman the boys caressed and plunged into in their sweltering dreams. That was the closest they got to her. In reality, she was totally inaccessible.

But the photograph was a piece of solid evidence many of the high school mothers quickly seized upon. They chided her father behind his back for being so cavalier as to let his daughter wear whatever she wanted to. The photograph hardened them in their suspicions, convincing them that she was the girl of easy virtue they had imagined all along. The fact that she was anything but Mediterranean further sharpened the intensity of their censure. She was a girl from India, and such girls were expected to maintain a certain level of decorum. Our finest traditions are slipping away, some mothers sighed.

They thought her behavior all the more inexplicable because Molly's home was something of a cultural citadel that attracted Indian religious men as frequently as singers and musicians. They came from India, often seemingly penurious but agreeably disposed towards North American hospitality in a spirit of unblushing immodesty. But they also came from Detroit and Philadelphia, Toronto and California, lured by the large concentrations of their fellow Indians. "I will build my temple here," said one, "and galvanize the world's attention towards New Jersey." For a time, a *sitar* player of illustrious heritage set up a music school in the city and the enrolment promptly shot up to seventeen in a matter of weeks. There were daughters of rich Indian doctors as well as a millionaire doctor himself who, deciding that his investments with Bears Stearns more than guaranteed a secure future, said goodbye to his medical practice and settled down to a lifetime strumming the strings of the sitar.

Molly lay back in bed staring at the glowing patch of blue sky framed against her window, preparing herself to be nice during her father's evening visit. But her mind kept slipping back to memories of Uncle Kerry.

Kerry Ahluwalia was fearless and outspoken about the rights of Hindus and Sikhs to build temples or *gurdwaras* wherever they could or wanted to. If churches could flourish in any neighborhood, why did temples need to be tucked away in slummier industrial districts? Kerry Ahluwalia died fighting for the survival of cultural symbols.

That's how *India Today & Tomorrow* began his obituary. But the truth was that his daughter Sonya desperately wanted to pass her driving test before her nineteenth birthday. So he had promised her an entire weekend of driving lessons. That proved fatal.

It was Sunday, and Sonya was doing just fine. But she was slow making a left turn on a busy intersection. The impatient driver in a van behind her persisted in blowing his horn, adding to her confusion and nervousness. Finally, Kerry rolled down the window beside him and showed the man a glistening, unambiguous middle finger. The van followed Kerry and Sonya right back to their house. "You fuckin' cabbagehead. Cock suckin' Paki'" yelled the man as he blew away Kerry's side with a single shotgun blast.

The truth about Kerry's death hardly mattered anymore, thought Vikram, as he stared at the white birches standing outside his window. It was early in October, and the trees were beginning to be touched with colour. The leaves danced in the wind like feathers on the heads of primitive dancers. The berries were gone from the berry trees, but tiny sparrows and waxwings still darted through the slender branches searching for food. A solitary robin sat untempted on the higher branches and, higher still, against a pale blue sky mottled with puffs of white clouds, flocks of returning geese hurried south in strict formation, filling the air with their panting and honking.

On late afternoons such as these, the softly rustling breeze and the gentle warmth brushing over his skin always stopped short of putting him to sleep. Back home at this time, with Calcutta's heat slowly sucking life out of him, sleep was precisely what he might have surrendered himself to. Here, the effect was somewhat hypnotic. It dredged up the past and scattered it like husks before his eyes. But there was a difference today. The husks were more elusive than ever. He couldn't see beyond the trees or the patch of sky against which they shone. The tears in his eyes blurred everything.

Vikram waited to visit his daughter, weighed down by a paralyzing heaviness which seemed to drain his legs of strength. A schoolbus ground its way up the hill, breaking the stillness for a time. He never saw it, but knew it by its sound. On a normal day, the schoolbus would've dropped the youngest Ahluwalia kid, Raj, at his home six houses down the street. He knew the boy hadn't gone to school today, not on a day they had cremated his father. He had seen Raj and Sonya, and shed tears with Mrs. Ahluwalia at the funeral service earlier that morning.

Kerry Ahluwalia was more than a neighbor. He was a friend, and he continued to grieve silently for him. His real name was Kirpal Singh Ahluwalia. Reluctantly, almost against his will, he had allowed the name to be corrupted to Kerry. When Ted Sexton of Ted's Auto Imports decided to sell his auto repair business and drive off to the California sunset in his black Corvette, it seemed almost natural for Kerry, the chief mechanic, to buy the business off of him. "Why go to California?" Kerry asked Ted. "How come you ended up in New Jersey?" Ted retorted, without answering Kerry. "Must be destiny," replied Kerry, smiling.

Vikram had drifted to Montclair in pursuit of a job with a food brokerage company importing large quantities of Indian tea. There had to be changes galore. The name Malini had shrunk to Molly in a matter of weeks. Mindful of the fate that had befallen his own name, Kerry insisted with Vikram that he refuse to give in. "Go talk to the principal," he said, "and insist that she be called Malini. There's so much beauty, so much purity in our traditional names. Why Molly?" Vikram smiled, but did nothing else.

Now he was weeping in silence, knowing it was too late to do anything. Somewhere, he seemed to have given up on his daughter. It was not easy, and he felt his heart ripped out of him. The new world was proving too much for him. At times, he wanted simply to curl up and die. It was hard to imagine that only a few weeks ago he was jubilant over her acceptance at Smith College. At least Malini would now not be too far from New Jersey, a little closer than when she went to school in Newton, Massachusetts. He used to believe once that a moment of sorrow lived isolated in time. It could not touch past pleasures, or future ones, each a point of light stretching out of the mother's womb all the way to death. He knew he was wrong.

It was not my wish to be one of you, thought Malini from her hospital bed. It was the pain of not being one of you, the pain and humiliation my M 'n M's helped me forget. But there came a time when the little monsters left her neither with pain nor pleasure, helped her neither to forget nor remember.

Malini reached under her pillow in an attempt to remember one last time. She found her little diary, one of those which started on 1 December. When she opened the first page, it was as if she didn't remember anything before that date. It had all been totally wiped out, with memories of her mother and the love she felt for her poor father. Would this be the record of the last year of my life? thought Malini, as she began to flip through the pages.

15 December	Broke up with Stephen.
16 December	Went out with Stephen for the last time.
30 December	Appointment with Tracy. Gave prescription for birth control pills.
19 January	Dinner with Marc at Prudential. Car towed away.
26 January	Went to New York with Marc. Met Craig.
11 March	FBI came to Marc's house. Questioned for three hours.
17 March	Spent night with Marc at Ramada Inn. Met Christopher at Marc's house. Craig arranged lawyer Feldman for Marc and I.
27 March	Return home. Fought with Craig. A real creep.
30 March	Marc visits Nathan Street. Takes me out for a couple of drinks.

3 April	Back to school.
17 April	Eliot came to visit. Went out with him and Marc.
20 April	Out with the girls. Met Eliot in town for clubbing. Ran into Marc. Rode on his bike. He gave twenty soapers to sell for him.
25 April	Dinner and cocktails with Stephanie.
26 April	Saw Marc.
28 April	Not too keen, visited Craig in hospital just the same.
2 May	Spent night with Marc. Eliot came to visit. All went out.
4 May	Party at Wellesley College.
6 May	Saw Marc at night Went out with Craig during day.
8 May	Saw Stephanie at office to get blank tax forms. Marc called. Wasn't in to speak to him. Craig came by. Wasn't in to see him. Acceptance letter from Smith.
9 May	Saw Marc in Newton Centre on his bike around 3:30. Afro-American classes cancelled.
10 May	Call Stephanie before 10. Final phone bill due. Have paper for Freddie. Eliot and Derek came here. Marc and I take them to 'The Other Side' and 'Mondo's'. Spent night with Marc.
12 May	Returned to dorm at 9:00 a.m. Josephine came. Marc and I go to New York. We spent night at Gary's. Said hello to Dad. Lied. A depressing visit.
13 May	Final exams due in Spanish and Biology.
14 May	Final exam in Afro. End of classes. Bike riding with Marc after dinner. He called me an hour later with a lame excuse for not seeing me at nine.
15 May	Finalize summer residence plans. Here or Nathan

	Street? Shopping with Margaret. Out with Marc.
18 May	Graduation practice. Transcripts to Smith. Check with Registrar. Party at the Linwood. Marc never called.
21 May	Got to stay on. Receive dorm keys from office. Marc and I spend night in the dorm.
22 May	Parent's reception at 4:00. Susan a proper nuisance.
17 June	Saw Marc twice during the day. He was thrown out of the dorm. Also high on smack.
19 June	Looked at apartments with Marc and Josephine. Concert at the Fen's. Dropped Marc's motorcycle keys.
27 June	Dad made a surprise visit. Where did he turn up from? Saw Marc, looked at Mercedes, ate at the Green Jade.
28 June	Ate at Highlands Pizza. Went over to Marc. Had another falling out session which proved nothing. Showed a car to buyer, then spent night together.
30 June	Watched Marc play tennis. Sylvia called from New York.
5 July	Marc sold car. Left for the Berkshires.
17 July	Saw 8 1/2. Couldn't make any sense. Walked through the Combat Zone, then went to Church of Scientology.
20 July	Marc came with Bobby. We went swimming. Later returned to Marc's apartment and spent the night.
27 July	Appointment with Tracy. Got a new prescription Had chest x-ray. Went to the movies. Spent night with Marc.
28 July	Marc down with tonsilitis.
30 July	Dad thinking of moving East. Went out with

	Ellison. Marc came back early and found out. Spent night with him. Fought for a while. Took a soaper and fell asleep on him.
31 July	Expenses: 1 Rix Cosmetics 3.00 1 Cherry & Webb Shoes 19.90 2 4 Seasons Movie 2.75 2 Talbert's Pharmacy Deodorant 2.30 3 Cherry & Webb Underwear 9.95 3 Garb Drugs Birth control pill 2.25 14 CVS Cosmetics 5.67 16 Continental Haircut 15.25 18 Newton Pizza dinner 2.35 18 New England Telephone 11.40 20 Drycleaner 2 coats 3.50 22 Cherry & Webb Shirt 12.60 23 Rexal Drug Vitamins 2.82 26 Abbey Cinema Movies 3.00 31 Garb Drug Birth Control Pills 2.25 GRAND TOTAL 78.99
17 August	Marc brought over his laundry in new BMW. Got stoned with beanie and went to see 'Camelot'.
20 August	Heard about Marc's insurance company ripoff. Went out with him trying to sell BMW. Took a dolphin. My M 'n M's come in such beautiful color. Smoked a lot. Got fucked up. Stopped at Jay A's in Cambridge for a drink. Spent night with Marc. First time fornicated during period.
25 August	Spent day on the Cape. Marc returned at night. Evening at Music Hall. Spent night together.
7 Sept	Marc cooked brunch. Fooled around. Bought grass from Kate. Climbed up the Prudential, then ate at

	Charlie's Eating & Drinking. Another fight.
9 Sept	Josephine got into accident with Ruby's car. Doubled with Josephine and Ruby to Orson Welles. All spent night at Marc's house.
13 Sept	Marc picked up. Dad found out about us. Returned home.

And then there was nothing. Malini put aside the book. This was her secret life, hidden from all but a few. How dreary it all seemed now. Marc and Craig and Stephen mere names along the way.

Malini walked over unsteadily to the window. From her twelfth floor room, the trees and shrubs below all seemed part of the gathering darkness, a sea inviting her to plunge into its depths, firm in the knowledge that a return to the surface was only a matter of practiced movements. She thought about the sensation as she walked back to the bed somewhat decisively. Perhaps she would feel like a little insect stumbling blindly across the sprawling body of a vast, mysterious creature. She sat on the edge of her bed and stared at the darkness outside. Then she pulled out the diary one more time to write something she had remembered. "M 'n M's are not what they're cracked up to be," she wrote. The sad sentence sloped down to the edge of the page and trailed off into uncertainty and silence.

When Alice heard the news of Malini's death she was filled with self-reproach at first. She should've kept touch with the girl in Boston, she told herself, and this mightn't have happened. Malini's life and death defied understanding. Alice herself had once been inches away from death, and seemed to be waiting for the moment without fear ever since. That moment between life and death lay frozen in her mind. Every so often, she saw herself sitting in one corner of a clattering railway compartment as it alternately puffed and whistled into the unfolding day. A narrow slit of dull pink stretched across the entire length of the horizon where the night had parted from the earth. Massed over this pink streak, there lay deepening shades of blue that dissolved into the sky with a pale moon suspended in the starless void. Alice did not care to remember beyond the moment, not when she heard about the death, nor when she decided to attend the funeral.

"It seems so pointless," she said with a hollow laugh, 'to live through hell only to o.d. in Montclair, New Jersey."

Vikram didn't answer. He stared at the ground for a long time, trying to hide his tears. Finally he looked up at Alice and asked, "Will you come and live with me, if you're free to do so."

A faint smile played across her face. "I've waited a long time to know and understand men," she said. "I think I understand you. Yes."

Later that evening, Alice and Vikram ate dinner in silence, each trying to understand the absurdity of Malini's life, the absurdity of Kirpal Singh's Ahluwalia's death. If Vikram and Kerry were neighbors in America, it was inconceivable that in the land of their birth they would've lived in the same neighborhood or found reason to mix socially. A manager and a garage owner here, they were tea industry manager and truck driver in an earlier incarnation. Destiny had brought them together one day when Vikram and Krishna set out on the road to Chirribilli.

So much had happened since that terror-laden day and night when, suddenly, not far from the towering and awesome majesty of Everest and Kanchenjungha sworn to eternal silence, several lives collided and every life seemed changed forever. Kirpal was there.

Before Kirpal Singh and the others left the Chirribilli area for Calcutta, only Alice was well enough to express her thanks to the men who had saved her. Vikram was still in a daze. "You must come and visit us in America some day. I live in New England, a city called Boston," she said.

Kirpal Singh did not have the faintest notion of where Boston was. But the name New England stuck in his mind and leapt out when, many years later, a U.S. official interviewed him in Delhi for immigration. She asked Kirpal if he had any preferred states where he would like to live and work once he was in America. He promptly said New England. Unfortunately, none of the New England state names cited by the amused official came anywhere close the name he had in mind. New Jersey came the closest, and he was prepared to settle for that.

Three

TAPEWORMS. Tapeworms, like flukes—whatever they may be — are parasitic forms that can cause serious, and sometimes fatal, diseases among vertebrates. Noor Mohammed, an impoverished fifty-one year old night-shift clerk in a Calcutta hospital did not know, and had no means of knowing, that he was a vertebrate. What he did know was that he felt very weak on sultry summer nights. It was different from those other summers when the sweet, sickly stench of fruit and filth inspired in him a deep longing to get back to the open spaces and the blue skies of his village up north. This time it was something inside his body, a constant gnawing hunger in his guts and a clammy spell of weakness and apathy hanging over him all day. So Noor Mohammed began by asking some of the young interns for any pill that might make him feel better. The interns gladly obliged him with innocuous substances from the medicine cabinet, but nothing happened.

Finally, at the urgings of his son Hamid, Noor Mohammed lined up at the hospital's outdoor clinic at six o'clock on a Monday morning behind three hundred other patients who had already beaten him to the door. Through constant entreaties to the peons controlling the flow of patients, Noor Mohammed and his son eventually came to the cubicle of Rahul Chaudhury, an intern, who unbuttoned his shirt, looked him up and down, and said there seemed nothing the matter with him. For once, the timid Noor Mohammed screwed up enough courage to say there was indeed something the matter with him, that he thought he was dying. Rahul felt compelled to open a rusty medicine cabinet and pull out a long flashlight. He asked Noor Mohammed to draw closer and open up his mouth as wide as possible.

Rahul threw a beam of light deep inside Noor Mohammed's mouth and gasped in horror. Then he began to laugh. He called out to his fellow interns working the adjoining cubicles. Soon there were no less than twelve doctors peering into Noor Mohammed's mouth, nodding their heads in dismay. Hamid stood silently in one corner of the little room, frightened and fearful of the worst. When Rahul noticed him, he asked him also to look down his father's throat. Hamid became aware of something moving at the far end of his father's mouth, something pale, slimy, worm-like. Rahul took pains to explain to father and son that it was a tape worm, possibly the longest one that Rahul and the other doctors had ever seen, maybe four yards long, maybe five or six. But there was nothing to worry. Rahul was going to purge the devil out of Noor Mohammed's system with a powerful prescription which he then proceeded to write out for the old man.

Noor Mohammed seemed to share none of the doctor's optimism as he nodded his bald head dubiously and folded the prescription into his shirt pocket. Still, father and son thanked Rahul politely as they left the cubicle, pushed their way past another throng of three hundred patients or more waiting to be seen, and disappeared among the three thousand or so that walked or waited outside the hospital's ever-open gates almost any hour of the day or night.

Noor Mohammed had only a vague sense of what the others had seen inside his mouth. Hamid explained that it looked like a little bit of a worm. Noor Mohammed asked if it had eyes or a mouth, but Hamid couldn't recall having seen such things. It didn't matter whether the object had eyes or not, said Noor Mohammed, for he himself suddenly felt gifted with a hundred eyes. He didn't care if it had a mouth or not, for he felt he was growing a hundred tongues. There were strange things he was beginning to see, deep chasms opening up to reveal their secrets to his mind. But he dared not speak. These were terrible secrets which he could never bring out into the open, terrible secrets with terrible consequences.

It didn't surprise him in the least that he must have harboured the worm within his body for many months. Nor was he surprised by the stunning suddenness with which he became aware of his powers. What surprised him was that he had always associated the worm with such unclean meat as pork. And since he had never once tasted of that vile flesh, how could he have developed this malady, this gift?

Noor Mohammed was still puzzling over the mystery at the start of his night shift when two policemen brought in a corpse for the hospital morgue. As Noor Mohammed looked down at the stretcher on the floor, his eyes met the dead man's. Almost instantly, a burning light flashed through his brain. In that light he found the early spring sun casting shadows over the land where, not far away, the Railway Protection Police had found a crumpled body lying beside the tracks that shoot out from Sealdah Station like a giant tongue ribbed with steel. One of the policemen prodded the body with a baton as it lay on the blackened canvas stretcher. His comrade nonchalantly picked his teeth with a pencil from Noor Mohammed's desk. Noor Mohammed pretended to be busy with the paperwork even as he called out to his son.

Hamid was doing his arithmetic on a bench in one corner of the room, as he normally did most nights until he simply fell asleep. With the policemen chatting with one another, Noor Mohammed asked Hamid if there was any way he could quickly reach the young doctor who had examined him earlier in the day.

While Hamid went looking for Rahul in the section of the hospital where most interns usually had their quarters, Noor Mohammed asked the policemen why they couldn't give the morgue a break once in a while. This was getting to be too much. The refrigeration system which had battled sizzling tropical temperatures for eleven years had finally given up, much to the annoyance of those whose job it was to stack one 'unidentified dead' over another in the overflowing trays. And the city continued to spew out a rich harvest of dead young men, nameless.

When he saw no signs of Hamid returning with the information he needed, Noor Mohammed allowed the body to pass on to other clerical hands. He was certain there was something about this body that needed to be brought to the attention of the young intern. Little did Noor Mohammed know what really lay ahead in the days to follow, or he might have had reservations, perhaps even a certain skepticism, about using his freshy acquired gift for unravelling the past. Hamid returned after a fruitless search.

It was the next day before Hamid caught up with Rahul while he was once again on duty. He identified his brother Sanjit's body without any trace of emotion. What did surprise him was Noor Mohammed's uncanny instinct urging Hamid to pass the information on to him.

I didn't know how to refuse Rahul when he called me up to go to Bishnupur with a message for his father. He said he was asking me to do this out of love and concern for his father. Then he left the hospital to break the news to his sister, Krishna.

Coward that I am, I was not equal to the task. It was Krishna's telegram that eventually sent Sambhu Narain and Janaki Devi rushing from Bishnupur to Calcutta. It also gave the young Chanchal an opportunity to involve himself in their lives. He would accompany them too, for he was certain the family would need helping hands in the days ahead.

Rahul headed for the front door as soon as his parents entered the house. This was the marble palace belonging to Krishna's in-laws. There was a certain bitterness and uneasiness in the air, and if he stopped short of vanishing into the outside world, it was because of the pity he felt for his sister. Krishna's face was swollen from crying all night. She burst into uncontrollable sobs as soon as she saw her mother.

The day wore on, and Rahul didn't leave. News of Sanjit's death spread among friends and relatives. The mourners continued to gather in Sir Ajoy's house, questioning what had happened, lamenting what had happened, and heaping silent abuse on a radical political group known as the Naxalites, the inevitable villains that came to mind those days when people were faced with unexplained deaths or murders.

Sambhu Narain rested for a while. Vikram persuaded him to come and speak to some of the mourners. He was immediately confronted by a distant relative who thrust the morning paper towards him. He said Sambhu Narain mightn't have had a chance to read the news, but he should know the police had a pretty good idea who was behind Sanjit's death. Then, allowing the revelation to sink in, the man edged a little closer to Sambhu Narain and whispered in his ears, "How can you, a responsible person, allow your son Rahul to be a part of this murderous gang?"

Sambhu Narain looked up and saw Rahul reading silently near a window. For a long time, he said nothing, in spite of the shock of the discovery to which his considerate cousin had led him. He refused to believe it at first, even though vague rumours had reached his ears in Bishnupur. But the mourners kept goading him with their looks. Their accusing glances moved back and forth, and the weight of all the gossip and innuendo began to exact its toll. Sambhu Narain walked over to Rahul with tired footsteps. He looked old and defeated in front of his handsome, defiant son. He asked him about the propriety of his being there in view of what people were saying about him.

Still without any trace of emotion lighting up his face, Rahul looked at his father. But he looked down before anyone could see the anger in his eyes. He carefully marked the page he was reading, closed the book, and walked out of the house without a word.

Whispers broke out in various corners of the room. It seemed to some that a spirit had been exorcised. Sambhu Narain was left staring at the floor with a hollow expression in his eyes. Krishna and her mother were both unaware of what had happened. There was no time even to say goodbye to Rahul, who soon disappeared round a corner.

The darkness closed in outside. Fires sprang to life in the overcrowded tenements in the distance, and the air became thick and pungent as the smoke simply refused to rise up, swirling back and forth instead along the ground and over walls laden with graffiti and cow dung. The smoke and the overriding concern with the funeral details left people no time to admire the elegance of Sir Ajoy's house.

Chanchal continued to take in every detail, revelling inwardly in the wealth spread around him. For someone from the rural backwoods, he proved to be a smooth operator with plenty of city connections.

With a few quick phonecalls to the army headquarters and some of his political friends, he procured the use of an army truck and assurances of bureaucratic cooperation as he set forth with Sambhu Narain to recover Sanjit's body.

It started with endless rounds of tea, biscuits and cigarettes for shrivelled men hunched over peeling ledgers and rubber stamps, dazzling their supplicants with unexpected bursts of power. It wasn't enough to cross their palms with silver. When Sambhu Narain wearily asked how much more the men wanted before they would release the body, one of the clerks made a face and asked, "Would twenty rupees be too much? The body's smelling pretty bad."

Then Chanchal took charge of the situation. With an unmistakable air of authority, he asked the clerk to rise from his desk. He pointed him to a snub-nosed military truck silhouetted on the driveway about fifty feet away. This was transportation provided by the garrison commander at Fort William as a mark of deference for a member of the armed forces. He said, "There are ten soldiers sitting in that truck, each one armed with a rifle and a bayonet. . . ." He did not need to complete the sentence before the clerk, his voice quivering in panic, yelled to his invisible underlings to get the body to the truck immediately.

Before the clerk, now gushing with humility and flattery, could return to his chair, four coolies had delivered the litter to the soldiers. They stood sullenly in the shadows, hoping for some *baksheesh* to the bitter end. The soldiers secured the litter to the floor of the truck, then stood by the metal uprights, each one clutching a rag over his face.

As Sambhu Narain climbed into the truck, he saw two enormous pigs standing alongside the coolies, their startled grunts echoing the men's resentment over this show of force which had upset the equation of power. Sambhu Narain could barely stop himself from getting sick as the ugliness and obscenity lashed across his face like a blast of hot air.

Noor Mohammed wasn't around because there was no question of Hindus sharing gratuities with a Muslim. But he seemed to know everything that was going on. As the truck pulled away from the charnel house, in another section of the building, Noor Mohammed put his hand on Hamid's shoulder and said, "They've taken the body away, but they'll not leave you in peace, my son."

The truck ground along to the cremation grounds through swarming crowds carrying the last of the clay images of the goddess Saraswati to homes or public squares for the following day's festivities. They would've put up all the Saraswati images in Bishnupur today, remarked Chanchal in a voice so full of emotion that Sambhu Narain turned to look at him, wondering what was going through his mind, a little surprised at the overflowing tide of his concern.

❋

It was getting late. There were fewer people on the streets. The clattering tramcars passed at longer intervals. The huge diesel trucks and tankers sighed louder and deeper as they stopped at the traffic lights. Friends and members of the family waited patiently for the truck outside the walls of the cremation grounds.

They moved the body away from the truck. Soon the road, the lights, the tramcars and the diesels became one with every other invisible presence that lurked over the grounds. These included the strident sounds of a wedding which poured out into the night songs of passion and longing over a crackling battery of loudspeakers. As they entered the grounds, Sambhu Narain looked at Chanchal leading the group, and there was something in his eyes which said, "I don't trust you."

Moments later, they formed one more group of mourners gathered under umbrellas near a pathetic stream, more a muddy trough than a brook, their umbrellas held aloft in anticipation of a shower that looked imminent only a short while ago. The dark clouds shed a few drops of rain on the silent group and then moved away. They continued to stand under their umbrellas, quite oblivious of the playful moon looking down on them from time to time, then diving silently into the churning sky. There were eight, maybe ten, men, dark under the pallid light from three naked electric bulbs strung across two bamboo poles teetering in the wind. No one was giving away anything of himself, each one writing in silence his own epitaph for the dead.

A fire sprang to life before their eyes, transfixing them where they stood, embalming them in thoughts of mortality. The fire kept roaring in the wind. An hour or so passed, and Sambhu Narain broke away from the group, walking over to a *banyan* tree shrouded in darkness. He sat down against its trunk, and soon the others followed.

"They will stay here a few more hours," murmured Sambhu Narain, , without turning to anyone in particular. "There'll be time to look back for us all, time to feel our way through sunset fields of paddy, to linger on deserted dunes and watch the moon riveted to the water. They seem so distant now, as distant as lonely men who trawl the waters all night, floating in little boats like specks of darkness. As distant as the dreams of youth which never return, at least not in the totality of their first wondrous awakening."

Then he turned to some of the men seated around him and said mysteriously, "I see myself stretched on the dunes, stretched over miles and miles of windy undulations, I can hear crickets chirping, see the water dissolve its silver mane around curious fish darting to the surface. I lift up my collar and button my coat against the phantom spray, and lick the phantom salt off my lips. The pity of it. Our visions are but the debris of an innocent happiness blighted like all others. To think that I repeated my lines over and over again, memorized all the inflexions. Is this what remains?" Then he fell silent.

I think we all felt the chasm widen between Sambhu Narain and ourselves, as we saw the moon shrink slowly to a sickle, and heard old men laugh mockingly at us. In spite of it all, we felt a surge of hope and strength as if we too were destined to become spirits of the night and, who knew, maybe we'd find the water all aquiver with fairies. Once in a while the chasm might seal itself and we might all walk down the paved moonbeams with the old man and find ourselves in the midst of elves, demons, and other harmless companions of a vanished youth. I think Sambhu Narain knew where happiness lay. We didn't.

Time passed. There were many with him at the time. They would crawl back to their separate worlds before dawn. They would return again, thought Sambhu Narain, some of them, like himself, for he had been to places like this so often, awake and in his dreams. In the early hours of the morning, in the blazing sun, in the evening when the smoke hung low. He preferred cremations at night, when faces are dark and shadowy and no one sees the tears. He found himself struggling to remember the totality which eluded his grasp. He felt tears welling up in his eyes and wondered why he persisted in asking the same questions over and over again. "We persist," he said, turning to the others, "to avoid the shame we push aside each night. These are the only realities truly ineffable," he said, "for joy never tears, mangles, sears, and scars like pain.

They continued to sit in silence beneath the ancient tree, Rahul's ineffectual messenger to his village among them. Suddenly, we found another wave of ecstasy sending shivers through our bodies as other blurred figures came into view in the distance. Some folks were standing, others sitting around another burning pyre whose tongues defied the muddiness of the stream that flowed by and seemed to rise from the burnished surface of the water itself. I realized that my sense of joy came from a sense of togetherness in the face of death, for I was one with other witnesses to death and wished I could be with them forever, for this was where men disowned and cast away all pride, where spirits met.

Sambhu Narain startled everyone by saying he could see the faces of his father, his father's father, and other faces. There was sorrow on the faces of those he had loved, derision in the eyes of his enemies. "It's gone now," he said, "visions and memories all poured into a pit sucking into its eddies the prince's pride, the soldier's fervour, and the saint's saintliness. Not caring whether the prince's remorse was any more real than the hunger of those he drove away from their lands, nor whether the soldier's penitence more moving than the terror in the eyes of those he slew. Unmindful of the priest's contrition and the heretic's forgiveness at the stakes."

His voice rose like a gathering storm as he prayed, "Have pity on our fathers, O Lord, for they knew all the answers but decided they were not important. Have mercy on us, O Lord, for we know all the questions, but they slip through our fingers like sand."

Our silent lips moved to echo his prayers, seeking forgiveness for forgetfulness, seeking to cast out the demon of forgetfulness, until the moon disappeared and large raindrops began falling once more, muffling the sound of human voices. The umbrellas burst open over the mourners' heads, and heaven only knew what their last prayers were as they started to drift away from the smouldering fire.

I think Sambhu Narain knew in his heart that last prayers would remain unanswered, for last prayers are always late. All one could do was to remain patient, to wait one's turn for deliverance, wait for the muddy waters to cleanse their cold bodies, their inert bodies past the reach of contempt and abuse. For was it not in front of their eyes that the holiest rivers met, where all pilgrimages converged, where there was neither any beginning nor end. Till the beginning met the end and closed the circle, pain would return, horrors recur, and the minstrel's songs and the mother's lullabies swell and smother in the wind.

Sambhu Narain did not return home with the others. Rumour had it that early in the morning he boarded a train going north out of Sealdah Station, perhaps buying a ticket to Darjeeling, perhaps not knowing where he wanted to go, certain only that he was not prepared to go home. Later the following day the truth dawned upon his wife too as she wiped a teardrop from the corner of her eye and whispered to her daughter, "He's still like a child. How can anyone expect him to act like a man?"

Krishna sensed the unspeakable pain in her heart but did not know how Janaki Devi would prepare herself to face the loneliness that lay ahead.

Four

RAHUL AND Sharmila ran into each other at Boston's Museum of Fine Arts one afternoon. Two of a kind in a sea of strangers, they were quickly drawn to one another. He was in the country on a Rotary Fellowship. She was . . . well, she left it somewhat mysterious. They had hundreds of things to talk about, how they were going to change themselves and the world. Soon his academic obligations began to seem totally irrelevant.

As they got to know each other better, they agreed to go out searching, inexplicably, for New England ducks and mallards. It struck them both as a very civilized way to spend their idle hours. In the process, they kept stumbling upon unexpected lakes all the way from Boston to Bangor and beyond. They circled Walden Pond endlessly, and Rahul spent days wrestling with his thoughts, trying to understand what Gandhi saw in Thoreau.

What exquisite peace he found walking round the wooded bank until it grew dark and his careless steps frightened the birds into flight. And so he took care to walk only where the thick carpet of dry pine needles betrayed their presence to no one. But Sharmila had other thoughts on her mind, and soon asked him over to an exquisite home on Chestnut Hill where she taught him what it was to make love to a woman.

It was a beautiful summer, and every day Rahul found himself drunk with Sharmila's many breathtaking faces. Tall and willowy, she looked like a gypsy one day, a princess the next, and it flattered him to think that she had offered him something inaccessible to others. Enchanted by her body, his attention naturally turned to his own. He took up running so passionately that he virtually moved in with Sharmila if only to take advantage of the fine trails near her house where, as he put it, he could run for hours and pretend he was in the countryside.

"Don't worry about Bill," she told him. "He's a friend of my dad's from their days together at Wharton."

Bill Woodcock seemed to spend most of his time in Japan, his wife and two kids having moved out after one last battle which left behind twenty thousand dollars in damage to plate glass windows and Persian rugs. Rahul didn't know what Bill Woodcock thought of his involvement with Sharmila, but the arrangement seemed splendid and untroubled.

Summer moved along. While some of the heady excitement of their first sexual encounters began to wear off, it still seemed natural for them to make love as often as possible. Before summer came to an end, this became as much a part of their daily routine as his runs. Sharmila was working in Harvard's audio-visual lab, but she seemed to know the whole world. It was easy for her to find him a job at an electronics store in downtown Boston. Payment in cash, so the taxman wouldn't know, and the Immigration and Naturalization people were too dumb anyway. It was mindless work for someone trained in medicine, but before long, it became a part of his daily routine as well.

William Woodcock, Jr. threw Sharmila out of his Chestnut Hill house one day and Rahul's idyll came to an end. It was an emotionless farewell. She simply took the train to New York and the next available Air-India flight out of the country. Not long afterwards, Rahul decided it was also time to kiss the Rotary fellowship goodbye.

❋

They got together again once they were both back in Calcutta.

But there was no longer any sex in their relationship. Now it was all ideology. It must be climate that inspires fidelity, discourages sleeping around, he remarked one day. "No, one simply gets used to each other's body odours," she said. That's the basis of tradition, they concluded.

Tradition demanded that the period of mourning for Sanjit's death end with a big feast. The dead must rest easy on our full stomachs. Everyone present at the cremation had to be invited. People of means always invite other relatives and friends as well. Normally, the feast would have taken place in the village of Bishnupur. But few from Calcutta would've attended. With Sambhu Narain's disappearance, Bishnupur now seemed out of the question.

Sir Ajoy's massive house was built for feasts. Certainly large gatherings, if not feasts. The house took on a different complexion from the moment it was decided that the funeral feast would be held there. Until then, there were equal measures of pain, anger, and disbelief in the air. Everyone carried a burden, everyone was suffering in silence.

Except for one person, little Malini, who only cried from time to time protesting the neglect being heaped upon her. She could barely sense what was going on around her, and the strangeness of it all made her fearful.

As the dinner got under way, Sharmila dropped by. Rahul escorted her to the living room where the women had gathered around Krishna, her mother, and her mother-in-law, Lady Ranu. Conversation had been difficult between Rahul and members of his family ever since he had walked away from Sambhu Narain three weeks ago. Sharmila's presence somehow made the others better disposed towards him almost instantly. Krishna even allowed a flicker of a smile to express her curiosity about what might come from his friendship with this beautiful woman.

Rahul was about to sit down to eat when one of the servants informed him that a young man was waiting to see him at the door.

He recognized him right away as the son of the tape-worm freak. "My father sent me to you to ask for a job," said Hamid. The inappropriateness of the time didn't seem to bother Rahul or the young lad. He laughed and asked how he supposed he could find him a job. "Where?" Rahul asked emphatically.

"Right here or in your sister's house," replied Hamid without a moment's hesitation.

How did he know about his sister? Did the boy have the family cased for a major robbery perhaps? Rahul shrugged off these suspicions right away. There was something about the boy's eyes that he found hard to take his own eyes off. Something compelling. He asked him to wait and went inside to get Krishna.

Krishna loved her brother too much, and it didn't take him long to convince her. But there was in the city a long-standing fear of young male servants. That Hamid was a Muslim was another point against him. He looked tough and well built for the fifteen years that he claimed to be his age. But servants were hard to come by, and Hamid also had a very engaging smile. Krishna soon relented and promised she would take care of the situation and convince her husband to hire the boy.

Vikram's approval was somewhat more difficult to get than she had imagined. Vikram found Rahul's presence distasteful, was deeply suspicious of the company he kept, and disdainful of the coming revolution that Rahul took pleasure in cautioning him about. But he was no match for brother and sister as they conspired through an understanding that united their blood.

There was another conspiracy that neither Vikram nor Krishna liked the looks of. Wherever they looked, they saw Chanchal following Janaki Devi around like a puppy dog. Vikram didn't approve.

On one occasion, he heard Malini crying from her room and was making his way to her when Chanchal's voice from an adjoining room made him stop and listen. Janaki Devi was asking Chanchal to return to Bishnupur where he had so much work to do. Chanchal replied, "I know there's always work. But I came with you and your husband here, and my responsibilities remain with me until I've seen you safely back home again." In a voice choking with emotion, Chanchal added, "I'll never be rid of my responsibility towards you unless you release me from it."

Upto this time, Vikram had never felt a great sense of concern for Janaki Devi even though she had lost a son, had seen another turn into a Maoist by all accounts, and seen her husband walk out of her life. He knew she still had Krishna's indomitable spirit to rely on, and her own, for Krishna loved to tell how her mother believed oppression was nothing, loneliness nothing, deprivation nothing, that everything lay with the human will. And how strongly she willed, against all established norms, that Krishna receive the kind of college education that she herself had been denied. Still, there was something of a snake about Chanchal.

"Well, I'm releasing you from it," Janaki Devi said to him, with a note of amusement in her voice. But Chanchal stayed around.

Before the evening ended, Vikram's new found peace with Rahul would suffer another blow, thanks once again to the same relative who had forced Sambhu Narain to confront his son. After the meal, this man suddenly whipped out a newspaper cutting containing the names of several students arrested in connection with the death of the young Indian Air Force officer, Sanjit Chaudhury. He taunted Vikram to find out how many of the students had been Rahul's friends in medical school or earlier. This conversation took place within his hearing. Rahul smiled politely, shrugged his shoulders, and walked away. He did not wish to provoke Vikram and reopen the question of Hamid's job which had been settled earlier to his and Krishna's satisfaction.

For several days afterwards, Rahul remained somewhat distracted. Something was turning over and over in his mind. It started with a letter Krishna read to him, a letter Sambhu Narain had left behind for Janaki Devi.

You have the power I dream of, wrote Sambhu Narain, the power I lack. Now I must step beyond your life to be better able to return to it, to remake the truth. If we knew the truth about ourselves, perhaps we would no longer feel the craving to live. I hear a call in my dreams, telling me the world is too alive, too wrapped up in itself for me to break out of my dreams. I must answer the call, must find in the peace of the forest that part of me which fled my weak body years ago — the will to exist, the will to resist. The will, not the desire. There are easy escapes open to each one of us. Some of us simply don't care to make them our own.

Rahul grew even more pensive, withdrew more into himself, when he ran into Noor Mohammed a few days later at the hospital. He felt nervous and agitated when Noor Mohammed expressed sorrow over Sambhu Narain's disappearance and told Rahul quite firmly that he was being tested by his father. "I don't have to play any games with him," said Rahul after a long silence. Noor Mohammed, glowing in his prophetic powers, said that Rahul would then have to play games with himself, and walked away.

"But where do I begin?" asked Rahul, quickly catching up with Noor Mohammed. The old man told him to look no further than the railway yard where Sanjit's body was found.

And so it was that on the following morning, grey and damp, Rahul went to a rusty, abandoned warehouse in the general area Noor Mohammed had suggested. The structure lay smothered in fog, but lost none of its grim ugliness for it. Masses of scum and weeds sprawled lifelessly on the pond separating the building from the railway tracks. An occasional duck poked its way through the fog, shooting its neck underwater in search of food, breaking the syrupy surface with a click but barely a ripple. A young boy sat on the water's edge, fearful of snakes, and emptied his bowels into the pond. Rahul called out to the lad asking if he had seen Kartick Sirdar. The boy's reply was lost in the sounds of an invisible locomotive engine suddenly blowing its whistle, followed by clanking metal, bursts of steam gushing out of valves, more whistles, then silence once more.

The sudden bedlam triggered a wave of activity around the warehouse. A dozen men ran out of an opening in the wall and disappeared through the fog in the direction of the tracks. Rahul did not need to ask the boy, perched even more precariously on the pond's edge as he now cleaned himself in the water. The man he was looking for walked out of the fog, calm and unhurried, in the wake of his disappearing cohorts. As he neared Rahul, he seemed to grow large with a bewildering suddenness. It was one of those tricks fog and the temperature play on the eyes.

The heavily pock-marked face and oily curls of thick black hair gave to this giant of a man the air of a mythical demon. The two had known each other for a year or so, during which period Kartick had been an unfailing supplier of small arms and other necessities to Rahul and his political friends. Kartick was surprised to see Rahul this morning since he couldn't remember if they had some transaction he might have forgotten.

"I came to see you" said Rahul, "because I've been feeling bothered and annoyed over my brother. You never met him. They found his body near the tracks only a mile or so from here exactly three weeks ago today. Would you know anything about it?" He added that the police had naturally arrested some of his friends on murder charges.

The *sirdar's* face lit up like fireworks against a darkened sky and he burst into peals of laughter. All the meanness, all the filth of the earth, must somehow be a part of him and his miserable men, for where else could it survive but in the muck and stench in which he lived? he asked. Of course, students and respectable men could no more think of murder and rape than he could hope for virtue and heaven. Rahul knew he was teasing him. He joined in his laughter. This was the right thing to do as it took the edge off his sarcasm and drew from Kartick a promise to get to the truth. The *sirdar* held sway for miles around, and getting the information was a matter of honour for him.

Kartick Sirdar turned somber again. But he had a natural flair for drama. In a moment he turned his darkened face and flaming eyes towards me and asked, "Who is this man?"

"I am his occasional messenger," I replied, pointing to Rahul, who assured him that I was a friend and could be trusted.

Kartick's men began to return one by one, bent double under the weight on their backs, slowly making their way into the warehouse. As soon as they dropped their loads, they went running back to the rail tracks once more. Kartick explained that they would've cleaned the wagons of sixty bags of rice and forty chests of tea that morning, all for the price of two bottles of Scotch. One for the Anglo-Indian engineer, the other for the South Indian guard. The way Kartick used the words Anglo-Indian and South Indian suggested that he did not consider them a part of intelligent forms of life on earth. After all, the Scotch was adulterated anyway. There was little the two railmen could do since they would have to pass by his humble abode some time or the other. They cooperated or they were dead. Kartick chose to pay them simply to humour them, to make it less difficult for them and give them a reason to work with him.

Kartick jerked his head around as he called out to one of the men scuttling out of the warehouse, a big powerful man who was reduced to cowering in fear in front of the *sirdar*. His voice reverberating like thunder, he told him he wanted some quick information on a body found near the Pathshala signal box three weeks ago. If anyone had picked off some personal belongings he wanted that returned too.

In a matter of minutes the man returned, tall and self-assured this time, pushing in front of him a small, pale man with fearful eyes bulging out of their sockets. He moved forward with heavy, mechanical footsteps as the larger man held him by the scruff of his neck and proudly told the *sirdar* he had brought him his man. He pushed him to his knees and roared, "Show Sirdar what you've got, you bastard."

The little man was clutching a bundle close to his chest which he laid reverently at Kartick Sirdar's feet and hastily undid the knots. A pair of trousers, a shirt, a wallet, a pair of shoes and a watch, that's all the bundle held. Rahul kept staring at the objects. He bent down, picked up the wallet, looked through the few papers remaining, and murmured sadly that it was Sanjit's all right.

Now Kartick Sirdar's eyes turned into balls of fire. The kneeling man looked at him once and wilted with fear. He kept whimpering and swearing that he had not killed the man. All the while Kartick kept trembling with rage until his right foot suddenly flew out from under him and struck the man squarely across the jaw, sending him shrieking with pain, squirming backwards on the ground, swearing upon his mother and his sister's honour that he had found the man dead, that the blood on the clothes was already there when he found him. The man had already bled to death.

Kartick looked at the crowd of his followers who had gathered in a semi-circle in the distance. He ordered them to get back to work and to take with them the worm grovelling at his feet. When the men had disappeared from sight, Kartick, now thoughtful and composed, turned and said he believed the man was telling the truth. He was almost certain it was the police who had probably done it out of mistaken identity, since Sanjit was not in his air force uniform at the time. Everyone knew that undercover policemen were regularly pushing young men out of railway compartments or shooting them and dumping their bodies in parks. Some were indeed radical students. Most were not.

We left the place with Kartick Sirdar's parting words echoing in our ears. "There are no accidents in these troubled times," he said, "there's almost nothing that's not planned in advance."

And it was meticulous planning that Rahul got down to right away. I kept telling him he was crazy, but there was a fiery glint in his eyes and an avenger's brittle edge in his voice. If this was how his father was testing him, he said, then he would show him a thing or two. I persuaded Noor Mohammed, now feeling a little less sure of himself after the massive purges prescribed by Rahul and other interns, that this was surely not what Sambhu Narain might've had in mind. It was too late.

Rahul had taken it upon himself as a duty to see that his friends arrested for Sanjit's death should go free. His friends shared his contempt for the legal system and it was easy to persuade a few of them, including Sharmila, to join him in this personal vendetta. To his utter amazement, Hamid volunteered as well. "How the hell did you know what we're planning to do?" asked Rahul, somewhat fearful and alarmed. "My father told me everything," said Hamid, switching on his angelic smile.

So it was that I found myself in Rahul's company on another visit to Kartick Sirdar's fiefdom. This time I couldn't help feeling overcome by a strange weariness, a sense of futility. As I looked at Rahul, I couldn't help wondering about the revolution and change to which he seemed to have foresworn his life. He walked and talked like a crusader, a breed apart from the masses for whose cause he was fighting. The masses around us in Kartick Sirdar's hideout didn't inspire much confidence. I shuddered inwardly to think Rahul was fighting for humans whose aspirations might scarcely exceed those of animals, out of necessity rather than choice.

The morning fog was just starting to lift when Sharmila drove up to the warehouse in a black Ambassador car, banishing all greyness, all dullness, from the scene. She evoked visions of violent love rather than revolutionary change, but it was a matter of time before one realised she was tough as steel and that the lure of her sensuous body was one of those supreme illusions it was a pleasure to remain under. "Ah! Sharmila," said Kartick Sirdar, greeting her warmly, "forget your duty, your instructions, for once. Make me your victim today and make me proud. I'd gladly die a thousand deaths at your hands."

"But you're immortal, Kartick," Sharmila reminded him. "You're the one God who gives as generously to saints as to sinners. The saints receive from God a surfeit of illusions. But you, you dispense reality to whoever appeals to your fancy and your wallet."

Kartick protested that Sharmila was wrong to kill him with her tongue rather than her hands. Rahul interrupted him. "Look Kartick," he said, pointing to a shiny, late model Ford which had crept noiselessly to the edge of the pond, "there are other devotees at your door this morning."

A chauffeur stepped out nimbly and opened the door for a man of obvious distinction. He walked with a pronounced limp, and though the ivory cane he twirled in his hand lent a certain elegance to the limp, the total effect was somewhat comical. "And what brings the Chairman of Epic Industries to you, Kartick?" asked Rahul mockingly, not unduly concerned over proprieties.

He knew what Mr. Jhunjhunwala was after, and wasn't at all surprised that the big man had personally come to see Kartick who scorned dealing with flunkies. In a country where many goods were perpetually scarce, Mr. Jhunjhunwala displayed an insatiable appetite for contraband. That he possessed other healthy appetites as well seemed evident from the lustful gaze with which he devoured Sharmila. Why had Kartick never told him he had such beautiful friends? His voice was plaintive as a child's begging for a cookie.

Kartick replied that this was where he did business, and if Mr. Jhunjhunwala ever invited him to one of his fancy clubs he would be glad to let him into his circle of friends. Jhunjhunwala pretended to be stung by the remark and promised Kartick he could have an invitation any time he wanted. Then, looking more closely at Rahul and me, he asked if they could move away a little to do business. The *sirdar* would have none of it. He assured Jhunjhunwala that everyone there was a friend and suggested that they begin without any formalities.

Rahul and Sharmila were not interested in Jhunjhunwala. They lowered their voices and began to discuss a concern bothering Rahul since the moment he had finished speaking to Sharmila over the phone that morning. They had spent hours going over their plans, and now Sharmila informed him of some last minute changes. She reminded him that the party executive often made last minute changes in plans to throw off informers. Rahul wanted to get on with it and hoped Kartick would quickly dispose of Jhunjhunwala and give them the two revolvers he wanted.

Jhunjhunwala looked furtively in our direction a few times as he told Kartick that his company was expecting a large consignment of the painkiller, Pethidine, within the next forty eight hours. He promised to pay him handsomely if Kartick intercepted the medicines before the wagons were unloaded. The terms remained to be worked out. Jhunjhunwala scratched his chin thoughtfully and said that the consignment was valued at a hundred and forty thousand rupees. So he imagined that sixteen thousand, or a little more than ten per cent, should be ample for Kartick.

Kartick turned away from him and asked him to quit joking. There were others in the trade, and Jhunjhunwala should go to one of them. Limping fast, Jhunjhunwala quickly stepped over to him and grabbed his wrist. He wanted to apologize if he had offended Kartick. He assured him that Kartick was the best, that he would never go to anyone else, then informed him confidentially that there was talk of trouble with Pakistan and that the government was spending a lot of money in the east. Kartick had to help him quickly build up a large inventory.

There's always talk of trouble with Pakistan, retorted Kartick, but he would settle with Jhunjhunwala for thirty five thousand. The merchant gasped in disbelief. Kartick waited for an answer and then started to walk back towards us. Jhunjhunwala promptly agreed to the terms. He asked Kartick if he needed any other information, like wagon markings for instance. Kartick waved him goodbye saying he had all the information he needed. His men couldn't read anyway.

Rahul asked him why he had dealings with crooks like Jhunjhunwala. He was quickly silenced when Kartick pointed out that it gave him a chance to deal with people like Rahul. True, he felt a little guilty robbing a consignment for which the merchant would claim against his insurance and then obtain a fresh licence from the government for a new consignment which he could sell on the black market or arrange to be stolen, or whatever. But it's all destined, isn't it? he asked. Kartick was amused at how little Rahul knew about trade. Revolutionaries like him would gladly banish trade from the face of the earth, but what would they do with people like Jhunjhunwala?

The wind died down, the fog lifted, the city came alive, and the road bared its ugly potholes, gouged out by rain and neglect, to the sky. A strange, overpowering smell, half sweet and half greasy, rose from the ground and enveloped the uncollected heaps of garbage at street corners. It didn't spare the wailing beggars with glazed eyes and wrinkled skin and parchment breasts. It went on to knock on the doors of brick mansions towering over the sidewalks, mansions with shuttered windows and colourful balconies at whose doors sat armed guards in khaki uniforms, twirling their whiskers all day and night. Through it all, the city clung to a flicker of its old life. It flickered in the Grand Hotel, freshly whitewashed, windows trimmed in baby blue, rising like a giant birthday cake over the litter surrounding it. It flickered in the frayed awnings on top of Firpo's Restaurant, looking more and more soiled and tattered each day. It was anything but alive behind the barricaded windows of the United States Information Services — defensive on Vietnam, but always aggressive about the homespun values back home. Rahul admitted he missed it all sometimes. Gallons of beer some felt so privileged to drink at quiet parties with strange white men and women, so deferential and curious about India. Dave Brubeck and Charlie Mingus creating the spell and magic of America. He couldn't help wondering if it was more real than the long lines of movie fans spilling away from the box office of Metro Cinema presenting *Mother India* in glorious technicolour, 3:00, 6:00

and 9:00 p.m.

His mind slipped back in time, to his father declaiming on the triumph of virtue from his rickety stage in Bishnupur, triumphs bought with a terrible price. Bishnupur and Calcutta and other points on the face of the earth seemed no more than points straddled by the feet of a compass, its towering arch celebrating an irrevocable unity of mind, time and space.

Rahul reached inside his jacket, felt the warmth of the revolver, and smiled at me reassuringly. Sharmila grew thoughtful. Echoing some of my earlier thoughts, she wondered aloud if it wasn't a mistake, somewhat premature, to believe that people were crying out for change. Did anyone need social change any more than their friends needed to get killed? Rahul silenced her saying there was no point digging a hole in the sand, sticking one's head in, and pretending everything was dark, silent and untroubled. There may be doubts as to whether the Naxalites shouldn't have continued in the rural north before taking on the cities, questions about the very top leadership having been infiltrated. The answer lay in getting on with the job. Nobody won a battle who didn't fight. When you acknowledge a leadership, he said, you acknowledge the possibility of errors.

"Do you know about Srinivasan?" he asked me. "They called him the serpent. Serpent Srinivasan, the chief of police. Last month he and his men murdered nearly two hundred of his comrades, most of them shot in cold blood in front of their families. There was another hundred the month before, and the month before. Two thousand members under arrest, with no hopes of a trial in the near future. The party's falling apart. Nobody's sure who's a friend and who's not. What have we got to lose?" he said.

We passed the deserted zoo, passed the public gardens where a display of roses was drawing the jaded and the deprived by the hundreds. Sharmila parked the car on a side street, placed her pocket book inside the glove compartment, and stepped out. Rahul shook his legs as if loosening his muscles and asked Sharmila if she was all set to go. No doubts and misgivings? "None," she said.

We walked over casually to the main prison entrance where the crowd of visitors had already grown to fifty or so. They were late in opening the gates that morning. Among the people massed ten deep in front of the gates, Rahul spotted Hamid clad in his favorite lemon yellow shirt which Krishna had found for him. He exchanged quick glances with two other friends also there, Ravindra and Barin. I fell back on purpose and kept close to Sharmila.

A khaki-clad police officer started shouting, "Form a queue, form a queue. We'll not open the gates until you're all queued up." He brandished a baton and fondled a service revolver resting menacingly against his ample waist. Watching him, I lost Sharmila.

With a loud and prolonged clatter the wooden doors swung open. Not fully, only just enough to permit one person to pass through at a time. As the visitors walked in, one by one, it was like entering the dark and dank womb of a monster. Most of the visitors were awed into silence by the thick red walls and the enormous wooden doors studded with iron bolts. An old man stopped in front of an officer and said, "You opened the gates fifteen minutes late today. Does that mean we can stay inside fifteen minutes longer?" The officer grinned malevolently and replied that the old man could spend the rest of his life inside if he wanted to. He looked eagerly at the faces ranged in front of him, expecting some laughter. No one smiled even as the old man, mortified, walked quickly into the cold hallway.

At a spot where the queue ended for no particular reason, I found a cluster of men just hanging around. It was in their midst that I planted myself, my eyes fixed on a set of iron doors about twenty feet beyond the main entrance. Two young men sat behind tables arranged on either side of the main door, registering visitors, asking for the name of the inmate they wanted to see, and directing them to a body search as soon as they crossed the second set of doors. Rahul and his friends planned to keep their revolvers near their genitals in the hope that the puritanical squeamishness of the prison officials would keep their fingers away from the private parts. If anyone was caught, the others had orders to shoot from wherever they were. The next step was to grab some hostages and use them as shields or pawns as the circumstances demanded.

Hamid, Ravindra, and Barin had already gone inside by the time Rahul registered and crossed the second set of doors. Even in the dim light, I was surprised to see the security guards wave him on without a search, pointing him to one corner of the caged enclosure to await the prisoner he wanted to meet. Then I saw Sharmila again, following the person who had stood behind Rahul. As this person went in, Sharmila spoke to one of the prison officials, "I'm here to see Mary Tyler."

The officer repeated the name and asked if it was Mary Tyler, the girl from England. Yes, Mary was the person Sharmila wanted to see. The officer bared his teeth in a wide grin and informed Sharmila that Mary Tyler was no longer in Alipore Jail. She had been transferred to Hazaribagh Central Jail the night before.

'"hat shall I do now?" asked Sharmila, surprised. The officer smiled again and told her there was little to do but go home and order a cup of tea.

Visibly concerned over the holdup, Rahul stepped back towards the second set of doors. He felt an instinctive urge to protect Sharmila, to make sure she got in without a hitch. But Sharmila had already started to back away. I stepped forward to get a better view. A grim-faced Sharmila brushed past me without a word. I thought I noticed the slightest flicker of nervousness flash across Rahul's face. Then I lost him to the damp hall inside the prison.

There was something cold and frightening about that moment. When I looked around once more, I found no one I knew. I thought I was fully in command of my senses, but knew secretly that I was a coward. I was not armed, and Rahul did not expect any heroics from me. I turned and started to walk back towards the main entrance and, eventually, the car. Perhaps I had hoped to catch up with Sharmila. She wasn't near the car. Where could she be? A strange premonition seized my mind and I remembered the notebook she had carefully stowed away inside the glove compartment. The car was unregistered, so it didn't matter if we left it behind. But if the police had gotten wind of our plans, I was at least determined not to let Sharmila's pocket book fall into their hands.

I picked up a piece of brick, smashed a hole through the window, opened the car door, and reached for the pocket book. I opened the clasp and was immediately overcome with fear and confusion. There wasn't a shred of paper in the bag, which was just as well. But I found something that shouldn't have been there. Sharmila's revolver.

Had she lost her nerve at the last moment? I picked up the revolver uncertainly, thrust it inside my shirt, and started to walk away from the car. Just then, all hell seemed to break loose around the prison walls. As I look back over the terrible events of that day, I grow certain that there was some towering, pervasive power guiding our actions, leading us every inch of the way, even through our failures.

I came to the main street and saw people running and screaming wildly around the prison gate. Suddenly, Ravindra, a menacing revolver in one hand, pushed a staggering Hamid towards me. Blood was pouring from Hamid's hand. Cold and frightened, I somehow caught him in my arms. Weaving in and out of people rushing at us, I pushed my way into a cab waiting at the taxi stand. The cab driver took one look at us and refused to budge.

I had never before pointed a revolver at anyone till that day. Trying desperately to calm my trembling hands, I pulled out the weapon and placed the end of the barrel against the cabbie's head. I wasn't sure I could speak, but found my voice. "You'll not live very long, you'll not raise any children," I warned the man, "if you stay here now or talk to the police later." It didn't take him long to get going.

We left him at the door of the Nilratan Medical College. I was beginning to like my role and warned the cabbie even more strongly as we left. Hamid was in obvious pain and didn't utter a sound. Being Noor Mohammed's son, he was a familiar face in the hospital. One of Rahul's friends attended to his wound right away. I wasted no time in getting him a fresh change of clothes from Rahul's locker in the duty room. I handed the blood stained ones to Noor Mohammed in a plastic bag and told him to destroy them immediately. I promised him I would come and see him the next day. With that, I quickly led Hamid out of the hospital, hailed another cab, and went straight to Krishna's house in Ballygunge.

There was never any doubt in my mind that Krishna would do everything in her power to protect Hamid. Vikram was a different matter. It took a lot of persuasion, a lot of emotion from Krishna, to prepare him for the cover-up. By the time it was all settled, Krishna was pale and trembling with fear. "You must go back and bring me news of Rahul," she told me.

I spent a frantic evening and most of the night in the areas surrounding the prison, trying to piece together what had happened. I heard wild and conflicting stories. Some of the store-keepers were plainly suspicious of me. Others refused to speak. I didn't go back to Krishna that night. I had nothing to tell her.

Early next morning, I went to visit Noor Mohammed as promised. I was too late. He was moaning in agony when I found him in his room in the dingy quarters the hospital provided to some. His eyes were the colour and size of large white onions. I quickly got some interns to come and fill him up with painkillers. It did not take me long to discover that the police had visited Noor Mohammed early in the morning. He couldn't tell them what they wanted to know, or wouldn't. So they left him after injecting acid in his eyes. As the painkillers took effect, Noor Mohammed held my hand firmly clasped in his and whispered slowly, "Tell Rahul sahib to stop now. He has done enough to calm his father's doubts." Shortly before sleep numbed his tongue he roused himself a little, blessed me, and said some of his visionary powers would seep into my soul, of this he was certain. I wanted to know what they had done to Rahul. I couldn't see the answer right away, and Noor Mohammed was asleep before I could ask him.

Later that day, some of Noor Mohammed's acquaintances took the blind man to his village up north. To this day, I do not know what powers, if any, he passed on to me. But there was something that took hold of my imagination that morning, a clarity of perception born of the indescribable pain I felt while clutching Noor Mohammed's hand. A new awareness started to grow in me. I seemed to see and know all that had happened in and around the prison the previous day. Surely I was dreaming, I told myself. I became fearful of the experience when Rahul later told me what I had seen and felt was indeed true. The enormity of what Sharmila had done to her friends also became clear to me. From the moment she let Rahul step past the prison security guards into what was, for all intents and purposes, a cage and a trap, she not only abandoned him and his friends, but betrayed them as well.

Once past the guards, Rahul was in reality in a space bounded by cages on three sides. The open space formed a sort of quadrangle. Standing there, the bars of the adjoining cages gave the visitor the impression that he, a free man, was himself in a cage. The weak, pale light in the dark hall did not give Rahul a chance to see where Hamid and the others were. What he did see was that none of the visitors who had checked in were talking to any inmates on the other side. As he contemplated the lock which he was to force the guards to open, Rahul realized that the prisoner he had asked to see was not appearing either. It was then that he decided to make his presence known to his friends.

Rahul began shouting, "Mr. Guard, Mr. Guard, what has happened to my friend Shiben Talukdar? Is he coming to see me or not?"

The baton twirling officer we had seen on the way in now mimicked the name 'Shiben Talukdar' sarcastically. "Where do you think you are?" he asked. "The university coffee house perhaps."

Rahul did not respond to him. He had just spotted Hamid, and began to edge closer to him. Suddenly the prison walls rang with the sound of gunfire. Then came screams and other crashing sounds. Panic seized the visitors. As soon as the first shock wore off, they charged for the inside door which was still open to allow the last of the visitors to come in. Rahul, Hamid, Barin and Ravindra quickly closed in towards each other. Plucking their weapons from out of their clothes, they dashed towards the door.

The officer was waiting for them. His first shot struck Hamid in his arm, but Ravindra swept him past the officer and through a cluster of unresponsive guards outside. The officer's second shot tore through Barin's heart at point-blank range. He dropped soundlessly to the floor before being trampled by those behind him. Rahul paused for an instant to lift up his fallen friend. It was no use. The fleeing visitors were all over him. He quickly straightened up on the run and fired a single shot. The bullet pierced the officer in the right eye, and his face exploded like a ripe orange smashed against a concrete wall.

Rahul pushed his way past the scrambling visitors. In the chaos outside, he found a half dozen policemen, bayonets at the ready, taking up positions immediately in front of the gates. Street urchins and curious onlookers were beginning to converge upon the spot, adding to the chaos. Some of the visitors who had not gone past the security check were turning back and trying to break through the line of policemen. The policemen made threatening gestures to keep them back. For the moment, they had no orders to fire. The officer assigned to them was beyond all earthly orders by now. After a brief test of nerves, the men managed to breach the ranks of the policemen, spilled out onto Judges Court Road, and ran for their lives.

Ravindra had meanwhile passed Hamid over to me and slipped back inside the milling circle to join Rahul. They met up, exchanged glances, and decided to take advantage of the confusion to rush past the guards. Still clutching their weapons, they sprinted down a sidewalk to a narrow bridge leading towards Russa Road. Nobody tried to stop them. Street vendors leapt back from their wares and their vegetables to make way for them. The road sloped slightly upwards as it neared the bridge, and it was here that Ravindra stopped to look back. He had not seen Barin go down.

"I'm going for Barin," he shouted as he raced back towards the prison. Rahul was already some distance ahead when he heard him. He turned back and shouted to him not to go. "Barin's dead. Barin's dead," he yelled. "Come back."

The crowd of outsiders was thick around the prison gates. They had heard the shots, heard wild rumours. They were curious, and sensed blood and excitement in the air. The policemen had tightened their ring, and no one seemed to be coming out of the prison any more. Seeing Ravindra running towards them, a few of the policemen turned to face him. Ravindra stopped abruptly. It was only then that he seemed to hear Rahul. Three of the policemen had started advancing towards him. "Quick, Ravindra, quick," Rahul kept shouting. Ravindra turned round.

The reason the guards stayed their fire was probably because of the presence of the bystanders who now began to scatter in all directions. But the traffic along Judges Court Road hadn't yet realized what was happening. A tramcar rattled past the prison gates, unconcerned, followed by another. Taxis and other cars slowed down a little as they approached the crowd at the gates, but speeded up as they sensed there was something wrong.

With the crowd scattering, Rahul knew it was a matter of seconds before the guards took a shot at Ravindra. He would try to distract them. Hoping to split up the firepower, Rahul crossed over to the other side of the street until he stood directly under the prison walls. He had hardly any time to catch his breath and take aim before the walls towering over his head exploded with a deafening roar. Guards had opened fire at the opposite sidewalk from the towers jutting above the prison walls.

Two innocent bystanders were the first to go down. One sprawled headlong across the sidewalk and lay still at the feet of an old man selling puffed rice. The man was trembling like a leaf against the wall rising from the edge of the sidewalk. There was nowhere he could run to. He simply stared in horror at the prostrate figure whose breast was bathed in blood.

Ravindra looked stunned at the sight of the two men going down. He stopped dead in his tracks and turned round to face the advancing guards. He stood waiting, waiting for them to get within range, and then started to fire. He ran out of bullets before he could stop his pursuers. They were upon him in no time. One thrust his bayonet into Ravindra's neck. Two more beyonets pierced his sides in quick succession. Ravindra threw his head to the sky as his body whipped back under the thrust of the knives. Slowly, he rolled over and fell upon the heap of puffed rice which scattered under his body. The old man cringed against the wall and looked on in disbelief as his fair merchandise gradually turned a deep red colour.

Sick with fear, trembling with rage, Rahul saw all this too. A passing bus momentarily blocked his line of vision and gave him a chance to plot out his next moves. He decided his best chance of escape lay in walking away from the scene as casually as possible. He had hardly taken ten steps when he heard a fresh chorus of voices behind him. There's also a third man, someone shouted. "Which way did he go?" asked someone else. "To the bridge," yelled one of the jubilant guards thirsting for more blood.

Rahul quickened his pace a little, hoping none of the bystanders would give him away to the police. He was almost on the bridge, with the police gaining on him every second, when he heard a powerful voice call out, "Better not go on the bridge. Just follow me."

Rahul looked with surprise at the man who had spoken, wondering if he could be trusted, hoping he was not walking into another trap. But he had few options left. He made up his mind and stepped towards him. The man slipped down from a drum of tar on which he sat and briskly started down a set of steps leading from the top of the bridge to the bank of the river below.

As was only natural this time of the year, the river was almost dry. A flourishing colony of shacks had sprung up on its dry bed. It was to one of these shacks, put together with flattened kerosene drums, cardboard boxes, crates, and bamboo mats, that the man led Rahul. He almost pushed him into the shack. Since there wasn't enough room to stand inside, Rahul let himself collapse into one corner. It was then that he had his first clear glimpse of Kaloo.

Naked from the waist up in spite of the cold, Kaloo's hair fell on his shoulders in a thick cluster. His dark body shone with strength in every rippling muscle. His eyes glowed like diamonds. "You remind me"' said Kaloo, "of a person I saw some weeks ago in the burning grounds when they were cremating a young man your age. But for your beard, you could be an exact double for the older man. I can't seem to forget him. There was something about his eyes."

There was no disguising the fact that they were very close to the cremation grounds. Only a hundred yards or so and one was there. As if to prove the point, a puff of wind drove the smell of burning flesh into Rahul's nostrils. "I had no idea we were so close," said Rahul.

Kaloo laughed. "We're always close to that place, my friend," he said. "Only a breath or a gasp away." He explained how he was always there, making sure things were going smoothly, the fires burning, no vandals running away with half cremated bodies. "For the bones, you know," he offered by way of explanation.

Rahul's plight was gradually beginning to sink in. With it, his heart felt as if it would explode over the loss of his friends. Kaloo interrupted his thoughts. In answer to his question about what he was doing inside the jail, Rahul denied he was doing anything. He added that he seemed to get caught in something terrible that was certainly not his making. Kaloo had only seen the shooting outside. He sighed and asked if his friend whom the police had killed would've had the same story. Rahul chose not to answer. In the silence that followed, Kaloo poked his head past a piece of rag flapping over the entrance to the shack. He said he was going outside to take a look.

Rahul felt cold and nervous. His eyes adjusting to the gloom, he looked around to find three other persons crammed inside the hut. Two men, both middle aged, squatted on their haunches, their eyes closed, swaying from side to side, smiling faintly one moment and turning somber the next. They twirled round and round in their hand a glass with some frothy drink in it. From the sweet smell hanging in the air, Rahul concluded the stuff must be toddy. The other person, now surveying Rahul intently, was a young girl, not more than twelve or thirteen. She sat cross-legged and cramped between the cardboard wall on one side and a battered cash box on the other. Several small earthen pitchers of toddy stood in front of her.

Rahul was relieved to find Kaloo returning alone. He stepped inside and said the police were unlikely to come looking for him there. "Sometimes it's a blessing to be an untouchable," he said. He smiled amiably at Rahul and added, "I can guess from your face and your clothes that you are a high caste person. But, I should warn you that I handle carrion. I am a *dom*." Rahul returned his smile and said he knew that all along. It didn't make any difference to him.

Kaloo tried to sound diffident and good humoured as he asked another question. Was Rahul the only person to come out of the jailbreak alive?

Rahul looked puzzled, even annoyed. He didn't know anything about a jailbreak. Kaloo nodded his head doubtfully and said he couldn't make up his mind whether Rahul was an actor or an innocent victim. His looks would surely have qualified him for the films; perhaps a little more flesh around the jaws, the cheeks, the waist, but not much more. Rahul interrupted him to say he was telling the truth, that he was no escapee.

"Didn't you hear the hellish firing just before you met me?" asked Kaloo. "I don't mean the shots that killed the two men on the road. I mean the firing that took place inside at about the same time. I just found out that thirty prisoners are dead, maybe a hundred."

Rahul writhed inside in helpless anger. This was the government's way of getting rid of prisoners and making way for more. Everything nicely stage managed. "Are you blind, little one," Kaloo spoke softly, turning to the young girl, "can't you pour out a drink for the gentleman here?"

Rahul didn't want any, but that didn't seem to offend Kaloo. He only reminded Rahul that, before the day was over, he would probably need a lot of fire in his veins. Rahul suggested he should be getting along soon.

Kaloo couldn't hide his impatience. "You may not be an escapee, but you're mad to think of going out'" he said. "By now every greedy son of a bitch vendor in the neighborhood must've promised to act as a police informer." It was safer for Rahul to lie low for the moment. As long as he was with untouchables, it was a safe bet that he was untouchable himself.

Kaloo offered to fix him up a bed for the night. That was one of their trades on the side. Even though the beds were pretty tacky, they had beds galore, picked off the cremation grounds by the score. Quite a few got sold each week since they were always in great demand. Yes, the supply was endless too, but there wasn't much by way of quality. Once upon a time they brought aristocrats for cremation on rosewood beds, beautiful furniture. Now it was all the same — aristocrats and *babus* all coming on crates. This tide of information helped Rahul forget his grief, if only for a brief moment.

He politely declined the offer of a bed but did agree to spend the night with Kaloo. Later, he moved to another shack which was somewhat larger and where the blue smoke from the evening fires seemed a little less suffocating. There was nothing to do here but stare through the chinks in the wall at the gathering darkness outside, a darkness pierced by sudden illuminations as new pyres burst into life in the distance. Kaloo came and went, busy with whatever had to be done around the place, pausing to talk of the death of friends and strangers, which seemed a perfectly natural thing to do.

Rahul dubbed Kaloo the local expert on death and asked him, somewhat distractedly, if there was really any need for the police to bayonet his friend to death. The expert pointed out how much better it was to be stuck with bayonets than to have rugs pushed up one's ass with batons, or have hungry rats in little cages nibbling away at one's penis. Kaloo assured Rahul that his friend's death was no more than symbolic, meant to be a lesson, as all deaths are meant to be. He had been told that the police had left the sidewalk strewn with puffed rice, now caked and dyed red in blood.

Kaloo's wife brought him some dinner. Rahul had no appetite left, but there was no escape. Kaloo, his wife, and the young girl sat silently on the mud floor in front of him while he plodded through the rice, a piece of fish, and a small bowl of lentils cooked with string beans. When he had finished, the young girl, at a gentle push from Kaloo's wife, helped Rahul clean his fingers with water. She then took the brass utensils to be scoured in the stream.

Rahul felt as touched by their kindness as he felt transfixed by the distant fires. In a somewhat mellow and philosophical spirit, he asked Kaloo if he thought the fires were trying to tell him something.

"These things are beyond me, a poor untouchable," he replied with a shy grin. "But this I know. Though the raging fire prevails for a time, when all is finished and done with, it is the ashes that remain. Not the fire." Seeing Rahul staring into the night, he told him again how much Rahul reminded him of the old man with the unforgettable eyes. Like him, and thousands of others before him, the old man too was staring at the fires that burn. Kaloo wished he knew whether the man found any answers there.

Rahul did not know if it was his father Kaloo was referring to. But he was beginning to see his destiny woven with his father's like he had never seen before. He was not different. He could never be different from his father. Rahul heard the sounds of drums and cymbals and wailing conch shells in the night, and it suddenly occurred to him there was not a single note of sorrow in the air. Yet, he knew for certain that sadness lay heavy over the land. As he fell asleep, he imagined the sadness was as vast as the land itself.

It was not the next day, but the day after, that Rahul ventured out of his sanctuary and made the phonecall I had been waiting anxiously for. I assured him Sharmila and Hamid were both safe. We agreed that there was only one thing for him to do and that was to get out of the city. Getting out of the country appealed to him more. I took it upon my shoulders to try and arrange this. I consulted with Krishna and felt there was nothing wrong in approaching Dan Cohen of the United States Information Services for help. After all, Dan had served for months as a spiritual mentor to many of the Naxalites now dead or languishing in jail. If anyone could help, it would be Dan.

I suffered my first setback when I discovered that Dan Cohen had left Calcutta on indefinite leave. I was forced to deal with his churlish successor, Alan Briscoe, who first told me he hadn't a clue who Rahul was, then reminded me drily that the U.S.I.S. wasn't in the business of issuing passports or visas. I heard him out patiently, then suggested that he should somehow get in touch with Dan wherever he was and check out the facts about Rahul before risking having the whole affair blown up in the newspapers. When I phoned the next day, I found Allan a different man, charming and considerate, who invited me to drop by with a recent photograph of Rahul's and stay for a cold beer. He promised the papers would be ready in a week.

Meanwhile, Rahul was growing bored and restless. I had convinced him he should stay where he was. It gave him something to do when Kaloo suggested he should shave off his beard for a better disguise. He sent for an old barber who, he claimed, possessed a memory even weaker than his eyesight, a person affectionately known to everyone as Uncle.

Uncle's glasses were so thick and Uncle himself looked so feeble that Rahul couldn't bring himself to trust his face to the man. So he borrowed his razor, his cup of soap and the worn out brush, and painstakingly shaved off his beard himself.

"Uncle usually shaves only the dead," said Kaloo after the man had taken his leave. "They're less fussy than you."

Sensing his increasing anxiety, Kaloo finally persuaded Rahul to join him in three hours of meditation that afternoon. He was impressed by the ease with which Rahul slipped into meditation, how much better he felt for it. Immediately after the evening meal, he said to Rahul, "I've something interesting in store for you. I think you'll enjoy meeting my friend Guru Shaktiramji tonight." Rahul felt himself in as good a frame of mind as he would ever be to face the unexpected, even the supernatural. He agreed.

While experts in the American Consulate continued to fix up his papers, Rahul spent a week dabbling in *Tantric* practices, quietly submitting to every one of the Guru's demands. There were rituals he took part in that might have outraged him earlier. Now, it didn't matter any more. He found his appetite for the unreal suddenly growing. It helped him forget Barin and Ravindra, helped him forget the city he was so fond of. As I handed him the airline ticket, the passport and visa, I could sense he had already set himself adrift on some inner voyage. He was at some point beyond this land. Even as he stepped out of the passenger lounge at Dum Dum, the land of his birth shrunk to a pinpoint of light and his family and friends joined the phantoms wandering in his mind.

Five

A surly immigration officer in Boston kept looking back and forth between his passport and Rahul's face. When he asked Rahul why he had shaved off his beard, Rahul scratched his chin and said, "Dermatitis."

"I should quarantine you," said the officer without a smile as he stamped his passport and set him free.

No computer stores this time. Rahul was surprised how quickly he found a researcher's position in a Cambridge lab. It was headed by a Nobel laureate who was fond of saying, "Blessed are the children of the rich, for many a door will open itself unto them." This time, Rahul was determined not to throw it all away. Having seen much of it on his earlier visit, he had no desire to explore the land. He was also determined to avoid women. Even though he did not know the truth about Sharmila, he began to see women in a different light. His new emotions about them were more confusing and ambivalent than before.

His life was routine, his work was fun. Rahul liked it that way. He tried to understand the Vietnam War but felt largely untouched by it. The closest he came to any form of protest was when he witheld his telephone tax and mailed his cheque to Bell Telephone without postage and without a return address on the envelope. He puzzled endlessly over the innocence and naivete of these public reactions, conceding eventually that he was a much inferior human being compared to a

Gandhi or Martin Luther King. But the truth was he had always been impatient of pacifists.

In the Spring of nineteen seventy he discovered a cause in Bangladesh and found a moral, if not ideological, ally in Senator Edward Kennedy. He also found a villain in Richard Nixon for siding with West Pakistan against the Bengalis of East Pakistan. Suddenly, all the pent up fury of the past two years exploded and seized every moment of his waking hours. He found friends on both sides of the Charles River who debated endlessly on human rights and Nixon's love for military rulers. But much of it ran out of steam one Friday evening on Boston Harbour where a ship, supposedly carrying U.S. arms from Savannah to West Pakistan and coming to Boston to pick up additional supplies, never showed up.

Determined to prevent the ship from docking at Boston, Rahul and his friends sat out the day in eleven boats. They turned back towards the shore at four the next morning, too exhausted to persist with their vigil. They were invited over for hot chocolate and muffins by Alice Newton, a young woman who had dropped by with others to give them encouragement from the pier.

Rahul had barely finished his second cup of hot chocolate before he fell asleep in one corner of the family room. Alice didn't have the heart to wake him up. When he was startled out of his sleep late in the afternoon, Rahul found the family busy preparing for a party that evening. He apologized for falling asleep and prepared to take his leave. John Newton, Alice's father, wouldn't hear of it. He had just come back after a year in Zambia, and wanted to talk to Rahul about India and Bangladesh. Rahul needed at least a shower and a shave, and it fell upon Alice to help him out. She even found him one of her dad's shirts. Afterwards, she led him into the dining room and poured him a glass of punch.

They stood beside each other, silently watching John's slide presentation. Their eyes were riveted to the wild colours flashing across the screen. There, out there against the wall, the opaque and luminous patch glowed with splashes of yellow, orange, blue, grey, and black. An odd combination, but it hardly mattered. Certainly not to the intense audience spilling out of chairs and sofas on the Oriental rugs. Larger than life on the screen, slightly left of center, two women stood frozen in their flowing robes. One smiled, black and shiny, with a black and shiny child sleeping on her back. The other had an expression of total peace and happiness on her face. Above them, blue and cloudless, the African sky seemed waiting for something to happen. Waiting for what, for whom? thought Rahul. Waiting for experts like John, he imagined, and the moving finger that would seed the clouds with rain and milk and push up the G.N.P.

Hah! who cared for John Newton's slides? Well, John did. His voice rose triumphantly from the darkness and slithered past the curling after-shave lotion coloured coils of cigarette fumes churning in the projector's beam. "This is the Barclay's Bank at Lusaka, DCO," he announced. A murmur like a mountain stream's, steady and predictable, flowed through the room. Words rose to the ceiling and became lost in some black hole in space, clear and distinct one moment, forgotten the next.

"Those lovely Zambian ladies'" said someone. "The intensity of the colour," gasped a majestic blonde, sheathed in black, stretched like a panther, licking her honeyed lips with a silken tongue, reclining as if for a portrait by Goya. Annoyed for staring at her when the lights came on, Rahul forced himself to look away. As he did so, he caught a sparkle in little Susan's eyes.

"Know what?" asked Alice's little sister. "We dropped daddy at the bank. Then Mummy and I went shopping."

"It's only her imagination," John said quickly. He and his wife had separated shortly after their return from Zambia. It was almost as if Mummy was an unwelcome intrusion in the evening's agenda. John's voice was suffused with pride a moment later. "I waited twenty five minutes to catch the women under the mural. Well worth it, don't you think?" he asked. No one answered. Did they really give a damn, thought Rahul. The silence didn't seem to bother John. "Hit the button, Susan," he called out to his daughter. Susan's response was immediate.

"This one was taken at Carols by Candlelight," continued John, happy and unhurried. Then something upset his mood. As the groans and murmurs began, he cried, "Jesus! the slide's all wrong." Then he shouted under his breath, "Move, Susan. More. One more. There, that's better."

Pale faces in the pale light. Susan clicked along. Her father's voice followed at a steady pace. "That's a foxglove," announced John. "Oooh!" cried the voices. "A hibiscus," he said. "Now a poinsettia. This one, let's see . . . can't seem to remember its name. Water lillies here." The voices responded, "Aaaah!"

The sight of the flowers cast a quiet spell upon everyone in the room. John shattered it with another cry, "Hit the button, Susan." She lunged for the switch with a sudden start.

The scotch and soda in his hand began to take effect. John's nostalgia grew deeper. "And here," he continued, "here they're playing tennis at the United Nations Club." Dressed in white linen, shod in white sneakers, they leaped and stretched on the clay court. The faces came and went. More pale faces, old faces, young faces, giving way to new faces. Until finally a single face, fleshy and jowled, lay stuck on the screen. The camera had caught him gazing intently upon a still-life of baked beans, sausages, and ketchup frozen against white china on a table. "An Afrikaaner friend who liked to lunch at the club," said John. "Looks well fed, doesn't he?" John laughed as a disembodied voice from the darkness commented that the man looked harmless enough.

"Man, wait till you see him stare a nigger down in Joburg," commented someone else.

"How come Indians do so well in Africa, but the Blacks can't?" asked John. If he was expecting Rahul to take up the question, Rahul wasn't prepared to oblige. Instead, someone suggested better genes and laid the matter to rest.

Pale face, master race, thought Rahul, as the machine suddenly jammed. The pudgy face kept smiling benevolently, the ketchup turned a deeper red, the sausages glistened, and the beans sank deeper in their gooey mess. "Susan, back one'" cried John. "SUSAN," he shouted. Then, somewhat abruptly and not very gently, he snatched the controls from her. He seemed contrite the very next moment. "Maybe you'd like to go into the other room and play there," he suggested. "Maybe you're getting tired."

Susan walked away in a huff. But the pained expression soon

vanished from her face as she allowed herself once more to be seduced by her father's slides and his fond memories. Free at last of the machine and its irksome demands, she soon found her voice and began to chatter excitedly. "Know what?" she asked. "That there's a lion. It's an angry lion. Somebody threw a paper bag at him. It had peanuts. That's why he's angry."

Rahul's thoughts went back to Krishna's daughter, Malini. He had never been very close to her, simply because he chose not to visit the house too often. Even if he had, he wondered how close he could've ever gotten to the girl who was practically blind. "She's impossible, isn't she?" Alice interrupted his thoughts. Rahul looked at her and smiled. He had almost forgotten about her presence till now.

John was not to be put off by these interruptions. "This is one of my very best," he said. "Notice the deep wounds in the hippo's body. Can you see them? Look closely and you'll see blood dripping near its mouth." Click, the next frame. "That's a banded mongoose, also snapped on the walking safari. They eat snakes." Then John turned his head and peered into the darkness behind him. "We have an Indian expert in our midst tonight. He'll tell you India is famous for its mongooses."

"Mongooses or mongeese?" questioned an anonymous voice causing another stir in the audience. John didn't move the slide, expecting Rahul to straighten out the correct plural form. Again, he remained silent, not amused for having been singled out for attention over such a trivial matter. We have indeed, he thought angrily, but minus the bands.

"Have you never heard of Rikki?" he asked softly, almost inaudibly, turning towards Alice. "Rikki Tikki Tavi, with his little eyes like hot coals, weaving and dancing around the cobra. And the cobra, coiled like a watch spring, flailing the earth, hissing through the grass like a whiplash flicked across a horse's neck." His face hardened unconsciously. He wasn't sure if it was the expression on his face that made Alice turn pale before his eyes and sway a little. "Are you all right?" he asked her. Alice touched her forehead with her fingers and pushed the golden hair from her face. "It's nothing," she said.

The slide show went on. Rahul grew pensive once more and was startled to hear Alice say, "A penny for your thoughts."

"Mind's a complete blank," he lied.

"I'll tell you." She was once more in control of herself. "There's resentment in your eyes. There's something in each one of us we don't like others to touch, a little secret which no one pries into. Dad touched you, and it made me sick."

Rahul was impressed. There was a life, an identity, in Alice he hadn't suspected before. "I must try to get to the bottom of this resentment," he said, smiling. The African slides made him uncomfortable. He wasn't sure any more whether he really should have stayed to watch. How would he have felt about Indian slides, he asked himself.

The little chandelier in the dining room cast a deathly pallor on every face. In another place and time, he would've wondered if they were alive or dead, such is the perception of the darker races. But were they alive to anything beyond their own existence? Few are, he reminded himself, with a warning to be less arrogant. For had they not offered him a new home. Maybe they were real, after all, but they still seemed beyond his understanding. Were the women as unselfconscious as they pretended to be? Were the men all self-possessed, confident, and invulnerable? The white man's strength seemed so different from his own. His own, as far as he could tell, seemed to come from whatever he was. Here, even those who professed an obvious disdain for the outward trappings of wealth and power shared something with the rest, something which neither their long unwashed hair nor their faded Levis could hide. Was it the certain conviction in the finality of their beliefs? Had they abandoned doubt? The product of a culture which showed many shades of black and white, where assent could never be taken for agreement, nor any refusal so stern as to exclude all possibilities of a complete reversal, Rahul wanted desperately to get behind the essential uniformity of the people he was getting to know this time around - from Dr. Brock down to all the lab scientists and technicians to the folks now around him. Where were the others? Was it their absence that set him apart?

By now he had lost interest in the slides. He turned to examine each guest intently in the dim light, wondering what it would take to start a brief encounter, a fleeting intimacy, before enough secrets spilled out and there grew love, pity, or resentment. Such a different world from the world inside his lab. Were both a waste of time?

He was suddenly thirsty and longed to get out of the room. Since Alice had disappeared, he turned to Susan who was still standing in front of him, captivated by the pictures. "Susan," he whispered, "where can I get a drink of water?"

"Come with me." She led him into the kitchen.

Rahul held the glass absent-mindedly beneath the kitchen tap. It suddenly split in two. He dropped the pieces in the sink as the hot water touched his fingers. Cursing softly under his breath, he drew another glass from the wall cupboard and took care this time to turn on the right knob for cold water. "It's all right," Susan assured him. "I broke many glasses and nobody was mad." She showed him the trashcan and waited for him to throw away the broken pieces.

"Know what? I can write a story."

"Write me one," said Rahul.

Susan made him wait near the table while she got herself a piece of paper, a pencil, and got down to the serious task of writing her story. Rahul turned his attention to the voices in the next room. Echoes, echoes, echoes. In the room the men come and go, talking of Zambiothello. Meester Kaaunda, hees permanent secretaries ees impermanent. Too much tribal whorefare. Meester John, our economic aardviser, hee teereefic. Now we has the most modern copper extrooding plant employ feefty Zaambians. Schloemann, automated Deutsche. Kaunda no buy Anaconda. He plan fartilizer plant too. Employ eighty seven Zambians. No guano, no no.

John Newton in Lusaka was so much like Harold Melville of the Ford Foundation in Calcutta, thought Rahul. Cognoscente of the world's transport systems, occasional visitor to their gatherings at the U.S.I.S., Harold Melville probably had his toilet paper shipped from Singapore, great scott F.O.B. on the S. S. Virgin Clipper, twin screw and stabilizer, flagship of the Royal Fallopian Lines. And San Miguel beer from Hong Kong, compliments of Douglas Macarthur. And Marcella Borghese skin cream for you, Mrs. Melville. Ooooh! Mrs. Melville, your breasts so tumescent. Yours squeezably, from the commissary in Saigon. What a man! What a plan! No more overcrowded buses and trams. Ford Foundation had deemed no more carriages dropping inhumans on the street mashed under the wheels, no more secretarial boobs rubbing maidenform mysteries on mongoose-pimpled scapulae as we go rolling rolling home sardined in double-decker subs. What a great subway it'll be. Good job, Mr. Melville, as Ford Foundation one, two, three, packed their bronze figurines, colonial lithographs, moghul rugs, incense burners, and humbler belongings in teakwood crates and bonvoyaged the Melvilles to Ithaca, tenure unbroken, tapestry unwoven, and lots of thank you, thank you, thank you's. Yes, it's the Russians now coming out of the subway, thousands of them. Who brought them in? Who showed them the way? That's what non-alignment is all about, you jerk, simple matter of which way you want to pee, Washington or Moscow.

Susan had finished. She was waving the piece of paper in Rahul's face. She couldn't wait to get on with her story: "Now there was a big bad wolf. One day he went up the hill. And he saw what he saw. And the big bad wolf he huffed and he puffed and he wuffed and blew the house down." She looked up expectantly at Rahul and said, "That's all."

Rahul told her it was a beautiful story, and she was ready with another right away. Here comes: "Once there was an alligator. He went up the hill too. And he saw what he saw. And he puffed and he wuffed and he huffed and he blew the house down."

"Marvelous," said Rahul, then turned to ask what happened to the developers. "Who are developers?" asked Susan. Rahul explained that they told stories too, funny stories, bedtime stories, to sell expensive houses.

Susan wasn't finished yet. "I'm coming to my best story," she said. "One day the big bad fox climbed up the hill. And he saw what he saw. And he wuffed and he puffed and he huffed. Nothing happened. So he climbed up the chimeney and sticked his head in. But the big bad fox slipped down the chimeney and fell into a pot. Inside the house the wee little pigs quickly closed the lid on the pot. And guess what they had for supper?" she asked. Rahul of course didn't know the answer. "I won't tell you, ha! ha! ha!" cried Susan, clapping her hands delightedly. Then, somewhat coyly, she said, "Maybe I will." The secret, the clue, came after a suspenseful pause. "Fox soup."

"I'm so dumb," said Rahul. "And you're such a clever story-teller. Let me take another look at the story." He picked up the sheet of paper, swarming with crosses and lines and A's dancing on one leg and mutant B's. "What's this?" he asked, pointing to a particularly exotic figure.

"That's how you write big bad wolf, silly. Don't you know that's a B?"

Rahul apologized for his ignorance. Susan offered to show him, step by step, how to write a B. But before that she had to tell him what a funny name he had. Then she began. "See, first you write a E, like this, then you cover it up with two rainbows like this. It's simple." While Rahul marvelled at the simplicity, Susan turned to him again. "Wanna hear more, Rahool?" Without giving him a chance to answer, she was off. "Do you know that some cows are bulls?" she asked, looking thoughtfully at Rahul. "I know the story of a lady hippopotamus that put on lipstick one night before she went to sleep. And the man hippopotamus was so scared he ran away from the river and never returned."

Enter John Newton. "Well, Rahul," he exclaimed, clasping his hand warmly. "How nice you could stay." All the lights had been turned on. The guests were shaking themselves off the ground, from their chairs, filling up their glasses, perhaps taking stock of their neighbors. "Quite a crowd here, eh?" asked John, looking around appreciatively. He wanted Rahul to make sure he met some of his friends before he left. He called out to Alice inside the kitchen. "Why don't you pour Rahul a drink."

"I can help myself," he said, and walked over to Alice. She offered him a beer. "Guess you're quite used to having people run errands for you," she asked. "No," said Rahul, without betraying the slightest emotion or surprise.

"Tell me, Rahul," asked John Newton, drawing near. "Do you suppose there'll be a war between India and Pakistan?" Rahul was beginning to relax once more. He shrugged his shoulders and said, "When did they stop fighting?"

John nodded his head understandingly. "Yes, I know exactly how you feel. Terrible business this. Senators like Kennedy are quite outraged. How do you suppose America can really help?"

"But you are helping, John. I'm sure we have tons of stuff flowing in. What else can the free world do but feed the hungry, clothe the naked, and arm the weak? They say Dum Dum airport looks like a huge supermarket when the transports come in. The place is stacked to the beams with milk powder and wheat, gift of the people of the United . . . free world."

"I know the feeling"' said John.

"They say it's the white man's burden," Alice broke in.

Other voices drew near as the guests moved towards supper. In the growing babble of voices, the reasons why General Electric had sold its computer operations to Honeywell seemed to generate as much heat as the New York Times Book Review. "I knew Sennett," exclaimed a voice. "What a godawful teacher. Mercifully, they refused him tenure." Someone else said, "GE sold out for less than two hundred million and claimed they didn't take a loss. Creative book keeping." And on it went. Someone commenting on what a damning review it was, someone insisting that the reviewer blew it in the end, and someone else hoping that Skinner wasn't as tightassed as Bell. "Nice crowd, eh?" asked John, looking around once more.

It was at this point that the blonde drew near, her plate loaded with chili and a slice of pizza. "Have I seen you before?" she asked.

"We all tend to look the same, don't we?"

"My, my," she said, refusing to give up and walk away. "Who are you, a Black Panther or the Red Brigade?"

"We're black, we're red, we're khaki." There was a friendly smile on his face which said 'peace'. "What difference does it make?"

Just then Susan popped up in front of them. "Know what?" she asked, touching Rahul gently on the wrist. "I once saw a tin tray flying in the sky, twinkling like a. . . ."

"Stop interrupting, Susan," John Newton's voice was loud and clear. "Don't you think it's time you were in bed"'

"But I wasn't terrupting," she cried, breaking into tears. Alice quickly stepped out of the crowd, looking vexed and uncertain. She picked Susan up in her arms and began to comfort her. "I wasn't terrupting, Alice," she whimpered, "like Mommy teached me never to."

"It's all right, Susan. Let's go up and I'm going to tuck you into your warm bed."

"Will you make me some waffles tomorrow?" she asked, wiping away her tears. Alice assured her she would make her the biggest pancakes instead and that was enough to make her smile again. They both disappeared up the stairs.

"Goodnight, daddy," a voice floated down. "Goodnight everyone."

Goodnight. Goodnight. Goodnight.

John looked embarrassed. "Sorry about that," he said, turning from Rahul to the blonde. He introduced her as Ginny. Then, pointing to Rahul, he said, "Here's the right person to ask what Care, Oxfam, or Caritas might be doing in India."

"Why, were you interested?" Rahul asked Ginny.

"As a matter of fact I was."

"I know nothing specific about their operations," apologized Rahul, "except what I read in the papers."

"Hm!" said Ginny, a slice of pizza poised in front of her lips. "I've thought of working with the refugees."

"With or for?" asked John, feigning alarm.

"Oh, I don't know," said Ginny with a hint of irritation. "What difference does it make?"

John put his arm on her shoulder. "My dear Ginny," he said, "life is still hidden from your pretty eyes. One must do everything not to get sucked into local problems to which we're strangers, things we don't understand. I simply don't believe in meddling in other nation's affairs. As a person who knows the Third World reasonably well, I can say this with confidence."

Guests began to gather round them. The speaker had his audience. John continued. "That doesn't mean we can't take sides or express sympathy. I'm sure both Ginny and I have strong feelings about what's going on there. But will her presence in a hospital or a camp emphasize anything that's not all too obvious? There's trouble in all of Asia. They don't want us. I think they don't even need us. My advice is, let's keep out of trouble that's not of our making."

Alice came and joined him just as another guest moved over in his direction. "Very interesting," he began, clearing his throat. He introduced himself. "I'm Michael Thorndike. You know, I myself came very close to similar trouble in nineteen sixty eight. March, sixty eight, to be precise. We were on one of those A.F.A. tours, my wife and I. Excellent tours, very selective. Moghul Adventure, they called this one. Except for me and a couple of other poor professors, they were all lawyers, bankers and doctors. Harvard, Yale, you name it. Next year, they'll invite Dartmouth and Chicago. As I was saying, we were in New Delhi and waiting to go to Calcutta. They were killing policemen there. Yes. murdering them. There wasn't a snowball's chance in hell any of us would go." Then turning directly to Rahul, he asked, "Didn't we do right?"

"I guess so," he replied, looking at Alice. "I'm from Calcutta. At the time we were changing a government. Do it all the time in Bengal. One gets used to it after a while."

The professor ignored Rahul. "So you see," he said, nodding emphatically at Ginny, "John is absolutely right about staying out of trouble."

"Don't pay any attention to him," whispered Alice. "He's a real asshole."

"Oh!" Rahul lowered his voice. "Someone should tell the professor we were making drums with the gizzards of white men and impregnating white women in three seconds flat and carving them up three hours later to be served in communal feasts as Madras curry."

Alice started to laugh. "You're crazy." She wasn't offended.

March, nineteen sixty eight. The professor's words kept echoing in his ears as he piled chili and salad on his plate. What was he doing here, he asked himself again, in this elegant Brookline home, thousands of miles away from his own people. Is this really where he belonged? He felt his insides wrenched by a terrible longing. Alice came back and asked if he'd like a glass of wine.

"I'd like to go to India myself," she said, watching for his reaction. Rahul said nothing. "I met a tea planter in Europe last summer and he's invited me to taste his tea and enjoy his hospitality. Lives somewhere near Darjeeling. Grows oranges too. Do you think I should go?"

"Oh, you must," replied Rahul. "It's a beautiful part of the country."

"I thought so." Alice smiled. "The fellow told me that when one peeled his oranges, one could not only smell the tangy peel but the fresh leaves as well. Must be a rare experience."

Rahul couldn't help laughing. "I wouldn't believe everything those planters tell you. They're crazier than hell."

Professor Thorndike joined them again. "What beautiful cities you have. I'll never forget the changing of the guards at the President's Palace in New Delhi. What a spectacle, what thrilling music, and the mounted horseguards in white and red turbans. Ohhh!" The man nodded dreamily, staring into his glass, savouring the rising images.

Rahul stepped away towards the bar. Alice edged towards him. "The guy won't forget Srinagar either," he said to her, "or the beautiful vale of Kashmir and the canopied house-boats and the frail *shikaras* skimming over leaf-strewn Nagin Lake, or the valley of Pahalgam overhung with forests of blue pine and fir, the splendour of the Taj Mahal, the curious mystery of the Gateway of India, or the Ganga at Benares, seething with pilgrims. Ah! what peace, what quintessential harmony sipping iced gin n'tonic on the edge of the shimmering pool at the Oberoi Inter Continental, all aquiver with the martial passion of piped-in Finlandia." Alice doubled up with laughter.

The professor was irrepressible. "I was tempted to take another trip this summer to Persepolis. Should've been fun. Did you know, they celebrated Persia's twenty fifth hundred anniversary. Twenty fifth hundred. But I had to attend this damned conference in Buffalo. Science before culture." He laughed heartily, spilling his drink.

John and Ginny re-entered the room together. Alice looked at them and quickly caught Rahul's eyes. He suspected there was something going on between them. Still, he felt absolutely devastated by the curves on Ginny's underbelly. John interrupted his thoughts. "First thing tomorrow morning," he said to Ginny, "write out a check for Oxfam or Save the Children and you'll feel much better. Galbraith has the nicest things to say about them. He ought to know. He knows that scene better than any American."

"But he prefers Saint Tropez any day," piped in Professor Thorndike. John moved along, so did Michael Thorndike, but Ginny lingered. Rahul wished her luck with the refugees. He wished himself luck with her. He should be going. He looked around for Alice to say goodbye. She wasn't to be seen. Instead, his eyes met Ginny's. She drew closer. "Could we talk about this a little more sometime?" she asked.

That sounded like an interesting idea.

The cold night air hit him sharply on his face and turned his thoughts back to Ginny. She raised a faint exhiliration in his mind, but the pleasure of her memory was marred by a gnawing suspicion that he was not where he should be. As Ginny's face and body receded to one corner of his mind, Rahul realized with a slight feeling of loss that his passion didn't have much to do with getting into bed. Maybe it was from boredom.

The train was practically empty. As he stretched himself in the over-heated car, the wine and the rocking car contrived to put him to sleep. And ride in triumph through Persepolis. The words kept repeating in his mind as the bone-weary Green Line train rattled along its tracks.

Six

THERE WAS as much love as hate in his affair with Ginny, as much pity as cowardice. Things really began to look bad in the Fall. Rahul wasn't sure what it was except that the empty spaces in the day and night seemed to be getting larger. He knew Ginny would've left for work as he climbed up the steep driveway at the end of his run this morning. The trees were silent and rich in colour at that hour. Rahul stood with his fingers curled around the shining brass doorknob. With his left hand he drew a happy face across the silvery mist from his breath spreading itself on the glass. Three half moons within a circle. Or were they upside down rainbows? Rahul stood and watched in silence as the lines broke apart and disappeared into large drops of water. Like tears in a beautiful woman's eyes, he thought, as he held the door open. Like drops of water clinging to Ginny's breasts as she stepped out of the sea last summer in Chilmark, he remembered, as he stepped into the house. The epic solidity of Ginny's flesh, he murmured wistfully as he stepped into the shower.

But the loss of innocence. Or was it all an illusion? He wondered, as he fixed himself a quick breakfast. It just happens. It has to happen, he told himself. One is left with a tarnished innocence, and when that goes too? Perhaps we are wrong in trying to smooth out the rough edges, in trying to placate the passions, in rolling with the punches. How difficult it is to feel freedom if one has never known chains.

Perhaps Ginny was right. Perhaps relationships are like rooms with open doors, through which one walks in and out at will. But she had to learn that one always turned one's back to the doors in anger and regret. Oh! what a lesson he would teach her someday. Compassion, had he lost that too? Who needed compassion, he thought, as he finished breakfast.

Rahul walked along briskly, keeping some disance away from the voices in his head, glad to hear the sound of other footsteps as a group of children came shuffling, bouncing, dragging themselves to school. Rahul heard their footsteps, and then they stopped. Arrested by a sudden movement behind the bushes, one of the children halted excitedly. Another went down on his knees to examine some treasure the earth had yielded during the night. Yet another flung back his golden mane, blinked into the early morning glare, and contemplated the gulls wheeling in lazy circles below the clouds. Rahul wished he could share something with the children. If not something from their lives, at least a part of himself. But it was no use. He couldn't reach them. His mind had gone dead to the sense of wonder.

The unseen ghost of winter, the stripped carcass of spring, both were stalking him every inch of the way. It was in vain that he slowed down, quite unconsciously, trying to match his steps with those of the children. It seemed futile. They found meanings in fresh, uncertain rhythms, while he had lost himself in an immense, paralyzing certitude. Before long, his trail broke away from the children's as he turned off for the subway station.

He was alone. Maybe he was early. Maybe the others had all woken up late that morning, all those strangers whose faces he was getting to know so well. Nothing moved. The station was familiar, no longer of interest to him. The emptiness in his mind began to grow heavy. Moments after he had stepped out of the front door, the delicate beauty of the morning had reached out and touched his soul. It called out to him to forgive, to forget. It moved him with a sense of his own martyrdom. Sex is not for the possessive, she had said. A wave of horror swept over him even to think of it. Rahul knew a fiery jet of anger still burned fitfully somewhere inside of him.

As the children turned the corner, only the sound of his shoes on the wet concrete followed him. A short flight of steps led him from the street down to the tracks. The steps were damp and slippery today. Rahul had never been a careful man. Always one for taking chances. But today he slowed down. The sounds ended abruptly as he planted himself in his usual spot under the station clock.

He remembered the clock and lifted his eyes to it with a sudden motion of his head. The arms of a clock reminded him of those of a puppeteer to whom he had given away a large portion of his life, to whom he would probably give up whatever else was left of it. Every carefree impulse, and even his growing passion for order. Must he learn to measure his life by the hour, to parcel it out to others in thin slices, never to accept anything from others which couldn't be neatly balanced in his ledgers? Rahul recalled some of his earlier rock-like convictions and sighed to think of them. I can, and shall, be generous, he said. His sigh was like a little crack in the silence thickening around him, a silence that was beginning to fold him gently in its wings and transform the reality surrounding him. Soon the railway platform seemed to him no more than a gash in the landscape, and he himself a blade of grass no taller than a pin stuck on the edge of a precipice.

The clock stood still at twenty after eight. It suddenly occurred to Rahul that he had willed himself to an eternity of twenty after eights in order to wait for the Eight Thirty Inbound. Twenty after eight seemed to have swallowed the tracks from east to west in a vacuum of time. Now it was possible to travel in more than one direction simultaneously, even complete the journey, while time stood still. Rahul found excitement in this thought as train after train after train hurtled through his meditation, the orange colour of the cars an uneven blur over the unending blue of the steel rails. It's strange, thought Rahul, that all the trains were headed outbounds today. And why was the platform still deserted? Did nobody stop here anymore? No one to be picked up anymore? The blurred shadows in the windows flashing past seemed those of lives no longer recognizable, of lives spent. Except one, the shadow of his own life, thirty years fading to nothing.

What if this was the day his unconscious mind had been waiting for so long? A strange exultation stirred within him. Maybe the eight thirty inbound will not come today. Oh God! could it be true? What if terrorists had ripped up the tracks downtown? That means no one, no one, no one will ever, oh God! get to Copley, Arlington, Park Street. Ah! maybe they've left the outbound tracks open. Merciful radicals! Yes, get away while you can. Oh, thank you, thank you, Miss Fonda. Thank you, Angela Davis. There was still time, a little time, for honest housewives, jaded white collar workers, frustrated VPs and stern meter-maids to escape.

There they were, more outbound trains, accelerated by panic and fear. No wonder he couldn't see the faces of the passengers. Rahul broke into a cold sweat. What next? When will they blow up Louisberg Square? When will the whistling rubble of Beacon Hill shower death and destruction on Government Center, the Two O' Clock Lounge, Sodom and Gomorrah? Quivering with excitement, he turned his eyes to the grey east, waiting breathlessly for the sky to erupt in a blaze of fierce red, the promised dawn of the new age, the renaissance of the working classes. But nothing happened.

The unbridled violence of his thoughts filled him briefly with a sense of guilt and shame. The brave words forming on his tongue remained unspoken. The hell with the new age, he was about to say, when a lone blackbird crossed his line of vision. Rahul could not say whether its hoarse screech, before it vanished to the west, suggested encouragement or derision. Perhaps there's a divine message for me, he thought, in the flight of the blackbird.

Perhaps the blackbird carried a message from Ginny. Maybe she was already waiting for him somewhere out there, somewhere in the Berkshires, the Appalachians, the Adirondacks, bathing her beautiful body in some lake, crowned in an arabesque of ferns and lilies. He smiled at his fancy, unmindful of the lump he felt growing inside his throat. "My darling, Ginny'" he wanted to ask, "can you see the new world, luminous and golden, waiting to find its fulfillment in us?" God, he even heard her answer, her voice choking with emotion. "Yes, Rahul. Yes. Yes." He pictured her, as she said this, throwing her arms over her head in a wanton gesture of self-surrender. But he brushed the image aside. There was no time to be lost in idle reveries, a voice inside his head warned him. Time to move on.

From where he stood, the tracks climbed westward in an easy

gradient. They sloped just as gently towards the city. When the ground is wet and slippery, said the voice, it's always easier to walk uphill. Go west! That way, argued the voice — causing him to smile — he was less likely to slip and break his neck on the rails. Heaven forbid he should die or mutilate himself like his brother.

Rahul felt happy and surprised when a new train swept into the platform, opened a set of orange doors noisily in front of him, and sucked him up into its freight of nodding heads, pallid faces, and fresh-smelling newsprint. There were no vacant seats. Rahul was content to anchor himself precariously in a sea of rolling faces rushing past houses, trees, parks and fences until he reached out and found a familiar hand-rail and felt reassured at the touch of its polished smoothness. It seemed the train was rushing past time as well, leaving behind fall and winter, entering spring, just as Rahul himself felt poised on the verge of a new awakening.

He was no longer the same man, slightly depressed, slightly rejected, who had walked out of Ginny's home earlier in the morning. He now rejoiced in the certainty that the lover, the revolutionary, still lurked in some secret corner of his soul. He congratulated himself on the triumph of his imagination pinioned so long. A little shiver crept through him as he realized that his aesthetic regeneration was about to begin. Ginny, cried the voice in his head, you and I, together we'll sing our native woodnotes wild, live off pear trees and grapevines, live, live, live . . . (here the voice faltered, if only briefly)... like a goddamned sheikh, the sheikh of . . . oh! who cared. I'll worship you, he whispered. But immediately, the voice, and his sense of history, stepped in with a correction. Sheikhs don't worship women, they turn them into obelisks. But that didn't sound quite right. Obelisk or odalisk? Odalisk or obelisk?

This problem too, like the earlier problem of Rikki, he decided to leave alone for the time being. There'll be time enough, he told himself, to refine my vocabulary in our warm log cabin in some murmurous haunt of birds and birch trees way up somewhere. Maybe Wyoming. Montana. Ginny, my Ginny, I'll worship you there. I'll prostrate myself, if need be, at the tips of your golden feet. I'll cling for redemption to your warm, round, downy arms. Oh! I'll drown myself in the fountains of your breasts. Just then, the voice slipped in a somewhat wicked thought. May I, it asked, burn a pot of incense in your navel?

Rahul couldn't help laughing at this. A few curious passengers looked up at him, met his eyes, and turned away instantly in embarrassment. What if he was greying at the temples prematurely, he still possessed the sensibility of a mystic, the virility of an athlete. He hadn't grown up in the east for nothing. May I, asked the voice again, the pot of incense?

Rahul pictured her, pink and glistening, writhing in the grass in delicious agony, smoke curling out of the crimson crater of her belly button. Ooooh! she cried. Take it away, take it away, stop tickling me, you wicked satyr, you dirty old man. The train lurched to a stop, and her voice shattered in his mind, scattering the words in jagged little pieces.

Old man, old man, OLD MAN . . . Christ! wish people would see where they're walking. A-R-L-I-N-G-T-O-N, the conductor's voice rang out like a bell and pushed the jagged pieces into his flesh. He shook himself with a start, changed over to the Red Line, and prepared to face the reality that awaited him in his million dollar lab, in the sickness that festered outside the lab, on the street, and in the parking lot outside his window.

Ginny came empty handed to their midday rendezvous. He was surprised she hadn't brought anything to eat. She ignored his question about food and stared vacantly at the water where some gulls were masquerading as ducks and trying to snatch up pieces of bread a young man threw at them. "Rahul," she finally said, "I have a confession to make." She then told him of her decision to go back to John Newton. She said they'd like to start all over again. "I talked this over with Alice as well, and she understood," Ginny paused and bent down to pick up a blade of grass. Twirling the blade between her fingers, she said, "So you see, I'd have to ask you to move." She thanked him for the good times and everything else. Rahul sat there dumbly and watched her cross the traffic and disappear into the crowd just as a swan-boat loaded with chattering children glided into his view.

He would forget her, erase her from his memory. He should've known the affair was doomed from the start. How obsessive, how shameful, his demands had lately grown to be! And what did he have to show for himself? My God, he told himself, how desolate, how cheerless a figure he must seem to others. Yet, there was a time he could laugh. Only last month, drunk in Quebec City, nodding off to sleep in Ginny's golden hair, laughing himself sick over the effervescent lights. . . . *Non, non, monsieur. La lumiere, c'est bien*! c'est *parfait! Mais, votre tete, helas*! . . . "No, Rahul, no! don't pull it down. It's my telegraph line to the moon," cried Susan on the Cape. All that remained in the morning was no more than a piece of string tied to a piece of driftwood on the beach, and not a trace of the kite. And a sprint to the sands every morning, before Susan could finish her cereal, to get a new kite into the air so she would think her connection indestructible. A summer of such madness, lost forever.

How old is old, thought Rahul, as he dropped by his lab to check the mail. Surely, it was a matter of circumstance, climate, and compatibility, answered the voice in his head. Rahul walked through his door and sat down heavily in the chair. Yes, there was no question he was tired. When he lifted himself out of his chair, it was like a tired old man. Must do something about the print on the wall, he thought. He felt he couldn't stand Hans Hoffman another day. 'Song of a Nightingale (1964)' —abstract art, my foot! He brushed past the painting and stared outside his window.

Down below, everything moved so slowly. So it seemed to him. On a sudden impulse, Rahul flung open the window. The wind rushed in swiftly and scattered the papers off his desk. Rahul held himself back from lunging after them, watching in fascination as the gathering darkness on the street below swallowed them up. He would go and pack up his things at Ginny's. He pictured the subway leading him through the frozen brilliance of the sunset once more on his way west. He wondered if the bleeding skies, where every bird looked black and the same, could offer him the strength to face the tomorrows that lay ahead. Could one look at the sky and grow strong? The Guru – he remembered Kaloo - would certainly have said yes.

Rahul's thoughts were far away as he left the office and started towards the subway stop. Before he knew it, he was walking around aimlessly—past a group of brawling kids, past lonely old folk walking an inch at a time, past weeds growing high in vacant lots, past abandoned hopscotches too slow to fade away. Suddenly it dawned upon him that perhaps there was no further purpose left to his life. Groping for images from the poets he loved, Rahul assured himself that he had no desire to glorify the inevitable annoyances of his balding days, to dance like a bobbing egg in the cauldron of anonymity, no desire to be struck through the crown by the unerring swipe of the calculated insult.

He knew he could do what had to be done. When at last he walked up the driveway, for a moment he couldn't recognize Ginny's home in the semi-darkness. The enormous glass windows shone like white marble reflecting nothing but emptiness. Rahul felt surrounded by this cold whiteness. As he looked around, shadows began to dance and form on the walls. When the shadows stood still, they formed Ginny's face to his right, and Ginny's face to his left. Directly ahead of him, his own face. Rahul walked through his face, through the wall as it were, and stepped into the house. It was freezing cold inside, and totally dark. All he wanted was sleep. Was it tomorrow that Ginny wanted him to leave? It hardly mattered. But there was this letter he wanted to write to his sister. Rahul turned on the light in the study and sat down in front of the typewriter. It exploded under the fury of his fingers.

The quest for artistic fulfilment and wordly satisfaction can, and must, be yoked together, he wrote. Daedalus must be resurrected in Harvard Square. This land is one of dreamers trapped by their dreams, head high up in the clouds, one foot stuck in the Bay of Pigs, the other in the Gulf of Tonkin. The point is, dearest sister, it's not what you think you are that matters, it's where you end up that really counts. It so happens I'm here. But do I have the time to watch the birds come and go, time to thrill over the seagull plummeting from the sky with its shrill, piercing cry? As I had imagined I would. No, we roam as if lost and must somehow cope with the need to speak. I crave speech too, all the time. I see fingers tapping absent-minded codes on the arm of a chair and I want to reach out, to tattoo together. But one move and the tapping stops. We stare at each other as if through a wall of glass whose thickness swallows up the voice and numbs desire until, burning, screaming, I rush to the edge of what seems existence itself. And the horizon spins before my eyes, hissing my name into my ears at every turn. Suddenly, I don't know who I am. Yet always, but always, I have manouevered myself into irretrievable disasters, precipitous isolation, always wanting to bury myself under a mountain of light and contemplate my many faces turning in the frosty glow. Now I'm caught in the middle, cheated out of beginnings and ends. Tell me, Krishna, must I creep under the shadow stretched between the anticipated and the unknown, to lick my wounds? I need help understanding these inscrutable feelings closing in upon me. Father's abandoned us, mother's at peace with her world, but you hold love in your hands. I know I can count on you, even as I find myself soaring over the towers of Manhattan one moment, scraping the bellies of pendulous clouds, or find myself squashed and reconstituted the next, a piece of bubblegum stuck under a seat in the theater. But do you know what frightens me the most? Thinking I'm a firefly trapped in a locked car in a deserted parking lot.

And then the cursed Selectric jammed!

Rahul got up, stretched himself, poured himself a beer, and sat down again. The past year had been one of discoveries, altogether a pleasant year. Really? He had discovered that the things one wants desperately are indeed some of the most accessible. Then one finds that's not it, after all. Time, he also discovered, exacts its unfailing toll between the wanting and the getting. He had almost resigned himself, for the rest of his life, to the consecrated slopes of this wooded property with nothing between him and the solemn ritual of the sunrise. Nothing, that is, except the sharp crack of some insomniac golfer mulling over traps and bunkers. What, he asked himself, was there to look forward to but the equally solemn ritual of the sunset? He realized he had a problem, but believed it wasn't half as remarkable or uncommon as one might imagine.

Perhaps it's because I have steeped myself in my senses, he thought, rather than my sensibilities. He had tuned the former, his senses, to such an extraordinary pitch that, once upon a time, the parting of sun and moon never burst upon his consciousness but with a flood of sound and colour. With his eyes shut, alone in a darkened room, he could sense the beginnings of night and day moving through his blood, punctuating his moods and phases. Primal metamorphosis, was how he had tried to explain it to Ginny, without much success. All it meant was that beginnings were mere continuations, and conclusions yawns signifying boredom. Rahul believed that under normal circumstances this perception itself would've led intuitively to inner peace, fortitude, and other qualities which sustain spiritual leaders. But when are circumstances normal, he asked himself, except in an unreal subjugation to incomprehensible forces — that is to say, a subversion of reality? No, no, these rambling thoughts weren't the diabolical whispers of his disintegration. It must be the East calling out to him. He knew too well that once the East gets you it grows into your soul like Forster's *Passage*. Never admitted to Sambhu Narain that he loved the book. Yes, a man can never stay away from the caves of his mind. It's dark in there, and stifling, but the shadows are everything one tries to push out of one's mind.

Since he was unable to get on with the letter to Krishna, Rahul began to toy with the idea of going for a run. He wondered what it would be like outside at that hour. Sometimes, when he walked out of the driveway, the wind hurtled like waves through the topmost branches and the tall pines creaked like the masts and yards of tired schooners. If he then shivered under his shirt, he was amazed to find that it was something deep within him that shivered, not his body. Of a sudden, dark, obscure corners of his mind would dissolve in light and expose barbaric forests where naked men poured wailing music out of hollowed branches and naked women flailed their arms at the sky. He would peer cautiously into this edge of time and exult in the blind power surging through him, until he felt himself moving with the wind, one with the power of the wind. But sometimes the wind was still, and he would see the hot sun striking down petals that had flared too quickly, too passionately.

No, it was no time to go for a run. His imagination transformed his runs into a nightmare where he saw himself as a bloated earthworm lying on the sidewalk under the pale green leaves of summer, and running feet thundering past, until one pounded him to the ground and the earth ceased its trembling.

Now there was little in his mind but emptiness, and it didn't matter whether one said 'No' to Gallo or whether multinational drug companies were a force for good or evil. Ginny used to say he was too hard on himself. He just hoped he wouldn't goof up and wake up in the hospital. He was certain there was villainy there the last time they had visited Steve and Jane. Poor kids! stuck with a roomful of expensive toys which no one but Goodwill seemed to want. Also an antique crib, a fortune in ribbons and laces, an inexplicable smell of babies, and Dr. Robinson's voice echoing eternally in Steve's head: "A bum sperm has gone and ruined a perfectly good egg."

Steve and Jane would wait all evening for them to come to dinner, and when they wouldn't show up, probably drink themselves silly on Chablis. Heaven preserve him from hospitals. There was a smiling villain behind every surgeon's mask. A medical man himself, he knew it all too well.

After he finished the beer, Rahul left the study and went upstairs. He threw a rope over one of the low beams. They looked so beautiful and stark when left exposed. Then he fashioned with infinite care a running bowline on one end. Afterwards, he raised it practically to the level of the beam. Having wrapped the free end several times around it, he tied it firmly into a granny. From inside, the upstairs windows all seemed to have been boarded up. Rahul could see nothing outside. No street lights, no signs, not even the distant glow of the city. But he knew which way the city lay. Motionless behind a pall of rust, it thrust its bed of concrete to the sky. It loomed over the verdant treetops and watched him like a beast of prey. It seemed to wait for the grass to grow and bury all, leaving the rest to winter. But it couldn't end like this. He still had to finish the letter.

Miraculously, everything functioned perfectly this time. He had missed his vocation in electronics. The ultimate in technology, the very perfection, the little ball no longer danced like a thing possessed, no infernal hum rose from the bowels of the machine. Everything made such splendid sense all of a sudden—what life was all about, what love added up to, even honesty, purity, and simple decency. But there was also the realization of his own nothingness. Was this the ultimate humiliation? Ah! today's entertainment was but the nightmarish biography of tomorrow. Somehow, in this realization he found his own immunity. This surely was his triumph. They would all inherit his sense of nothingness, all who came after him. His sickness he owed to all who habitually confounded compassion with the object of compassion, love with the object of love, and self-pity with self. For the present, the only hope lay in *shantih*. "*Shantih! Shantih! Shantih!*" echoed Rahul, after the priests and the poet.

He thought he heard footsteps outside as he walked upstairs once more. He even thought he heard the sound of laughter. Hah! so they mock me now. Yes, yes, he thought. I've emptied my store of exquisite moments. Now I must play the jester to the eternal bauble and watch the colour turn brittle on my skin, and bow my head under the gathering storm. Once again, the sound in his ears was the wind in the trees, and the hellish gurgling was the sea thrashing at his feet, falling back for another assault, another, and another.

Again they laughed, nearer this time. He could recognize them now. Sambhu Narain, Hamid, Sharmila, and Krishna, his sister of the sorrowful smile, telling him it was all a lie, that the mockery was in his ears, not in the laughter. They were all with him now. They've been with me all along, he thought, buried under the pile of memories, the deserts of time, all but forgotten. The clock. His attention was suddenly drawn to the clock. Through their laughter they had entwined themselves round the hands of the clock at midnight. For once, the sun and the moon stood still. Yes, he could read it all in his blood, his fatal gift. A piece of the sun, was that not his father's promise to him? Soon everything would lie buried under a pale gold sea. Who was that? Was it the wind knocking at the door, demanding an unrequited debt, its wergild? The sun, yes, the first time he had made love to Ginny he said her hair was made out of strands of the sun.

Rahul heard footsteps coming up the stairs. It was Alice. She walked up to him, took his hand firmly in her own. She led him down the stairs to her car parked on the driveway. It had started to rain. Alice turned on the ignition and the wiper blades and the radio sprang to life at the same time. Like a great swarm of insects, the raindrops swirled past the street lights, confused by the wind, and swept aside by the hypnotic swish of the wiper blades keeping time to Schumann. Long after the *Prophet Bird* had stopped dancing around its single message of harmony, dancing with its fluttering steps, its measured trills, long after it had dissolved into the vibrant *Waldscenen,* the blades still ticked away mindlessly. Alice reached over, put her arms round Rahul's neck, and kissed him gently, lovingly. As she drove out into the street, Rahul turned to look at the house one more time. The front door was wide open. The house was like an empty cage.

Seven

THERE WERE troubled days ahead for Rahul as he fought the sickness trying to break him apart. Alice was there wherever he turned, and he found strength in her presence. She was there when the city woke up in the early hours of the morning and created that rare harmony between man and machine which seldom survived beyond the eight o'clock commuter traffic. Together, they stared in wonder at the trucks and vans on the road at the break of dawn, at the labourers drinking coffee, getting ready for work quietly, cheerfully, at the purposeful movement of strong bodies committed to the care and sustenance of fellow human beings. They delighted in their walks around Haymarket, wet from having been hosed down while it's still dark. Clashing gears, squealing brakes, beeping trucks, all added to a happy confusion of crates and bottles and big men calling out to one another in Mediterranean accents, joking and swearing in the midst of tough, ball-splitting work.

Alice had made her plans to go to India. Rahul was afraid of the void that would face him when she was gone. He decided he too would go away somewhere. His landlady was getting to him, Mrs. Armstrong had a secret dread of miscegenation. She had visions of mutants and anarchists germinating slowly behind the doors of Rahul's room. She therefore resented the frequency as well as the length of Alice's visits to Rahul's apartment. They escaped from her to Provincetown and Bar Harbor to watch the ocean, to watch Fall chained in the wildest colours, hoping there would be changes in Rahul's inner moods as well.

There still remained a final rude awakening for Rahul — a telegram from Sharmila. For a while, the past had almost ceased to exist for him. Sharmila sent it spinning back into focus. The faces he had forgotten in Alice's company now swung into view once more.

Within hours of receiving the telegram, Rahul found himself doing something he would normally never have thought of. In his distraction, he started reaching into a pile of beer cans jammed in his refrigerator for a little party some friends had arranged in his apartment later that evening. He loaded his stereo system with some rock albums and started drinking alone. He hoped to exorcise the ghosts raising their heads in his mind.

By the time friends started to arrive, he had surrendered himself to a listless euphoria. He wondered where the folks were coming from, two by two, and why the room was getting warmer and noisier. Alice came alone. She decided to leave him alone as well.

Before long, he found himself imprisoned in music. It fashioned impenetrable walls around him, walls through which he could see, but walls nevertheless. He felt like a little fish anchored to a leaf, breathing, bubbling, breathing all night long, and a pair of brown eyes staring out of a familiar face, watching, watching in surprise and wonder. He realized it was he who was watching himself, as if his spirit had streaked away into the past and was only just oscillating back to the present before moving into the future. At the lowest point on this arc, Rahul looked down and was amazed to find himself hanging from a meat-hook with his flailing feet slowly getting embedded in a gigantic bowl of rice krispies. But when one is dancing, particularly when one is dancing in the air, one has no time to think. And so he pressed a peach coloured button floating by. Klack-klack-klick-klackety-klack-furrr-whooosh-hmmmm. "Well, what do you know, you've got yourself a perfect date. Congratulations, Rahul. Good luck."

"How're you makin' out, honey?"

"Unh hunh."

"Feel like. . . . Beware, ye people of Massachusetts, for the hour of judgement is at hand. The incidence of venereal disease in Boston is twice the national average and rising. Stop fornicating. Remember, if you got V.D. you got it from someone. Pray for that someone. Amen. Or better still, get help if you're touched by the curse. Come to God."

"Ever had a girl smell like Kentucky Fried Chicken?"

"Wake up, wake up," someone else was telling him. Must be Jerry Mulligan splashing cold water on his face. It cascaded down the windows, oozed through the ceiling in jagged trickles, pierced the walls like a thousand hammers crashing one after the other. He looked up and saw the ceiling corrugate itself into creaming waves. The little willow trees on the wallpaper grew larger and larger and moved away to a cold, green, silent faraway. The carnations in the corner dissolved before his eyes and vapourized into puffs of evening sky and hung diffused at the edges of his world. Jimmy and Janice rose from the sea, mounted the clouds, and became one with the blue-white, orange-grey, baby pink evening. And a voice called out to him, "Ra-a-a-hool." And once again, "Ra-a-a-hool." And again.

The music stopped. There was something obsessive about the intentness with which he listened, painfully, breathlessly, waiting for the sound to renew itself. Oh! the relief. It was like realizing he hadn't missed the last train after all.

The music started once more and pushed its way through a cackle of voices, some happy and hysteric, some sombre and ominous. Rahul climbed back on his gibbet and knew that his time had run out, that he had already started to die. It was far from a traditional death. But what a fine way to spend his final hours—stalking the guests through the viewless rooms, peering into their bloodshot eyes from the bottom of a glass of Michelob, plummeting from the void to snatch their words, baited, honeyed, and barbed.

A dark tree—was it a maple? — stood against the window. It shook a few leaves, twitched some vestigial twigs, as if warning him of its life. It seemed to bring him back to life, but only to make him feel old and wrinkled and drained of will. No will to answer Cathy who kept repeating every so often, "C'mon Rahul, come away from there. We need you." What was earlier a vague feeling of dissatisfaction within him, an inability to plot his presence either within the apartment or outside, seemed now to fill him with a sense of debasement. Rahul looked over his shoulder and saw Stephen talking dramatically to a bored and drugged audience. Cathy was curled up contentedly in Peter's lap. He seemed to know all the faces, but few of the names. Alice looked up uncertainly, caught his eyes, and pretended to be preoccupied with the record albums strewn around her on the rug.

"Come away, Rahul. Be a sport." Am I disposed to sportive dalliance, he thought to himself. Must I expose myself to the shaded lamps till every face shines in stupor and the lips settle to their unrehearsed drill? Circles of peach. Apricot squares. Perverse parallels. Pout one. Flick two. He hated faces that broke forth in pimples of alcoholic sweat, pimples of anticipation, pimples of satisfaction.

Lights came on behind several windows in the apartments across the street. Luminous squares, perhaps antiseptic and anaesthetised behind curtains from Sears. So soft and defenceless. A fresh army of spirits invaded his mind. "Ha, ha, I won't let you cheat me today," said one. "Cheat, sir?" asked Ahmed Khan incredulously. Smiling, whining, avaricious Ahmed Khan of Calcutta's Hogg Market held the chicken pinioned by its wings while Rahul gently stroked the down on its pink belly before jabbing his fingers for proof of tenderness prior to consent. The down, the fine veins and delicate bones visible beneath the diaphanous film of skin, all gave the little belly a lace-like texture. Khan passed the paralyzed bird to Junior Khan, his son, who deftly knifed through the bird's neck. He tossed it fluttering into a dirty, stained bin, slammed down the lid, and placed a brick on top to keep the lid from flying away. The bin suddenly came to life like a frenetic drum as the bird played out its bloody stomp. Sir Stuart Hogg. A remarkable achievement for such a name to rise to the knighthood, or was Victoria crazy?

The drumming ceased. Ahmed's son removed the brick, uncovered the lid, thrust his arm into the stinking abyss, and behold! a new bird plumed in brilliant red. He lowered it reverentially on the brick. "Let me caper a little more. No, no, no, I haven't finished yet." Was that what the half severed head jerked and twitched and tried to say? In two swift movements, the silent bird was stripped of its feathers. Pink and shining, its foolish heart still keeping time. How much longer? The bird was ready for the fire. Then they vanished. Blood, knife, chicken and all. One of the windows pulled down its blinds and became one with the night. Life suffused the night, infinite, shadowy, bright, perpetuating its blind cycle. Scores of automobiles whispered past the window, writing their secrets on the glass with yellow, amber, and red, blinking in disbelief as they approached an intersection not far away.

Belief? yes, that was it. He couldn't believe the telegram. Western Union Telex Service. Western Union Telex Service. Western Union Telex Service. WUD066MBI20MLLCI21K-YPDFTDNNEW YORKN. Y. 13.200pcdt. Rahul could not believe the telegram. He could not take his eyes off it. He had gone through it, impatiently at first. The letters smudged out of focus as he rushed past them to grasp what followed. It didn't make sense. He decided to wait on each word, wait for each to find a place in the folds of his mind. He waited, but the paper turned heavy and cold. His hands shook as the chisel worked its way on the stone. Sparks flew over the clashing of hammer and chisel. Through the flames the words appeared THOU SHALT NOT KILL. And drops of blood congealed in the grooves, overflowed the edges, and soaked his hands.

He hoped he had absorbed every letter of each word. It still didn't make sense. He could feel the paper curl up and become brittle against his fingers, ready to disintegrate into specks of dust perhaps, or sand. But the truth was that each minute it was growing grimy and limp with the sweat creeping down his hands.

From his seat by the window, Rahul noticed a couple watching him. He was surpised to think how long they might've been watching. They stood under the tree, staring at him like he was a rare four-legged ostrich risen from the bogs. He felt distrustful of them, even angry, but was amazed how quickly these feelings turned to one of indifference. There they were, children of the sun, holding each other against the night, waiting for the sun to rise again and the waves to roll in. And he, a lonely man, his body far from what it used to be, his complexion pale and sickly, eyes without lustre. They acknowledged his resurrection with a smile and moved on. He saw them laughing as they moved away and wondered if they were laughing at him.

The young man saw a crumpled can on the sidewalk and kicked it into the street. It clattered away from sight and yielded to the sidewalk a few stale drops of soda in its last, ignominious moments. The two laughed and kissed each other in a flood of golden hair and were gone. A tormented page of the *Globe*, caught in a sudden breeze, rose from the sidewalk and floated gutterwards to rest with the day's unburied — paper cups, cigarette packets, bottles, plastic straws, and cans.

The wind was a stranger locked out of his room. Rahul imagined its cold touch on his skin and shivered instinctively. He wanted to feel it swishing through his hair like before, and fought off a horrible impulse to slam through the glass in front of him. Imagine being impaled against the jagged edges in his flight, blood coughing out of his veins, the legs kicking weaker and weaker in agony, and the Fords and Datsuns passing by oblivious. What an insane idea. But wait. Perhaps his golden friend would return and take pity on him. And maybe the golden haired girl would care for him enough to cradle his fevered head in her lap, warm against her golden breasts, nursing him back to a forgotten dream. And he would peel off his wrinkles, and take wings, and perch himself on his maple tree. Was it a maple? He would turn his back to the shattered window, his empty room, the unwashed mugs of coffee and the overflowing ashtrays of his restlessness. He would wait through the Fall, and with the coming of the first snowflakes fly away to the sea.

Was it a dream? Was it possible to be looking at a deserted sidewalk and heaving street and dream unblinkingly in a super-heated room?

But surely, there they were once again, her head on his shoulder, their arms encircling each other. Had they forgotten the rare four-legged ostrich dredged out of the bog? They did not notice his crypt as they passed by the window and into the night. In an insane fit of jealousy, Rahul picked up an ashtray and hurled it at the window, butts, matches, ashes, and all.

"O Rahul, why did you do that?" asked Alice, running to him. She held him by the arms. She was afraid. The confusion in her eyes, the flush on her cheeks, the trembling of her fingers, all said she was afraid. Rahul slowly became aware of the murmuring group in front of him. He did not care. He searched their faces impassively as he crushed the telegram into a ball, slowly and deliberately. He swung round, and in one easy movement tossed the telegram out through the gaping hole in the window.

People moved away to the other room. Rahul was conscious of Peter or John asking, "Is he crazy or something?" Cathy, possibly out of a sense of loyalty, firmly answered, "No."

There was an urgent knock on the door and Mrs. Armstrong burst into the room. She was panting for breath. Her face glowed from the exertion of rushing down two flights of stairs. She clapped her hands over her heaving, pendulous chest and fought to regain her breath. "What happened?" she asked. "What's going on?" Everyone started to feel sorry for her.

"I'm going mad, Mrs. Armstrong," said Rahul.

She turned pale at the sight of the broken glass. "My window. What have you done to my window?"

"I'm really sorry."

"How did it happen?" she demanded. "I must know how it happened."

"I tried to empty an ashtray in the street," replied Rahul.

Her eyes swept over the furniture and came to rest on the writing desk. "O my God! Not my crystal ashtray? I should never have left it here. My darling Donald loved it so." Her voice trailed off sadly. "Donald would sit beside it every evening from the day we were married."

"I wish I could tell you how sorry I am, Mrs. Armstrong." Rahul tried to sound as apologetic as possible.

Mrs. Armstrong didn't seem to hear. "I wanted so much to put poor Donald's ashes in that Venetian thing," she continued. "It would've been kind of fitting. He was so fond of it. Instead, they insisted on that terrible casket called an urn or something."

"I had no idea your husband was cremated," said Rahul.

"Yes, he was," she sobbed. "He always thought of me. Always. Said it would be easier on me since the insurance wouldn't pay all the expenses of a burial."

"I didn't know. I'm sorry," repeated Rahul. "Shall I try to find the pieces on the street?"

He shouldn't have said that. His solicitude was lost on Mrs. Armstrong. She stood up, her face drawn, her eyes narrow slits that radiated hate. "Why don't you people go back to your goddam country," she hissed. "You've been no end of trouble to us." With that she swept out of the room.

Soon they all left. The party fell to pieces. Alice and Rahul were left to themselves. "I love you, Alice," he said, and she pulled him to her heart and held him there. They cried. "I wish you weren't going."

Eight

Alice left for India late in April. She had been his strongest ally against the scenes and voices from the past that were determined not to let Rahul be. The foolish jail rescue attempt was one scene he wanted to have nothing to do with. Nor did he wish to speculate on Sharmila's role that day. What did she want from him now? How did she know where to find him? She was drawing nearer to him against a backdrop of violence. Earlier, he might have only felt uneasy. Now he was afraid.

Her telegram was inoccuous enough: Meet Trailways Downtown Boston six p.m. on second. Speaking at Providence May third. Signed, Sharmila. He really didn't want to meet her. But there was also a tiny willingness, a small longing to go back into one's history. He sensed he might be in some danger. The veil he had wrapped himself in with such care, once destroyed, would never come back to him. Still, it was with a sense of expectation that Rahul stood behind the fence at the Trailways terminal and watched the Peter Pan bus from Amherst unload its ruffled cargo. In the dim twilight, Rahul realized she was just as ravishing as he remembered her from years past. Quite unexpectedly, she swept into his arms, surprising him with an embrace whose passion he was not prepared for.

"You look lovelier than ever," he said, quickly recovering his composure. She seemed relentless as she kissed him again and again on his lips.

"It's so nice to see you again," she whispered breathlessly. Words tumbled out of her mouth. "No, no hotels," she said. "I'm staying in Denise's apartment. But she won't be there. Like all sensible people, she spends her weekends on the Cape."

"I see," replied Rahul, trying in vain to take charge of his thoughts. The last thing he had on his mind was sex. But the high priestess had already set up temple, kindled the incense, and was waiting all afire. Even as a wave of revulsion swept over him, Rahul felt himself seized by a curious intoxication. It was the perfume in her hair and the animal odors of her body that were beginning to paralyze his senses like before.

"It's funny to see you on the lecture circuit," said Rahul. "You must keep good company."

"I have a great agent," she said. "But my humble beginnings keep calling back to me, and sometimes I weaken. Like tonight." Effusive and arrogant, she was clearly at her best. She was on a South Asian Studies faculty in Washington, D.C. "An insignificant departmental minion," she assured him. "A humble lecturer." But Rahul was impressed. When he asked her what she was going to be speaking on, she replied quite casually, "Oh! The liberated Indian woman."

Why not the unicorn, thought Rahul unkindly. But before he could utter a word or make a wisecrack, Sharmila swamped him with another torrent of words. "Been married over two years now." There was no time for Rahul to register surprise. "Yes, there's this superb honesty between me and my husband. My friends envy us because we never suffer from guilt while they're perishing from it. I forgot the meaning of guilt the day I left India two years ago." She laughed nervously, but there was also a touch of mockery in her voice. "Life has been so exhilirating, so liberating here. That's why I believe we'll have a stable marriage. You know, my Chairman's wife simply went to pieces while he played around with graduate students. After a while, they didn't have anything to say to each other. She slit her wrists one day."

Sharmila looked at Rahul, trying to sense what was going through his mind. He was lost in his thoughts as they walked steadily through the public gardens towards Beacon Hill, but Sharmila had no idea what they were. In the semi-darkness, he was more determined than ever to be in control of his emotions.

"No, no children," she went on. "My friends tell me I ought to start a baby soon, that I would adore it from the moment of its conception, that love would grow each day. Ugh! can you imagine anything more ugly. To love a protuberance inside the body. Love it more the larger and uglier it grows?" Her voice turned harsher, and Rahul couldn't understand why. "Puking, muling, dirty little things. I'd never damn my body to their avid suction. It'll learn to walk, to stand on its feet. I've only to imagine the obnoxious wart standing before my eyes, and poof! love vanishes. Children are epicene relics transmitted through concupiscence. I've decided to leave to others the vacuous nothingness and atavistic egotism of motherhood." Sharmila looked down at the pensive Rahul from her extravagant heights. "What about you?" she asked. "I seem to be doing all the talking."

I know nothing of what you're talking about, thought Rahul. He realized with a jolting suddenness that he had indeed seen very few children. Susan was the only one he knew. Did they all believe as she did, he wondered. No, it couldn't be true. One didn't have to live in the suburbs to get pregnant. Even those for whom love was a shooting gallery of one night stands sometimes loved children. Even those knocked around by blubbering, insensate lips. Or goaded by a handful of hot flesh, leaping like a frog, weeping like an infected sore, drunk on a thimbleful of... opaque luminosity. He stopped in his tracks. He had to get a hold of himself.

Rahul thought of Susan. Yes, there were many who even loved unwanted children. But Sharmila made a virtue of her disgust. "No, keep talking," he told her. "I'm enjoying every moment of it." Then, somewhat lamely, he added, "No children, eh?"

"Can you love a wart?" she asked.

"No, of course not. But I could invest in a Skinner Box," he said, brightening up.

Sharmila went on. "We decided long ago we would never have children, never own any property. That's why we live in rented places. We'll retain nothing, however valuable, that will clutter up our lives."

"But why did you get married?" he asked.

"We really didn't want to at first. We lived together for nearly six months. Then one day we got married. I guess there was an edge of hypocrisy to our earlier relationship. We had to push that aside. Things have changed so much in the last couple of years. We used to deceive people when we lived together. I stayed away from Georgetown as much as possible, changed apartments often, gave people crazy addresses and telephone numbers simply to confuse them. It got so dull after a while." She sighed as she paused. They were standing right in front of Denise's apartment. "That's it," she said, "it got so dull we felt we had to get married."

They thanked Mr. Minelli, the caretaker, for the keys. "Yes, we'll find the apartment for sure'" Rahul told him.

"What a beautiful place," she exclaimed, as soon as they stepped inside. "Quick, Rahul, see if there's any food in the fridge."

Rahul grew depressed immediately. The lovely homes were always someone else's. All his life he had lived in little rooms, even as a child in their large house. Then came rooms without windows, or windows barred. Rooms shaking with the sound of the world surging to hold him, and the sound of his fury screaming to be heard. Was he destined to live forever in little rooms? Or in rooms leaning against maple trees?

All he found was some whiskey. They set upon it with a vengeance. "Thank you, dearest Denise," said Sharmila, "for this your whiskey we're about to deduct from your bounty." They drank silently. "I'm famished," she said, breaking the silence. "Fish. I must taste some seafood. This whiskey is awful. Awful." Rahul concurred.

He told her he knew a great place for seafood. Sharmila remembered it from her Chestnut Hill days. They walked to the subway and headed for Harvard Square. The Friday night crowd was returning late from work. Sharmila felt touched by their solitude. Whatever excitement the office held for them seemed entirely drained out by evening. "Maybe they won't look so lonely once they get home," he told her.

"You know nothing of loneliness," she said, suddenly switching from English to Bengali. "I've been through it all. All. The loneliest I've been was during my first trip out of India. I was in Hong Kong. I never told this to anyone before. I stood naked by a window and watched the lights of battleships and destroyers pinned in the phosphorescence of the harbour below. And all the while my host in Hong Kong, my lithe Egyptian friend, leaned against the wall, fixing me with a crisp, crackling gaze. I almost developed stigmata on my spine. Can you imagine anything more ridiculous than an Indian girl laid by an Egyptian diplomat on Victoria Peak in Hong Kong? I liked him because of his white Aston Martin and also because I didn't know another soul on the island. Seems such bad taste in retrospect. Can't remember exactly what I felt like then. I loathed his voice though, rough as a grasshopper, as he plowed through me. The insufferable chauvinist. Gift of the Pharoahs, he kept calling it. We made love in the bathroom, while his wife entertained other guests." She grew pensive. "Would you believe it?" she asked. "Bill Holden lived on the floor above. We actually saw him in the elevator."

"Mark Elliot in search of Suzie Wong, or the other way around," said Rahul, looking at her with undisguised amazement.

"You might think it was the bathtub. But no, the tub held a week's precious supply of water. Hong Kong was going through a terrible drought at the time. The taps were dead. The reservoirs were dry. Of course, Mao wouldn't let Downing Street down. Ships brought in water from the mainland. Water was coming through pipes across the New Territories. But it was only a trickle. Every drop had to be preserved. We made love in a mist of lavender deodorant. On a toilet seat, if you please. Afterwards, when I lifted the cover I nearly fainted. He caught me just in time or I might've ended up in Aberdeen Harbour. Of course, there wasn't any water in the toilet. Just tons of shit. 'You've got to twy harder with Twyfords,' my seducer told me."

Denise's whiskey certainly made Sharmila rather amusing. But Rahul's thoughts were becoming clouded under the combined effect of the drinks and the cold air whipping against his face as they came to the surface in Cambridge. Now she had no fear of shocking strangers, so Sharmila went back to English.

She had come in a red *sari*, carrying a red hat. "What's the hat for?" asked Rahul.

"Mabel gave it to me. Said it would go well with my *sari*. Must've cost her at least twenty bucks. Now that I have a hat, maybe I'll go buy a belt."

"Take mine," he said, playfully.

"Oh! I couldn't possibly."

"Take it," he insisted. "It's genuine crocodile skin. I can keep up my trousers without it."

He was a little drunk. He told her that the hat cloven at the top looked obscene on her lap. She thought it was funny. "I wear a dress on Tuesdays," she said. "Other days I wear a *sari*. And on certain days I wish I was teaching in the raw. Can you imagine my class gazing longingly at me across their desks, pressing down on their proximate erections with Markandaya's *Nectar in a Sieve?* Guess I'll have to teach in the raw if I need to seduce a student like Michael again."

"Who's Michael?"

"He's the guy I'm going to sleep with in Providence tomorrow night. He's so good looking. Michael was twenty two when he first slept with me. For some reason, it simply blew his mind. Walked up to my husband afterwards, said he wanted to speak to him. He was totally incoherent. Kept stuttering and choking until a great big glass of bourbon finally calmed him down. What don't we do with our pitiful lives."

They remained silent as Rahul busied himself building a pyramid with a handful of french fries. She said she had to tell him things she hadn't told him before. Like the story of her very first full time lover, S.K., back from Harrow and Oxford, reeking from every measured accent. "Our farewell was so full of drama. There stood S.K. by the window, sobbing. Later, he went to his car and brought me all his marvelous paintings from the trunk. Then he left. Now he has settled down to the sedate life of a guru in L.A. We don't know what to do with the paintings. There's no market for them. Do you suppose he might want them back someday?"

"I doubt it," he said, looking up, as the unsupported french fries crumpled into the platter in a pile.

"We've left the paintings in storage, just in case. I hated it when he cried. Towards the end he would break into tears at the slightest pretext. Why do Indians cry so much?"

"Who knows?" Rahul shrugged his shoulders. "They never told us in med school."

She looked lovely in her red *sari* as they each drank a bottle of cheap Vouvray, ruminated over french fries and fried scallops, and thought the waitresses all looked the same. She nicked her finger on the knife and said, "I'm superstitous. This blood's probably a good omen."

While looking at the cut, Rahul couldn't help noticing some old burn marks on her fingers. She knew he was curious and quickly volunteered the information. "These? Happened when we were playing Truth one night. Ever played the game?" Rahul nodded and said no. "Well," she continued, "I said fire didn't worry me. That was the truth and I had to prove it. Here's where I held the cigarette against my skin for twenty seconds. Thirty-five seconds here. This one on my wrist was over a minute. Jesus! this one hurt for weeks."

The wine was getting in the way of his hearing. His thoughts in fact had turned to Alice. As the scallops grew cold and hard, and the Vouvray disappeared from the bottle, it was Alice taking hold of his mind. He saw a great flood hurtling down on her, but Alice didn't seem to notice. Frightened and childlike, her eyes kept reaching out for his unspoken thoughts like they had done a wild day not long ago, the day they first made love in the woods. "They say you shorten your life a little every time you make love," he remembered telling Alice as they clung to each other. A feeling of immense wonder swept over him as Rahul remembered their loving, its sweetness and its hopelessness. But the image of the flood bothered him. He wished her well in her travels.

Yes, it was Alice he was thinking of as he walked up Beacon Hill, not of Sharmila and her strange world, or of her faceless, nameless husband whose vague presence seemed somehow to be following them. As he said goodbye to her at Denise's door, both felt overcome by a sudden fear. She feared the loneliness of the night. He, the prospect of being nailed to his solitary bed, tortured by his dreams. "Promise me," she whispered, "you'll forget this request the instant I ask you. Can you remember that I haven't spent this night with you in Boston?"

Rahul stood at the doorway, swaying, while his mind crept backwards in time. And he thanked the pale light of that immortal presence which had led him through highways and country roads, through streets gouged out of teeming cities, through paths unfolding moist and dank like soiled bandages along valleys and forests, roads burying the graves of remote ancestors, through limitless roads, to Alice. As he held her in his arms, he told her of the sickness he had seen on the road. There was one bathed in bile, wearing a gutted liver on his sleeves. A consumptive donned a scarlet flush and smiled bravely at the world. He recalled rushing to a frail woman on fire. 'No,' she cried, wrapping herself in flames, 'You're young. Let me die.' Then a grey shadow shook itself out of the morning mist and barred his way. And he stopped. 'Physician, heal thyself,' murmured the shadow as it fell apart. Pieces of the shadowy figure floated away, fell to the earth, dodging his outstretched arms like timid feathers, like love. Rahul raged in his dream, clutching vainly at emptiness. Hot tears surged across his face, blood dripped from his torn fists. Then a woman, shaped like a leaf, covered with brown scales, entered his dream. 'I rusted in Harlem,' she cried. 'How come my seed was white as yours?' Then she disappeared too, making way for a dying man. He flashed a lipless smile at his fear, and with hard, icy fingers pressed him to his black, blasted body. Rahul thought he would surely die. Even as this pageant repeated itself in his mind, Rahul had Alice in his arms. "It's so nice to die in a misty day in the Fall," he said. "Today is not to die," she said, sealing his lips with a kiss.

The vision passed. He decided to stay in spite of his better instincts. He wondered what it was Sharmila wanted from him as they sat ensconced in warmth, parrying with little rapiers dipped in ennui. "Would you rather you slept with me again?" he asked.

She remained silent, looking at him thoughtfully, tormentingly, encouragingly for a long time, as if waiting for him to say more. "No, I'm sorry I couldn't," she said. "We've got to know each other all over again. This thing, this desire, has to grow upon me. Like it has to grow out of something. Like a piece of conversation. I've got to speak through the act of love. I didn't know how to before." Rahul's eyes were closing. He opened them with an effort and nodded several times.

"It's not that I'll never reconsider it," she said hastily. "Or that the question must be dropped, once and for all. I like you. You're attractive.

And you flatter me. Of course, I half expected the suggestion to arise. I feel drunk." She went for a glass of water.

Next moment, she was yelling from the kitchen. "Can you imagine us fucking away in Denise's bed? I think it would be positively embarrassing. Liking is not enough, you know. I liked you a lot once. I'd like to, but I need something more." She was standing in front of him with a glass in her hand. "If you hadn't asked me, I would've thought there was something wrong with me."

Rahul was trying to stay awake by piling cushions one on top of the other on his lap. Though he didn't seem interested in what she was saying, she continued, "Thanks anyway. I think it was awfully sweet of you."

Rahul yawned. He was glad he was not at his persuasive best. He let her go on. "It's so boring," she said. "Don't you think it's almost comic if it isn't the culmination of something significant preceding it?"

Damn it, thought Rahul, he would have to speak after all. "Culmination?" he asked. "Why culmination? Why can't it be something that precedes nothing but itself? Like something that is, and is not. Like being nothing, in being whole. You know? Like a cabbage, preceding nothing but the resounding fart, thunder of the gods chained and bull-whipped inside the body."

She wasn't to be intimidated. "Hey," she cried, "you're becoming metaphysical. I have some great insights I'd love to hear you expound on."

"You picked the wrong guy, sweetheart, to discuss metaphysics with. And the wrong time."

"Why?" she asked. "It's easy. You be my critic, my audience, my tormentor."

"I'm drunk and I'm half asleep."

"You know," she said, wriggling into a more comfortable position on the couch. "Nobody'll believe we didn't sleep with each other."

"Nobody's to know you spent the night with me, right," Rahul reminded her. "Perhaps it's just as well we shouldn't." Then, turning abruptly towards her, he asked, "What happened at the prison that day? Where did you disappear afterwards?"

She looked back at him uncertainly and said nothing at first. A look of sadness came over her face. "Must we reopen that chapter of our lives?" she asked.

"I guess not." The pages held much pain for him too. "Forget it." Moments later, he added with a smile, "But beware the wind. It may blow open the pages when you're not looking."

"Shall I put on some music?" she asked, trying to lighten the awkwardness creeping in between them. "Shall I dance? I love dancing." When Rahul showed no enthusiasm, she said, "But no. Not tonight. Hell, no! We'll dance and dance and soon we'll be screwing madly on the rug. That's not what I want."

"People tell me rugs introduce a deeper emotional content into copulation," said Rahul.

"Copulation and prayer," replied Sharmila, folding her hands in a prayerful gesture. "But not this rug," she said. "This is a real cheapie."

Rahul felt drawn into the conversation. "Like prayer, the act of love must begin somewhere between profound spontaneity and intense dedication. Casual encounters are merely promiscuous. But too much dedication wears out your balls. You can't be a pro and not act like one. You'd be exposed in a flash. Can't pretend to be that which you're not. I marvel at you, Sharmila. You have a great future."

The color rose to her face. "I'm really very transparent, am I not? Not a complicated person at all. Still, I find it awkward to sleep with every second person I run into. Michael's the only guy I took to bed within twenty minutes of our first meeting. Poor Michael, Irish and so very neurotic. Father's a redneck lawyer constantly talking about morality and issuing dire warnings on the future of the white race. You're my own kind, but much as I'd love to, I couldn't sleep with you tonight. Do you know, I haven't had a fellow countryman fuck me in three years. I think they should all be circumcised first."

"I was not thinking of going to bed," interrupted Rahul. "I'm only trying to figure you out how come you're here in the first place? Whatever happened to our master plan for the New Society? But you're right. We're far too removed from it all."

A fire engine shattered the stillness outside. It also woke him up a little more. "I'm very curious to know what happened to all our friends. Kartick, Jhunjhunwala, Dan and the rest. Perhaps what they say back home is true – don't dig for a worm, you might find a snake."

For an instant, Sharmila was startled. "I know what happened to Hamid. He seems fine in your sister's house."

"Now there's a splendid Indian for you. What if he's a servant. He's circumcised. You know, Sharmila, you might have a point about circumcision. Yes, I think circumcision should be made mandatory throughout the world. Its implementation examined and controlled by an Inspector of Foreskins. Be great for breaking down cultural barriers."

"What about the funding?" she asked.

"Why, from the United Nations Secretariat. Ministry of Prepuces. Where else?"

There followed a long pause. Sharmila began to hum to herself. Soon she began to sing. Her voice was rich. She sang songs from Tagore, songs he was beginning to forget. "My body's getting old and decrepit," she said. "So I have to rely on my tongue."

"Why did you come to Boston?"

"To see you."

"I'm touched. But couldn't you have gone straight from Amherst to Providence?"

"I wanted to chat with you," she said. "Like old times. Thought we would spend a refined, cultured evening discussing profundities. It sort of fell on its face, didn't it? Swamped by infantile suggestions, deplorable gambits."

"Gambits deplorably phrased, perhaps."

"Problem is, I'm drunk," she said. "I'm so drunk. Really, this whiskey is bloody awful. Must've been Denise's cooking whiskey."

She rose from the couch and wandered away into the kitchen. "Oh Denise," she wailed. "You didn't leave any food in the fridge. You're miserable. No cigarettes either. Only this vile whiskey. Your apartment's spooky."

"It hasn't any possibilities left, has it?" Rahul raised his voice so Sharmila could hear him. "When does Denise return from the Cape?"

"Sunday night. She has gone there with a horrible person."

"Why did she go with him?"

"Because she likes him, that's why." He heard her opening drawers and cabinets until she cried out jubilantly, "Hey, look what I found." She danced back into the room. "I found some cigarettes, I found some cigarettes," she sang. She held up the packet in front of him. "True. Ever smoked them?"

Rahul picked out a cigarette. He lighted it carefully, took in a lungful of smoke, and walked away to the bedroom. He pulled out a blanket from one of the cupboards and prepared to go to sleep on the couch. Sharmila pranced around him for a while like a stalking lizard. Then she began to laugh hysterically. "You look like a bag of beans," she cried. "Lima beans."

The entire situation was becoming very bizarre, thought Rahul. He decided to wait for her next move. But then he lost his patience and asked, "Why don't you go to bed like a good girl?"

"I'm really not very good in bed," she replied. "I'm a good girl though. I am. I am a religious girl." As she said that, she dropped herself on her knees upon the carpet. After a moment in that posture of prayer, she flung her head and arms forward and was soon resting on all fours. Then, curling herself into an oval shape she started to hum 'On the sunny side of the street'.

She was like a supple rasher of bacon curling up and down on a skillet. "Do you always sleep in that foetal position?" he asked.

"I feel like a horse, a donkey," she cried joyfully. "Wanna piggyback? Wanna piggyback?" she kept asking.

Rahul groaned in discomfort. "Did you know that Holofernes made the Queen of Aleppo clip a donkey so he would spare her son's life?" he asked. Then he killed the Queen's son afterwards. Why can't you be a little more original, Sharmila?"

"What's original?" she hissed back. "My cunt's no more original than your prick, you sonofabitch."

There seemed something totally out of place about the words coming out of her lips. He could've sworn she would choke over such obscenities only a few years ago. What wondrous changes time and place bring about? "Shall I bring you Denise's pillows?" he finally asked.

"I don't want Denise's pillows," she cried petulantly. "I don't want

Denise's blankets. I don't want her whiskey, her True's. I don't want nothing."

Rahul sensed a fleeting chance to provoke her, and couldn't let it pass. "I think you're being very childish," he said.

"Who's childish?" she exploded. "You pitiable worm. I have a new name, a new husband, a new country. All you've got out of your women are weak contractions, right? I'm not childish. I'm free. Something you are not."

"Relax'" he said, goading her further. "I know what's on your mind. One can't rush into it violently. It's like a game. One takes turns being serious and mocking, crude and sophisticated. I have a feeling you're asking me to screw you like some animal."

She glared back at him angrily. "Look chum," she said, "you couldn't fuck me in a year of Sundays if I didn't feel like it."

Rahul remained silent, lettting her seethe and simmer. When she spoke again, it was in a mellower, pensive voice. "It's terrible when you don't want it. Like someone sandpapering inside you. Do you know, the first time I made love, I liked it so much I kept hearing the Indian national anthem."

"I've always thought of having the national anthem tattooed under the navel," he said.

"That's hardly necessary." She was beginning to sound cheerful again. "Nowadays I feel stars and stripes running down my thighs."

"I can believe it," he said. "Celestial star spangled harmonies as you come and go."

She told him she planned to return to India next year. Go alone, since her husband probably wouldn't want to go. "He's terrified of Indian taxi drivers. Thinks one of them will drive away with me someday and commit unspeakable acts on my body. He believes a man should always step into an Indian taxi before a woman."

"Your husband probably doesn't know there are gay and bisexual cab drivers in India too. Enormous cocks. Tourists love them on the Delhi-Agra excursions."

"You're a proper bastard'" she said, returning to the kitchen.

"Tell me," he called out behind her, "what else does your husband think of India."

She said nothing as she returned with two mugs of coffee. She planted the mugs on the table and sat down on the edge of his couch. He was drifting off to sleep. She ran her fingers through his hair. Her lips were close to his ears. "You're not angry with me, are you, Rahul?" she asked very softly.

He looked back at her through half-open eyes and smiled. But the next moment he leapt up in terror as he saw, dimly, the kitchen knife in Sharmila's hand. "What're you doing with that?" he yelled.

There was just a spark of fear in her eyes. She sat silently looking down at the floor and allowed Rahul to disarm her without a word. "I wanted you to play with me,' she said, suddenly ripping off her clothes. Her breasts trembled slightly, level with the knife Rahul held poised in front of them.

"Don't tell me someone asked you to kill me," he said, drawing circles around her nipples with the tip of the blade.

"I told you I wanted to play with you," she said quietly. "I'm really burning for you."

"I'm not," he said sharply. "Are these the sort of games you and your spouse play?" He watched her wince as he slowly moved the blade down to her belly.

"No," she said, standing up.

"You can get hurt you know." Rahul backed away from her.

"I know'" she answered, wrenching the rest of her clothes away. She took a step forward and was almost upon him. "But I can save you," she whispered.

"What do you mean?" he asked.

"I mean the warrant for your arrest back home. The murder rap."

"It's a bum rap," he replied angrily. "And you know it." A sudden surge of blood rushed into his eyes. His nerves jumped up in a familar way. His hands moved up to her neck menacingly. But she was quicker. Before he knew what was happening, his lips were locked upon his. Her dissembling lips want to send me back home, or prove I am a coward, he thought. He had no idea what she stood to gain from either possibility.

But either way, he had Alice to think of. He remembered how her face fell when he told her about the uninvited guest. He wished he had never met Sharmila that evening. But the night was brief after all.

"You'll miss your flight if we don't leave now," he said, drawing away from her and picking up the packet of cigarettes from the table. "Have another True."

She refused the cigarettes. "The cigarettes are foul," she said. "Like everything else in this place."

"Make a nice name for condoms," he muttered, lighting a cigarette. "The one and only True. Give a damn; use a True, man. Be a True-man, always!"

"I'll try to be in Boston over Thanksgiving," she said, as they stepped out of the apartment. "Don't know where I'll stay though. Guess it'll be too cold for Denise to be screwing on the Cape. If I come, I'll let you know where."

Overflowing and half-filled trashcans, plastic bags bloated with garbage, all greeted their departure for Park Street Station. The gas-faked street lamps burned noiselessly, yellow-green and steady. A single ruby-tinted glass lamp on the corner of Joy and Mount Vernon glowed like an evil eye. Rahul shivered and turned up the collar of his jacket. Cartons, twisted, decaying and soiled, saluted them. Stand me on my feet. This way, said the box, in bold letters hard to miss. An old man stooped under an oak tree, sniffing like a water rat through moisture laden heaps of sandwich wrap and other inglorious rubbish. A veil of haze covered him, setting him off against the suffused glow of the street lights like a radiant penumbra. "Don't walk on the grass," she said. "You'll ruin your shoes in the dew."

Dawn came to Logan Airport. The silent cranes standing like giant oil rigs probed, unimpressed, the rosy-fingered dawn. Eastern's Flight 751 to Providence. Gate number nine. Seven thirty-five. The reflection of the lighted holes in the ceiling fell on the massive glass windows of the airport and stretched into the early morning sky. As the morning grew clearer, the reflections grew fainter. Towering smokestacks zoomed into view, their ashen breath swarming between the clouds. Sharmila sounded a bit subdued. "I hope you'll understand, Rahul," she said. "My blood pressure's real high. I can't take any pills any more." Then, lowering her voice, she said, "Michael always brings his things along. Why don't you? Wonder if Boston has any drugstores open at two in the morning."

"Oh well!" said Rahul absent-mindedly. "Maybe it deserves a study." Then something caught his attention, the initials S.C. branded in gold in one corner of her bag. They were calling for the passengers to board. Sharmila took a step in the direction of the gate. "What's the C for?" he asked, pointing to the initials.

"C for Cohen, silly," she said, kissing him goodbye. "Didn't you know I married Dan?"

"I'll be damned," he said, puzzling even more over the purpose of her visit.

Free, carefree, she departed for her lover's embrace with a wave of her hand. A slender, beautiful vestal stifled by her joyous pangs. In a burst of hatred, he imagined her gasping for a reversal of life's immutable irrascibility as ghostly men immured her in brick and concrete for ever. Once blessed by kings with gold, frankincense and myrrh, the kings of the East. Sold lately on the auction block for a cockleshell.

As the plane flew off, he realized that all Dan needed to do was report his police records to INS and they'd ship him back home the next day.

Nine

KAYNCHASAYWHEYEARGOOINMAN? New Yok. New Yok. Goin' Carlton Towers, man, three two two east sixty-first. Should've looked where I was walking, thought Rahul. Not walking, but floating. Floating through the sculptured hollows that are Manhattan streets, bouncing against stone eyes that will not see what they see, sliding on rain-soaked sidewalks, hoping to touch someone, wanting to hold a hand. Lonely, lovely New York City.

At first, Dan Cohen was not prepared to see him. He reminded him curtly of a deal they had made through the American Consulate to stay clear of each other's paths. He relented when Rahul asked him how long he expected him to live this lie, his unreal existence. Set me free, Dan, he pleaded. He was going to be in New York. Dan told him to come and meet him there.

What warmth, what unexpected gladness in Dan's welcome after Rahul had checked through the lobby under the watchful eyes of an armed security man. They kept needling each other on trivial matters for a while. Then Rahul asked Dan about Sharmila and saw a strange look come over his face. He wasn't sure whether to believe him or not when he said, "She decided to leave me."

"But why?" asked Rahul.

Dan could only say he wished he knew. They lapsed into a long silence, broken when Dan asked if Rahul knew that Dan's mother had passed away. Rahul remembered her as a kind and lovable person whom the servants adored. She was interested in the smallest details of their lives and prepared to do anything to help them. They began to talk about Dan's cook, Subramani, and how Dan had negotiated his wages — thirty-two dollars a month if Dan's mother was to do the shopping, only twenty dollars if Subramani were to do it.

They slowly warmed up to one another and Dan said how sorry he was over the poor shape Rahul's party was in. Three more attempted jailbreaks in the past five months. They were always overpowering the guards at first, always getting caught scaling the walls. "I didn't know all you guys were so suicidal," said Dan ruefully. Bodies stretched out for the press. Scythes, knives, ropes and ladders all thrown in for good measure. "Make great photographs'" said Dan. "I've seen quite a few in the State Department."

"I really wonder sometimes why we got mixed up in all that," asked Rahul. "Do you know why?"

"I know why, Rahul. You believed you could change the world in the image of some idealized vision. You thought you had only to raise the flag, blow the whistle, move forward, and all hell would break loose behind you. You were so naive, so trusting."

"Did you think we were right in believing what we did?"

Dan smiled. "I really don't know whether you were right and I was wrong, or whether we were all wrong."

Rahul was amused at the way Dan moved from one guarded opinion to the other, always staying clear of extremes. Such was the pragmatic way of the Western mind. "But you didn't feel this way, Dan Cohen. Not once upon a time," he said. "No! not when we bolted down the imported lox in your airconditioned apartment, and the Dutch cheese and the smoked ham. I remember sitting there carving my initials on the chilled beer cans like I was writing my name in dew, fully believing we had only to walk out of that room to step into a new dawn. You chilled our souls. Dan. You made us believe that a new order was well within our reach."

"So we led you down the garden path?"

"I never said you did," replied Rahul. "I think you were a kindred spirit, or believed you were, and excited us with the idea of change. You told us what we liked to hear. Somebody else in the State Department or the Hoover Institute or wherever had no doubt convinced you earlier that it was really all you needed to tell us. You fathered our spirit, fanned the flames, and then walked out on us. But why?" Rahul smiled as he saw Dan scowling at him.

Dan waited until he had poured Rahul another drink and carefully dropped two ice cubes in the glass. "Listen to me, Rahul. I had finished my term in Calcutta. I simply had to go."

"Yes, Dan, you had done a great job and returned to Washington for your reward." Rahul wasn't going to leave him in peace. "But why didn't the next guy at the Consulate lift a finger to help us when we needed it most? Was it because the Marxist threat to the State Government was no longer so strong? Did you set us up to be radicals only for that single purpose, to wipe out the Marxist government with an even greater radical threat? And strengthen Mrs. Gandhi's hands in New Delhi?"

"Don't say Allan didn't help you," interrupted Dan, pointing an accusing finger at Rahul.

"Of course he did, but only because of you. If it hadn't been for your request, I'd probably never have left the country. You might have found me in one of the photographs in State, stretched out for the press. The truth is we've all been had. Isn't that so, Dan?"

"Not by me, Rahul, I swear."

Rahul started to laugh. There was an unmistakable note of mockery in his voice. "Don't swear to me, Mephistopheles. You never kept your part of the bargain. When your hour struck, you simply turned away, leaving us all fucked up."

"I'm sorry, Rahul, but when I gathered you and your friends into our little circle out there, I really believed the movement for rural change up north could work in the rest of the state. All we needed was the support of the educated and the committed."

There was a faraway look in Rahul's eyes. "I know, Dan. I wanted to build us a world where I could look every human being straight in the eye without shame or fear, where I could return home each night to a decent home and a warm meal without having to feel guilty, without having to thank God for his grace in giving to me and not to others."

"I'm sorry," said Dan simply.

They sat drinking quietly for a long time. "At least you succeeded," said Rahul after a while. "I think you and your bosses succeeded beyond your wildest dreams. Even the Russians failed to call your shots as you castrated their pals, the Communist government in Bengal. People deserted their ranks and came to us because we believed only in revolutionary change. The Communists still kidded themselves with democracy. Mrs. Gandhi screwed the Communists first, according to the law, then let loose her butchers against us. We used to dream of help from the Chinese. They'll never help us, will they?"

"I doubt it," said Dan.

"Yes. Especially now when Henry is snuggling up to Mao and his friends. Now America must turn a deaf ear even to Bangladesh." Rahul finished the rest of his drink in one gulp and stood up to leave. "You don't know what you are doing to us, Dan. When the white man first walked on our land, it was to steal our wealth. Now they haunt the land to steal our useless secrets. Your forefathers wanted to mellow our savagery and so took away our freedom. You say you want to protect our freedom, and end up goading us into savagery." Rahul walked up to Dan and touched him on his shoulder. "Now help me get back, Dan. Please."

Dan sighed and looked away at the towers of light almost touching the window. In a strange way, Sharmila no longer meant very much to either of them. Neither did their many differences. Before the night was over, Dan had promised to get Rahul an American passport.

"I dare not renew my Indian passport and tip off the Indian police," said Rahul. "I must have a new passport."

"What I'll get you won't prevent you from getting killed," said Dan. "It might simply give you some legal clout should the police get too close to your ass."

TEN

AS HE waited for Dan to send the promised papers from Washington, Rahul's mind was filled with doubts once more. Freedom, the very idea of which drew him most to America had no meaning if he couldn't move in and out of the country at will. Why had he gotten himself into a situation where he couldn't do so? When his anger and sense of having been wronged wore off, he imagined it must all be *maya*, the workings of Lord Krishna's whimsical law of life. Freedom is an illusion, he told himself. It was possible for a person to believe, sincerely, that racism was nothing, blacks were born to be inferior, men more dependable than women, and Hiroshima a morally ordained vindication of the superiority of the Aryan race. A person could believe all this and swear unflinchingly that America was the ultimate bastion of freedom. Was it? Was it possible that the spirit needed servility, to ideas at least? There was no longer any need for servitude to a fearsome, vengeful God. Ah! what sweet promise lay in the playful Krishna, forever making music out of his flute, and a world out of his kaleidoscope.

Rahul could afford to leave such thoughts alone now that Alice was back. But Fall was gone, its colours gone, gone was Rahul's interest in his research. Even in the middle of the most exciting seminars, his mind was far away. Each day brought news of fresh outrages in Bangladesh. War between India and Pakistan seemed near. Rahul grew more and more restless.

It was also time for Rahul to break the news to Alice. She had come home, but it was almost as if she had never left Boston. She gave him little or no information about her visit. She did tell him however that Krishna had not come back. It took him a few days to recover from the despondency that followed this news.

It seemed a shame to break off his relationship with Alice. As he sat in his apartment looking idly through a pile of mail and casual jottings, he hoped his papers would reach him soon. The moment of truth was almost near.

The afternoon was still. It was an afternoon that sharpened one's instincts, brought options into focus. Rahul looked up from his desk. He had been trying for over two hours now to create some semblance of order in his scribbled notes and unanswered letters. The old trashcan would soon give way at the seams. He could see it coming. His thumbs were raw from ripping sheets of paper and stuffing the pieces in the can. He couldn't rip up this last bunch. His wrists were tired. Divide them into lots, he thought. That should make it easier. Who would want to read his trash anyway? Deciding not to bother any more, he flung the whole pile into the bin. He missed, and the papers scattered on the floor. In it, not at it, you bloody fool! Where had be seen that sign? Ah! yes, on an urinal in the Grand Hotel. Passengers will please refrain, from urinating in the train . . . funny song that! ...... when the train is standing at the station.

Rahul gathered the papers from the floor and stood up. He pushed his foot deep inside the trashcan, trying to create space. Click! That did it. Its joints split open. The trashcan yawned stupidly at him. Scraps of paper slid out of the crack and returned to the floor. It was time to give up. "Alice," he called out. "How about a nice walk?"

"I'm coming," she answered from the next room, "as soon as I've finished this." It was a few minutes before she left her knitting on the bed and came up to Rahul.

"What're you knitting?"

"Oh, just a little something. Something for Malini."

A distant look came into his eyes. But Alice flung her arms round his neck and surprised him in the middle of his thoughts. Would he have the courage, he wondered, to take back home this woman he loved. But why would she want to go? It was a wild, impractical thought. Even before he could get to the question of his own honesty, there was the question of the law. Besides, he ought to do something about Krishna, dead or alive. A fear he had not known before seized him as he thought of his family. Could it be that life for them had changed a lot from what he knew it to be? Was it possible for someone from his own family to give him away to the police? He imagined a shining boot lift from the floor and smash into his groin. A crimson world swam before his eyes. It danced faster and faster. Whoever died in a paddywagon or a police lock-up? But they did. Dozens of his friends, nocturnal creatures, slid back into the morgue, a surreal mess of staring eyes, crooked arms and yellowing flesh, iced in leaky, galvanized iron trays.

He wrenched his thoughts away and turned to Alice. His hands moved to her waist. He stood holding her silently, not realizing his nails were biting into her flesh. "Stop it, you're hurting me," she cried.

His hands dropped to his side with a start. "I forgot myself," he apologized. "It's so beautiful outside." His lips brushed her nose as he stood swaying in her arms. "Your eyes are so beautiful, Alice. Can you promise never to grow old?"

She said nothing, simply closed her eyes and drew nearer to him.

"I must tell you I have to go home."

She looked up at his face, finding it hard to believe him. "Shall we go for a walk?" he asked. "I'll miss my walks with you, Alice. The city belongs to us when we walk through it, doesn't it? I'll miss you too. More than I can tell you."

Two teardrops rolled down her cheeks. Rahul tried to kiss them away. "Let's go," she said, regaining her composure.

The quiet confusion of his mind was something Rahul had not bargained for as he stepped into the sunlight and the gently stinging air. The presumed happiness of his first footsteps soon settled down to a melancholic rhythm.

They crossed Kenmore Square and stepped into Commonwealth Avenue. The hazy sunlight bathed the houses in gentle dyes. Brownstones, white and beige bricks, stood proudly sharing their tales with the clinging ivy. The delicate balconies, forged out of iron with patient care reached out to the moosewoods, redbuds, and silver maples growing below. The timid volutes, dark fossils from a quieter age, shivered below the roof's edge as they remembered the time and started counting their days. In the middle of the avenue, ancient oaks, lindens, and maidenhairs flinched from the traffic roaring down on both sides. Like Brahmins forced into a butcher shop, they stood dismayed and invoked the name of winter in anger. And the leaves fell, murmurous and sad, dancing in the air.

In the shade of the trees and on the grass, there sprawled groups of young men and women, turning over in their minds the ills that troubled the land, burying the leaves under discarded cans and paper bags. The concierge of the Somerset Hotel stood at the top of the steps, wrapped in earnest conversation with some English tourists. Clean and elegant, he averted his eyes from the decay drawing ever closer to the beautiful hotel. Even he had seen better days.

They stopped in front of a tubular scaffold on which a work crew were busy picking the bones of a once proud home. The wind swirled unchecked through the gutted skeleton.

Rahul was startled by a stranger. "Spare some change for a meal, sir?" he asked, in a level, matter of fact voice. It was the voice, not the question, that surprised him. He found himself looking into a pair of blue eyes. Through them, he was looking into a sultry afternoon of despair and hopelessness. He was back home, escorting on behalf of the Indo-American Friendship Society George and Mildred McCarthy from Syracuse. "It's a fine city you have here," said George, drawing out the 'fine' in a way Rahul had not heard before. Hour after hour, long as the sun was up, he gazed enthralled at the city. Just kept looking through his Pentax until, at a red traffic light, he found a young woman with a cowering face, imploring eyes, and a naked child in her lap, licking the mush from his nose, smiling. The woman held out an emaciated arm to them. George kept on clicking. Mildred fumbled through her purse for a suitable coin. There were francs, dinars, Dutch florins, Thai ticals. "George, I thought you had given the pennies away." The light turned green and the cars behind grew impatient. The taxi slowly got under way. The woman stepped back to the sidewalk without a word. "Ah! I've found one at last," said

Mildred. "Too bad you couldn't find it earlier," said George. "I got a real beaut, though." Another beggar approached them at the Park Street lights and the McCarthys unloaded some of their coins on him and felt good. They had parted at the American Consulate on fashionable Harrington Street with a profusion of thank you's and *au reviors*. How he laughed when he read in the papers the next morning that the Marxist government had renamed Harrington Street, home of the U.S. Consulate in Calcutta, to Ho Chi Minh Avenue. He should remember to ask Dan if the Consulate ever changed its stationery. Rahul happily parted with a quarter. "All I can spare," he said.

"Thanks a lot. Thanks again." A smile lit up the handsome blond face as the young man bowed and went his way. One of the workmen suddenly opened up with a heavy drill and peppered them with tiny chips of stone. It was time to move on.

"Help me get these stones out of my hair, Rahul."

"Why don't you shake your head real hard," he said.

"Shall I?"

"Yes," Rahul encouraged her.

Alice placed her hands on her hips with a flourish, planted her feet on the sidewalk, and toseed her head from side to side for half a minute or so. "Are they still there?" she asked, stopping and running her fingers gingerly through her hair. "They're all over," she cried disgustedly, and started shaking her head once more. The few people around looked at them curiously and decided she was probably stoned.

"It's no good," she said. "My head's reeling." Exhausted, Alice sat down on the steps of a brownstone. "They're bothering me. Please take them out for me, Rahul."

"I'll try."

Alice crossed her hands over her knees, laid her head on her hands, and let her hair fall to her ankles. Rahul knelt on the street in front of her and began to pluck out the offending particles one by one. A man in his forties or fifties stuck his head out of a window. "What's going on down there?" he shouted.

Rahul looked up and shouted back in just as loud a voice. "She's sick."

"What's wrong?" asked the man. "Did she pass out?"

"No, she has got the mallophaga," explained Rahul

"What's that?"

"Lice," he shouted back gleefully.

"Jesus Christ," exclaimed the man. "She should clean her hair more often." He looked quite disgusted. "Go away. Get off my steps," he shouted angrily. "Don't want vermin crawling all over my front step."

Rahul stood up and stared menacingly at his adversary. "Sir," he said slowly and deliberately, "you may not be aware, but this is the only method authorized by the Holy Koran for the extermination of lice from heathen bodies." He paused and stepped closer to the window till he was face to face with the man. "Have you any objections to that?"

The man was obviously taken aback. "I didn't know that," he said defensively. "Just get on with whatever you're up to." With that, he disappeared inside the house.

Some people had gathered to look. Rahul let his eyes sweep over them with feigned disdain as he returned to Alice. She hadn't moved at all. A wild impulse got into his head. "Inshallah!" he suddenly cried out. The onlookers drew back apprehensively and stared even harder at him. He whirled around dramatically and touched Alice lightly on her shoulder. "Come away, Magdalena," he cried. "This air breeds poison. And these, my gawking friends here, are spirits risen from the grave. Let us go."

Alice stood up looking like a wild creature. She could barely see through the hair covering her face. Rahul led her by the hand through the hushed audience.

They walked a hundred steps or so before Alice crumpled over his chest. "O Rahul," she cried, choking with laughter. Just as suddenly, she grew strangely silent. Her voice was plaintive when she spoke again. "Take me with you," she said. "Please let me come."

He pushed the hair away from her face and watched the tangled strands settle over her smooth shoulders. He was pleased with his performance but was beginning to suspect it was done more in pain than jest.

She had no time to wait for an answer before she came upon a pretty patch of flowers, no doubt the last of the season. "Look at those flowers," she said. "Wouldn't it be nice if there were just flowers here, no houses, no people."

"I could live without flowers," he said.

"I couldn't," said Alice, smiling. Patting his hand in a gesture of understanding, she said, "I care for them most when they're wilted, when they're dying. Then I ask myself why they blossomed, why they were plucked from the branches in the first place."

Rahul looked away from the flowers. Their unexpected presence surprised him. He looked at the house in front and tried to imagine who they were who cleaned the weeds, then planted, watered, and watched the flowers bloom. Were they young and disenchanted? Were they old and angry? His questions remained unanswered since no one came to the window. Just then, a shaggy spaniel bounded out of a corner, paused by the flowers, sniffed, cocked a leg, and let fly a warm jet. The frail stems of asters and gerardias shivered in the ureic shower.

"Rahul, will you take me back with you?" she asked again. What did she really want? Could she honestly tell him that? "I want to hold Malini in my arms."

The evening, which the flowers had made light and magical only a little while ago, grew heavy. Malini's name began to press down on his spirit. He felt uneasy thinking about her, about Krishna, about Hamid. A bird cried unseen on one of the trees. A frightened bird. A piercing cry. It cried *poowhittettoo, poowhittettoo,* again and again. There was no answering call. He could not understand his sadness and wished it was the bird, nothing else, that fathered his mood. But he knew it was not so.

The evening grew silent in the public garden and the traffic settled to a steady murmur. The greens rolled lazily under their feet, still lush with life and some flowers. How different from the early morning darkness. He'd probably be gone before Thanskgiving. With Alice, it was so much easier to capture simple feelings on the grass, to love, to promise, to dream. But the pigeons distracted him. To poison pigeons with popcorn? No. What will you poison when you grow up, my children?

The dancing devotees loomed into view as they cut across the Common. The air echoed with the tinkling cymbals as a blessed trio danced a prelapsarian half twist, sang *Hare Krishna, Hare Rama,* and waited in ecstasy for their absent god. Rahul supposed Krishna was waiting too. Haloed and phosphorescent, perhaps he was frolicking with his nubile groupies in Cape Kennedy, waiting for the countdown that would send him, resplendent in a blazing gold chariot, down the Freedom Trail and into the American Way followed by a heavenly host of cherubic Rockettes. The *thung-thunh-thing-thung* sounded more hypnotic the farther away they went. The sound rose and fell with the throbbing in his veins. The cymbals reminded him of minstrels who came to sing at the fair in Bishnupur and left behind forgotten legends of lost love.

"How far are we walking?" she asked. "Aren't you tired?"

"A little."

They were in a small public park. They found a bench and decided to rest awhile. Paul Revere's statue loomed in front of them. Some irreverent joker had given Paul a cigarette. It was pushed between his lips. Paul let the cigarette tilt rakishly from his mouth, stared defiantly at Bullfinch's sturdy church in front, and proferred his right arm for more. Dusk was upon them.

"I've been asking you something all evening, Rahul," said Alice, "but you haven't answered me. Will you take me with you?"

"Take you where, Alice?"

"Wherever you're going."

He looked sad as he turned towards her. She was like a bird that had flown into his life from a sunset sky. She asked no questions, stated no terms, simply wove her life into his. The idea of life together with Alice was tender and frightening at the same time. In spite of his deep affection for her, Rahul wasn't sure there was really a future for them side by side. She would probably end up going her own way. Just like him.

"Where do you think I'm going? Do you suppose it's a better place I'm going to, a land of gentler, kinder people? We hate, more bitterly and violently than you can imagine. It's not a land of mock turtles and gryphons. Can't you see I can't take you. This is where you belong, Alice."

For a moment, she looked frantic, even fearful and hurt. But her voice was quiet and wistful. "I thought we belonged to no one but ourselves. That's what I've believed so long. But maybe you're right."

'I know I am,' said Rahul. 'We belong to everyone but ourselves.'

Alice looked away from him. Not far away, there were children playing with baseball bats. Like flaming swords that turned every way, desperately trying to ward off the serpent waiting to bruise their heels, said Rahul, describing for her a scene from one of his father's plays. It was late to be playing out of doors. But there they were, happy and unconcerned. On the sidewalks, old men spoke in Italian. And butchers shredded tripe in deserted shops.

She stroked his hand with her fingers. "Must it end this way?" In moments less desperate, Alice sometimes thought of life with Rahul. No matter where. Life with children. Now the walls around her proclaimed the triumph of procreation but mocked her thoughts. Increase Mather, father of Cotton Mather and Harvard today, plaqued on the walls of the mall till doomsday. What glory! What pride! What little difference it made! The bone of my bones, flesh of my flesh, she thought, remembering his heart beating against her own. And she remembered the voice in the garden: I was afraid because I was naked and I hid myself.

There were promises he had thought of making to her, but they stuck in his throat. He couldn't bring himself to lie to her, to tell her he would return. It would've been so easy.

It was dark when they walked away from the cobblestoned mall. Did she see two lanterns swaying from the Old North Church? No, it was only his imagination. Perhaps the battle was already fought and lost. What was there to find in the ruins?

They kept walking aimlessly. There was a time when he wanted to be one with the conquerors of the earth. He would ride the crest and never grow old. There was hope and exhiliration in his encounter with the new world. He had designed his days with some care, looked for purpose in every corner. It seemed so long ago. Now his life, however badly ordered, was teetering over his head once more, ready to bury him in rubble. "We are drawn together on such slight pretexts," he said.

"Yes," said Alice. "We drift apart on even slighter ones."

The darkness thickened a little more. Rahul looked around and realized there wasn't a soul in sight. What he hadn't noticed earlier was that the surrounding houses were all dark and deserted. The buildings all looked like they were waiting to be torn down. Doors facing the street were firmly boarded up. The street itself was strewn with broken glass. The vacant windows stared out like ghosts charred in hell. Every house looked the same in the pale street light. Suddenly, the buildings seemed to be closing in on them. Noiselessly, on padded feet, inch by measured inch.

Rahul felt the hair stand on his neck. He pulled Alice by her hand and started to run. The hollow, gaping windows sucked up the sound of their feet charging through the street and turned it into echoes that laughed back at them. The road stretched into what seemed an eternity and, any moment, Rahul feared he would hear feeble pox-ridden voices squeaking for help behind the boarded doors. The ghosts didn't whine. They didn't call out. But Rahul imagined that their rotting bodies, yellow and pustular, flowed thickly under the boards and congealed in the street under their feet.

They flung themselves on the steps of City Hall. The echoes died down, but the sound of their gasping lungs filled the air. She had felt the same fear as him. "Oh Rahul!" sobbed Alice. "What was it? It was so awful. I thought it would never end." She buried her face in his neck and began to cry softly. Rahul felt her shaking against him and wondered what frightening madness had seized them both so suddenly.

It was a strange night. Something strange was happening near the fountain. They walked across the paved promenade and found an old man clutching the edge of the pool and doing hard push-ups to the bare stands, an empty Colosseum. The muscles and tendons in his arms looked like they would snap any moment and catapult his unbleached bones into some ossuary in space. Burn it up, burn it up, burn it all up, his silent lips seemed to be saying. They watched him in fascination for many minutes until the man seemed unable to go on. Ignoring their presence altogether, he swung himself out of the water and stood up. Somewhat unsteadily, he shuffled away, shoes squelching, water dripping from his wet trousers, head hanging low in defeat. Now there was silence once more. Nothing moved, except a massive pizza of scum which bobbed up and swivelled across the pool.

If the night was strange, the following day was even stranger for Rahul. He waited for Alice all day, and found out late in the evening that she had left for India. Without an address, without a word of farewell for him. Rahul still had a few days left. Till then, he would have to learn to live with loneliness.

While he waited, he walked alone to Coolidge Hill one day to a point where he could see much of the serene, pastoral graveyard and imagine himself lying somewhere in the ground. Rahul pictured it changing its appearance with the seasons — pale or glistening green, orange or yellow, ashen and bare. Rahul would come and watch the fields every day until it was time for him to leave the country. On the final day, he suddenly realized that the fields were watching him too, and he was afraid. I must take up running again, he told himself, alone.

Eleven

There was only a faint touch of winter in the air the day Rahul landed in Bombay's Santa Cruz Airport. If there was a war on, it seemed to exist on paper. The Mig fighters standing on the edge of the southern runway were real enough, but no more real than the ice cubes colliding in martinis at the Sun-n-Sands Hotel. Here, off-duty servicemen zeroed in on targets nearer home, victims eager to surrender themselves to the nation's finest. Since the stalking hunter and the willing prey both wished to forget the world outside, the Charlie Dorsey Goan Band obligingly filled the main ballroom with the sound of dance music. Even at night, no one paid much attention to the world outside which, blacked out by orders from Delhi, hid nervously behind the crackling leaves of the palm trees.

Contrary to official orders, the moon leapt out of the sea at its appointed hour. It bathed the pleasure seekers on the beach with the pallor of fresh cadavers. This was not the mysterious East of Thomas Cook or American Express. Here was theme park Fort Lauderdale after a power failure. If anyone tried to wrap himself in his mind's peace and quiet, reality swiftly bore down upon him, burying it all under a flood of Burt Bacharach, central air conditioning, room service, and awful French cuisine.

Rahul wished to see more of the city during the day. He could've done so easily if the Customs hadn't taken three hours to get to his baggage. "What're you bringing these in for?" asked an official, pointing to packets of Kool-Aid and Carnation Instant Breakfast.

"I wanted to give them away to friends," explained Rahul.

"Give them away, eh?" asked the resident narcotics expert. "Well, you can start right here," he said, as he systematically opened every packet.

"So you're now an American," sneered the security officer examining his passport. Rahul stopped short of explaining to him that he remained an Indian at heart even though he carried an American passport. He decided it would sound utterly stupid.

A younger and more affable officer now turned his attention towards him. "Does Mr. Nixon suffer from Portnoy's complaint?" he asked, dissolving in laughter.

Rahul stood feigning an embarrassed silence. He saw no point in saying any more than he had to. Bombay remained true to his earliest recollections, neither here nor there, a Janus-faced monstrosity playing a deadly game of reviving the past while clutching at the glitter and promise of an unknown future, mixing its hymns to Krishna with 'Lucy in the Sky with Diamonds'. As he had half expected, not all the gods and well-meaning agents could get him on a flight to Calcutta that day. Trying to make it easier for him, they suggested that he try the buffet lunch at the Taj Hotel that afternoon. "After all," said one of them, "you're carrying American dollars. You can afford to have a good time."

The hotel was only a few blocks away. Rahul pursued the suggestion up a plush red stairway into an enormous hall echoing to the rhythms of Strauss. Nobody was dancing. Nobody seemed interested. To most of the two hundred patrons, even the food seemed quite incidental. Not to Rahul. The sight of the endless rows of tables laden with colourful foods from East and West awakened in him a ravenous hunger. He moved impatiently past waiters melting with deference, past polite and rude glances, and snatches of conversation punctuated with names of great hotels in Paris, Geneva, Rome, or San Francisco.

There were some tables in the wide corridor outside the hall. It was here that Rahul sat down, beside the glass windows overlooking the Arabian Sea. From where he sat, India Gate was visible less as a gate than a wedge of cheese. The gate did not face him squarely, but merely presented one side to his view. The spectacular arch looked no wider than a narrow passage. Intrepid tourists, heedless of the war, still passed through it, marching down a flight of steps for the cruise to the Elephanta Caves.

Back at the airport, an agent examining his ticket said, "There are dangers you and I don't know of." Then, somewhat more gravely, he asked, "What is the U.S. Seventh Fleet doing in the Bay of Bengal anyway?"

A man hunched over a nearby desk came suddenly to life. "Loading the last consignment of *hilsa* fish for the White House," he said, shaking with laughter.

"No," volunteered someone else. "They can't take the stench of rotten bodies in the Gulf of Tonkin any more." Another perceptive commentator suggested that the Chinese and American cavalry, working in close cooperation, would soon come galloping down the Himalayas and snatch the Pakistan army from the jaws of a humiliating defeat. "The Seventh Fleet is only a diversion," he said wisely.

Rahul slept through the flight to Calcutta. He dreamt that the jet was banking steeply and levelling off towards a different ocean. There was Paris, a limitless spawning ground of pearls, its bright lights shimmering in the night air. London tilted precariously against the window and vanished. Then there was New York, strewn with opals. When he woke up, the Indian Airlines captain was announcing their arrival in Dum Dum. One look through the oval window and Rahul knew nothing had changed.

The airlines bus brought him right into the city. Rahul decided to use public transportation from there, rather than a taxi, to get to his sister's house. As usual, the bus was packed beyond its capacity. Rahul wriggled his body into the solid mass of other bodies and kept eyeing an empty seat marked 'For Ladies Only'. But the solitary woman who sat beside the empty space showed no interest in sharing the seat with a stranger. Without her explicit invitation, Rahul knew he would probably be courting a rebuff in asking if he could sit beside her. The bus raced through the traffic, lurching forward of a sudden, then braking with equal suddenness, the latter having the effect of packing in the passengers even more tightly and miraculously making room for others waiting at the bus stops. Rahul stepped off at one of these.

He hoisted his bag over his shoulder and decided to walk over to Krishna's house. It was only a short distance away from the bus stop. The bag was heavy, but he walked quickly along the streets he knew so well. He drew curious stares, mournful appeals for alms, and even some rude comments. He looked an uncommon traveller and there was no way he could hide this fact. Something about his appearance gave him away as someone living outside the country.

The longer he walked, the more powerfully he realized that something had changed indeed. This was evident from his own inner response to the city. He realized the change might be within himself, in his mind, but it was change just the same. There was, for instance, nothing wrong with him physically, yet he was finding it increasingly difficult to walk. It was as if this sprawling city had suddenly grown hills beneath his feet. It was as if he was dragging his body, climbing uphill, his feet slipping under him. He reached out in his mind to the tips of his hands and feet, reassuring his limbs, testing their reflexes. Slightly ahead of him, the narrow asphalt road levelled off or sloped down. He couldn't tell from where he was. And all the while he knew, these ups and downs, these unexpected twists, they all existed in his mind.

He made an effort to shift his thoughts away from his immediate surroundings. He succeeded, but his mind reminded him immediately of the pain plucking at the tendons in his feet. Rahul looked up at the sky waiting for him at the top of the road, bright, clear, of no single colour in particular. Several indefinable shades blended together, so that the sky looked simply pale. His thoughts bounced off it, and finding the certitude of the street more dependable, renewed their questioning of his feet.

Rahul stopped, rose slowly on his toes, and felt the pain climb to the calves and to the muscles in his thighs. The sunlight fell over some of the houses, avoided some of the others, each a prisoner held in place between neighbours, unchanging from day to day, year to year. It's just the inhabitants who come and go, he thought, as he looked up and saw a mother and son on a balcony. He couldn't remember them living there three years ago. The boy sat with a red blanket draped over his legs. He waved at Rahul, but something prevented him from waving back, from establishing the boy's face as anything more than a blur in his mind.

He thought he knew what the trouble was. Perhaps he was not alive any more. This suspicion grew stronger the closer he came to Krishna's house. Again, he couldn't remember which way the road went up ahead. The rows of houses radiated away from him left and right. The sky came down with its pale vastness on the houses and the road. It was winter. But those couldn't be trees pointing up from the children's park in front. Maybe they were not trees, just men and women.

A few yards from Krishna's house, his feet simply refused to move any more. The windows of the upper floor received the last of the daylight while the rest of the house lay engulfed in shadows. At that place and hour, the windows of the upper floor were little pools of light standing fast against the creeping dusk, the trim white frames dividing each window into four squares of silver.

Rahul was drawn by a slight movement behind one of the windows. When the movement stopped, he could see the outline of a face. Only the face seemed to catch the sun. The rest of the body remained in darkness. As if to make it impossible for him to recognize the face, a flaw in the glass distorted it to a frightening ugliness. The face seemed to dissolve in the light. One eye grew to an immense size and lodged itself in one corner of a giant head. The other eye melted and disappeared altogether. The mouth, or rather one corner of the mouth, drew itself out like pliant glass and dipped delicately to one side, as if waiting for the next breath through the blower's tube.

The face moved. It drew closer to the glass. As the person moved away from the window and the flaw in the glass created another hideous bulge on the face, there was nothing to suggest that the person on the other side had recognized Rahul. He kept standing in front of the house, looking up. Even if his feet would let him, Rahul felt he would be making a mistake in crossing his sister's threshold, now that she was no longer there. Of his own free will, he had made himself a stranger to his people. Could he reverse that and assert his earlier ties so easily?

Krishna would've welcomed him with open arms. He was not so sure of Vikram. There seemed no point in walking through the iron gate and pressing the doorbell. Rahul turned and started to walk away. He felt no pain any more.

If he had waited just a little longer, he might have discovered that the person behind the glass was Alice. She saw him, and waited only because she couldn't believe her eyes. She expected him to walk into the house. By the time she came down to the road below, he was gone.

She took a few uncertain, frantic steps on the road until a purple, sausage-shaped balloon floated in front of her as if from nowhere. She looked up instinctively at the sky. Pale as before, the sky offered no clues to the ownership. The balloon escaped her hands and came to rest at her feet. But only for a moment. There was a slight breeze, and trapped in it, the balloon jumped about like a fat pigeon hesitating between food and fright.

"Thank you, lady," said an unseen voice. "Could I have the balloon back, please?"

It was a child's voice. Alice stopped in her tracks, trying to place it without turning her head away from the road.

Another voice said, "I'm here." A woman's face, gaunt and ravaged by age, looked down from a window. "I'll come down and get it."

It was for her son, she said. He was a cripple, been that way from birth. Alice returned her the balloon and walked back distractedly to the house.

Twelve

When Rahul called me at home later that evening, I was out of town. I met him two days later, surprised over the name of the hotel my servant passed on to me. He seemed perfectly happy in a grimy, smelly hotel room on Ezra Street. He was surrounded by piles of newspapers and magazines, and seemed quite unconcerned about the endless commotion outside his window.

Directly below the window, facing the street, was the hotel kitchen. Till the early hours of the morning, it sent up the smell and sounds of mouth watering *kebabs* and egg rolls. Rahul walked down to the kitchen every few hours to satisfy his hunger. In the process, he endeared himself to just about everyone in the hotel. It didn't matter to the Muslim hotel owner that Rahul was a Hindu. What impressed him more was the fact that Rahul had just stepped off a plane from America.

"My own city refuses to recognize me and my hotel for the quality of my food and service," said the owner to one of his regular customers, "but my patrons come from foreign lands where they know my real worth." The customer was unimpressed at first when the man pointed to Rahul and announced that here was a gentleman from America. "But he looks like one of us," said the surprised customer.

"Looks can be very deceiving," said the owner, nodding his head wisely. Turning to Rahul, he said, "A few years ago we even had an

American *guru* spend two months in my hotel, in the very room you're now occupying." Then, pointing to a tubewell standing on the sidewalk in front of the hotel, he laughed, adding, "But nobody ever saw him take a bath." Later, as if to prove his point, the man rummaged through his cash-box and produced a dollar bill on which was written — To my friend, Salim Ali, from A. Ginsberg.

The invisible war asserted itself through the daily headlines. Again, the city reflected nothing of it. Calcutta seemed preoccupied only with itself. There was some talk of the millions of refugees herded into camps only twenty miles from the city. But like the war, they too were invisible. At least one couldn't see them unless one drove for miles. It wasn't a pleasant drive, hardly worth the stench and squalor waiting at the other end.

Rahul was a bit diffident about asking the proprietor, a Muslim, what he thought of the war. The man himself brought up the topic on the second day of his stay. "I suppose," he said, "you've come to write about the war and the refugees like those white-skins with their expensive cameras in the Grand Hotel and the Great Eastern." Salim Ali ignored Rahul's protests about not being a war correspondent. "Let me tell you," he continued, lowering his voice a little, "it's all humbug."

Rahul looked at him curiously. "You mean there isn't a war?"

"No," replied Salim Ali quite firmly. "Ayub Khan and the Pakistani army needed some whores, so they went after them. Mujib's men also need the same things, so they end up whoring in Calcutta. It's all to do with women, see?"

Before Salim Ali started boasting to his customers that he too had a war correspondent in his hotel, Rahul made it clear to him that he had no business in the city, that he was going home to his village in Bishnupur up north.

"That's pretty close to the border, isn't it?" asked Salim Ali slyly.

"Yes," replied Rahul. "But it's the village next to it that's smack on the border. Hazariganj, it's a largely Muslim village. I've no business at the border."

"I remember," said Salim Ali, "it was beyond Hazariganj that we crossed over from West to East Bengal after the partition. There used to be a pretty village on the other side. It's name was Hasnabad. I think it was December, ninety forty seven, when they tore up the tracks between Hasnabad and Hazariganj. It was such a long time ago." Salim Ali sounded sad. "It was to keep us, Muslims and Hindus, apart from each other, was it not?" He nodded thoughtfully. "But blood runs thicker than religion. That's what I think."

"I don't know," said Rahul, turning his face to the smoke rising from the kitchen fires.

I knew Rahul was headed for Bishnupur. "This time there's no reason for you to come," he said to me. "I guess it's my father still pushing me on, testing me, pushing me to the brink." I wanted to go with Rahul, but he was insistent. "There's no need for you to take on this burden."

When he reached Bishnupur the next morning, Rahul was surprised to see a mountain of construction material lying alongside the platform." "What's this all about?" he casually asked the station master.

"You must be a stranger here," said the man. "All that stuff is for the Railwaymen's Convention due to begin here in a few weeks. The Railway Minister will himself preside over the closing session. I'm afraid you'll hardly be able to recognize our little village in a week or two. First the convention, then the annual fair."

"I thought the fair was usually held earlier," said Rahul.

"That's true," replied the station master, "but this year it has not been the same. The phoney war, you know, and the refugees."

"And Sambhu Narain's plays?" asked Rahul.

"All that's in the past," replied the station master with a wistful smile, "even though Sambhu Narain's back. Suddenly turned up one day just like that, after his daughter went missing. Many travellers from the north say they've seen him in the company of holy men. He comes and goes as he pleases. Speaks very little."

"And what about Janaki Devi?" asked Rahul.

"You ask too many questions, stranger." The station master had grown suspicious. He stepped closer to Rahul to take a good look at his face. "Who may you be?" he asked.

"I'm Rahul Chaudhury. Sambhu Narain's son."

The station master gasped in disbelief. His spectacles slid down to the tip of his nose. "Oh my God!" he exclaimed, embracing Rahul and starting to cry. "Your mother's a very holy person or you wouldn't have been sent here in her hour of need." He released Rahul and glanced around him fearfully. He whispered to him to follow him into the ticket office for it was not safe to be standing where they were.

The train blew its whistle and painfully pulled out of the station as Rahul and the station master walked the length of the platform and entered the modest station building. The old man promptly secured the ticket window and bolted the door from inside. Rahul could barely hide his impatience as he asked him what was going on. The man collapsed into a chair and said he had a long story to tell. But he would try to be brief with Rahul.

He began by reminding Rahul that his brother's death and Sambhu Narain's disappearance left Janaki Devi totally helpless in Bishnupur. They were always ready to help his mother, he said. Unfortunately, before they knew what was happening, the local Congress boss had moved into her home. Chanchal Sircar, the very man the government had sent to Bishnupur as a social worker. Rahul admitted he had never met him. The station master lowered his voice still further and declared emphatically that there was no truth to what many detractors were whispering behind their backs. The truth simply was that Janaki Devi welcomed Chanchal into her home as a son, only to be cheated out of everything. Sambhu Narain's recent return had not made the slightest difference. "He lives in a world apart. We've watched this with pain and anguish, but Chanchal's a powerful man and nobody dares say anything in public. Thank God you've finally come home." He wiped away his tears and clasped Rahul's hands in his.

A passing thought arrested the old man. He asked Rahul what he himself had been up to all these years. Rahul replied that he had been studying abroad, which wasn't such a good answer because the station master promptly asked if he had forgotten how to write in his mother tongue. Rahul had little choice but to inform his inquisitor that he had been studying in an ashram run by an Indian guru, and had been totally secluded. The man seemed silenced and impressed by Rahul's explanation.

Rahul was a bit uncertain as to what might be expected of him in Bishnupur. The station master wasted no time in telling him quite sharply that the rascal Chanchal had usurped his rightful position. It was upto him to recover what was legally his, up to him to take charge of the Chaudhury household once more. Rahul had no intentions of telling the old man that the last thing he wanted to do was take charge of his family estate. But he did enquire about his mother, whether she had given up everything without a murmur of protest.

"Without protest," he said. "Whatever interest she might've had, it was all gone when Krishna disappeared. I've seen her at the station from time to time. She never complains. Not even to Durga Chakravartty, the priest, who feels just as outraged and sees her much more frequently over prayers."

Janaki Devi wasn't in Bishnupur at the time. "I think she left for Calcutta sometime last week," recalled the station master. "She goes there often to stay with Malini, your sister's little girl. Poor girl. But Sambhu Narain might turn up any time. There's no telling when."

Perhaps he ought to go home and wait for his father's return, said Rahul. But the station master cautioned him to be careful and not to mention their conversation to anyone.

Rahul wasn't at all prepared for the surprise that awaited him at home. Chanchal couldn't be more cordial, more deferential. "Your mother has wept day and night these three years," he said, "waiting for your return, waiting for your sister's return. She has wept and prayed. So have we. These have been very difficult years, but we've done our best and hope you'll approve."

Chanchal said his mother might be home any day, for she seldom stayed in Calcutta more than a couple of weeks at a time. But when Rahul asked about his father, Chanchal looked troubled. "He lives in a world of his own. Comes and goes when he pleases."

Then he turned to Rahul and asked what wonderful adventures he had had these past few years. Rahul knew he would have to deal with such questions before long, but he had made up his mind to say nothing. He was saved for the moment as there suddenly appeared a slight, frail man who fell at his feet. The prostrate figure was paying his respects, but Rahul stepped back in embarrassment. When he saw it was the old servant, Panchu, he bent down and lifted him gently off the ground. "You've grown so big, master," he said, trying to hold back his tears.

Word spread quickly through the village. People began to drop by almost immediately and continued to do so all day long. With Sambhu Narain having given up control over his earthly possessions and ties, the return of his son held the suggestions of a new order in the house, if not the entire village. The many tragedies that visited the family in recent years touched every heart in Bishnupur. But neither the priest nor the postmaster or the grocer repeated anything of what the station master had said to Rahul, which bothered him.

Many came out of simple curiosity, to see a man who had travelled across the seas, the one solitary detail of his recent history Rahul had been compelled to disclose to his visitors. "Is it true," asked a young boy, "that in America, with science, they can turn donkeys into horses?" It had always been an exclamation of despair and disgust in Bengal to say you couldn't change one into the other, that fools would remain fools. Rahul stopped laughing and was about to explain that Americans were indeed very clever. But the boy's father yanked the lad by his ear out of the room for his impertinence, and so saved Rahul the need to champion American scientific ingenuity.

Chanchal looked after him well, making sure he was fed well and often. He rarely left his side, especially when visitors were around. In spite of all this care and attention, Rahul came down with high fever on the third night of his stay. Again, he thought he was going to die. At least, he was certain he had passed out in the middle of the night during one of his frequent sprints to the outhouse on the far side of the courtyard. He had no idea whether it was day or night when he finally regained his senses.

As he stirred out of his groggy sleep, his fevered eyes could only see fields that stretched uninterrupted behind the house for miles. There still wasn't enough light to bring into focus the trees silhouetted outside his window. Drunk with dew, they squatted low against the sky, sucking the colours from the horizon's edge.

A long time passed before Rahul heard the sparrows chirping outside. Uncertain and undecided, they scattered from the treetops like dust in the wind, then shot back just as suddenly to settle in the canopied trees. As they alternated between sudden fright and serenity, visible one moment and mere voices the next, Rahul knew it was morning. The morning still held some terror for the birds, terror from which they found shelter in the leaves and branches. He imagined he felt like the birds, felt his world descending upon him like a bird of prey, its eyes full of satanic duplicity, tempting him, humiliating him.

Rahul drew his quilt closer against his body and hoped he was free at last of the uncontrollable shivering which had seized him the night before. The fever had left him now, and invisible hands seemed busy wringing the sweat off his body. He badly needed a change of clothes. Those he had on were almost as wet as the quilt. Getting up seemed to require so much effort that he decided to wait a little longer, frightened that the trembling might return the moment he stepped off the bed. Malaria, dengue fever, enteric, names of familiar diseases passed through his mind as he set about trying to diagnose his symptoms. Even if he were to write himself a prescription, he hadn't the faintest idea where medicines might come from in a village like Bishnupur. Finally, he was pleased to leave the problem in the hands of a Dr. Bagchi whom the resourceful Panchu brought in to see him later that morning.

Dr. Bagchi chatted happily. His fees never varied. Two rupees for a prescription, two rupees for a simple examination, two rupees for a medical certificate to justify almost anything. But to charge money for examining Sambhu Narain's son, who was himself a doctor, would be nothing short of disgraceful. Having made this lofty statement, he pinched Rahul, looked into his eyes, made him breathe deeply, patted his tummy, and asked, "What did you eat last night?"

Smiling weakly, Rahul admitted he had eaten just about everything that had been placed in front of him. The same with the meal before that, and the one before that. The doctor interrupted him, saying he would now have to pay for his weakness. Nothing but barley water for the next forty eight hours.

Dr. Bagchi left promising to send some pills later in the day.

Panchu dutifully started bringing Rahul his barley water every few hours. Chanchal dropped in too, enquiring how he was feeling, asking if he needed anything to make himself comfortable. "There must've been one bad shrimp," he said thoughtfully, "enough to knock a strong person out." He proceeded to abuse Panchu for not examining the day's shopping more carefully. Panchu kept his head bowed and listened to Chanchal's tirade in silence. "I must leave you for a few hours," said Chanchal eventually. "I have to finish some business in the village. I'm sure I'll find you much better when I return."

As soon as Chanchal stepped out of the house, Panchu came and knelt down beside Rahul's bed. "You must leave this place as soon as you can," he said. He looked sick with worry. "It's not safe for you here."

In spite of his weakness, Rahul started to laugh. "You must've had more than your share of *ganja* this morning, Panchu," he said. "Who would want to harm me here, in my own house?"

Panchu was adamant, certain that someone had put something in his food the night before. Even though he told Panchu he was speaking utter nonsense, a tiny grain of suspicion began to grow in his mind. Sounding desperate, Panchu implored with him to go away for a few days at least, perhaps to Siliguri, and return when Janaki Devi was back. Rahul began to think it was not such a wild idea after all. He needed some dry clothes right away and some warm clothes as well. It could get quite chilly in the northern parts of the province. Panchu told him not to worry, for all of Sambhu Narain's clothes were still around. Rahul could happily take whatever he wanted. But he had to hurry. There was no time to lose.

For the first time in many years, the irony of his immediate needs came home to Rahul. Clothes, money, personal safety. There was a time when he would've scorned such concerns. Property he would most certainly have banished from his scheme of things. If he had any need for money, the need was confined to a world of cigarettes, coffee, and bus tickets. As a student, his mother never begrudged him whatever it all added up to. Sambhu Narain didn't seem to care. How he once loathed his father's world, his pretensions, his naive connivings, his subtle self-pity. Now he hated him more for having abandoned his mother. Poor father, nothing to remember him by except for all those despicable things he valued. Or did he really?

The one nice thing Rahul remembered about his father was a single image of Sambhu Narain towering above his head, tall and sturdy as a slim birch. Everything else was fading. Trying to capture these forgotten images was like walking into a deserted town. Only the empty shells, but no life one could relate to. Still, there was one image he was beginning to remember, the image of a winter's day, and little Rahul walking hand in hand with his father.

It came back to him now. Every time he ran, it was this single image that took hold of his mind for long periods. He would have loved to drive it out of his mind, if only he knew how. Every time he looked back over the hump that separated their lives, he was still walking with his hand in his father's. His sneakered feet still went pitter-patter over the glazed asphalt, still strained to keep pace with his father's enormous strides as they stepped out of a glorious avenue lined with trees and wandered south along the river.

How beautiful their house in Calcutta used to be then. One walked into the avenue as soon as one stepped out of the gates. There was a strange pleasure merely in walking in and out of those gates. It mattered little where one was walking to, and upon what errand. Rahul couldn't have been more than four years old then. He found it strange that he couldn't remember other occasions when he and Sambhu Narain must at least have been physically close to one another if nothing else. Something happened as he grew older. Could it be that, at a certain point, they had each made a conscious choice to go their separate ways. Or was it that he seemed merely to be retracing his father's steps, a little behind in time. Like his father, was he too picking up society's worn out hand-me-downs along the way?

He had no doubt his father had once belonged to an elite. There was always a great deal of adulation heaped upon him. Most of all, he was a hero to his family and relatives, the one son of his father who had broken away from his rustic beginnings in the ancestral village of Bishnupur and gained a degree of prominence and respect in the city. His two brothers died in Bishnupur even before their father, one of smallpox, the other of typhoid. So, it was left to Sambhu Narain to present himself as the one shining beacon to his far-flung relatives. With the looks of a fairy-tale prince, pretty secretaries slowed down as they walked past his glass-walled office during the day, hoping to catch his eyes or, better still, elicit some trivial request or irrelevant enquiry. His colleagues from the press, who looked derelict to the last man, reviled him for his outward appearance and, while they sipped their acrid coffee or cheap whiskey, regretted that the man didn't have more talent. But within the family, Sambhu Narain's excellence remained unchallenged. Your father wrote this, your father would never wear it, your father wouldn't be seen alive with him. Such were the absolute canons with which Rahul grew up. They came less from his mother than from his relatives. At the time, it never occurred to him to question them. Until they finally parted one day, everyone thought he was destined to remain faithful to his father's ways, in style if not in substance.

When Sambhu Narain moved to Bishnupur in nineteen fifty nine, there was great consternation within the family. A change was coming over him, and he seemed indifferent to what people thought. He still dressed well, carrying around his hardy British suits. They showed up each year at the end of summer when it was time to get them aired. They looked so limp and sad, they reminded Rahul of the feeling of emptiness one felt backstage at the end of a play. Like the first year in college when he worked with the student production of Julius Caesar. He had the mindless task of sorting out the *dhoties* that passed for togas, the wooden swords and the *papier-mache* helmets after everyone had gone home. It was dreadful work. He had the time of his life accounting for everything, especially on the final day when Caesar's ink-stained mantle and his parchment will couldn't be found. They suspected some poor servant had made off with the mantle, but who would steal Caesar's will? Who would want to wear his father's old clothes, Rahul asked himself, as he prepared to go through Sambhu Narain's possessions with Panchu.

Still somewhat weak, he moved slowly into the room where Panchu prepared to exhibit his master's former wardrobe with all the pride and flair he could muster. An enormous steel trunk unexpectedly disgorged the old British suits. Sambhu Narain had visited London in nineteen thirty nine, purchased four Seville Row suits for a fortune, and nursed them through repairs and alterations for the next twenty years. His sartorial standards having once been established, Sambhu Narain remained secretly contemptuous of Indian tailors for the rest of his life. As far as Rahul knew, only one tailor, an arthritic old man by the name of Farookh Rahman, ever found favour in his eyes. One single tailor in a land of five hundred million people! When questioned on this subject, Sambhu Narain replied, "That's not at all surprising. Out of every million Indians, how many bother to dress? Not more than a hundred, I'd say. And out of this hundred, perhaps one person knows what it is to dress with taste. Given this limited clientele, if there were others of the caliber of Farookh Rahman they'd all starve."

Rahul saw his father as a man of clashing contradictions, a man who had failed to find his place in time. He looked down at the English suits and saw the patches, worn and shiny, and other spots that had been skillfully darned. As the smell of mothballs and *neem* leaves rose to his nostrils, it occurred to him that there was one towering relationship in his father's life which seemed to dwarf all others. The fruitful and steady association — Rahul even thought of it as a collaboration — between Sambhu Narain and Farookh Rahman. Together, they had guided the English suits through two decades of structural change, working their way past fluctuating lapels and uncertain cuffs. Somehow, the thought appealed to Rahul. Happy in the thought that Farookh Rahman had indeed played his part well, Rahul picked up one of the darker suits. He assured Panchu that was all he'd need to tide him over the winter.

As he led Rahul back to his room, Panchu said, "You know, a young man came looking for you a few months ago. Chanchal wouldn't let him inside the house so he couldn't speak to your mother. He threatened to beat him up if he ever caught him on the Chaudhury estate again. He has changed a lot, but I'm sure that was the boy servant your sister took in about the time you went abroad."

Rahul wasn't sure if he had heard Panchu correctly. His face lit up with excitement. "Do you remember exactly when he came here?" he asked in a quiet voice. Panchu couldn't be sure. Maybe two months, maybe three. With that, he turned to leave the room, saying he would prepare a flask of barley for Rahul to take with him on the train.

"I won't be taking a train, Panchu. Instead, could you get me a bicycle?"

"You're in no shape to ride a bicycle," protested Panchu indignantly. But he soon relented, promising to get the bicycle as long as Rahul wouldn't leave without the barley water.

Thirteen

The path along which Rahul cycled to Hazariganj was narrow and pitted with holes. It was not a pleasant or easy path. As they travelled on it during the monsoons, people prayed that it wouldn't rain, for then it became almost impassable and one needed to fight with snakes for the right of way.

Of late, this path was one along which some people had travelled back and forth in search of Krishna. Each person carried with him a burden of guilt. Sambhu Narain's guilt was of a special kind, a father's guilt for bringing life to a child. He had wanted to possess her as only a father could. He had forgotten there were others intent on destroying her.

Hamid had been through here in the summer, searching for scraps of information, wanting to know if Krishna was dead or alive, hating himself for having failed when she needed him the most. He had seen them rip off her clothes and slash at her breasts with their knives. He had heard her scream. The memory of that poisoned his sleep forever. When alone, the pain was ever present. The murderous crowd rushing upon them, stepping over the lifeless bodies of Vikram and Malini, then carrying Krishna away as their prize. Reeling from the blow to his head, blinded and disoriented, Hamid ran until he could no longer see anything but flames in the distance. The shame of it when he realized what he had done. He was too late by the time he gathered enough courage to return. The convoy of trucks was pulling away with the bodies of Vikram and Malini. That much he had seen from the distance. He wanted to call out for them to stop. Shame held him by the throat, choking his voice.

Hamid promised himself he would not rest until he had tracked down Krishna's abductors. For weeks, he wandered from village to village, not knowing where the men had come from or where they had escaped with Krishna. Sooner or later, he had to end up in Hazariganj not only because it was one of the neighboring villages, but because it was still the nearest place to home.

His father was dead, but his mother was overjoyed to see him home at last. Hamid had no intentions of staying there. He would hardly stay in the village a day before he was gone somewhere else. Who came and went from the village was of little interest to him unless they could tell him something about Krishna. So it didn't matter one bit to him when a beautiful and mysterious woman showed up in Hazariganj one day.

No one recognized her as the half-crazed, half-naked Saira who once roamed the village fields and paths like a skulking animal. If her father had any suspicions, he laid them to rest the moment she opened the pages of her bank passbook. Even though the old man could barely read the figures in the passbook, one look at the woman standing in front convinced him there was no need of further proof beyond her expensive clothes and her jewelry. It had to be his daughter Saira.

Saira was also Chhotki. She had taken on a non-Muslim name in the gardens out of sheer necessity. Roger Ames, the British planter from Chirribilli, had provided handsomely for her before he left the Dooars. So well in fact that she walked right out of the tea graden quarters and her pimp's protection one fine day to return to the village from where she had been spirited away many months ago.

Saira settled down to an exemplary life in Hazariganj and charmed everyone. Soon people stopped whispering about her infamous past in Chirribilli. Hamid's mother even imagined her son settling down with this woman someday. None of this made any impression on Hamid. Obsessed with the thought of finding Krishna, he had all but forgotten Saira as the girl he once loved.

Hamid was away from the village the day a band of Pakistani

soldiers, chasing some Bangladesh freedom fighters, burst upon the village of Hazariganj. It was not part of formal military operations, and they had not intended to enter Indian territory. Once there, however, they didn't hesitate to beat up some innocent villagers. Saira interested them. When they left, they took her along. Over the next few weeks, many villages on Indian territory suffered similar outrages as the Pakistani soldiers secretly built up an enormous stable of local women.

He was also away the day Rahul came to Hazariganj. Hamid's mother insisted he wait in her poor hut for her son's return. So he waited. Two days later, he was blindfolded by a group of young men and led at night to a Mukti Bahini freedom fighters'camp. When they finally met one another in the camp, their wild emotions as they embraced each other moved the rest of the camp to lay out a feast in celebration. The camp leader, Jamal Hussain, demanded no token of Rahul's commitment to their cause. "We need everyone," he said, as he welcomed Rahul into the group. He was Hamid's friend after all, and Hamid had already proved himself to them.

It was a new life for Rahul. He imagined it was another turning point. Winter rains were upon them now. The mornings were cloudy and steamy. It always rained during the night, leaving the fields bathed in grey. A blanket of smoke hung upon the ground each morning. The smoke was heavy, and showed no signs of wishing to be one with the clouds above. It settled upon the earth like a giant moth and shrank its muslin wings little by little until, late in the day, it vanished like a puff of smoke. Everything looked grey, so that the green fields were not green and the brown earth all but invisible.

Rahul supposed that elsewhere the mornings were like mornings are supposed to be, full of sunshine and promise. But not here, where the news from Bangladesh was all bad. Mornings raised no hopes here, simply deepened the anger.

For a whole month, Rahul slept on a bed which was no bed at all, just three crates placed side by side on the ground. Empty ammunition crates. He woke up each morning eleven inches above the ground and imagined he was lying in the clouds. It was an illusion created by the layer of vapour which hung inches above his head and rubbed its flanks against the open flaps of his tent like a ponderous, shaggy monster. He was not sure whether it was this or the martial associations of his bed that often filled him with a strange sense of power even on the most depressing mornings. When he finally walked away from the bed, it was with a confidence which never deserted him for the rest of the day, even if few of the other camp members shared in it.

The rains came down relentlessly. Still they waited, spending cold nights under their patched-up army surplus tents of World War II vintage. They were holed up like rats in fifteen tents pitched in a sea of mud. From a distance, the camp gave the impression of an armada of overturned paper boats gradually being swallowed by the waves. Never having been in a shipwreck, Rahul wasn't sure if there was an element of adventure in at least its initial moments. If there was, his feelings at the time couldn't have been much different from those of the hapless voyager cast between the jaws of sky and ocean. Rahul felt both fear and exhiliration. But the rest of the camp never had too much of one or the other. What kept them going was the solid conviction that it would all end soon, one way or the other. Like many others before him, Jamal Hussain believed the world would be a better place for them after it was all over. If not the whole world, certainly a significant corner of it.

At times, it was like running, simply a matter of pushing oneself. With such an attitude, nothing was a pain except pain itself. All their inconveniences became sources of mirth. Shaving was abolished as time consuming and unnecessary. Bathing was declared decadent. They worked, exercised, ate and slept in the same clothes, taking time off only to pluck the leeches which hung like ripe plums from their skin every evening. The hair on their bodies worked its way through the clothes they wore. When the time came to take off their clothes, they were certain they would end up peeling off their skin in the process.

The worst of it was having to defecate in the surrounding fields. The rains not only transformed the fields into treacherous marshes but also blessed them with a harvest of snakes. Rahul and Hamid spent fearful moments out there each day, waving off the pesky greenheads and wishing they had their magical eyes and lightning reflexes. As he sat there, Rahul was at times so scared he wished he had not two, but two hundred eyes staring out of the back of his head, the back of his spine, and reaching way down to his bare buttocks. These he imagined to be particularly vulnerable to a reptile's fangs, for they were almost level with the mud and must have presented a target both immense and inviting. The slightest sound that broke through the ceaseless hum of the flies alerted him to possible danger. His heart-beat would quicken and the sphincters knot themselves into a horrible cramp as he waited tensely for the twin needles to tear through soft flesh and hurl him screaming to his death.

At night, Rahul and Hamid lay side by side. One had tales of America to tell; the other, of nothing in particular. "Pretty women out there, aren't they?" asked Hamid. "Nice breasts," he added as an afterthought. Yes, replied Rahul, pointing out it was all the same once one got between the sheets. Hamid asked about Sharmila one day. Rahul didn't say a word, remained utterly silent, and Hamid never brought up the subject again.

The young recruits at the camp were restless for action. They were only modestly armed but felt ready to take on the might of the Pakistani army. The Mukti Bahini relied on a network of supply points close to the Chinese border. Most of their weapons carried American markings. Even though there weren't any Chinese handling the distribution, almost everyone knew where the arms came from. Unfortunately, their camp was a low priority one and received very irregular supplies of arms and ammunition. Money was no problem since the Indian government made sure the Mukti Bahini had ample funds at its disposal.

Rahul suggested to Jamal Hussain one day that he might be able to get some arms from a friend in Calcutta. The idea appealed to Jamal. It would give his ragtag boys something worthwhile to do. Besides, there was a transmitting station at Hasnabad which the guerillas desperately needed to silence. If Jamal's band could finish off the job, it would earn them a lot of respect in the eyes of others. As if to give the entire operation an added emotional urgency, Jamal Hussain received a piece of information both Rahul and Hamid had been waiting for. Someone answering to Krishna's description had been seen in a group of women. They were confined in the soldiers' barracks in the cantonment town of Jessore not far from the border.

They decided to combine the attack on the transmitter with an attempt to look a little more closely at the information on Krishna before planning further action. With only eight fighters available and not fully equipped at the time, the adventure looked terribly risky. Hamid wouldn't hear of Rahul leading the attack on the transmitter. Jamal Hussain agreed. "Give me a chance to redeem myself in my own eyes," said Hamid. He wanted Rahul to join him in Jessore if and when he had some definite information to go on.

Jamal Hussain arranged for a Government of India jeep to give them a ride to the outskirts of Calcutta. Once there, they were to steal a car in which to bring back supplies from Kartick Sirdar. It was around noon that the jeep dropped them off at Barrackpore. Rahul and Hamid spotted a late model Ambassador car and decided that was what they wanted. It was the only car around.

The car was parked in front of a lowly, wayside restaurant into which the owner had probably gone for his mid-day meal. Even as they watched, the driver stepped out of the car and, leaving it unlocked, went round to the alley to urinate. Rahul eased himself into the driver's seat and turned on the ignition. Hamid settled down beside him. At the sound of the engine starting, the driver leapt up from the side of the open drain, no doubt throwing the muscles of his half empty bladder into total confusion. His frantic cries evoked a somewhat similar reaction from his master who came rushing from his table inside the restaurant and promptly landed a resounding slap on his servant's face for having left the car unattended. As Rahul drove away, master and servant stomped upon the ground in anger and desperation, the master beating the air with his right hand still lavishly smeared with rice and curry despite an earlier brush with the driver's face.

A short ride through crowded side-roads brought them near the giant railway marshalling yards. At last, they could see the tottering, rusty warehouse which once formed the centre of Kartick Sirdar's strength and wealth. Could it be that three years had changed everything for Kartick too? Rahul wondered if his men still plundered the railway wagons at will, buying off an engineer or guard when necessary, putting a bullet through those who were too greedy, too conscientious or uncooperative. They wanted to get a little closer but found their path barred by a very unfriendly man. That was as far as the car could go.

Kartick was happy to see Rahul once again. He seemed more preoccupied and distracted than when Rahul knew him last. He was cordial enough today, but lacked the time for casual, idle conversation. "Why do you come in a miserable car?" he asked sarcastically. "I could've filled you a truck today."

A truck requires much money, explained Rahul, and also permits for the police, neither of which they happened to have. Kartick lamented he had a terrible storage problem on his hands. "See, I don't have a regular warehouse," he said. "It becomes impossible when people don't lift their orders on time. The Bangladesh minister ordered two thousand blankets and my men have been crawling in and out of them for three weeks."

Rahul was curious to know if the minister had been in direct contact with Kartick. "No, no," replied Kartick with a faint smile. "They're too busy screwing around and getting drunk in the city. They placed their order with my most loyal customer, Mr. Jhunjhunwala, whom you must remember. God knows what happened to the man he sent me recently. Left me a good advance too."

Kartick took them to a corner of the abandoned shed, still on the point of sliding into the motionless pond. The entire structure seemed suspended in air. From the ground upwards, rust had eaten into the four sides, leaving the rest of the corrugated iron walls flopping like rags. An enormous iron door, worn and pitted, hung crookedly on its hinges and made way for a blast of smoke and stench whenever the wind was strong.

"Where are the ducks?" asked Rahul absent-mindedly.

"Oh, they come and go," replied Kartick.

There were nine men inside, lying on bales of Canadian blankets, some spilling on the floor. Around them lay a wide assortment of crates and bags, stained and sweating from long exposure to the damp floor. "Get up, men," shouted Kartick, clapping his hands. "We've got customers."

All but two of the men stumbled out of their berths. Two continued to moan in their blankets. They had been shot by the railway police the night before, explained Kartick. Nothing serious. His main problem was that he couldn't get doctors to come to the place, so they had to patch up their men the best they could. He added quietly that the police would soon get what was coming to them. Then he shouted in the ears of one of the wounded men and asked if he thought he'd live. If the man had any answer to offer, it never got past the yellow glaze covering his eyes. Kartick turned away from him with a resigned expression on his face. "Karma," he said, with a shrug of his shoulders. Looking at him, Rahul knew the man wouldn't outlive the evening. There was little he could do to help.

"Load those in that black car," he shouted to his men, pointing to a stack of rifles covered with blankets. "Are you sure you don't want anything other than rifles?" he asked, turning to Rahul. Rahul replied he was quite sure he didn't.

"How about some anti-personnel mines? I have a few crates here. Found them in the same wagon with the rest of the stuff."

"When the boys are a little more experienced maybe," said Hamid. "Right now they can barely hold their rifles straight."

"In that case," said Kartick, "I doubt they'll get much experience in anything but getting killed." With that, and a final look at the two dying men, they stepped outside. Rahul hesitated for a moment when he saw two uniformed policemen enter a small shack a short distance away. Kartick took no notice of them. Seeing the questioning look on Hamid's face, he said, "Don't worry, they're only going in for a cup of tea. They're as meek as lambs out here. In fifteen minutes they'll walk over to me for their monthly bonus, then they'll be gone."

They returned to the car, and Hamid offered to drive for the first stretch. Rahul wasn't sure how well Hamid could drive, but he welcomed the chance for some rest. He planned to let the cool breeze lull him to sleep. Soon the wind was whistling past his face. In his half-sleep, he brushed away its discordant notes and gathered round him the sounds he loved, sounds he believed the wind carried for him. As the tires licked the road monotonously, he thought he heard the long-lost sounds of crickets and of croaking frogs. The throbbing engine faded as he imagined the sound to be that of a distant waterfall. But deep sleep was impossible, as the road soon became winding and uneven. Rahul would doze off and find the speeding car rocking him violently against the door to his left or jerking his head into the emptiness to his right. He was convinced Hamid was a terrible driver.

Towards evening, they came upon a lonely check-point at a road junction. Quiet and defenceless, it stood over a vast plain with nothing but a few tall trees for company. There were fields and fields as far as the eye could see. To the east, they faded into shadows. To the west, they stirred the lilac sunset in its final moments. There were no barriers in sight. At the sound of the approaching car, an uniformed man stepped out of the cabin and stood in the middle of the road, waving a red flag. He waved it in ever-mounting panic, watching the car rushing at him, hoping it would stop in time.

Rahul was awake now, but he wasn't sure what Hamid planned to do. The car bore down upon the man, until his eyeballs grew so big they seemed to fill the entire windshield. Hamid showed no signs of slowing down. A fraction of a second before the eyes vanished from their sight, the man stopped waving the flag. He just stood there with his right hand held aloft until, at the instant before impact, he dived headlong to one side of the road. The car shot past the fallen figure. "The fool," murmured Hamid under his breath. When the car turned into a gas station a few miles later, Rahul wasted no time in taking over the wheel.

Early next morning, Rahul dropped Hamid at a rendezvous near the border. Hamid's disguise was to be that of a sign-painter. It was a clever disguise because the military authorities in Bangladesh needed painters all the time. They were needed not only to cover up offensive and provocative Mukti Bahini slogans, but also to subdue the local population with fresh ones carrying dire threats and warnings.

Hamid was joined by seven boys, as excited as they were nervous. They said their goodbyes because it was unsafe to drive any further. The car might warn agents on the other side of the river that something unusual was in the offing. Rahul stood watching the group until the nearest line of trees swallowed up the figures. At a bend in the river some distance ahead, a boat waited to carry them across. Still feeling tired, now a little lonely too, Rahul returned to Jamal Hussain's camp to deliver the remaining rifles and wait for word from Hamid.

Planning to attract the attention of the guards, Hamid deliberately approached the transmitting station along a narrow road leading up to it. He whistled and kept time with the paint brush, trying to make it as conspicuous as possible. But there was no paint in the can that dangled from his hand, only a few grenades the boys had brought along from the camp.

They worked their way slowly towards the transmitter. Hamid's companions were bare-bodied. They tried to make out they were heading for the fields with their scythes. The rifles were tied to their legs and lay hidden under the *lungis* they wore. The idea was to get as close to the transmitting station as possible before rushing it with blazing guns.

They got no closer than a hundred yards before the Pakistani guards opened fire with their automatic weapons. Leaving five of their comrades bleeding in the fields, the rest crawled back to the nearest village from where they had started off in the first place.

Hamid was one of the survivors, but he found little joy in his good fortune. Something warned him against getting inside the village. They had passed close enough to it on their way to the raid. Not one person spoke to them or looked them in the face except one young man who offered them tea and biscuits and wanted very much to come along with them. They had no guns to spare, and told him they would enlist his help some other time.

As they were now carefully skirting the village, this same man rushed out of his hut to receive them. He wept when he heard what happened. "You should've let me come," he said bitterly. "I have a score to settle with those Pathans. They raped my mother and sisters before my eyes and bayonetted them to death."

"Can you tell us where we can take cover until sundown?" asked

Hamid impatiently.

"Here, in this village?" asked the man incredulously. "They'll have their patrols combing through here within the hour. Your only hope is Jessore. It's a large enough town so you can hide. I know a way through the fields which'll be the safest for you."

The villages belonged to the freedom fighters as long as the Pakistani patrols were away. Hamid wasn't sure if he ought to try and reach the riverbank or move on towards Jessore. There seemed little they could do just then for the five dead or wounded they had left behind. Hamid didn't have any grenades, but he still carried his gun. The two boys hadn't even had a chance to untie theirs. Hamid didn't know if the man could be trusted, but he felt they were not totally defenceless against this one stranger. Besides, the path to the riverbank was fairly exposed. It led to the border and that was where the Pakistanis would most likely be looking for them. He quickly made up his mind and decided to follow him to Jessore.

A few children and a half dozen old men hovered around them nervously, trying hard to follow their conversation. When they saw them heading for the fields in the company of the young man, some of them tried weakly to attract Hamid's attention. But their tongues were paralyzed with fear, their voices too soft to be heard.

They walked in silence most of the day. From time to time, the young man talked about some of the soldiers' atrocities. When he turned to women, Hamid ventured to ask if there were many Bengali women in the barracks. He would like to find out about one in particular, he said. Jessore was still a few hours away. The young man promised to take them to a house where they'd find all the information they needed on the captive women of Jessore.

Fourteen

When brigadier Iftikar Ali first assumed command of the garrison at Jessore, the cantonment area sparkled like a picture. The roads, the trees, the bungalows, the barracks, everything seemed just right. Everything was bright and shining. The labourers worked hard on the flower beds, mowed the lawns with care, and trimmed the hedges to their proper height. The trees on the golf-course looked down on lush fairways, and the clubhouse waiters were always anxious to please. In the officer's mess, the trophies and regimental colours glittered night and day, and no one ever relaxed with an empty glass in front of him.

Seven weeks had changed everything. Now the grass grew wild, the flowers were dying, and the hedges looked rough and unkempt. Even the barracks looked sick and lifeless under their coat of green paint hastily applied under orders from the Pakistani high command. Every message indicated that full-scale war with India was imminent, furious military action only days away. But nothing happened. To the Brigadier's dismay, nothing seemed likely to happen. A few skirmishes, a few explosions in factories, a few bridges blown up by Indian sappers, and the Pakistani military administration was in total disarray.

Iftikar Ali considered himself a veteran. Trained in Dehra Dun and Sandhurst, he had seen action in two previous wars with India. He just didn't seem to understand this present one. Some of those handing down orders to him now were men he had fought with in

Kashmir. They too had changed. He couldn't read their minds any longer. All they seemed interested in doing now was to terrorize the Bengali population. They called it punitive action, and the directives from above pointed out in unambiguous terms what punitive action implied.

His instincts rebelled against the thought of striking at the innocent civilians for actions clearly planned and executed by the Indian army. But those were his orders. He looked the other way while his men raped, looted, and murdered. He was beginning to believe there might be something about the underlying politics of the situation which his military mind was incapable of grasping. "This isn't genocide, I insist," a senior general lectured to him. "On the contrary," he added with a wink, "our soldiers are helping these Bengali women to be truly productive." Iftikar Ali concluded that values were changing too fast around him.

He had stopped his weekly inspection of the barracks. There were too many women for his liking. His men had turned the long halls into cubicles through an ingenious arrangement of bamboo poles on which they hung curtains, trousers, saris, and just about anything else they could lay their hands on. Having permitted women inside the barracks, the Brigadier now felt compelled to allow them the little privacy they deserved. To a large extent, it was what the men wanted that mattered. Their morale needed to be kept up. The women deserved nothing. Whatever sympathy he might feel for them, he was certainly not prepared to play the mediator between the devil and the damned.

During the last week of June, when the first lot of women were herded into the barracks, the air was constantly charged with their shrieks. If their cries and screams weakened the Brigadier it was not for long. The wailing was at its worst during the night, and Iftikar Ali quickly made it a point not to spend his nights in the cantonment. There was a neat little cottage on Casuarina Avenue, not far away, where he and other junior officers felt much more at home. It was infinitely better than the officer's mess, the nights much more quiet and soothing.

✻

Although these soldiers had nothing to do with the attack on the car near Chirribilli, it was inside their barracks that Krishna eventually found herself. After weeks as a captive of her own people, mutilated and degraded, driven from village to village, she was at last in the hands of a known enemy. Her scarred breasts in particular held an intense fascination for the soldiers. But Krishna was past caring about any abuse they could heap upon her body. It was almost liberating to be in enemy hands.

Not surprisingly, she was at the forefront of a group of women determined to turn adversity into a means to freedom. Krishna herself came up with a game of straws where there was one piece of straw for every woman enslaved in the camp. There was always one straw much shorter than the rest. Whoever drew the short straw would drown herself in the river anytime the soldiers let the women loose to bathe in the waters at dusk.

On six different evenings, six women drew the short straw and gladly gave their lives to the river. If the soldiers missed them, they did nothing about it. On the seventh day, Krishna herself drew the short straw. But as she swam away from the cluster of women on the riverbank and willed the river to take her body, something inside told her she could not die. The current swiftly took her far away from Iftikar Ali's soldiers. In the darkness of the evening, she crept onto a secluded stretch of land where she heard the sound of women's voices, at peace with themselves and others. She knew then for sure she would live.

On the western bank of the river, she was among her own people. They clothed her, sheltered her, and sent word about her to neighboring villages. As they nursed her back to health, they told her of a bearded man with fiery eyes who was scouring the villages near Hazariganj and Bishnupur, all along the East Pakistan border, searching for his lost daughter. Krishna listened but said nothing. There was no emotion left in her.

If the other women had not been missed in the Jessore camp, it was not the same with Krishna. Word reached Iftikar Ali's ears that three young men on the run had come to Jessore enquiring about the woman with the mangled breasts, the one the soldiers called the breastless one. And now she had suddenly disappeared.

Iftikar Ali would deal with the problem later. For the moment, it was the message from Saira that was uppermost in his mind. Today, there was the prospect of escaping the boredom of the noon hours in bed with her. The Brigadier liked Saira. She was no rustic like the others. At times, he saw in her a woman of amazing sophistication quite at odds with her background. With Saira there was none of the theatricals which other women tried to pull off with his soldiers. Iftikar Ali respected her for her casual acceptance of the political realities of the day. If she had pledged herself to any other man in the past, she never bothered to discuss it with him. It was none of his business anyway. Neither was it his business if his men raped and killed under official orders. He at least was no rapist, although he certainly delighted in exploiting to the hilt the social advantages his military strength placed at his disposal. He no longer had a wife in West Pakistan, and saw nothing wrong in asserting himself over Saira. He confided to her there were times he even played with the idea of marrying her once things returned to normal. Saira laughed and reminded him she was a local girl, and he could claim the two thousand rupees reward which the government in Islamabad had offered for such unions.

It was sometime before the first message had gone out to the Brigadier that Hamid and his companions reached the outskirts of Jessore. The cantonment was at the other end of town, several miles away. In the midday sun, even in winter, the roads were all but deserted. The cottages lining the roads nestled drowsily under the shade of the overhanging trees. Still mourning the loss of his young companions, Hamid felt too exhausted to question closely where he was going. With the two boys almost ready to collapse, he had no choice but to place his faith in the stranger leading them through the town.

The streets had no names, and the houses no numbers. They stopped in front of a particularly neat and attractive house. The young man's bold knocking was answered by someone peeping furtively through the curtains. Then the doors parted slightly. Bidding the others follow, the young man quickly stepped inside.

The woman who had opened the door was clad in a light *burqah*, her face completely covered. She folded her hands and greeted them with a bow as the man introduced them. "Our honoured friends from the other side of the border," he said. Then, with a slight nod in the direction of the woman, he added reassuringly, "Our sisters are all on our side."

Hamid noticed several other women, their faces also covered, looking into the room. They disappeared from the door as soon as their curiosity was satisfied.

There was no food inside the house, not for four unexpected guests. When the young man enquired if there were any shops open nearby, the woman sighed behind her veil and said the closest ones were as far as the main bazaar. "They'll look like they're closed," she said, "but most will serve you through the back door." The man asked Hamid and his friends to be comfortable and promised to come back with something to eat in half an hour.

As soon as she had shut the door behind the man, the woman quickly went to the two other doors leading out of the room. After satisfying herself there was no one eavesdropping behind the curtains, she walked up to Hamid and said, "It's a trap. You must leave right away."

It took Hamid a while to believe it was Saira who was speaking to him. She lifted the veil covering her face, and then he knew for sure. She told Hamid she knew why they were in Jessore, but the woman he was looking for was dead. She had drowned as part of a game of chance she had herself invented, as the soldiers discovered shortly afterwards. When he had overcome his sense of defeat and numbness at hearing the news, Hamid was filled with a terrible desire to rip Saira's veil and hold her face in his hands. "I will not leave without you," he said.

"No, no'" Saira pleaded, "there's no time to lose. You must go immediately. Please go back the way you came."

With a supreme effort of the will, Hamid started walking towards the door. His uncomprehending companions scrambled behind him to follow. Hamid turned back once more at the door and said, "I will come back for you. I will."

By now, Saira was almost pushing the men out of the house.

"Please don't even think of it," she said tearfully, as she shut the door behind them.

As they cowered on the banks of the river, the weeds, the tall grass, the mud, and the swift current all helped to weave around them an indestructible armour, a magical spell, to ward off the menacing patrols which a furious Iftikar Ali sent after the fugitives. The breastless one had suddenly become an important piece in a puzzle that left the Brigadier baffled and disturbed.

Under cover of darkness, they swam across to the other side. Hamid had begun to sense the river as a living presence. Almost in the spirit of a religion he had been taught by the *mullahs* to hate, he felt an immense gratitude towards it. He hoped that the river's benevolence had been merciful with Krishna, that it would somehow reach out and touch Saira too, wash away all the pain and sorrow as if nothing ever happened, and destroy in one cataclysmic flood the bridge of time that had kept them apart so long.

They were still far from safe. Even before they came to the first village on the Indian side of the river, they realized that the Pakistanis hadn't hesitated to cross into Indian territory either. Half the village was in flames. Villagers who hadn't run away to the nearby woods now stood some distance away from the fire and watched their homes burn with sorrowful eyes.

The villagers were only too glad to help Hamid once they were satisfied they were from the Mukti Bahini and not Pakistani collaborators. Hamid and his friends needed bicycles to link up with Jamal Hussain once more. To allay any suspicions the villagers might have, Hamid asked three of them to accompany him and return with the bicycles later.

They discovered along the way that the Pakistani attack might have been provoked by the suspicion that the villagers were sheltering a woman they wanted. The soldiers kept asking about a young woman, the breastless one as they called her. Hamid found she had managed to escape only hours before the attack. The village headman had found two boys to accompany her down the river. The boat would take them to a point near Benapole from where she might find transportation to Calcutta. Could this be Krishna? Now Hamid was truly confused.

When Hamid finally met up with Rahul at the camp, Jamal Hussain wasted no time in arranging for a jeep to take them to Benapole. "This may not be your sister," he told Rahul, "but why don't you find out for yourself."

Fifteen

Now there were nights when Sambhu Narain didn't sleep at all, nights laced with dreams and fragrance when he suddenly woke up gasping for breath, moaning and clutching at invisible hands for support. He wrestled with demons in his mind, wrestled with the spirits he believed he had inherited from his daughter. Her expressionless eyes stared out of barred windows from a lonely room, blind to the lush trees and thick clumps of bamboo casting deep shadows across her face, deaf to the crackling crows piercing the heat of the afternoon. To her, the trees and the birds were insubstantial, and the jackals howling at the gathering dusk no more than shadowless mimes. Sambhu Narain knew then that her spirit had fled, even if life hadn't.

As he fought and raged against these demons, Sambhu Narain worked himself to a frenzy and his violent moods struck terror in the hearts of servants and the villagers in Bishnupur. For his wife, Janaki Devi, it merely evoked a tinge of pity and sadness. Of all the people around him, she was the one person who really understood. She understood and said nothing as he stormed out of the house to walk the fields for hours. He'd go off on sudden visits to villages on the border, to outposts like Benapole. There he mixed as freely with the Indian customs officers as with the more amiable villagers from both sides of the border who came to rest at the tea-stalls. They talked of whores and thieves in loud voices and of generals and collaborators in somewhat hushed and careful tones. They also spoke of hunger and the death of loved ones.

What Sambhu Narain really wanted to hear had nothing to do with whores and villains. He was certain his daughter was out there somewhere, for if she had died he would've found her in his soul. He had fasted and prayed, and searched for her in his prayers. She was nowhere to be found. Janaki Devi's heart was broken too, but seated in front of her golden gods she forgot all the pain. Only the haunting memory of her beautiful girl would never go away. The tears stopped mysteriously and life took on the aspects of a play which one watched with emotion, but left with dignity. It was not the same with Sambhu Narain. His wild eyes kept searching the horizon for signs. His ears waited for the sound of that single voice that would put an end to his quest.

Even if he happened to pick up some names during his visits, Sambhu Narain got no closer to the flesh and bones which bore the names he stalked, flesh he was ready to rip apart with his bare hands and suck out the warm blood to calm the fires tormenting him. It was this resolve that brought him so often in his rusty jeep to Benapole. Looking every inch like a god, he sat somberly beside his driver and held a trident upright in his hand. The stall-owners laughed at his appearance, but loved his generosity.

Inspector Sinha of the Customs was equally glad over the visits because Sambhu Narain's presence promised him a brief escape from the company of savages in whose midst he had been thrown ever since his transfer to Benapole. The most insufferable savage of them all was Ramcharan Goswami, the shifty-eyed sub-inspector.

Goswami's cavernous stomach grew larger by the day as he complained to whoever would listen how excessive work was reducing him to a shadow of his former self. With all the humility he could muster, he now asked Inspector Sinha if he might prepare tea since the so-called *Nawab* of Bishnupur had just driven into the village in a cloud of dust. Sambhu Narain brought an aura of aristocracy which the servile Goswami yearned to get close to. He believed that could be one avenue for him to snatch away from Inspector Sinha his position in the bureaucratic hierarchy which seemed so formidable, unattainable, and tempting to Goswami at all times. He desperately needed a patron.

If Inspector Sinha was silently contemptuous of Goswami, Sambhu Narain was not. Goswami prized the company of both men, even though he had so far found little to comfort him or nourish his pride. But that was all right, because one of the two had been born to a position of power and respect while the other had risen to a position of power, if not respect, through the machinations of political friends in Calcutta no doubt. Or through some vile pandering not beyond Goswami's fertile imagination.

When Sambhu Narain stepped into the Inspector's office moments later, there was a friendly smile on his face. He remarked how quiet, how dead, the checkpost and its surroundings seemed that evening. Seeing Goswami pouring the tea, he warned him not to drown the cup in milk. After he had taken a sip or two, he patted Goswami approvingly on the back and assured him that not even the Chief Commissioner of Customs could surpass Goswami's skills in the art of brewing tea. In a rather expansive mood, he even suggested once that Goswami came close to the ideal brew which captured the grandest elements of the Himalayan landscape.

None of this conversation helped to put Inspector Sinha in a happy frame of mind today. As soon as Sambhu Narain settled down with his tea, he began a long tirade against bureaucratic rules, especially one which deprived Benapole of married accommodation for those on duty at the outpost. He was married six years ago in an eastern village, well before he came to Benapole. His parents wanted him to marry a Rajasthani girl instead of one of the local peasants. It was a good idea since the girl's father owned the only textile shop in their village. Shortly after the marriage, the father-in-law suffered a stroke which completely paralyzed his right side and forced him to sell his business and return to his native Rajasthan to die. Hargovind agreed it was only proper that his wife should accompany the father and stay with him until he either died or recovered sufficiently for his mother-in-law to look after him. That was the last he saw of his wife. Before long, she gave birth to a son whom he was yet to see in the flesh. And the irony of it was that, to the best of his knowledge, the father was as far away from death as he was four years ago, and no nearer to life.

"She's only doing her duty," pointed out Goswami, warming to the conversation. "Where would we be if our families didn't hold together? What's there for women outside the family but shame and degradation?" Then, affecting a gentler tone, he suggested that Hargovind should waste no time in paying a visit to his wife and child. "Don't worry," he said, "I'll look after this place with my life."

Sambhu Narain was more interested in getting out of the office and joining the villagers in the tea stalls outside. Goswami looked such a pathetic figure in his attempts to gain status that he couldn't help putting in a kind word for him. "Oh! he'll do very well, I know," Sambhu Narain said to Hargovind. "You have a very good man here."

Goswami was completely taken aback by this unexpected compliment. After a moment of silence, his mind swung into action as he groped for ways to press home what he saw as a very advantageous situation.

"I've no doubt Goswami Bhai will be very good," said Hargovind grudgingly. "But, you see, it's a question of money." Without giving Sambhu Narain an opportunity to leave, he began to explain how he was entitled to four weeks statutory leave each year. The family being so far away, only the railfare to and from their village would be ninety rupees at least. Three years ago it would've been sixty. How he regretted not having gone then. Take ninety, then add the cost of meals for the three days in the train. He was thankful for being a vegetarian. Even then, meals would cost twelve rupees. He'd change trains at Benares, Kanpur, and Ajmer. Say, another ten rupees for the porters at these railway stations. Then the gifts. A sari for his wife would be thirty, one for his mother-in-law twenty perhaps, toys for his son another ten. He stopped to add up the figures.

"Are you paying attention, Sambhu Narainji?" he asked. Sambhu Narain shook his head and said he certainly was. Goswami used the pause to pour out more tea. Hargovind confessed his mind boggled at the total. How could anyone expect him to go home on his monthly salary of one hundred eighty rupees? He knew people would wonder whether everything was running smoothly between him and his wife. But then he'd look around this terrible place, not even a post office here, and he'd ask himself who really cared if he went home to his wife or stayed here.

"Yes," muttered Sambhu Narain sympathetically, putting aside his cup and standing up to leave. Goswami leapt to his feet and said he wouldn't allow Sambhu Narain to leave so soon, for he had after all visited them only once in the last fortnight. Sambhu Narain finally relented and promised to come back later in the evening and share a simple meal with them. For the moment, he wanted to take a walk through the shops in the village.

Hargovind left the office first, agreeing to bake the bread. Goswami remained behind, thinking of a meal that might truly win over his patron's heart. Who knew what preferment it might lead to eventually.

Hargovind continued to feel strangely depressed. He was also very tired. There was still some light in the sky. Blue above, a deep purple where it touched the land in the west. The colours made no impression on him. He prepared to cook his evening meal, sitting down on a low wooden stool and tearing off little pieces of dough listlessly. On other days, he felt a sensuous thrill as his fingers shaped the soft rounds with slow, deliberate movements. He would stare in fascination at the moist balls before flattening them between the palms and slapping them swiftly on the stone slab. Tonight, it seemed a futile thing to do as he sat with his legs stretched out on the uneven, crumbling floor.

It was only sitting this way that he could hold the stone slab firmly between the knees in order to roll the dough. He reached out for his well-worn rolling pin and rocked himself gently to and fro as he flattened the dough into thin pieces like the full moon. He felt himself hardening between the legs, but the sense of sudden release that calmed the boiling feelings, bubbling and bursting in his blood on other nights, eluded him. He sat there, empty, even after he had finished rolling all eighteen chappatis and tossed them back into the brass *thali*. Tonight, nothing happened.

He lifted himself off the floor with a sigh and walked up to the window at the back of the room. Dusk was falling quickly. The sky was streaked with angry orange welts that filled the night with a strange expectancy. There were sounds of gunfire in the distance. The earth quivered and threatened to burst into flames. The banana trees swayed their enormous leaves with a lazy grace. A solitary frog croaked awkwardly from a nearby pond and, finding no answer, fell silent.

About fifteen yards away, in a cabin directly opposite his window, sub-inspector Goswami was singing to himself as he prepared the rest of the meal. Hargovind brought his face close to the wooden slats barring the window and listened for other sounds. Then he slowly unbuttoned his trousers and, leaving it dangling on his hips, unconscious of what he was doing, he gripped himself fiercely in his hand. As the tension drained out of his muscles, he turned away from the window and stumbled into his bed. The coir ropes woven under the flat cotton mattress stretched and squeaked under his weight, the noise fading away as he grew still. Later, he heard Goswami's voice through his drowsiness, crying out his name, asking if he was all right.

"Yes, yes," replied Hargovind as he sat up on his bed and rubbed the sleep off his eyes. "I'm all right."

"Then why haven't you switched on the light, sir?" shouted Goswami, stepping out of his cabin and striding across the small clearance which was to them a sort of courtyard. "I'm ready with the *dhal, bhaji,* and the curry. Shall I try and find Sambhu Narain to come and join us?"

Hargovind quickly switched on the light and asked Goswami to wait a while longer for he hadn't quite finished the *chappatis*.

Goswami's slippers flopped under his feet as he climbed up the porch and stuck his head through the open door. He chuckled with amusement at the sight of the unbaked bread. "Let me give you a hand," he said,"or the curry will get cold."

They worked quickly under the glow of a single light bulb, its element burning red through the brown film covering the glass shell. Smoke from the open fire on which Hargovind cooked his meals spared nothing in the room. Everything was stained. Even linen and clothes sucked in the smell of oil and held it forever. Hargovind, and everyone else around, always reeked of these oils regardless of the soap they used for bathing.

Sambhu Narain completed another futile evening of conversation.

As the stall owners prepared to lower the shutters for the night, he took their leave and walked over to Hargovind's cabin. He asked the driver to buy himself a meal before the shops closed, and to stay with the jeep.

The meal was a quick, quiet affair. Goswami tried to make some conversation at first, saying what a shame it was that Hargovind was such a strict vegetarian, missing out on some of the best export-import items at the border, like *hilsa* fish for instance. He hoped Sambhu Narain liked the fish and, even without waiting for an answer, belched loudly in announcing his personal verdict. His shining belly protruded through his unbuttoned shirt. He massaged it caressingly and belched once more, exclaiming that everything they had confiscated that morning was first class. The fish, the rice, the vegetables, everything.

Sambhu Narain pushed the *thali* away from him gently an inch or two, signalling the end of his meal. He was a very small eater. But Goswami wasn't one to give up easily. "I fear we'll have a very busy day tomorrow," he said after he had finished. "One of the guards told me a while ago there are over a hundred people waiting behind the barrier already, waiting to come in."

"At this late hour?" asked Hargovind, surprised. He found the prospect of more work somewhat irritating. "Something strange is happening over there," he said, turning to Sambhu Narain. "Why do you think so many people are suddenly trying to cross the border, and at this hour?"

Sambhu Narain remained silent. But Goswami was quick with an answer. "They say the Muslims are burning their villages and the Pathans are butchering all the men."

Hargovind cast an amused look at his fellow officer. "They always say that." His voice was full of skepticism. "I've been hearing it from the day I came here. But there has been more gunfire today."

"Maybe they want to earn some extra money harvesting our crops this year," suggested Goswami.

Hargovind laughed and assured him the only harvest going on at that hour was in people's beds. Goswami laughed heartily at this joke until there were tears in his eyes. Trying to change the topic in deference to Sambhu Narain's presence, Hargovind asked abruptly,

"Did we collect much revenue this morning?"

"Revenue?" Goswami started laughing again. "A big zero," he said, indicating a hole with his thumb and forefinger. "I tell you, they are bringing nothing, absolutely nothing, across the border. The only thing of any value we confiscated this morning was nine kilos of fish. Nine kilos from a hundred and seventy men and women." Regaining his composure slowly, he asked, "Why don't you eat some? Your wife won't know. The little I have will go bad by tomorrow morning."

"Why don't you give it away to the two guards?" said Hargovind.

"They already have their share, sir. You don't want to give them ideas above their station, do you?" asked Goswami, somewhat stiffly.

"I suppose not," said Hargovind, smiling at Sambhu Narain. Goswami rose and walked out to the dark porch to empty the *thali* at the bottom of the steps. A favorite haunt of dogs, cats, and jackals, that was where both men dumped their garbage. Hargovind took the opportunity to tell Sambhu Narain again how everything was rotting around him, how he needed to stir up the authorities for a transfer from the place. From morning till noon, all year round, the air smelled of fish. All that the peasants seemed interested in carting across the border was fish. Hargovind was content to allow Goswami to make his own arrangements with the big Calcutta fish merchants regarding his commission. From time to time, the sub-inspector gave him a shirt, a *dhotie*, or a *sari*, to keep him happy and looking the other way. Hargovind had obliged because the alternatives seemed tiresome.

They heard a child crying in the night. There were no children in the neighborhood, so the sound must have come from the barrier. He wished Goswami would take what food was left and give it to the child perhaps. Hargovind confessed he would've asked the guards to unlock the barrier. But he was sure it would cost him his job.

Sambhu Narain was preparing to take his leave when Goswami stopped him once more. "You must come to the office with me, please," he said excitedly. "I have something special for you."

Sambhu Narain gathered his shawl around him, picked up the trident, and reluctantly agreed to follow. Hargovind expressed some surprise at seeing the lights in the office burning so late in the evening. Goswami, speaking very quickly, assured him it was all right. What he was about to bring them to was a special offering for the great *Nawab* of Bishnupur.

Goswami pushed open the door from outside. As they stepped into the office, he pointed to a young woman sitting on a bench, looking through a window at the night outside. She kept staring through the vertical bars, unconcerned over the presence of the three men inside the room.

"She came with two young lads looking for a van that might give them a ride to Calcutta," said Goswami softly. "But I've sent the lads away on an errand." There was a triumphant smile on his face. "Isn't she good? Isn't she fair?" he asked, looking expectantly into Sambhu Narain's face. He was not prepared for what he saw, a terrifying look of scorn and anger as Sambhu Narain clenched his teeth and his knuckles tightened around the trident in his hand.

The woman had heard their voices, and now turned her face towards them. The blood seemed to drain out of Sambhu Narain's face. The cold fury disappeared from his eyes. He took a step forward, then another, and the woman was in his arms in an instant. Sambhu Narain dropped the trident with a clatter and buried his face in her hair.

Goswami broke out into nervous laughter. All his suspicions about the lustful appetites of people of rank and wealth were coming true. Visions of advancement with Sambhu Narain's help opened up before his eyes. Sambhu Narain heard him laugh and released the woman. With a quick movement, he picked up the trident from the floor. "You bastard," he hissed at Goswami, "this is my daughter." As he pierced Goswami's heart with his trident, he said, "The devil take your soul."

Hargovind was quick to recover from the horror before his eyes. He slowly backed away to a corner and pulled out a gun from a secret recess behind a filing cabinet. "You fool," murmured Sambhu Narain between his teeth, and lunged at Hargovind with his trident. The three tiny spears unerringly went through his neck even before he had a chance to lift the gun off the wall.

Krishna stood there without flinching. Sambhu Narain put his arm around her, switched off the light in the office, and walked out towards the jeep parked near the deserted stalls. He said he wished, for Hargovind's sake at least, that there was a fairer law of survival, one that took into account human goodness, good intentions, merit, and ignorance. But unfortunately there wasn't, and of this he was deeply sorry.

Sixteen

As they approached the Benapole checkpost from the Indian side, it had the appearance of a quiet, ordinary night. The two guards on duty snored peacefully in their brick cabin a half a mile or so from the village. The jeep bringing Rahul and Hamid was under orders to return immediately. The driver let them off near the first row of shuttered shops and left. The sound of the jeep would normally have caused quite a stir in the village. Tonight, not a single door opened, not one person showed up. The air was full of rumours, it was a time to stay inside. There were reports of fresh trouble in Dacca, of Mujib being packed off to prison in Islamabad. The villagers were frightened, in a hurry to return to their homes before sundown. Once inside, it felt like a victory of sorts in even the poorest household. Another day lay behind.

Rahul and Hamid made their way towards a cluster of small cottages in the distance. One of these looked like it might be an office. They drew closer and began to hear sounds they hadn't heard entering the village. They climbed the steps to the office. Rahul saw two figures huddled together in the shadows of the verandah. As he pointed his flashlight at them, he found them shaking violently. "Please don't hurt us," they both whimpered. They were young boys, barely fifteen.

Hamid bent down and pulled them off the floor. "Nobody's going to hurt you," he said, and put a reassuring arm round each. Rahul pushed the door open and gasped as the beam of light fell on a thick pool of blood and gore congealing around two dead men.

Hamid switched on the light inside the room. "We came up from the river this evening with a lady," said one of the boys. "This man sent us on a wild goose chase for a bus." He pointed to the lifeless body of Goswami. "But now the lady's nowhere. She's gone," he cried in a shrill voice, tears running down his cheeks.

Rahul and Hamid stared at each other. The thought that crossed their minds at the same time was whether she could've done it. But that seemed impossible. Rahul walked over to a large desk and quickly shuffled through a sheaf of papers piled on top of it. He picked up a letter, examined it closely, picked up a few more, and said to Hamid, "How curious! these letters signed by the Revenue Secretary, S. Srinivasan. Wonder if it's the same person, the Serpent, who was hounding us three years ago."

"If so, we may have one more score to settle," said Hamid. But for the time being, he suggested they check out the other cottages before deciding what to do next about the missing woman. Where could she possibly be?

The four carefully picked their way through patches of tomatoes and cauliflowers growing behind the office. They came to the shack which served as Hargovind's cottage. This little cabin was almost identical to the two others, in one of which lived Goswami. The other was shared by the four guards assigned to the outpost. The four structures faced four directions and formed a small quadrangle between them. During the monsoons, the spot became a slushy and impassable sewer into which the four cabins drained gallons of rainwater off their sloping corrugated iron roofs. When dry, it boasted patches of marigold and spinach, basil and chillies, tomatoes and peas, cabbages and cauliflowers. Hargovind and Goswami had first claim on the produce, the guards shared the rest. Finding all three cottages empty, they circled back to the office and were halfway up when they heard approaching footsteps. A solitary man was running across the dirt road towards them. "*Huzur, huzur,*" he cried in a frightened voice, "they're breaking down the barrier."

Almost instantly, the sounds that had filled the night air earlier grew stronger. The man stopped running, and stood panting heavily in front of them. He was one of the guards, Surju Singh. He was shaking, his face ashen in the moonlight. Surju Singh didn't even realize that he wasn't speaking to Hargovind or Goswami. "The barrier can't stand it, *huzur*," he repeated hoarsely. "Thousands of them," he added, turning around and pointing in the direction of a dark cluster of trees to his right.

"Where are the other guards?" asked Rahul.

"There, *huzur*," replied Surju Singh, pointing to another apparition emerging from the darkness. This man was struggling to fasten his khaki trousers around his waist and trying to run at the same time. As he came up to the office, he wailed, "We are doomed, *huzur*. Thousands, thousands, there are thousands of them."

"We're in charge of the office here now." Rahul's strong voice was such as to suggest unmistakable power and authority to the two frantic guards.

"Call the other guards," ordered Hamid. The unexpected roughness in his voice terrified Surju Singh into instant obedience. The others were off duty, he said, but he'd make sure they came to the office right away.

"And find out where the jeep is," added Rahul threateningly.

The office was the closest building to the wooden barrier about four hundred yards away. Its entrance faced the pitted dirt road which started at the border and disappeared into the village of Benapole after half a mile or so. As they entered the office once more, they heard Surju Singh cry out from the road outside, "They're gone, *huzur*, the motherfuckers. Bet they're out drinking in the village." Hamid quickly stepped out to the verandah and ordered Surju to go find them, pointing imperiously in the direction of the village.

Surju Singh and his fellow guard started running towards the village. That very moment, the deluge was upon them. Like magic, a billowing stream of men, women, and children came round a bend and milled like stampeding cattle across the narrow road. From the edge of the verandah, Rahul and the others could hardly believe their eyes. The sheer force of the crowd pushing from behind carried the people forward. The force was too strong for those in front to even stop and look at Rahul and the others, let alone speak to them.

Their voices rose and fell like howling winds in a storm, each one screaming, wailing, pleading to be heard. Directly in front of Rahul, a woman suddenly cried out in a shrill voice. Rahul saw her only for an instant before she was gone, hurtling forward in a seething wave of bodies. Children called out to their mothers. Mothers cried out for their children. But there was no time to stop and look for lost ones. Like victims of a shipwreck, each one had nothing but himself to hang on to, bobbing and pitching and waiting for the sea to spend its fury or blow them off to distant shores.

The road was lined with trees on both sides, and the moonlight danced with gossamer steps over the fluttering leaves. But the silvery radiance could not transform the misery of the human forms below. Rahul stood transfixed by this sight until he heard Surju's voice once again. "*Huzur*," he cried, 'the jeep's gone too. The bastards have taken it to the village for sure."

Surju Singh was trying painfully to creep back up the office steps when he was pushed aside by three men. The three shook themselves out of the moving mass and climbed up to them. They were young men in their early twenties, their slim, muscled bodies naked to the waist. Proud and silent, they stood like rapiers thrust above the surging torrent below.

"What can we do for you?" asked Rahul.

"We are like broken pieces of straw," said one of the men, "fleeing before a storm." A companion's hand reached out peremptorily toward his lips and the man fell silent.

The second person now stepped closer to Rahul. "We're from the villages across the border," he said. "We need food and shelter."

"What's going on?" asked Hamid, unable to hide his curiosity.

The second man smiled and waved an arm at the people below. "Ask your eyes," he said.

"But surely you owe us an explanation for coming through the barrier in this way," said Surju Singh, overcome with a sudden burst of courage.

It was the turn of the third stranger to speak now. His voice was cold and hard as steel. "Come with me," he said, grabbing Surju by his collar and pulling him down the steps. Surju's tormentor did not pull him down to the road, but simply left him standing on the lowest step, still anchored to his cruel fingers. With his other hand, the man reached out into the crowd and pulled out an elderly man, grabbing him roughly by the shoulders. With a single effortless movement, he brought the two faces to within inches of each other. "Look at him," he hissed at Surju. The old man was sobbing and murmuring "Allah! Allah!" under his breath.

"There's your explanation," the young man told Surju mockingly. He let go of both and climbed back to the verandah. Turning now to Rahul, he said, "There are many sick and wounded among us. Can you give us some space to look after them and cook some food?"

Rahul pointed to the office and asked, "Will this do?"

Yes, they said, Allah be with you. Hamid added there were three cabins at the back which they were free to use as well. The men nodded their heads gratefully. "Come," said Hamid, "I'll show you the way. It'll be quicker if we went through the back door."

The men stepped past the two dead bodies as if they were of no consequence, an everyday sight. On the way out, Rahul switched on all the lights in the office and on the porch. A loud cheer went up from the crowd outside and several men came rushing up the steps. They saw the two bodies, quickly dumped them in the field outside, brought out a couple of buckets of water from the adjoining washroom, and cleaned up the stains as best they could before opening the door again to the others.

In a matter of minutes, the room and the porch overflowed with bodies. From the two desks in the room dangled the spindly legs of children and adolescents who had climbed upon them. Mothers placed their children on the three filing cabinets standing against the wall, full of official forms and useless files. From their precarious perches, the children gleefully waved their arms and legs and shouted encouragement to other less fortunate children who had to satisfy themselves pulling out the desk drawers. Unfortunately for them, most of the drawers were firmly jammed under the weight of those already sitting on the desks.

Rahul reached the first cabin and led the men inside. Once more, he switched on all the lights and another thunderous cheer rose from the people. Before they could spill out of the main road and engulf this cabin too, the three men rushed out and ordered the crowd to move on.

"You may find some vegetables in the courtyard," said Hamid, "but wait till the morning."

Then Rahul said he would take leave of the men and try and find a jeep which was somewhere in Benapole village. He and Hamid would return in the morning if possible, but they had one favour to ask of the men. "Could we leave these two young boys in your care?" asked Rahul.

"You are like brothers to us," one of the men said to Rahul, embracing him. Another embraced Hamid and said, "We'll look after their safety with our lives."

The space around the vegetable patch was already crawling with activity as Rahul and Hamid took their leave. They saw three children, hardly four years old, rummaging through the filth. One of them held in his hands the uneaten chappatis Goswami had thrown away that evening. The child's fearful eyes stared straight into Rahul's. The others were too busy with their search to notice either of them. They found the lights most welcome as they eagerly sifted through the trash to see what else they could find. Hamid asked where they were going, and Rahul replied that he honestly didn't know. They simply kept going.

It would've been easier for them to cut across the fields and go straight to the village. But they didn't know the way and certainly didn't relish the idea of stepping over snakes in the dark. So they took to the road, Rahul deciding it would be easier to stick to the shoulder. They had taken only a few steps in that direction when they were swallowed by the human sea and propelled forward in a state of near weightlessness. Countless faces sped past Rahul's eyes in a blur of black and white. Thousands of words assailed his ears in an endlessly booming echo, and the heavy, acrid smell of the poor slammed into his nostrils. Surging forward with this uprooted mass of humanity, mud and filth clinging to their bodies, Rahul felt a strange sense of freedom. It was as if he too had been cast adrift from a sinking ship and was now spinning helplessly towards a shore he couldn't even see. It didn't matter though. Strangely, a flicker of understanding came to him even here. For one fleeting moment, he saw himself less as an avenger, more as a part of the family of man.

Pushed by and pushing against this moving wall of bodies, both he and Hamid made good progress towards the village. An emaciated old woman flung out her wrinkled arms at Rahul and cried,""What'll happen to us, my son?" Rahul shouted back over the tumult. "Nothing, everything'll work out," he said almost joyously, regretting the unintended irony moments later. God, *Ram*, *Allah*, the names tumbled freely from their lips as the faces flashed by.

Once in the village, the people broke away into little eddies and thronged around the local population. They swirled around the huts which were now ablaze with lights. The whole village was awake and busy commiserating with the plight of their fleeing neighbours. Never before had the tea stalls opened their shutters so late in the night. The other merchants also threw open their doors and were soon so rapt in hair-raising tales of murder and rape they hardly seemed to care whether their customers paid or not.

Rahul and Hamid wandered aimlessly in and out of the crowds until they found themselves on the southern fringes of the village. They entered a small, dark alley reeking of toddy, urine, and disinfectant. The lane stretched no more than twenty yards. On both sides there stood mud-walled huts packed so close together that each seemed an extension of the other. Eight wooden doors to the left and right of them gave access to the local whores, seven in number, if one were to exclude four apprentices between the ages of nine and thirteen. At the far end of the alley, next to the open fields, there stood the local tavern, the only one officially licensed by the government. Directly behind this pathetic structure of wood, board, and bamboo, they suddenly saw the official jeep in the distance. Instead of making a dash for it, they stopped in front of the tavern, the earthen vats inside of which took care of the needs of all the local *goondas* and bums.

It had been hours since the last drink was quaffed inside the dump, and the last *chillum* of grass passed around. As was customary for that hour of the night, several inert bodies lay sprawled on both sides of the front door. Hamid flashed his light methodically on each blissful face. The last man sat up with a sudden start, sidled up to the creaking wall, and started to sing. "Summer and winter, summer and winter, riches and holiness," he sang. Then, with an angelic grin, he slumped upon his neighbour. The other body promptly resurrected itself, temporarily, with a loud invocation to the private parts of his companion's grandmother.

Rahul and Hamid walked away to the jeep, laughing. Sure enough, the two remaining guards were inside the vehicle, sprawled over one another, snoring like buffaloes. Surju Singh was standing uncertainly beside the two men. When he saw Rahul and Hamid approaching, he began to prod their anatomies roughly at tender points. As a result, the two figures disentangled themselves with some effort and promptly collapsed on the grass.

Rahul and Hamid settled down inside the jeep. The two drunks propped themselves up beside Surju Singh one last time and, holding on to each other for support, threw a wobbly salute at them. After that, they started walking back unsteadily towards the tavern.

"What shall we do?" asked Rahul.

"Shall we not try to find the woman who finished off the two men?"

"If she did, I think she can take care of herself," said Rahul. "Besides, where do we start looking?"

"Well, it's up to you to decide. Maybe we should head back for Jamal's camp."

"No," said Rahul, "not tonight." He switched on the ignition. "Tonight we wipe all scum off the face of the earth," he shouted delightedly.

Hamid started to laugh at this new twist to the night. He banged his head heavily against the dashboard as the jeep jerked forward. "Let's squash the Serpent once and for all," he said.

"A great idea," agreed Rahul. "Let's teach the swine a lesson."

The knock brought tears to Hamid's eyes. He continued laughing till the teardrops were actually trickling down his cheeks. Soon, both were laughing like men possessed. The jeep picked up speed as it climbed out of the field and entered the highway. The wind whistled in their faces, bringing tears to their eyes one moment, drying them the next. Now the roar of voices faded away, replaced by the roar of the wind.

"Ninety-six Hare Street won't open its doors till ten tomorrow," shouted Rahul.

"No government office opens before ten o'clock," Hamid shouted back.

"No government officer shows up before eleven," yelled Rahul.

"No government clerk signs the attendance before noon," yelled Hamid.

"Sonagachi," shouted Rahul. "Sonagachi tonight, Hamid. To Sonagachi."

"Oh no! not Sonagachi," groaned Hamid. He was embarrassed at the suggestion. It was hard to tell whether Rahul was pulling his leg. But ninety minutes and forty miles later, the jeep slowed down and cruised softly into a dimly lit street lined with empty rickshaws.

Some of the rickshaw pullers who were still awake converged upon the jeep as it came to a halt under a sputtering gas lamp. Soon the rickshaw pullers were joined by four shady characters. Each fished out of his pocket stained, old photographs of scantily clad women. They waved these pictures under Rahul's nose and started to speak all at the same time.

Chinese, want Chinese? Egyptian, fit to be Shah's wife. One terrific French girl, almost virgin.

Brushing them all aside with an impatient gesture, Rahul said, "Give us something local and inexpensive. Women of the soil."

"How much?" they asked in chorus.

"Ten rupees each for me and my friend," replied Rahul.

"You're not serious, are you?" asked Hamid in a hushed voice.

"Let me do the talking," said Rahul, a wicked glint in his eyes.

The crowd was starting to melt away amidst a murmur of disparaging remarks. "For ten rupees," sneered one of the pimps, "you get gonorrhoea, not sex."

But Rahul persisted. "Ten rupees," he said firmly.

"Make it fifteen," whispered one of the pimps who was hanging back, "and I'll really make it worth your while."

"Can she sing?" asked Rahul suddenly.

"Sing?" asked the pimp incredulously. "She has the voice of a nightingale."

"That's all we want," said Rahul, thrusting thirty rupees into the pimp's eager hand.

She was no raving beauty. The quality of her voice remained a mystery to them as she bared a crooked set of teeth in a tired smile. It was nearly dawn, she said, her hour of levitation, but she would oblige the gentlemen just the same. "What kept you so long?" she asked with feigned concern.

"We were gathering information for the government," replied Rahul with mock solemnity.

The plump and cheerful whore was equal to the occasion. "I feel honoured to serve you," she said, tossing off her bra. "All in all it has been a good night," she said. "The last person made me promise I'd vote for him so he could form the next government."

"Are we to believe we're numbers two and three tonight?" asked Rahul.

"Three and four," she corrected him. "The first man promised me a free trip round the world anytime I wanted. When I pressed him for details, he laughed and said he'd show me the best stamp collection in the city. What a bastard! Of course, I might be interested in becoming a minister now that the Prime Minister has shown the world what a woman can do. Too bad my friend the politician never offered me a seat in his cabinet." Then, turning to Rahul she asked in a honeyed voice, "What'll you be promising me, my good looking friends?"

"Official secrets only," replied Rahul. "But why don't you cover yourself up and make yours'" asked the woman, alarmed. "I don't go for anything kinky."

"We're not asking for anything kinky," said Rahul. "We only want to hear you sing. We heard you had a beautiful voice."

"I'm flattered," said the woman, wriggling back into her clothes. "But you'll give me some of your secrets, won't you?"

"Ah!" said Rahul, "even our Prime Minister won't know of it till after breakfast, maybe even after lunch."

"Get on with it," she urged, "or I may not sing."

"Well, then," began Rahul, "our border gates are wide open as your thighs. Our old friends are pouring across it by the thousand."

"Oh that," she said, yawning with disappointment as she walked over to the washbasin.

"Can't you see, woman'" cried Hamid after her, "your business will boom. We'll be lucky to be number twenty three on your list next month."

"It's not the business that worries me," she replied. "It's the competition."

"In America," said Rahul, "they say it's impossible to keep a good woman down." While the others let the observation sink in, Rahul pulled up a couple of pillows and, tossing one to Hamid, settled down to hear the woman sing.

The night passed quickly as she sang in an indifferent voice. But the words somehow created a gentle spell over them, and they were sorry to hear her stop when she was too tired to sing any more.

As they stepped out of her stifling room, they saw the darkness lifting outside. Like a softly forming navel of gold, the sun was slowly making its way out of the river, heading for the skies.

Seventeen

RAHUL AND Hamid drove through the deserted city streets for a long time until they reached a wayside restaurant which had just opened its doors. The cook already had two vessels of oil heating over open fires. He was frying *kachoris* in one and *jalebies* in the other. He welcomed his two customers warmly, inviting them to what he promised would be a princely breakfast created before their very eyes. They were both extremely hungry. The owner, who was the cook, found it impossible to keep pace with their appetites. "Slow down, brothers," he cried. "One would think this was the last meal before you mount the scaffold."

Hamid laughed back at him and said, "With food as wonderful as yours, you could hang me four times a day and I wouldn't complain." The owner was immensely flattered and decided to pour them glasses of hot, milky tea, all on the house.

After breakfast, they drove around some more until they found a street corner where a hunchbacked barber sat on four bricks, ready for business. Rahul remained in the jeep and watched the city yawn and stretch itself awake while Hamid shaved and had his hair trimmed. Holding a broken mirror in front of his face, Hamid moved his head from side to side and subjected the barber's artistry to a penetrating scrutiny. Then, signifying his approval with a loud grunt, he shook himself up from the bricks. The barber brushed off the loose hair from his neck, his face, and his clothes with a flailing towel badly in need of a wash. Hamid paid him and walked over to a cigarette vendor who had just opened his stall and was busy arranging his display of Coke and Fanta bottles.

The barber aired his towel, brushed the bricks clean, and was ready for Rahul. Springing out of the jeep, Rahul lowered himself gently on the bricks and stretched out his legs on the sidewalk. With an ancient brush whose bristles had worn off to within half an inch of its base, the barber worked up a furious lather on his face. Rahul shut his mind to everything that lay beyond the pores of his skin as the man lightly pinched a corner of his cheek and brought the equally ancient razor smoothly down his face. He scraped off the lather on the back of his wrist and murmured with pride, "German."

Before turning his attention to Rahul's somewhat corrugated chin, the man fumbled through the street barber's ubiquitous black box and pulled out a shining whetstone. After several flashy sweeps of his hand on the stone, he lowered the razor once more on Rahul's face. Rahul could've swooned with ecstasy if only his back hadn't begun to tire. The smooth lump of alum rubbing against his skin, even the dark towel reeking of sweat and soap suds, all filled him with pleasure. The barber was a good salesman and promised him even greater joy. Rahul agreed to have his ears cleaned.

Delving back into his black box once more, the barber produced a wad of cotton wool and a fearsome array of long, blunt needles, each about six inches long. When the last chunks of wax had been dredged out, the barber produced a bottle of perfume which he waved with great flourish in front of Rahul's half-shut eyes. Then, soaking two pieces of cotton wool in the perfume, he stuffed the two pellets into Rahul's ears.

Overpowered by the smell, Hamid walked over and wanted to see the perfume bottle. He found on it a crude label showing a well-dressed man leaning suggestively over a woman reclining awkwardly on a sofa. Under the picture, the brand-name printed in bold letters: LOVE-FAIL-ME-NOT. Hamid started to walk away, trying to escape the fragrance. The barber assured him it was the finest perfume to come out of the holy city of Benares.

Rahul lingered. He now wanted to have his head massaged. The barber obligingly poured a generous quantity of warm coconut oil on his head, rubbed it into his scalp with a quick, circular motion of the fingers, then patted his head, tugged at the hair, and squeezed his skull. Rahul surrendered himself to the seductive rhythms in his brain. When he opened his eyes at the end of it all, he saw the houses leaning over him across the sidewalk, the ornate balconies threatening to topple over his head. He felt reluctant to leave, and hoped the mansions would remain pinned to the earth longer than he was destined to remain under his barber's hands.

While Rahul and Hamid played the fool at the barbershop and contemplated their next move, the Revenue Secretary, Mr. Srinivasan, dipped his stainless steel spoon in his stainless steel breakfast bowl and rocked his head gently from left to right. This indicated his pleasure over the *uppma* his wife Annama had served that morning. He liked it the way only his wife could cook, spiked with cinnamon and bay leaves, sprinkled over with fresh, moist, shredded coconut and coriander. Annama sat in front of him dutifully and gazed out of the apartment at the cloudless sky pressing down on a bed of green treetops. Below this green mass lay the drab, dusty city she hated.

Still, she was grateful for their tenth floor apartment and for the illusion it created of rural vegetation seen from a great height. It brought her close to her childhood in Kerala where everything was green regardless of whether one stood on the ground or on the hills. Hers had been a happy childhood there, but she didn't feel the same way about her own children. They seemed safe enough at that hour, playing with their *ayah* in the garden below. But only a brick wall separated them from the street outside where it was swarming with beggars, ruffians, and degenerates of every description, and uncollected garbage stewing in open pits. And the menace of the terrible Naxalites, had it not been for the splendid job her husband had done in an earlier assignment in ridding the city of their curse.

Annama would've liked the children to be with her all day, sharing with her the endless view of the trees to the west. A view broken only by the faint grey incision of the Hooghly working its way sluggishly to the sea. It was all so serene and peaceful that she wanted to share it oftener with them. But she knew it was a childish wish. Now the day was about to unfold with her husband finishing his breakfast, going for his shower, followed by a last searching look at the pages of the *Statesman,* and off to Hare Street. The children would wave him goodbye and grumble as the *ayah* pushed them into the elevator and brought them back to the apartment.

Mornings were so sacred to Mr. Srinivasan that he demanded absolute peace. Annama and the *ayah* cooperated by getting the children ready so they would be out of the apartment before Mr. Srinivasan picked up his pipe and settled down on the sofa with his morning papers. This was also the hour of the day when the servants began mopping up the bathroom floor and laid out Mr. Srinivasan's clothes or polished his shoes. They knew too well it was imperative they remain discreetly out of his sight.

When he first moved to Calcutta four years ago, he found the servants freely parading up and down the apartment. At first he tolerated them, for he had been told that good, reliable servants were hard to come by. One day, when one of the servants slipped on the polished floor and crashed into an ivory Buddha, it was the end of his tolerance. "Wherever I look I see thieves and imbeciles," he complained angrily. "In my home, in my office. I have no time to think. It's one phonecall after another, one favour after another, one disaster after another." He then started to take a strip off the poor servant and banished him from his sight, forever. Annama not only had to pacify her husband but also mollify the servant who felt he had been treated unfairly and threatened to leave. From that day onwards, Mr. Srinivasan had his mornings all to himself, so he could marshal his thoughts and cultivate the serenity he needed to face the day's complexities.

"This was very good," he said, smiling at his wife, pushing aside the empty bowl.

"I didn't put too much milk today," she replied, "because I know you like it a bit gritty."

"Yes," said her husband, lapsing into a final contemplation of what remained of the morning. Then the telephone began to ring.

Husband and wife quickly exchanged glances, trying to decide who would pick up the receiver. Since Mr. Srinivasan disliked phonecalls in the morning - it being another of his pet aversions - another intrusion upon the carefully guarded sanctity of his mornings, Annama received the call. When she called out from the living room, "It's Brigadier Jammail Singh," Mr. Srinivasan stood up in alarm, sensing trouble.

Annama handed him the receiver, walked back to the window, and reminded herself she should ask for the car after it had dropped the children at school. There was a bridge party at Mrs. Tarafdar's. Afterwards, maybe she'd return home and read a book or sleep for an hour or two until the children came back. Perhaps she could even persuade her husband to go to *The Bridge on the River Kwai* at the club. Although the highlights of the day did not excite her unduly, they were at least sufficient to protect her against boredom, which was one thing she dreaded. Her attention was suddenly drawn to her husband's voice, unusually high pitched and excited as he talked on the telephone. He hung up just as she walked through the door into the living room. He met her questioning stare with angry eyes. "More trouble," he said disgustedly.

In answer to Annama's question, he mentioned something happening at the Benapole checkpost. The Brigadier had called to find out if he had heard anything. Since the Brigadier had himself seen hundreds of men and women pouring out of Benapole into the main highway, Mr. Srinivasan decided to call the checkpost before the army started calling up the Chief Minister and God knows who else. He flipped through the pages of the phonebook and when he found the number he was looking for, carefully circled it with a pencil permanently attached to the book with a cord. He made the call.

"I want Inspector Hargovind Sinha," he barked angrily into the mouthpiece. A burst of sounds greeted him from the other end, adding to his irritation.

Everything was far from silent at the other end, for there was coming through the receiver many faint voices accompanied by the sound of objects crashing and being dragged across the floor, of children wailing and mothers screaming. When mixed together and filtered through the slender telephone wires, it began to sound like the end of the world. To Mr. Srinivasan, the sounds were meaningless but ominous. His fury kept on mounting, but the voice he sought wasn't there.

Only Surju Singh was there. Confused and forlorn, he had crawled back to the office and now sat quietly on the steps. He found the pandemonium raging around him somewhat scary. He ran the palm of his hand over the stubble on his face. He felt poor and dispossessed, the more so since one of the young men persuaded him to give up his cabin. Now he didn't even have a bed to sleep on. A short distance away, another guard, Oste Bahadur, sat and dozed against the wall. Once in a while, he would wake up with a start, his lolling head swinging away from the support of the wall and lurching towards the floor. When awakened, he'd tighten his grip on the rifle cradled uselessly on his lap. He would slowly doze off again.

Neither Surju nor Oste heard the phone ring, and the peasants packed in the office hadn't the slightest idea what to do with a phonecall. The first person to pick up the ringing receiver looked at it suspiciously for some time, drew up the earpiece to his mouth, then replaced it gingerly back to its original position on the cradle. "Better leave those infernal things alone," advised a wise old man. "They can sometimes give out a charge of electricity."

Mr. Srinivasan swore and raged and dialed once more. When the telephone rang this second time, no one seemed interested in picking it up. So the phone kept on ringing until a fearless young fellow, no more than four years old, ambled up to the instrument unobserved, lifted up the receiver, and filled it with his complete repertoire of words and sounds. As the *oooo-dagoo-dagoo-oooo* sounds rose above the other noises and poured into his ears, the expression on Mr. Srinivasan's face led his wife to fear he might be on the verge of an apopleptic seizure. But the boy's parents had meanwhile pounced upon the wayward child, pulled away the receiver from his hands, and replaced it once more where it belonged.

This child had already caused enough damage around the office and so was deservedly pulled away by his ear from the vicinity of the phone. Back in the washroom, this same child had brought a wall-type cistern crashing down when he suspended himself on the long, dangling chain and decided to swing to and fro with it. The heavy cast-iron cistern barely missed the child as it broke loose from its moorings on the wall and fell on the floor. His parents were determined to avoid further catastrophe.

Mr. Srinivasan once again found the phone dead in his hand. He next proceeded to take two major steps. Since his jaws had locked themselves in rage, it took a powerful effort of his will to unloosen them before his dentures became permanently damaged. Next, he summoned what was left of his patience and stopped himself from picking up the telephone, receiver and all, and flinging it out through the window. Having averted these two disasters, he called Benapole once more.

Word eventually went round to one of the young men, whom Surju immediately recognized as one of his tormentors, that the phone was ringing or had developed some noisy malfunction. He came running from the cabin next door just in time to prevent another attack from overcoming Mr. Srinivasan. "Hello," he said, picking up the receiver.

"Who are you?" shouted Mr. Srinivasan rudely.

"My name is Iqbal Ahmed," replied the stranger. "Can I be of any help to you?"

The sudden transition from infernal chaos to a measured, educated accent confused Mr. Srinivasan. But he hadn't spent two summers at the Administrative Staff Training College in vain. So, after a brief pause sufficient to help him regain his composure, he said, "I should be grateful if you could call Inspector Sinha." Adding, as an afterthought," That is, if I have the correct number for the checkpost at Benapole."

"You have indeed," replied Iqbal Ahmed. "Unfortunately, there's no inspector here. Perhaps you'd care to speak to someone else."

Once more, Mr. Srinivasan was beginning to lose his mind. "Is there a person by the name of Go-Go-Goswami there?" he stammered.

"There is someone here," replied Iqbal, "but I don't know his name." Iqbal would get him to speak to Mr. Srinivasan.

Surju still hadn't heard the phone, but that was because his mind was far away. In fact, at that moment it was crowded with dirty thoughts. In front of the office, on the far side of the road, was a tubewell. Two women sat in front of it rinsing some pots and pans. A third, obviously younger, leaned against the metal arm and pumped it vigorously with both hands. In the process, the free end of her sari trailed away from her shoulders and lay bunched up at the elbow, thereby exposing one glistening side of a single tapering breast. Surju's assessment of the woman's youth was supported by solid evidence, gathered in his imagination as he reached out with invisible fingers and tested the firmness and suppleness of her quivering body. Unfortunately, the stranger who had shaken him by the collar the night before now shook him out of this pleasant reverie as well. "Someone wants you on the phone," said Iqbal.

"Oh!" said Surju, hoisting himself up from the floor. Then, noticing Oste Bahadur asleep against the wall, he bent down and shook him awake. "Follow me," Surju told him. Oste Bahadur tightened his grip on the rifle and stood up. Surju motioned to him to follow. Having left behind his own rifle the night before, Surju wasn't going to be caught defenceless in the present situation. These were all beef-eating Muslims around him, and he had grown up with a congenital suspicion towards all Allah's believers.

His voice was small and timid as he picked up the phone and asked, "Hello! what do you want?" When the voice at the other end announced imperiously that it was Mr. Srinivasan, the Revenue Secretary, Surju Singh lost his voice altogether. He turned his head and looked at Iqbal Ahmed helplessly. Seeing his plight, Iqbal took the receiver away from him.

"What's going on there?" screamed Mr. Srinivasan.

"You fool," said Iqbal Ahmed, and put the phone down.

Mr. Srinivasan began to shake like a madman this time. Through bitter experience, Annama had learned to leave her husband alone in such moments of crisis. Like the servants, she too relegated herself to a dumb role in the background. The one difference was that she, unlike the servants, had nothing to do except go back to her view from the window.

For the first time in a brilliant career, Mr. Srinivasan felt he had failed, admittedly through no fault of his. But the perception of a perfect, closely-knit department, once shattered, would be very difficult to restore. The army knew, maybe half the world knew, what he should've been the first to know, the first to communicate to the powers above. Like the ignorant peasants, he too had his little gods. When the telephone rang a moment later and he heard the voice of one of them, the Chief Secretary this time, Mr. Srinivasan was certain his gods had turned against him. Mr. Patnaik, at the other end, made no secret of his irritation. "What's this I hear, Srinivasan?" he asked. "Is it true?"

"Very true, sir," answered Mr. Srinivasan seriously. "I've been trying to reach you, sir,' he said, 'but these damned cross-connections. . . ."

"The telephones stink," interrupted Mr. Patnaik, "but thank God somebody managed to get through to me. Caught me on the twelfth with a message, and, believe you me, I was playing well below my handicap."

"That's wonderful. We must have a game some time." Then, somewhat sadly, Mr. Srinivasan added, "I'm sorry my men couldn't hold out, sir. I understand several thousand Pakistanis have crossed our borders illegally since last night."

"There's nothing to apologize about, my dear chap. I quite understand." Mr. Patnaik's voice was definitely friendly now. "We have a checkpost there, not a fortress," he added consolingly.

Mr. Srinivasan agreed wholeheartedly but did not allow his professional instincts to desert him altogether. He needed to know where the Chief Secretary had found his information. "No doubt Brigadier Singh has informed you of the position, sir?" he asked. Pleased with the information he needed, he promptly busied himself with strategies for the future. "I suggest we seal the border immediately, sir," he said, "and then arrange for the people to go back."

"Splendid idea," agreed Mr. Patnaik. "The Brigadier is closest to Benapole. I'll call him right away."

Mr. Srinivasan, now warming up to the subject, had other splendid ideas still. He suggested they drive out and see the situation for themselves before reporting to New Delhi. They ended the conversation agreeing to meet at the Secretariat at eleven.

Mr. Srinivasan knew his gods were with him. He stepped into his shower with an easier mind. The tiny jets of water drummed on the floor, surrounding him in a hollow of sound, steam, and spray. Slowly, he began to recover the peace he loved so jealously.

It was in the shower that he led his mind to distant reaches of thought and speculation, undisturbed and unobserved. Here he'd arrive at the most difficult decisions, confident in his ultimate vindication as an uncompromising public servant. That is all that mattered to him in life. He wished he could carry this nobility of purpose intact through the day. He needed it most in his office where every action of his subordinates seemed calculated to offend, every hour of bureaucratic delay purposely engineered to discredit his noblest ideals of service and test his patience in the face of parochial hostility and middle class militancy.

Annama, who was waiting for him in the living room, felt relieved to see him looking much better. She would've liked to know what had upset him earlier, but was afraid that any curious remark about his work would offend him. Instead, she asked if she might have the car for a while after the children had been dropped off at school. Mr. Srinivasan pretended he had just remembered his appointment with the Chief Secretary and felt sorry he couldn't part with the car all day. Perhaps one of the servants could take the children in a taxi, and perhaps she could plan to do the following day whatever it was she wanted to do today.

Perhaps she could, thought Annama, as Mr. Srinivasan took a tentative step towards the door. At that moment, as if by a pre-arranged signal, one of the servants stepped out of the background with his briefcase and took up position five feet behind him. When all was ready, master and servant swept majestically out of the room.

A short drive later, Mr. Srinivasan again marched down the corridor of the Secretariat and strode into his office. He looked neither to the left nor right. Whenever he walked in and out of his room, he was in the habit of keeping his eyes fixed on an invisible spot directly ahead of his nose so he wouldn't catch the eye of anyone waiting to see him. Experience had taught him that eye contact diminished objectivity. He therefore didn't see Rahul and Hamid sitting on a long wooden bench placed in the corridor directly outside his door, a seat reserved for less important visitors waiting to see the Revenue Secretary.

It was also the seat used by Mr. Srinivasan's bearer who leapt out of the lotus position at the sound of his approaching footsteps. He stood to attention while concealing a half smoked *biri* behind his back. As soon as Mr. Srinivasan disappeared behind the green curtain, he took two more quick puffs on the *biri*, knocked off the burning head with a deft flick of his finger, and carefully secreted the remaining piece in a crack at the far end of the bench. He then turned to Rahul and waved a little slip of paper in his face. Rahul had written the name, Hargovind Sinha, on the slip. The bearer flashed him an ingratiating smile which was meant to suggest he would ensure the boss saw them as soon as possible. Then, withdrawing his hand from under Rahul's nose, he straightened himself to a full five feet five and walked into Mr. Srinivasan's office with soft, humble footsteps which seemed totally out of character.

There was no longer any doubt in Rahul's mind. This was the man. This was the Serpent who had terrorized and killed his comrades three years ago.

"Send them in," said Mr. Srinivasan, eager to get on with the business of the day. He didn't bother to look either at the bearer or the slip of paper he held in his outstretched hand. Before retreating from his master's presence, the bearer lifted a brass paper-weight and slipped the scrap of paper under it.

"You can go in now," he told Rahul and Hamid, in a tone suggesting again that the master would never have granted them the audience had the bearer not interceded on their behalf. His eyes measured Rahul slyly, calculating what he might expect as a tip at the end of the interview.

Rahul and Hamid walked the length of the room and were standing directly in front of his desk before Mr. Srinivasan lifted his eyes from his papers and saw them. He picked up the slip from under the paper-weight to check their names. As soon as he glanced at the paper, an expression of terrible anger clouded his face. "Which one of you is Inspector Sinha?" he asked.

Rahul identified himself as Hargovind. Mr. Srinivasan looked at him with withering scorn and said, "You rascal, how dare you show your cowardly face in front of me?" Then he was the cold professional once more. "I'm busy right now, Inspector," he said. "Come back tomorrow."

Seeing neither of them making a move towards the door, Mr. Srinivasan waved them away with his hand. "Go away, go away," he said. "I'll have to place you under suspension for grave dereliction of duty," he added as a threat.

Rahul quietly walked over to the side of the large desk. Mr. Srinivasan looked up at him, puzzled and surprised. "Your hands are covered with blood, you sanctimonious bastard," said Rahul, looking down into his eyes. "You ought to be shot for all the innocent lives you destroyed as Home Secretary," he said, pulling out his revolver and pointing it to his heart.

Mr. Srinivasan's eyes were like those of a frightened animal. But he had his wits around him still. He tried to move his fingers towards the buzzer.

"Stop," cried Hamid.

"You worm," said Rahul. "A bullet's too good to waste on you." He lifted the pistol and whipped the Revenue Secretary sharply across the temple. Mr. Srinivasan's eyes rolled over once, and then he crumpled unconscious on his desk.

Rahul and Hamid stepped out of the office and ran straight into the bearer's outstretched hand. They both stopped. Rahul took a step forward and saw a look of fear come over the man's face, fear that they might escape without giving him his due. The greedy smile had been replaced by a pitiful, imploring look. Rahul pulled out a rupee note which the bearer snatched out of his fingers. He had no further interest in the visitors. He perched himself back on the bench without even a word of thanks and proceeded to re-light his *biri*.

Eighteen

There seemed no reason for them to stay any longer in Calcutta. Rahul and Hamid headed straight for Jamal's camp. When he found time to reflect over his sudden meeting with Saira, Hamid wasn't sure if she told him of the death of the breastless one simply to get him out of Jessore. Who then was the woman the villagers told him about? He wasted no time in getting together with the two survivors from his last expedition and planning another trip to Jessore. They had invested so much of their energies in trying to find Krishna that Rahul couldn't bring himself to stop him.

He and Hamid decided to come into Jessore from different directions to arouse as little suspicion as possible. They would watch the house on Casuarina Avenue carefully and go in only when satisfied it was safe. They put on captured Pakistani army uniforms this time, and Hamid felt little fear as he boldly walked down Casuarina Avenue and knocked on the front door. His two companions followed him cautiously, armed and watchful.

It was not Saira who opened the door, but another woman in a *burqah*. "Please wait," she said, as she led them through the door and disappeared inside the house. She took a long time coming back, and Hamid and his nervous companions thought they heard the sound of heavy footsteps in the rooms upstairs. But their fears vanished as soon as Saira walked into the room, still clad in a *burqah*.

She spoke in an uncommonly loud voice, welcoming them, asking them if they would like some lemon water. But as she walked past Hamid she dropped her voice suddenly. "Oh! why did you come back, you fool?" she whispered. "There's no escape this time."

It was at this moment that the young man who had once been their guide to Jessore rushed into the room. He was not alone. Of the five uniformed men accompanying him, one was Brigadier Iftikar Ali of the Sind Regiment. They stormed into the room and pounced gleefully upon the three men. There was no occasion for any heroics as three men deftly tied their hands while a fourth waved his stengun over their heads. "What do we do with them, Brigadier?" asked the young civilian.

"What do I care?" replied Iftikar Ali with a shrug. With that he turned towards the veiled woman and put his swarthy arm around her. Then, whispering to themselves, the two turned their backs to the men and returned upstairs.

"Let's take them to the square for some fun first," suggested the young man to the others. And so they did.

There was an old well in the square. Nobody could remember when it had last yielded any water. The mouth of the well was covered over with a massive slab of concrete. The young men of the city gathered here every evening to smoke, to argue, to stare at passers by. When they had nothing else to do, they scrawled their names on the concrete with chalk, charcoal, and anything else capable of leaving an impression. Some had even tried to chisel their names on the surface. But the chisels either lost their edge or the hands grew tired before the names could be finished. Most names remained incomplete, random letters frozen without a context. The grooves were old and worn. Hardly anyone, it seemed, had tried to chisel their names in recent years.

In the early days of the West Pakistani crackdown, the concrete mysteriously blossomed each night with words of patriotism and hate. Of late, however, it was just another weather beaten stone face with nothing to say. Although the well was dry and sealed, the pillars and the arms which held the pulley still survived. In times less violent, street hawkers vied with each other every morning for this spot. If someone selling men's underwear got to the place first, the beam would soon be covered with a fluttering display of vests and briefs. On other days, there might be old issues of Indian magazines, women's and movie magazines flapping in the air, their dog-eared covers yellowing in the sun. One would find current newspapers and magazines on the concrete below. These days, there were no newspapers and no vendors.

In fact, there was no one in the square when they marched Hamid and the two boys to the old well. They tied the boys to the pillars. "They are our own men, brothers," said the young man, a crooked smile lighting up his face. "Traitors no doubt, but we'll be generous with them." He looked around with satisfaction at the small crowd which was slowly beginning to form in front of them. "But you," he cried, bringing his face close to Hamid's, "you're a mystery to us. You choose to leave your home and meddle in our affairs. You we'll treat as our special guest."

Hamid spat in the man's face and was rewarded with a kick in the groin.

While separate arrangements were being made for them, the square filled up quickly. Young men were conspicuous by their absence. Those present were either children in their teens or men bent with age. They huddled together in hushed silence. If they felt anything for the three men, they didn't show it in their faces. Only a faint murmur rippled through the crowd as the soldiers stripped Hamid of everything but his vest and underwear, then swiftly hoisted him by his legs and suspended him from the centre of the beam.

"Here, you cur," the man screamed at Hamid. "See how we deal with our Indian friends." The loose vest had fallen over Hamid's face. With a violent jerk, the young man tore it off his shoulders. "Sheikh Mujib is dead, my brothers," he cried this time. "A new Pakistan waits for us, but not for traitors." With that, he pulled out an evil looking knife and coolly gouged out a piece of Hamid's thigh. Not once did he scream, not a sound escaped his lips as the man hacked whimsically at other parts of his body.

When Hamid was nearly dead, and certainly no longer conscious, the dripping knife flashed in a huge arc and ripped open his stomach. The few stray dogs that were so long sniffing at the spectacle from a distance now rushed madly at the body as Hamid's entrails tumbled into the blood gushing over the concrete slab.

One by one, the men in the square began to turn away. Many of the children were already whimpering on their father's shoulders. The two boys had died a thousand deaths already. The Pakistanis untied them and pushed them roughly into a waiting jeep. Then they drove away in the direction of the cantonment.

Nineteen

At the very last moment, just as he was about to leave for Jessore, Jamal Hussain decided to come along with Rahul. They had been warned not to take any chances with Mukti Bahini snipers who might have mistaken them for Pakistani soldiers. Seeing there was no better disguise than their stolen Pakistani uniforms, the last two in the camp, they took care to skirt the villages along the way and came directly to Jessore. It was inevitable that they should pass the square where the last gentle rays of the sun still bathed the swollen and mutilated body hanging by the ankles.

It was his hair that gave Hamid away. But after the first gut-wrenching moment of recognition, Rahul felt nothing. It was as if he had suddenly hardened and dried up inside.

If he felt sorry at all it was only because he would no longer be able to look into Hamid's strange eyes. Set deep inside his face, they were almost lost in the shadows of his sweeping eyelashes and the dark sensuousness of his thick eyebrows. His hair, equally dark, ungroomed, spilled over half his forehead and further deepened the gloom surrounding those eyes. But it was easy to miss them. Sometimes, it was almost a relief to have missed them. Those who paused to peer into the gloom probably found themselves fascinated, frightened, or even repelled. Deep inside the shadows, there moved two points, small and incandescent, tempting the curious down a maze of mystery and passion that led, for those who didn't know him, to nowhere. They were extraordinary eyes, not penetrating in themselves, yet possessing the singular power to bewilder any stranger. Locked inside, as in a silent tomb, there lurked a spirit bursting with untold tales of adventure and excitement. It was as if Hamid's eyes held the unflinching wonder of a child who bides his time, heedless of life's terrors that await him.

Jamal Hussain looked at Rahul enquiringly, wondering perhaps if there was any need to go further. Others had already questioned why Rahul was endangering his life in the first place. "If Saira is to be brought back," said one of his comrades, "surely Hamid was the person to do it."

Rahul had smiled and said to him, "You don't seem to realize our destinies are woven together." Even Jamal Hussain saw no point in arguing. There was a small debt to Rahul and Hamid that he himself wanted to repay. So, rather than let him go alone, he decided to come along.

It was a long time before Rahul said a word. Then, since Jamal knew the city well, he asked him to lead him quickly to the house on Casuarina Avenue. He needed to find this woman, for the peace of Hamid's soul if not his own.

Jamal had no trouble finding his way around Jessore. "It's not a respectable house we're going to," he said. "I didn't want to break Hamid's heart by telling him everything."

"Doesn't make any difference now," said Rahul.

Thanks to their uniforms, they had no problem getting inside the house. One look, and Rahul knew they had entered a brothel, far more elegant than the one he and Hamid visited in Sonagachi. It was evening, and the women, resplendent without their *burqahs*, were obviously getting ready to begin their entertainment.

"You must be new around here," said the solitary man in their midst.

"Yes," replied Rahul, "we've just been transferred from Dacca."

"Ah! welcome," said the young man. "I must greet you with some tea and *halwa*." Eager to ingratiate himself with the visitors, the man quickly left the room to prepare tea.

Rahul wasted no time. "And which one of you is Saira?" he asked, looking from one pretty face to the other.

"I am," replied one of the women, after a moment's hesitation.

She was beautiful all right, thought Rahul. But a little used, a little coarse. His sense of loyalty to his friend wouldn't let him judge her too harshly. "Could I have a word with you in private?" he asked.

The other women giggled nervously. "Yes," said Saira, as she stood up from the sofa and led him to an adjoining room.

Rahul knew he had little time to lose. Since the women were ready to entertain guests, it meant other Pakistanis could drop by any moment. In fact, as he was following Saira out of the room, he felt a gnawing sense of doubt about her present loyalties. She seemed too much at home in the whorehouse. He therefore pushed aside the idea of revealing his identity to her, not for the time being at any rate. He would have to devise some clever subterfuge, thought Rahul, as he was leaving the room.

Jamal Hussain began tapping the coffee table and whistling to himself. He was starting to feel a little nervous himself. "It's been an exciting day, hasn't it?" asked one of the women, trying to break the ice.

"Yes," replied Jamal Hussain, "quite a day."

"It's all to the credit of Saira," said another woman. "It was she who tipped us off about the Indian spies. She was feeling terrible ever since she let them get away once before."

"Actually'" said the first woman, "Rizvi, our friend making the tea, played a big part too."

Jamal had already stopped whistling, now he abandoned the tapping as well. "Are you talking about the fellow cut up in the square?"

"Yes, yes." replied one of the women, "he was one of them." She turned to her friend and speculated he was probably the leader. "I'm told it's a terrible sight," she said, with a shiver and a grimace to emphasize her point.

Rahul and Saira returned to the room at this moment. "We're going out for a walk," said Rahul with a shy smile. "It's going to be such a beautiful night outside."

"I might join you a little later," said Jamal.

As Rahul and Saira opened the front door and stepped into the evening, Jamal stood up. He stretched himself and casually started to walk towards the kitchen. He hadn't gone very far before he ran into Rizvi returning with a tray loaded with cups of tea and plates of *halvah*. Something about the expression on Jamal's face frightened him. Sensing danger, cowering a little, he started to say, "Here's your. . . ." But Jamal didn't give him a chance to finish the sentence. A single shot rang out and Rizvi fell back against the door. The women screamed once and covered their mouths with their hands as they watched Jamal put his gun back in its holster and walk out of the house.

He soon caught up with Saira and Rahul. They heard his approaching footsteps and had stopped to wait for him.

"What was that?" asked Rahul, cautious and wary. Saira was also staring at him with fear and suspicion.

"Just an accident," said Jamal calmly. "Could I have a quick word with you," he said to Rahul, drawing him apart from Saira and whispering animatedly with him for a moment.

Rahul looked troubled. "I must get the truth from her," he said, "before we do anything."

Jamal grew impatient. He warned Rahul he wouldn't be able to keep up the charade indefinitely. Rahul suggested they just keep walking towards Hasnabad, adding that he hoped the way wouldn't prove too complicated. Jamal wished him luck in persuading Saira to walk with him, and Rahul thanked him for letting him handle the matter his own way. "I'll follow you out of sight," said Jamal, dropping back and allowing Rahul to catch up with Saira.

They walked together in silence for a long while until Saira began to complain she was cold and wondered if they shouldn't be turning back. Rahul looked behind him and saw Jamal had slipped into the shadows. "No, not yet," said Rahul, looking up at the gorgeous evening sky. "Let's walk a little bit longer."

As soon as they had turned off from Casuarina Avenue and gone some distance along the path leading to the river, Rahul told Saira he had come from the village of Hazariganj where the people loved her and wanted her back. He avoided any reference to Hamid, for they were still too close to the enemy for him to take any chances.

He thought he was tough enough to wipe Hamid completely out of his mind. He would try to be as objective as possible. Yet, he was beginning to feel Hamid was indeed a force to reckon with in his mind, with every step he took, every action he contemplated.

Saira didn't protest about having to walk, realizing perhaps it would be futile to argue with an armed man. She didn't say anything either at the mention of her village, Hazariganj. She just kept on walking.

It grew darker. Not a soul seemed to be around any more. The town appeared to be obeying an unwritten curfew. From its outer perimeter, Jessore looked eerie, a city without people or lights. They left the city behind, and still they continued to walk in silence.

There now lay some flat country ahead of them, but it became increasingly difficult to walk through the wild grass and the uneven ground that lay beneath it. Soon they found themselves in the rice fields, and Saira began to show signs of weariness. She was having trouble balancing herself in the mud, so she threw away her leather sandals since they were useless in the slush. With every step, the mud squirted through her toes like frosting coming down on a cake. The ooze climbing up to her ankles felt cool and soothing. Suddenly, Saira broke her silence to say she wished she could stand there forever, smelling the dank earth, counting the ripe grains scattering on her body.

The paddy was ready for harvest. But the war had driven away the farmers. Some had been burnt alive with their villages. Others now wandered through choking refugee camps across the Indian border. Swollen with life, bending under the grains, the fields rose and fell in the breeze, groaning for deliverance like a woman with child.

Suddenly, they saw the river ahead of them, burnished and circumspect like a bayonet lowered for the charge. They paused at the edge of the paddy field and saw the river in its fullness. Rahul felt no sense of elation, as he usually did, at the sight of water. Tonight, it seemed to promise nothing, least of all escape and freedom. It merely cut through an orbit of violence and destruction which Rahul, tired and lonely, wished he could put behind him.

She stood there beside Rahul, holding on to his shoulder for support. A single ear of paddy moved across Saira's face. She was about to push it aside and move forward, when she stopped. She tried to tear it off, but finding it impossible to do so with one hand, bit off the ear from the stalk and held it out for Rahul. "This is for luck," she said. Rahul stuck it behind his ear and quickened his pace.

"Be careful," he shouted a warning. But too late. A stifled cry escaped her lips as she knelt down in the mud and clutched her foot tightly in her hands. Rahul bent down and lifted up a jagged piece of glass. He held it close to his eyes where it looked dark and vicious, almost evil. He swore softly under his breath before tossing it away into the water.

"Let me have a look at it," he said to Saira, bending down once more. He fumbled through his pockets and brought out a handkerchief which he said would have to do for the time being. Saira tried to smile at him bravely, but winced as he wrapped the handkerchief over the wound and tied it with a knot. "I'll be all right," she said, smiling once more as they both got up.

The rising wind pushed the dark clouds to the north. Weaving in and out of the clouds' ponderous path, the moon covered the shining riverbank with mercurial flashes. But certain things remained untouched by the moon, and undisclosed. The blood which now stained the handkerchief and turned it into a rag seemed hardly red. Simply another large, black smudge. The mango trees in the distance were black. The railway station was squat and black. The burnt out hulk of the Patton tank, abandoned by fleeing West Pakistan soldiers, straddling the railway tracks was equally black. But the rails which crept from under the Patton and flew eastwards into the night still shone like a pair of incandescent arteries.

It didn't matter any more whether the rails rusted or shone. This was Hasnabad. Twenty-four years ago, many trains stopped here on their way to and from Calcutta. A hunch-backed station master and a lively pointsman presided over these comings and goings. Thrice each day, for anything from five to fifty minutes, passenger trains stopped here, presenting the only moments of drama in this bleak village station.

A half hour before the arrival of each train, the pointsman

vigorously rattled a steel rod inside an iron hoop suspended from the wall. This was the bell, at the sound of which the old station master hobbled from door to door, unlocking, getting ready for business. First, he unlocked the gate leading to the platform, then the third class passenger's waiting hall, and finally the broken down shed housing the urinals and a single toilet. The first class waiting room seldom required to be unlocked. Then the station master craned his neck from the edge of the platform to make sure the signal had been lowered. Satisfied that it was, he would hobble back to his room and perch himself with some difficulty on the high chair facing the ticket window.

He would sit there, each time a train came in, waiting and watching, while the air became thick with flying chicken feathers and dust kicked up from the unpaved platform. In summer, the smell of ripe mangoes rose over cries of interminable farewells and stern admonitions to the young lads heading for the temptations of Calcutta in search of work. Some of this changed from day to day, but not the peddlars running up and down the length of the train, shouting: 'Cigarettes, betel nuts, betel nuts, cigarettes, tea, hot tea, hot hot tea'.

Change came when, in nineteen forty-seven, the British government, partaking somewhat of the divinity which hedged a Christian king, carved up the land and served Calcutta to the Hindus of India and Hasnabad to the Muslims of East Pakistan. A few weeks later, a labour contractor and his team tore up the tracks between Hasnabad and Calcutta, as between several other points across the border, all the way to the massive bridge spanning the river. Gradually, few people and fewer trains came from Dacca to Hasnabad; from Calcutta, none.

With all the present confusion, trains from Dacca had stopped coming altogether. On this particular night, Hasnabad was spent and silent. The central span of the bridge had been blown up, giving the horizon the appearance of missing a tooth. Lower down, jagged chunks of concrete protruded over the lapping waves like coastal rocks. Behind the station, in the small field which was the village market place on Tuesdays, Thursdays, and Sundays, all that remained were some empty baskets, a few earthen pitchers, seven dead men, a few dead children, and a single dead dog. At other times, the place would've made one sick. But it was all right when the wind blew from the river to the sea, as it did tonight.

Mud is so deceptive, thought Rahul. Soft, cold, it was whatever the mind willed it to be. It was because it was January now that they could stand where they stood. In August, the river would've sucked them into her coils from that very spot. Like the paddy fields, the river too seemed packed with life. But it was of a different kind.

For many months, every evening the soldiers herded their women out of the slit-eyed bunkers now turned to rubble. They'd let the women enter the water like timorous brides washing themselves for their lover's arms. They wept and wailed as they bathed, and the villagers heard them and beat their breasts. Many a woman never returned from the river. Even without the game thought up by Krishna, many tied their own hands and feet and dived into the river's sprawling bed. They lay there until the tide pushed them back to the earth where they belonged. Those who returned to the hell gouged out of rock and clay lie there still, freed through the merciful blast of a shell or grenade.

Suddenly, the night became alive with the sound of battle. Mortars crashed in the distance, kicking up earth. The ground started to shake under their feet. Her face brushed by the crimson flashes, Saira looked afraid.

"Watch out," Rahul shouted again, pulling Saira away from a bloated corpse offering its silver buttocks to the moon. It was the sanctity of a woman's body, not fear, that caused his alarm. She was a woman all right, the mud-caked strands of her long hair spread out like the gnarled branches of an ancient *peepul* tree. In front of Rahul's eyes, the body grew and grew until its swollen vastness engulfed houses, trees, factories, bridges, cigarette ends, shell casings, broken bottles, all living things, and all dead objects. Like an enormous sausage, its skin taut like shiny vellum, it trapped atoms and steel girders, bricks and shattered hopes, wheels and bones, grinding them into little pieces glowing and twitching inside.

Quickly, they walked over to the station. He said they'd wait there till daybreak, and then back home.

The station was in ruins. There were massive holes in the walls. A small fire had also swept through part of it. The wind poked through the splintered beams resting on the floor, looked up through the blown roof which yawned with unconcern, knocked lightly upon a rusty safe peeping through a mass of rubble, and sniffed like a dog through the hundreds of train tickets scattered all over. First class, inter class, third class, Rajshahi, Chittagong, Khulna, Jessore, Comilla. Rahul took off his jacket and lay down in one corner of the floor.

Now he had all the time in the world, all the time to sharpen his fury. In the semi-darkness, Saira too began to take off her outer clothing, seemingly unabashed by Rahul's presence. Rahul suddenly remembered a brief encounter with Guru Shaktiramji which he had all but forgotten. No, he thought, it was just that he hadn't chosen to remember it till now. Shaktiramji was there right before his eyes. There he sat, the Guru, cross-legged, a bowl of milk in front of him, ordering Rahul to undress. Rahul unbuttoned his shirt slowly and carefully, pulled off his vest, and stepped out of his trousers when Guru cried halt. That will do nicely for the time being, he said, stroking his silver beard, watching him intently, asking if it was a mole under his left nipple.

Looking down at it for the first time, Rahul imagined one could call it that. "Hm! it's a good sign," said Guru, and pointing a finger at Rahul's crotch, asked him first to take off his briefs. Then changed his mind and clapped his hands, once, twice. Whereupon a pair of pink drapes parted slightly in the far end of the room, and out popped a head, then the rest of the body. What a body it was, impossible to look away from her dark, flshing eyes. Then Guru nodded and exquisite creature started to undress, her fluttering hands like butterflies unwinding her *sari* effortlessly and waiting, trying to check, but finally abandoning herself to a blush that spread from her cheeks and hung from her earlobes like crimson pearls. Until Guru nodded again and, hey presto! blouse came off, and bras too. A vacuous softness descending on the senses as Rahul cupped her small breasts in his hands. Embrace ready, kiss steady, go Scott go. Surely, the Antarctic was never so cold, hills, chasms all the same. Like sex in a roll of toilet tissue. Must conquer, Rahul warned himself, as there uncoiled in him a bright spark, an aspiration, a symbol, a concentration, mounting in ecstasy, curving in delight, telling him he must fight. Nipples spongy, unresponsive, negative. Hurray! he had a decisive victory in the peninsular war. And Guru's voice floated down imaginary sound system saying, "Yes, remember body's no more than a shit of paper, cellular construction, smooth texture, uniform sensitivity. Only thinking makes it otherwise."

Then a pregnant pause as Guru contemplated bowl of milk. Looking up, he ordered him to feel her belly, lower, still lower, probing, asking, "Is it different now? Think, *Think,* THINK. Is it er-moist?" Amazing, truly amazing, Rahul thought at the time, convinced sex was nothing but a crock. But Guru promptly back on the air, declaring, if fate willed him to know her better someday, he would find her a raging river, or a serpent, sleek, smooth, silent as a whisper. Piece of paper shows up only that which the moving finger writes, but the body may only reflect . . . a will. A pause, and then he intoned "E-r-e-c-t-i-o-n-s" slowly, solemnly, and as Guru snapped his fingers dicky leapt into the air, winked, and sang: *Karma, maya, dhyan;* what you kaint, I kyan. Then, ever so slowly, Guru inserted himself into bowl of unpasteurized milk. Slurp, slurp, bowl soon empty, siphoned wondrously. Ah! urethral miracle! umbilical harmonies!

Saira took off her clothes and lay down next to Rahul without a word. All his images, all his thoughts, receded swiftly from his mind. After a while, Saira unzipped his trousers and slipped her hand inside. Rahul didn't try to stop her. "Do you know," he said quietly, "you sent a friend of mine to his death. He loved you and would've married you someday. I'm talking about Hamid."

Saira continued to caress him. "I've known many men in my time," she said, "but I have few memories of Hamid except as a child. I saved him once, I couldn't a second time."

Rahul grew silent and unresponsive. Saira said she hated them all and would never betray a friend. Then she got tired of waiting and deftly covered his body with her own. Their loving was like something Rahul had never experienced before. He found himself driven beyond exhaustion till his mind was like a wasteland sprouting wretched scrub crying for justice to rain down upon the rents left by the sun's daggers. It was this awareness of his own body that suddenly exploded in a frightening vision of Hamid's, all bloated and mangled, helping him swiftly make up his mind.

Light as a feather she was, riding an ocean whose depths, if she could only see, would've driven her mad. She was not fair, but he assured her she was the fairest and imagined he made her happy. Flattered her buttery skin dissolving, between those cupcake breasts, like beaded crystals embroidered on dark satin. Through the gaping window, the moon looked old and wrinkled behind a withered tree whose branches drew dark welts across her face. Perhaps it was that which made her wonder how bruised her body would be in the morning mirror. And she stirred like a snail plunging back into its shell, grinding her body, holding her breath, closing her eyes, tearing at his hair as she came.

The last time, the crows were about in the sky, the cock crowing. The dead branches of the tree hung free of the moon. Yes, and she tossed him around like driftwood, and her face so peaceful as he covered it under his jacket. Yes, back she came with her nails slashing his shoulders, scarring him. Bucking, she kicked at invisible shadows bringing her feet crashing on him anchored deep within her. Yes, he rode her storm like a question that's deaf to answers. Saira was still warm and lovable as he lifted himself out of her silent body. Then he removed the jacket.

Her mouth hanging open in her twisted face, spittle on her cheeks dribbling down her neck and towards the eyes straining to come out of the face. How unlovely in death. If she could only see the faces of those she betrayed, he thought. Yes, I forget nothing, he reminded himself. Then he remembered one of her teeth with a gold filling. Yes, almost like his own.

Was it the sound of a train he heard? No, it was nothing, he told himself. He heard it again. It did sound strange, since there wasn't even a door or window left to creak on its hinges. Could it be Jamal Hussain? Rahul wondered how far he might be?

It seemed he saw the hunchbacked station master Salim Ali told him about. What was he trying to say? Buy a ticket, buy a ticket, buy a ticket. He said he wished Rahul was here the summer before. What a harvest it was? The river hid the floods in her heart and let the people be. And the men stacked the hay to the sky. And there was enough for the cows and the buffaloes, enough left over for the huts to have new roofs. And the children all had new clothes that made old folk feel really old. My little girl had sneakers, but she's gone, and there's only one sneaker left. What could he do with one? Rahul shut the voice and the image out of his mind as he slipped on his jacket and walked over to the edge of the platform.

He stood there scanning the horizon and measuring the progress of the waiting dawn, suddenly remembering a child's sneaker he had seen lying with the dead in the village square. Just then, a single shot rang out in the greying darkness.

Rahul clutched his side in horror. No, he told himself, it couldn't end like this. To be torn forever from the sunlight! Never again to see the wasp suspended by invisible threads. The white butterfly circling the yellow blossoms. The dark brown fly warming itself on dry pine needles. The *mynah* hopping from tree to tree. Leaves dancing in the wind, dying to free themselves from the branches. Must he now forget all these? And what about the landscape that fell gently away outside Alice's window? The land that rested in a tangled wilderness of pine and apple trees, widow's lace, yellow cowslips, wild roses, bluebells, and berries. The answering echoes of the railway engine's whistle, the chimes of a bell striking the hour, even the spiteful automobile revving up like a beast in heat. Surely, he couldn't forget these. These he tried to remember as, like a wall of ice, ripped out from a sheer mountain face, he stood poised against the cloudless sky. Then, wheeling round slowly on one foot, his outstretched arms reaching for the earth, Rahul slowly fell upon the rails.

Until this moment, Jamal Hussain had chosen to remain well away from the station building. Confused and surprised, he had seen some, imagined some, and was puzzling over what Rahul was up to when he saw him step over to the platform to stretch his arms and legs. The sound of a high-powered rifle was as much a shock to him as Rahul. Jamal waited to see if anyone approached the fallen body. It could be anyone. A fugitive soldier, and Indian patrol returning home. After some time, he slowly worked his way along the foot of the platform to where Rahul lay. He had a wound below the shoulder, and Jamal had no idea how serious it was. At least he was alive.

Still wary of some unseen sniper, Jamal dressed the wound as well as he could and decided to carry Rahul back to the camp. He imagined the distance to be only a few miles, but it took him over five hours to carry Rahul that distance. There, he and another comrade quickly made a decision to carry him over to Bishnupur, rather than Calcutta which was much further away. They still had the car Rahul and Hamid had walked away with a few days ago.

Jamal regretted his decision as soon as he entered the village. Unbeknown to him, the peaceful village had been pushed into the national limelight almost overnight. He had heard of course that Bishnupur had been transformed by the annual fair and the Railwaymen's Convention, and he was certain there'd be medical help available because of that. For the past five days, oblivious of the undeclared war, the village had been crawling with merchants, tradesmen, itinerant *sadhus*, and delegates with flags and armbands. Dozens of tents and makeshift washrooms had sprouted all over the village. All this was common knowledge.

What Jamal and his companion didn't know was that an explosion had wrecked the main podium the previous evening. It was a bomb planted by a terrorist or a Pakistani agent. Three persons had died, among them the distinguished Railway Minister himself. Although everyone knew the man was a scoundrel and many rejoiced secretly at his passing, it was unfortunately an incident which the ruling Congress party couldn't pass over without retaliating in some way.

Within hours of the explosion, Bishnupur was teeming with police investigators. There began a series of random arrests, especially among the delegates. Through it all, a band of local bullies roamed with impunity, settling old scores, beating up whoever they could lay their hands on. The police saw no point in taking them on or their leader, Chanchal Sircar. He and his men stopped the car as soon as it entered the village.

Jamal had turned in their guns the moment he reached his camp. He felt helpless being unarmed. It was bad enough for him and his companion to be recognized as Muslims. What was worse was that Chanchal recognized the semi-conscious figure in the rear as Rahul. The mob was already tense and excited. Here were Muslims nobody really cared for, certainly not in Bishnupur.

It needed only a single voice, Chanchal's, to rally them. The crowd massing around the car began to clamour for blood. In no time, they had pulled the three men out. After they had rained blows upon them for sometime and felled them to the ground, the attackers brought out their knives. Suddenly, a thunderous voice rose above the confusion, followed by shrieks of pain and fear. A section of the crowd seemed to melt away, and through this space there appeared the figure of a half-naked *sadhu*. His body was covered with ashes, his matted hair streamed wildly behind him. In his hand he carried a fearsome trident, poised and ready to strike.

Chanchal was lifting a bloodied knife over the unconscious Rahul when he saw the wild man lunging for his eyes with the trident. He dropped the knife and fell back on the ground, cowering like a dog. The holy man held the trident inches away from his eyes, ready to push the sharp blades to the innermost recesses of his brain.

The crowd had grown deathly silent. Not a hand was raised against the holy man. "Leave my son alone," he commanded. The fire in his eyes seared the hearts of those who dared look up at him. The first of those to recognize him prostrated themselves at his feet. The first whispers of his son's name soon swelled to a roar. But Sambhu Narain didn't seem to hear, and didn't utter one more word. He cast a parting look of withering scorn at Chanchal and drew the trident away from his face. Then, slinging it across his shoulder, he knelt down and picked up Rahul in his arms.

The crowd made way as he stood up effortlessly and began moving towards his home a short distance away. Jamal Hussain and his friend were bleeding too. But they were able to get up by themselves and follow the wild man walking with his son in his arms.

Twenty

THE LEAVES fell, brushed against his face, and kept falling. His feet pounded over the dead and dying leaves until he stopped at the water's edge and saw them lying below the water as well, shimmering under glassy furrows in their blazing colours.

Run. Run. Run to the ends of the earth. Run to whoever will listen. Run to Dan. Maybe Sharmila wanted to play after all. So hard to find a rhythm the first few minutes. The darkness and the cold make it worse. Did Dan really want him home? What's in it for him? Must keep my mouth shut or someone'll get me for sure. What fun striding down Fifth Avenue, watching his reflection in Cartier's and Steuben Glass, moving with the crowds like a king. A sea of hardtops thrashing, lava hissing, down First, Second, ad infinitum avenues, towers of bonds and equities, intrigues and inequities, frozen empires of steel, oil, and bananas swaying in the wind, brown mist of soot and fumes knocking on the windows.

He found peace as he settled down to an easy pace. Like the waters of the lake he so often dreamed about, his mind became a mirror reflecting past and present, making new images out of old, catching every brightness that seemed inaccessible at the start. So deep his involvement with the images springing up within his mind, he soon had a life of his own cut off from the world outside. The cars didn't bother him, the stop lights didn't. If he responded to them, it was through simple, almost blind, reflexes.

He found his second wind, and it became even easier. Would he see the lights of New York ever again, the magic in those lights that made him feel like a child? When will it all crumble to dust, he wondered. Will Harvard Bridge span the Charles three thousand years from now? Impossible to say, except that, for the time being, Harvard Bridge wasn't tumbling down. In fact, it remained superbly solid under his feet, while the Charles slept a fretful sleep in its ancient vat, troubled breathing a gentle sulphurous mist over the city, soap bubbling, phosphate snoring, good plum brandy good for royal Charles, glub, yes, glub.

Must get back in form, he thought. Must train. Battle stations, what? Need something like the Harriers here. Weave the community together into a mass of runners, some running away, some running to. Ah! the S-O-N-E-S-T-A lights still burning, but thrifty Jordan Marsh snuffs life out of fur storage lights giving the lie to academic illusions. The Charles a sea of cobalt every evening beautiful to see from the Mugar, earphones clapped to the head re-living Carmen. Cars picking up speed overtake. Seeyah later if Honeywell don't score Bachmai bullseye again. Dreams of glory, wonder if same has gotten to the head! Slept all day yesterday, woke up early, what time? Leave now for dogs and apes, for sun still ploughing through the Atlantic, long long time to go. Head light but body still flab. New saffron tracksuit hardly used smelling of solvents and my holiness. Bending down to brush dust off running shoes too much effort seemed almost took breath away. Ah! moving at last.

Across the river the towers masked in grey haze, still sleeping, lying, lieing if you will, to each his own, except when no one's looking.

The world at my feet, he thought. The irony of it, he thought. The pity of it. Can see Saira, Alice. Can see you Sharmila now in Providence now cradling poor Michael in now your trembling thighs. All husbands to Aleppo gone. Masters o'the tigress. Bmaah! Lookie Mickey babay, Mama's brought two little titties all the way from Trichy, dipped in frankincense myrrh and cream of tartar. Glubb! Plupp! Mnaah! Baby, baby, never satisfied want the other baby. But see, domed MIT crouched behind the trees like a cauldron round which go and in the poisoned entrails throw. Charles wriggling ugh with fillet of fenny snake, eye of newt, and toe of frog. Liver of blaspheming Jew too. Aleppo, ho! ho! It's Hue where the action is. Welcome home, horsemen of the Apocalypse!

There were others out this morning running. In the distance wasn't it Mike Gaines? Rahul quickened his pace. His body was now warm. The cold didn't bother him a bit. Different earlier on, the air nibbling at him with little beaks. What he saw of himself in the early morning mirror was enough to make him sick. Weak, old, weak. As others see us. Mirror tell me true. Wish Mike was running with. When man is frightened what is there to do but run. Guru Shaktiramji what a scream. Him and his meditative transcendence of fear. Up yours, your Holiness! Up mine more accurate, he thought. What a sucker I. Nighttime. And riverbank too. With Shaktiramji one more time.

Smoke and fog and smell of burning flesh heavy over the bald cremation grounds. Riverbank too. Dream of a nightmare. After-dinner chitchat of carcasses. Hard to come by stiffs. Nature and modern technology side by side serving people who have ceased to be. Broken down electric crematorium back in operation. Russian technicians to the rescue. Or wasn't it the Czechs that time?

Fond memories die hard. Maybe thirty yards away, two, maybe three pyres slowly dying out. Shame people still burning wood when government crying out Save Forests. Also crying out Stop Babies, Tie Tubes, clip clop clip clop. Ecology like casting pearls before swine. Scene gets awful messy when it starts raining halfway through. What's one to do with half-cooked mammal hallowed with the spark of divinity? Get the hell out of, before it starts raining, that's the general idea. Leave the *doms* to their foul deeds. Edible perhaps, give you the creeps. Non-vegetarians traditionally non-fussy. Slaughtered beast may well have been on its way to, blissfully unaware of pap test, frog test, or Kahn test. Electric furnace infinitely better. Roof over one's head and over that of the departed soul. Not as pretty as funeral parlors with fountains and cherubs with flutes and Crossley carpets and muzak. What do you expect for four rupees? About fifty cents, right? Incredible, and the priest's incantations thrown in free. Pickles cost a lot. Ask Tut, he knows.

Now and then dying embers spit out forked tongues to the playful wind. Rest, Aeolus, rest in peace. A hundred pounds maybe more of dissolving flesh and bones all yours. *Shantih*! *Shantih*! Fooled ya with Sanskrit, huh? Yeah, *sans* creed. Developing nations, you know. *Sans* everything but potent pricks. Someone coughed, a signal suggesting everything was ready. Kaloo returned, his folded hands entreating the Guru to proceed.

"She was a whore," said Kaloo, "a common one-rupee whore. Nobody came to claim her body. Tee bee." His men asked the hospital clerk for it. Ten rupees under the table. Lucky if she made that much in a week. Dead now for four or five hours maximum. Guru pats scavenger king appreciatively on the back. King beams with pleasure. "Poor, miserable whore," he said. "Didn't have no home. Called her Pagli. Saw her often on the streets. Word got around she had TB and no one would sleep with her, not even for half a rupee. The luck of the poor."

"The fate of the damned," said Guru, casting his eyes towards heaven and murmuring, "*Maya*." Then he looked tenderly at the inert body and said, "Money has its blessings. She her blessings too. Sometimes it comes early, sometimes late. She's blessed. She's happy now. Her life has not been wasted."

Kaloo knelt down and touched Guru's toes. He'd have to leave them, he said humbly. Till the morning. But his men would be around, armed with sticks to chase away jackals and dogs. They'd walk to the ends of the earth for a meal.

Guru blesses Kaloo and darkness swallows him up. Guru turned to Rahul. "In the morning you'll be free of fear forever," he said. "This is the ultimate fear for most. But behind it lurks the supreme hope. Reincarnation. Fear fear only, not its cause. It grazes only in the body weakened by lust and pride." He stops and smiles, flashing his saintly teeth. "I'll be under that distant tree," he said, "but I don't think you'll need me." With that, Guru swallowed up in darkness too. But he affirmed his galactical presence by lighting up grass in his earthen waxing waning *chillum*. *Chillum* bloomed orange with every puff, faded and bloomed again. Guru belched loudly. "*Hare Ram. Hare Om,*" he praised the Lord. *Ooooooooooom*, bayed the hungry jackals nearby as the sweet smell of grass got to them.

Rahul prayed in silence, prayed that the uncontrollable shaking in his body would stop. That the night would soon end. He lowered himself slowly. Wave of revulsion. Must fight, he thought. *Tantric* self-discipline. Too late to run away. He sat down on the corpse. Wobbly but not too soft. Bony. He hoped the darned thing wouldn't cave in under. TB. Maybe thorax a complete hollow. Maybe he'd get used to it by and by. By and by so easily said. Suddenly the body moves. *Baapray baap!* Like it was trying to get up. Scarier than anatomy demos. Like it was trying to shake off his weight. Rahul's throat went dry. He couldn't remember his blood running cold or hot. Pulse hammering away like crazy metronome, he remembered. He tried to shout. "Ooooooom," a low muffled animal scream escaped his lips.

Yes, imagination only. Rigidity. Happens before and after death too. Why? Spirit trying to beat it fast looking for suitable orifice escape hatch, frantic. Terrible if trapped in flames or shoved into bowels of mother earth. Who wants another heaven on earth? Find it in heaven nobody too sure anymore. Still, worth the risk, by Jove! Phew! No breath no. If mirror fogs up why, she lives. No mirror. No flashlight. No dilation of pupils. Soul birdied once and for all. Didn't seem to relish prospect of return. No thank you.

Opal-eyed jackals scurry around in the darkness. Unseen vultures fan themselves with impatient wings. Helped keep the bugs away. Perhaps metabolism running low. Vultures commute to and fro from the golf course. Shuttles all the time. Golf, last dregs of the Raj. Lining the fairways, lovely banyan trees and flame trees where the vultures sit and applaud. Soothing break for them. Take time off to scatter heavy, granular, yellow-green droppings. No danger if one stuck to the fairways. But hook or slice into the jungle, and you've had it. Blessed for sure. Injun women going for game in a big way. Compare social notes between drives and putts. "Adarsh in London for the weekend man. Much too busy for my liking. What about yours man? Wah! Wah! what a beautiful drive man. On the fourteenth I say we should both look smart and go for a hole in one man. What?"

Guru steps out of dirty, smoggy halflight to embrace Rahul. Not far away, the *doms* pile up half burnt logs and sprinkle them with kerosene. Then they put Pagli on top of the logs, her head like a rag doll's. Wood finished, so they scatter some dry twigs and straw on her, covering up her face. *Finis*. Small face, dark and round, devoid of rancour. For your blessings, your holiness, much thanks. No hard feelings for what you've done to me. What would she truly say is she found her voice? He owed her something for sure. Courage maybe.

Dissembling liar. Blackguard.

Michael Gaines drew nearer and smiled. Raising a clenched fist, he growled Hi! in a deep voice all but drowned by a boat's horn. Two quick notes, the sound spread and lingered over the waters. Slowing down to see. Varsity eight pulling away, Percy Griffith stroking. Blonde brutes, *sieg heil*! Coach Cabot, hair streaming in the breeze, wields bullhorn and follows in another boat. Magic in his booming voice. Bellows once and the rating shoots up, boat flicks through water like a knife.

"Nice morning," said Rahul, marking time.

"How're you, Rah?" asked the other, doing the same.

"Just fine."

"Still hangin' round that broad?"

"C'mon , Mike, she's all right. Done you guys no harm. It's me that's all messed up."

"Aren't we all? Say, party at Carl's tonight."

"No wheels, Mike."

"Use your legs, man, or gimme a shout."

Ballbuster Brigitte came bouncing behind Mike. Rahul smiled at her. She pretended not to see him. But she must have felt, he was sure, to the marrow of her bones, his mortal presence passing. Pleasant vision early in the morning. Shakes you up. And so the world pursues. Jug jug to dirty cars. Terrible for business. Veeps by the dozen hanging themselves with twisted bra straps. Fashion models taking to the streets. Bad for old men blood running thin. Should know better, displaying themselves like that. Firm now and defiant. But wait seven years. Sweep, dust, mop floors with. Slap your face with. Could knock a man out. Yeah! with pendulous passage of time, use 'em to hunt men like wild animals. Screw ball, Fred Flintstone. What next? Use it on each other. Two to our one, instruments of defoliation, weapons of destruction.

South of the river, the smokestacked university blew its first smoke rings of the day into the sky. Broiled Aristotle for breakfast. Milk of human knowledge too much for the old bladder. Bibliophiles spend hours relieving themselves, carving odes to devirgination on the school's sacred walls. Me in you, dick Nixon before he dicks you! One word and he could stop the carnage. President has this thing about women. Politics he digs, not the politics of sex. A head of state's a pain in the ass. Oh! to live and die on TV. Indira back home a goddess to millions. Pallas Athena rises in Delhi's Akbar Road, unhooks death's ponderous sickle, sends it swishing through the land. Fuck freedom at home, save it across the border.

On the other side of the river, the B-school grounds so green. Purer than the placid river motionless in its green jelly mold. Hedges trimmed with such infinite care. Silent and serene like an Aegean church. Spotless windows flashing between milk white mullions. Fresh sunlight fell in a tangled heap over puffs of cloud shielding the glorious trees shielding the Arcadian loveliness. But power mower coming round buildings, advancing *chugchuhgachuhg* towards the green, spoiling all ruining everything. Illusion exploding like a firecracker. Baker Hall roof shooting into the sky, bricks fall crashing into the river. They came running through the flames in their Brooks Brothers pajamas, cream of the corporate world. Police sirens wail in despair. Fire engines come screaming from Salem. From Bunker Hill, spectators watch the reddening sky in silent awe. But it's too late, always is. With every charred body that falls thrashing on the ground, the Dow Jones sinks lower and lower. Five hundred. Three hundred ninety seven. Eleven. What happens at zero? The bull's put to sleep and the bear goes back to Alaska. Flustered undertakers weave in and out of the crowd. Aetna, Allstate, INA, CNA, Mutual of Omaha. Could they survive the payout? Suicides in Lloyds of London. The Swiss Embassy closes its doors in Washington. Suddenly Wallace Stevens appears from nowhere, hovers over the raging inferno. Wringing his plastic wings in sorrow, he cries, "The river is moving. The blackguard must be flying." And the FBI ferrets out the arch-villain of the piece. They line him up against the wall after a quick trial in McDonald's. But the hail of bullets crumple like petals from blown roses at Father

Berrigan's feet after genuflecting briefly before his open breviary.

Bet you Mike doesn't show up tonight with his car. Wanted little to do with whites. Scared he'd take Alice to the party. Can't sleep white and think black, he says. Been kicked in the ass by white folks too long. That's the story of the computer whiz who went from L.A. to Okinawa, from Heidelberg to Ankara, serving his country. At school now for one last chance, one more chance for white brothers to embrace him as their own.

Call him after nine, he thought. Before midnight. What good's a telephone if no one receives it? Probably laying a sister. Once black brother bangs up white sister she'll keep wanting it all the time. Myth or reality? Academic, thought Rahul. The ripeness is all. Dispense sex without regard to colour, race, or religion. No shame in it. Do it top of your bent. Out in Fenway Park maybe. Boston Gardens? Nighttime too cold. Dawn better. Beguiling hues. Lateral-posterior. Do it like the doggies do. Will happen. Anno Domini nineteen eighty nine for sure. Nature's way the only way. Strawberry fields forever. Pity no bushes. But wait! Arboretum infinitely better. Bigger capacity. Hold at least a million couples. But too far to go. MTA bloody awful. Too slow. Too irregular. Waiting. Cramps in the scrotum. Bad for BP. Maybe spill on platform slimy slippery syrupy. Make females mad. Savage, eh? Speak for yourself, sexist pig. Bah! Waiting bad for mating. Bound to be riots. Public demands more cars on the Arborway line. Governor Sargeant take notice. What Boston needs is faster fuckin' facilities. Doors slam on faces. Doors jack-knife on vital male appendages. What indignity! Call the ambulance, double quick. No, not the principals, just the subsidiaries. Fellow had his pecker up trying to get in. Knife-edged doors. Instant amputation.

State of Massachusetts versus U.R. Dildo. Your honour, negligence is absolutely denied. Our doors perfectly safe. Rubberized. We submit that the investment banker's philoprogenitive attributes simply dropped off in the crowd. We have his medical history. Exhibit A. Grafted in the Trucial Oman by a Brazilian surgeon. What can you expect from Latino quacks? Case dismissed.

Next, Irina Scatalina. Fractured her fuckin' hip, your Honour. Sargeant here went afer her with a swingin' baton near Copley. Slipped on the blubber. Ruined for life. The defense rises. Conditions, your Honour, were a bit slippery on the day of the convention. According to Dr. Missner of MIT (May the Pentagon bless this hallowed shrine) there was an unusual deposit of tallow on the platform that night. FBI agents inclined to hold the SDS responsible. God! we'll teach them a lesson. This'll be their last subversive act. Them flamin' pacifists want to ruin our manhood, peace, apple pie, and the American way. Gandhi, King, bah! What chance has a man without his gun? We tried your best, your Honour. We pumped the unholy slime up to the street level. Soon as we started we were served with a restraining order. Some environmentalist fags charged us with polluting the city's water.

Order. Order. What was the convention all about?

Who cares, your Honour?

Right. Now the verdict. Freeze dry the stuff and ship it to Bangladesh. They say there's no food. This is high protein stuff. Stuff that makes hair grow on your knuckles. Restore the population balance in Asia. Genocide? What the hell does it mean ? Bring out the OED. Three million dead? Ships turning back from the ports? I sentence hardy Pathans to ten hours in Chittagong. Infuse fresh blood into the inferior races. Awaken them to the power of the work ethic. Ease them up the evolutionary ladder.

Press Secretary says White House remorseful now. Too many women raped. A Pathan, what a man! A whore in every bunker, dear Henry! dear Henry! Do it six times each night. Allah's injustice. Too few women. Do it with men. Animals too. Koran says, yes, when hungry eat bread of sacrament. No harmful for that. Ah! Yahyah! now there's a man for ya. Deceitful bastards, Indians. Bring Indira to Capitol Hill. Teach her a thing or two. Chinese sex life, from our observation, much more rational today. No Confucian. Henry'll publish his red book soon, illustrated with Mao's pings and pongs. And those delectable little feet. Hindoos strange. Breed like pigs on the plains. Do it on temples. Profane. Brothels in temples. Get thee to a nunnery, who said that? Good for the high priests. True, why shouldst thou be a breeder of sinners when you can buy condoms three for two cents? Spread out on every sidewalk. Taj Mahal, Rothmans, Charminars, Durex. Annual production in China now up to four hundred million. Chou's happy.

Thank God we've taken care of New Year's Eve, he declared.

And you, my dear, my dew-kissed, flower-fresh chickadee. How come you got into this den of iniquity? The State of Massachusetts clears its throat. Indecent exposure, your Honour. Came out screaming from the MFA trying to board the subway. She's confessed she's gaga over money and pickassholes.

Suddenly it's all over. The judge starts to scream from the tormenting itching of hemorrhoidal tissues and adjourns the case.

Tired. Time to return. Aiyeee! hold me, hold me. Hold me back. Swine. Left, left, leftrightleft. Rat, rat, rattatatat. Ah, Emil, you were the greatest. Always your left hand, left fist, thumping against your left. . . . Balls! you should've been in America. For your pains at Wembley, what did you get? A statue? Dime a dozen. Liberty's a statue too. Try punching the heart with fist as I run. Like this, always on the right foot. Quicken the circulation. Too bad, you missed the boat, Emil. Blew it with Dubcek. What does one do with beautiful people who're reactionaries? Give 'em a stretch at the tractor plant in Pilsen. Mop lavatories. No, no, not Belsen. Ajax, Chlorinex, Schlitz, and Budweiser. They say the best things in life are free. In death too? Yes, Emil, they would've honoured you for certain. No junk heap for you here, corporal. With Jim Thorpe in the Hall of Fame. Maybe curtains at Arlington. The Iron Curtain, joke of the century. Piece of paper, man. One prick and out you are, from the fire to the frying pan. Wish you were here, Emil. . . from one prick to another.

Running can be such fun. To push the earth spinning away from under the feet. Watch things near flash past as from a railway carriage. Azaleas and lilacs lost in a vast canvas of blurred colours. But stop for a moment and everything snaps back into place. Azaleas and lilacs heads held high over the blades of grass. Stop and see things as they really are. Must stop.

Rahul thought he would die. He wasn't particularly nervous at the prospect. What worried him was a lack of consistency. One moment the thoughts were so clear he could clearly put them to words. The next, they spun out of his reach, and he felt disturbed not knowing what the future promised. Thoughts danced away from him, taunting him. He felt an intense pressure growing in his chest, squeezing it, making it difficult for him to breathe at times. He recalled seeing a constrictor squeeze the life out of a giant rat, and felt now what the animal must've felt then, its incisors bared in a silent scream. He could almost feel the rat's pain shuddering through his body, feel his ribs cracking in the coils of some evil, beady-eyed serpent.

There came tears to his eyes, and he didn't know why. I shouldn't be crying, he told himself. There was a refuge in tears for those who feared death or loved life too much. He had always nursed nothing but contempt for such persons. In his final hours, he suspected that Hamid too saw the world exactly as he saw it now, a maze of shapes and colours drawn out of objects they had been a part of simply for the convenience of the human eye. This is what it must've been at the beginning, molten mountains like syrup in a vat, oceans of steam hissing and whistling to a sky cleft between the leaping tongues of fire and the sullen darkness of the waiting doom. Yes, he liked it this way, a very private death. There was a secret elation inside of him. He felt he was being primed for the vision of God.

From his bed, he could see at least one door leading out of the room. He knew it was there because a short while ago the door opened ever so slightly. He had seen doors opening before, but this one was like nothing he could remember. Instead of a person walking through it, there was a shaft of light which turned and faltered for a moment in his direction, and then slowly disappeared. Somebody was watching him for sure. Somebody he couldn't see behind the glare from the shaft of light.

He did not die. Later, his thoughts became a little clearer. He found the pain in his body defining the ebb and flow of memories, shadows bridging the oceans he had crossed. Memories framed the faces he remembered, not as they might really be in life or death, but as he cared to remember them. There was Alice, Hamid, and all the rest. He felt great playing God, enthroned in the heart of things, looking out, thrilling at appearances seen as on a clear day, from a distance, larger than life.

His body began to tire and his mind started to drift. The mist rolled in and the rain began to knock on his window. The morning turned grey and windy. The wind whistling and rattling against the shutters sounded like children playing with sticks along the backyard fence or like consumptive old men dying little by little. Alice stood naked and trembling by the window. He was standing with her.

The fog rolled away, the sun came out, and they saw an emerald lake in front of them, vaulted over by a sky of the deepest blue. The lake was a mirror, and Alice blushed in it with the warm colours of a Renoir. The tapering, finely veined alabaster of her fingers and toes stood apart from the veldts of golden brown rolling over muscle and tendon, dipping into warm chasms and moist corners, swivelling into a vortex, eddying, emulsifying, silent as the frost, clear as a summer's day. Her hair, the colour of chilled honey, floated over this sea, this cage, her body, like a tendril tossed into the waves, as she stood there, rare, untramelled, unveiled like Lucrece, or wrapped in mystery like a goddess.

She heard strange footsteps behind and turned away from the lake, her mirror, to glance fearfully at the door. Was it he, Rahul, standing behind it, or some Tarquin with overflowing ardour and sword unsheathed? The footsteps receded in lengthening cadences, sighing, fading in a pianissimo, releasing her to return to her mirror. A rare mirror, a connoisseur, it accepted only what it valued, retained that which was mint and unalloyed. It rejected all that might be attractive to meaner lives, shut out sounds of human breathing and the smell of human decay.

As Alice lifted her hands to her breasts, the mirror, hungry, followed as a flash, then flipped the image swiftly like a kaleidoscope as she planted her fingers over the burning aura of her nipples. The mirror drank slowly the vintage dyes that shook themselves awake at the touch of her fingers and spread like shame across its face. But its homage was only a reflection of its hopeless playfulness, for the mirror could never keep anything it touched. Alice's young body would remain out of its reach. It knew nothing of desire that rose like a fevered pulse and tugged at the fibers in her womb as Rahul walked up behind her in silence, pushed his hands past her hair, locked his fingers on her sculptured neck, and let his eyes embrace hers in the mirror. Her eyes wavered behind the stinging tears which gathered at the corners until, sated and bursting, they tumbled down her cheeks and disappeared in the grass at her feet.

Alice vanished too and there appeared instead a fearful Teiresias stumbling through dark, uncharted alleys, divining the dread echoes of the future germinating in the now, the moment streaking by. From over the distant hills there came a strange, flapping sound, stopping just as suddenly as it began. One moment, it was a vulture hunched between its giant wings. The next moment it turned into an eagle, climbing over the water, looping and swooping across the sky, scraping the colours off the sunset. Rahul bent down and picked up a shell from the water's edge and heard an even stranger sound as he held it against his ear. He heard the sea shore sighs of a woman's sadness echoing in a snail's deserted mansion of winds.

The eagle came down and perched on his shoulder and seemed to be listening too. Its beak bent in breast-piercing hate, its eyes blazing like the sun, its feathers all puffed up as its blood rose in a tide. And Rahul knew they had both heard the sound of a mother's voice calling out to her children across deserted paths that led to yesterday. They saw his mother search the fields and cry for her children to rise. Only a few palsied blades of grass shook themselves from the blackened, burnt out heaps of scrub, trying to answer. The sound grew louder and unbearable. Rahul began to run from it, but it followed.

Soon there opened before his eyes a purple path along which he ran until he came upon a seamy side-street strewn with fruits. A crowd converged upon him, offering him melons. Everyone was into melons. Ripe, blood red melons. Then, laughing and dribbling, they ran back to the water now seething like an ocean. They danced in the sea, stripped naked to the sea. In the phosphorescent afterglow, Rahul found himself annointed in a shower of cobalt. Then the eagle descended on his shoulder once more. As Rahul turned to look at it, it suddenly popped like a parasol revealing a scarred and bloodied Moses underneath, grieving he had spent forty hundred years in vain. Moses was on fire, hot tears bubbled on his cheeks, and his beard dissolved in clouds of dust.

Rahul heard a woman cry in his dreams until the ocean rolled in and drowned her voice. The mountain which had cradled the vision of Moses slowly started to sink, dragging the stars to the ocean floor. Forks of lightning shot up from the water and struck the last remaining planet in the sky. The planet exploded with the sound of thunder and spread fluttering coffins in the air. As they fell and smashed against the water, they flung out children, scattering them like seed. Hundreds of thousands of children. From some of the coffins, there flew out like doves the souls of unborn children. Where the sky once was, there now appeared an upside down rainbow made simply of bands of black and white.

Rahul woke up exhausted, his lips thirsting for water. "Oh Alice!" he murmured softly, "bring down your mouth to my kisses. While the world is still under my feet, while I have strength to climb forbidden pinnacles, before the clouds hurtle me down and drench me once more with fire and blood." Oh! is it not passing brave to be a king, he thought, and ride in triumph through Persepolis.

"Pray for me, Alice," he whispered once more. "Let your prayer be a song."

Alice brought her face close to his. "I'm here," she said. "I'm with you."

"Will you stay?"

"Perhaps."

THE END